The Magic Begins

"Friendship is Magic, Parts 1 & 2"

Written by
Lauren Faust

Adaptation by
Justin Eisinger

Edits by
Alonzo Simon

Lettering and Design by
Tom B. Long

MEET THE PONIES

Twilight Sparkle

TWILIGHT SPARKLE TRIES TO FIND THE ANSWER TO EVERY QUESTION! WHETHER STUDYING A BOOK OR SPENDING TIME WITH PONY FRIENDS, SHE ALWAYS LEARNS SOMETHING NEW!

Spike

SPIKE IS TWILIGHT SPARKLE'S BEST FRIEND AND NUMBER ONE ASSISTANT. HIS FIRE BREATH CAN DELIVER SCROLLS DIRECTLY TO PRINCESS CELESTIA!

Applejack

APPLEJACK IS HONEST, FRIENDLY, AND SWEET TO THE CORE! SHE LOVES TO BE OUTSIDE, AND HER PONY FRIENDS KNOW THEY CAN ALWAYS COUNT ON HER.

My Little Pony
The Magic Begins

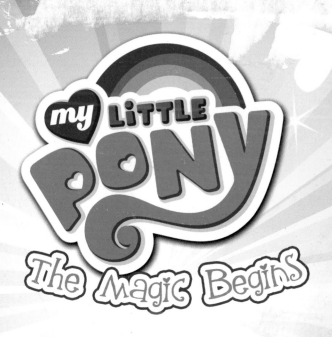

Special thanks to Erin Comella, Robert Fewkes, Heather Hopkins, Valerie Jurries, Ed Lane, Brian Lenard, Marissa Mansolillo, Donna Tobin, Michael Vogel, Mark Wiesenhahn, and Michael Kelly for their invaluable assistance.

ISBN: 978-1-61377-754-1
20 19 18 17   5 6 7 8
www.IDWPUBLISHING.com

Licensed By:

Fluttershy

FLUTTERSHY IS A KIND AND GENTLE PONY WITH A BIG HEART. SHE LIKES TO TAKE CARE OF OTHERS, ESPECIALLY HER LITTLE ANIMAL FRIENDS.

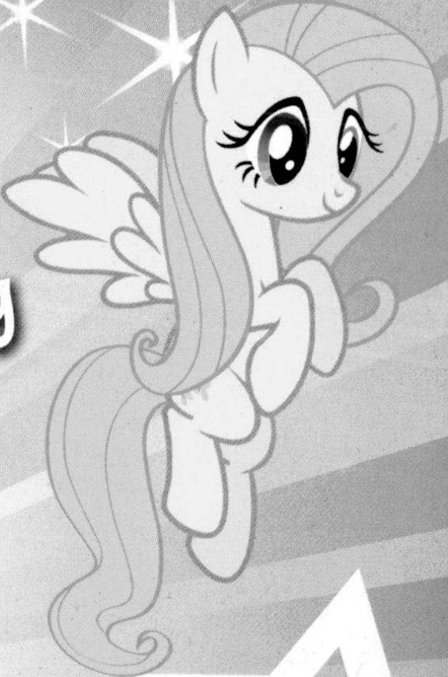

Rarity

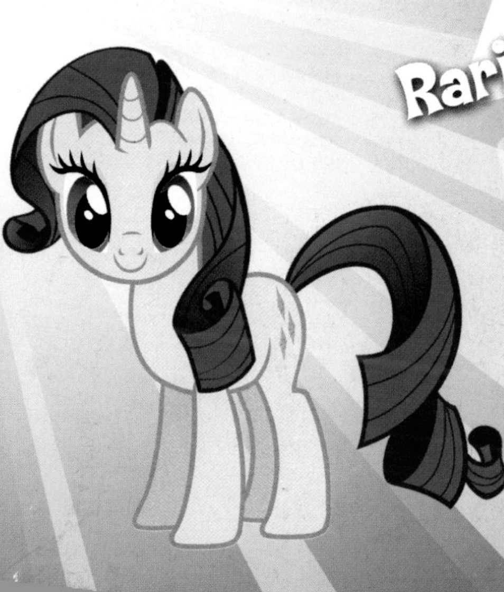

RARITY KNOWS HOW TO ADD SPARKLE TO ANY OUTFIT! SHE LOVES TO GIVE HER PONY FRIENDS ADVICE ON THE LATEST PONY FASHIONS AND HAIRSTYLES.

Pinkie Pie

PINKIE PIE KEEPS HER PONY FRIENDS LAUGHING AND SMILING ALL DAY! CHEERFUL AND PLAYFUL, SHE ALWAYS LOOKS ON THE BRIGHT SIDE.

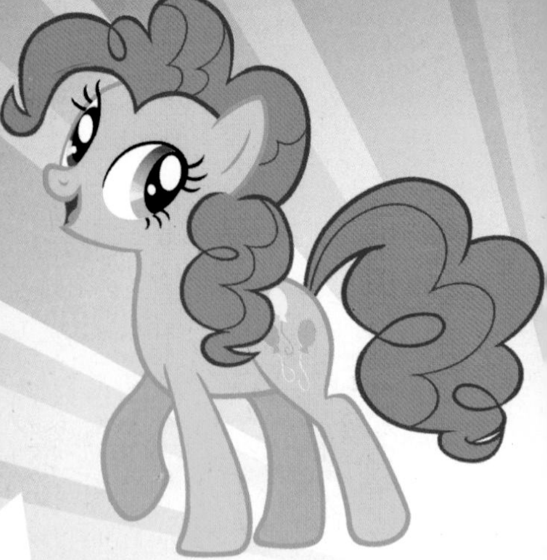

Rainbow Dash

RAINBOW DASH LOVES TO FLY AS FAST AS SHE CAN! SHE IS ALWAYS READY TO PLAY A GAME, GO ON AN ADVENTURE, OR HELP OUT ONE OF HER PONY FRIENDS.

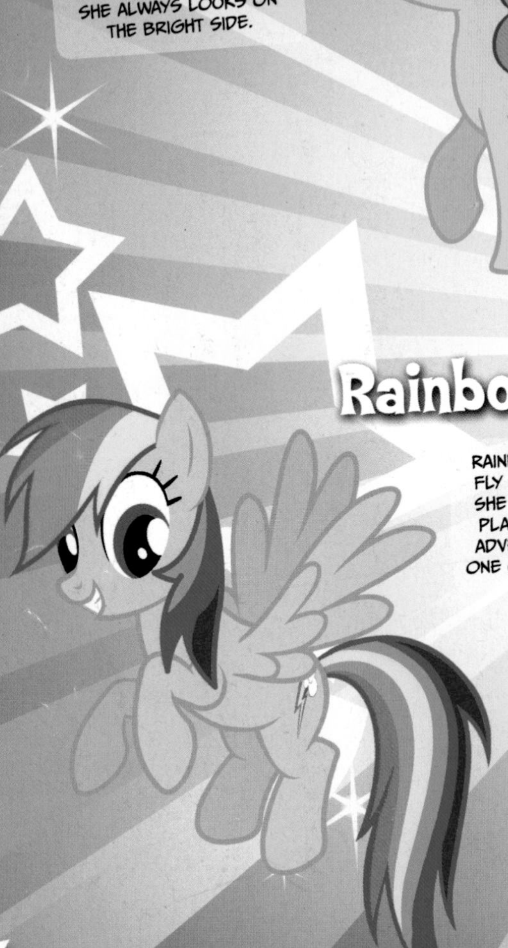

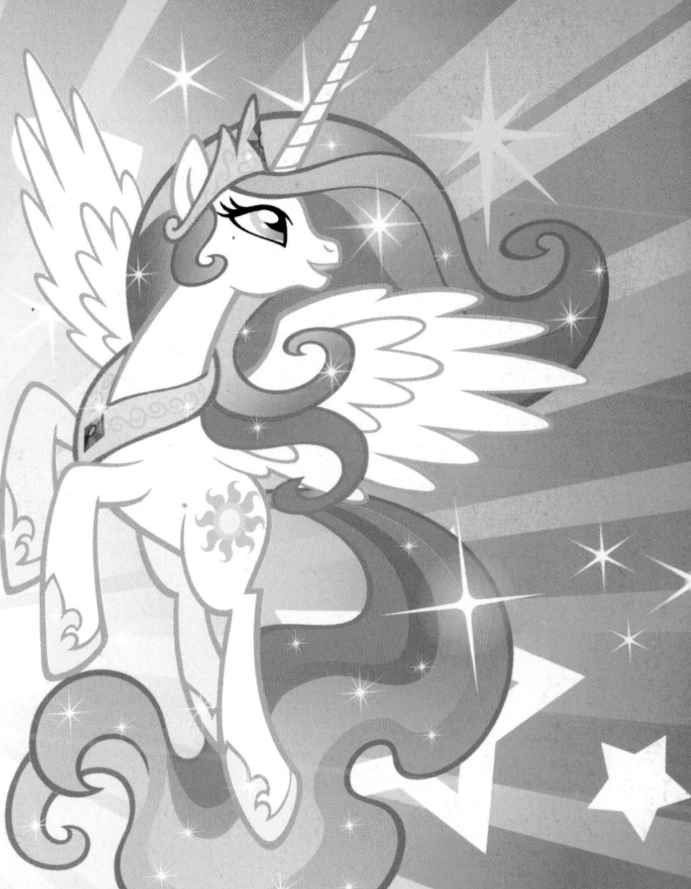

Princess Celestia

PRINCESS CELESTIA IS A MAGICAL AND BEAUTIFUL PONY WHO RULES THE LAND OF ESQUESTRIA. ALL OF THE PONIES IN PONYVILLE LOOK UP TO HER!

FRIENDSHIP is MAGIC™

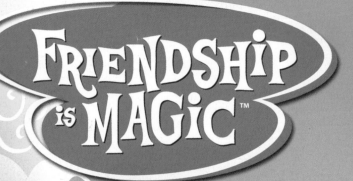

AND THE STORY BEGINS.

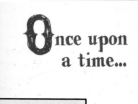

Once upon a time...

"ONCE UPON A TIME...

"...IN THE MAGICAL LAND OF EQUESTRIA..."

...THERE WERE TWO REGAL SISTERS WHO RULED TOGETHER AND CREATED HARMONY FOR ALL THE LAND.

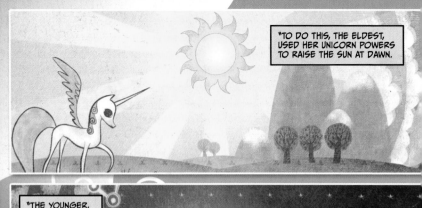

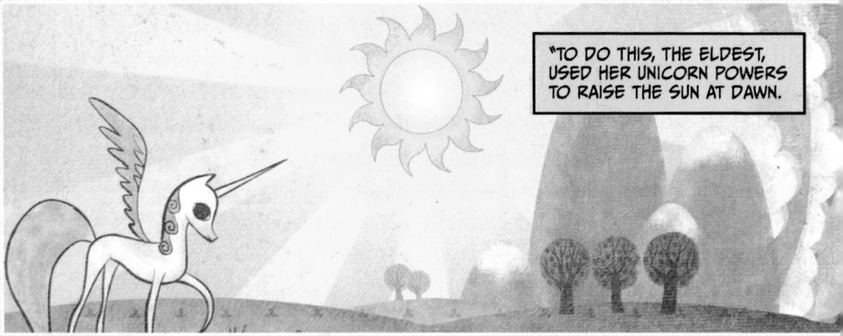
"TO DO THIS, THE ELDEST, USED HER UNICORN POWERS TO RAISE THE SUN AT DAWN.

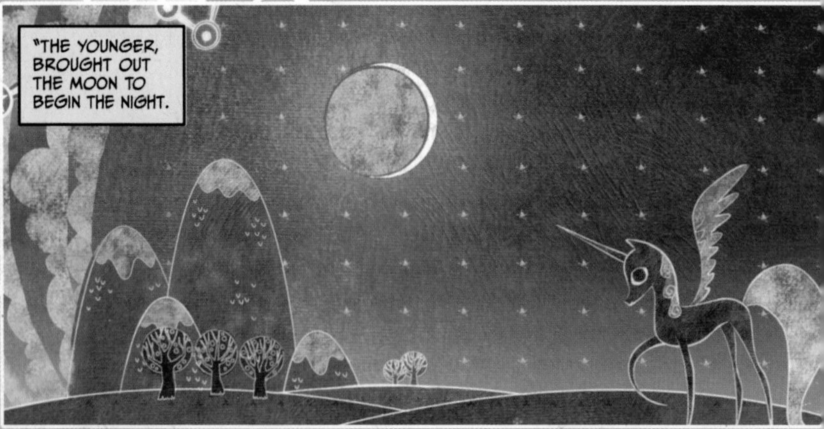
"THE YOUNGER, BROUGHT OUT THE MOON TO BEGIN THE NIGHT.

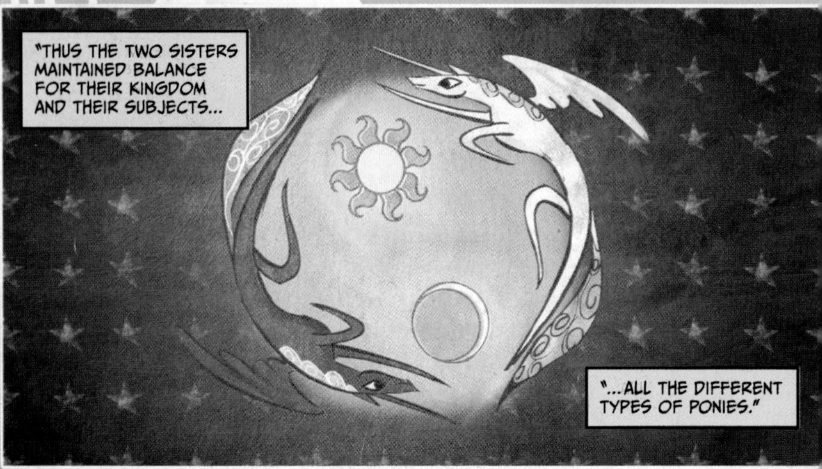
"THUS THE TWO SISTERS MAINTAINED BALANCE FOR THEIR KINGDOM AND THEIR SUBJECTS...
"...ALL THE DIFFERENT TYPES OF PONIES."

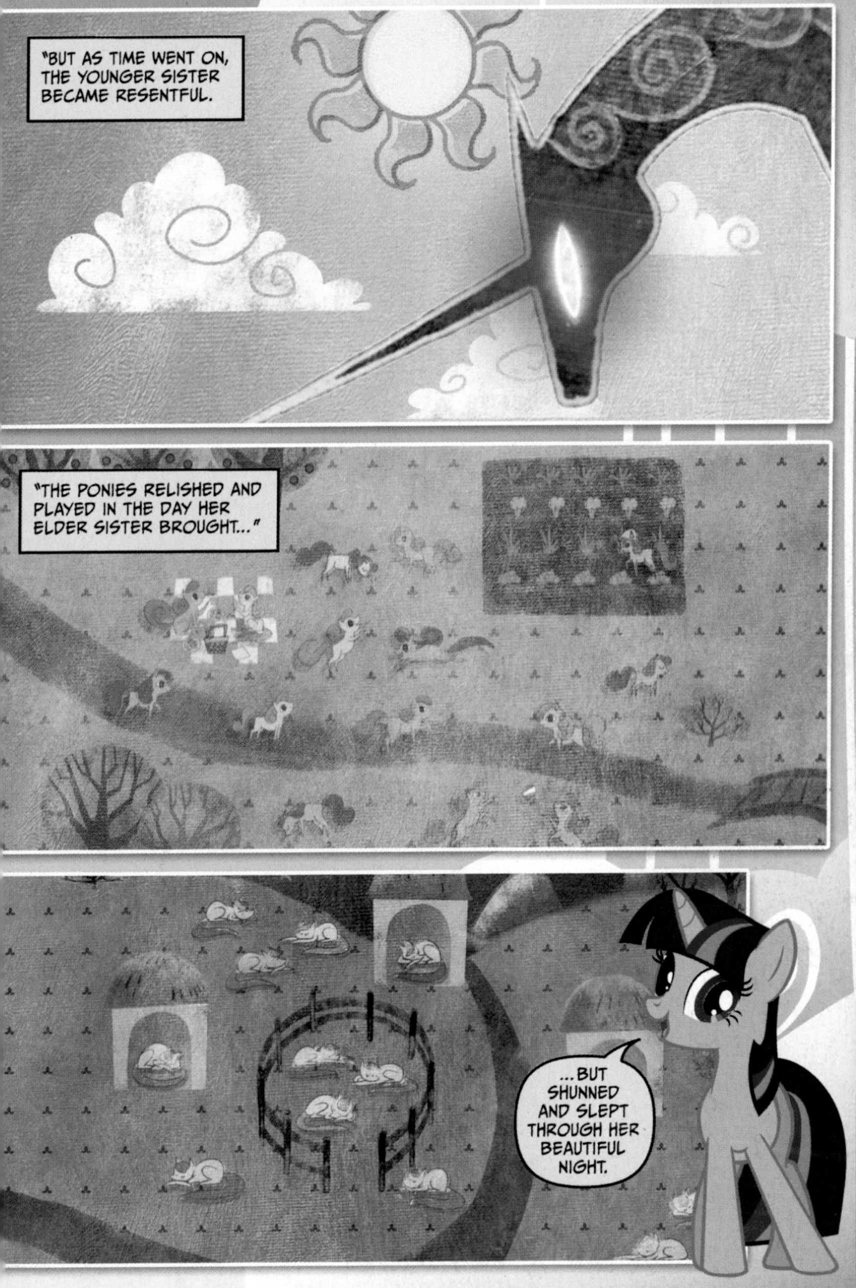
"BUT AS TIME WENT ON, THE YOUNGER SISTER BECAME RESENTFUL.
"THE PONIES RELISHED AND PLAYED IN THE DAY HER ELDER SISTER BROUGHT..."
...BUT SHUNNED AND SLEPT THROUGH HER BEAUTIFUL NIGHT.

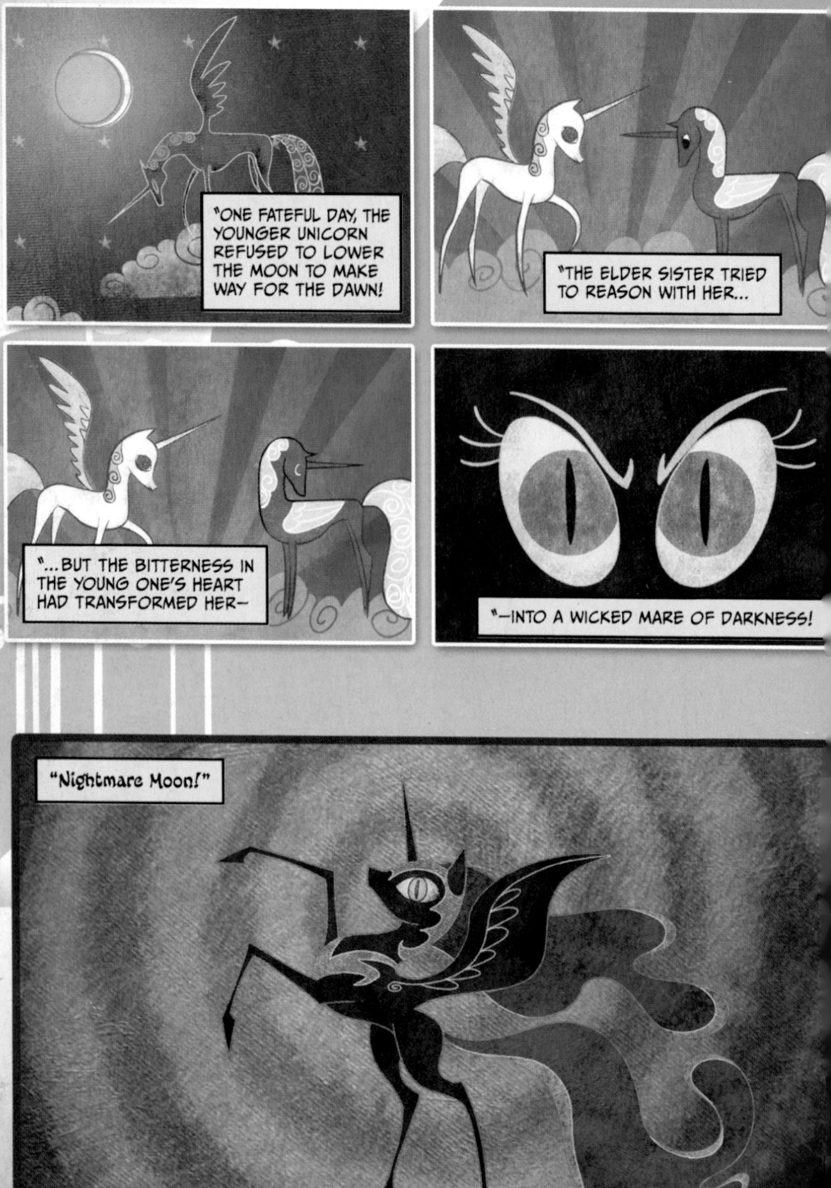
"ONE FATEFUL DAY, THE YOUNGER UNICORN REFUSED TO LOWER THE MOON TO MAKE WAY FOR THE DAWN!
"THE ELDER SISTER TRIED TO REASON WITH HER...
"...BUT THE BITTERNESS IN THE YOUNG ONE'S HEART HAD TRANSFORMED HER–
"–INTO A WICKED MARE OF DARKNESS!
"Nightmare Moon!"

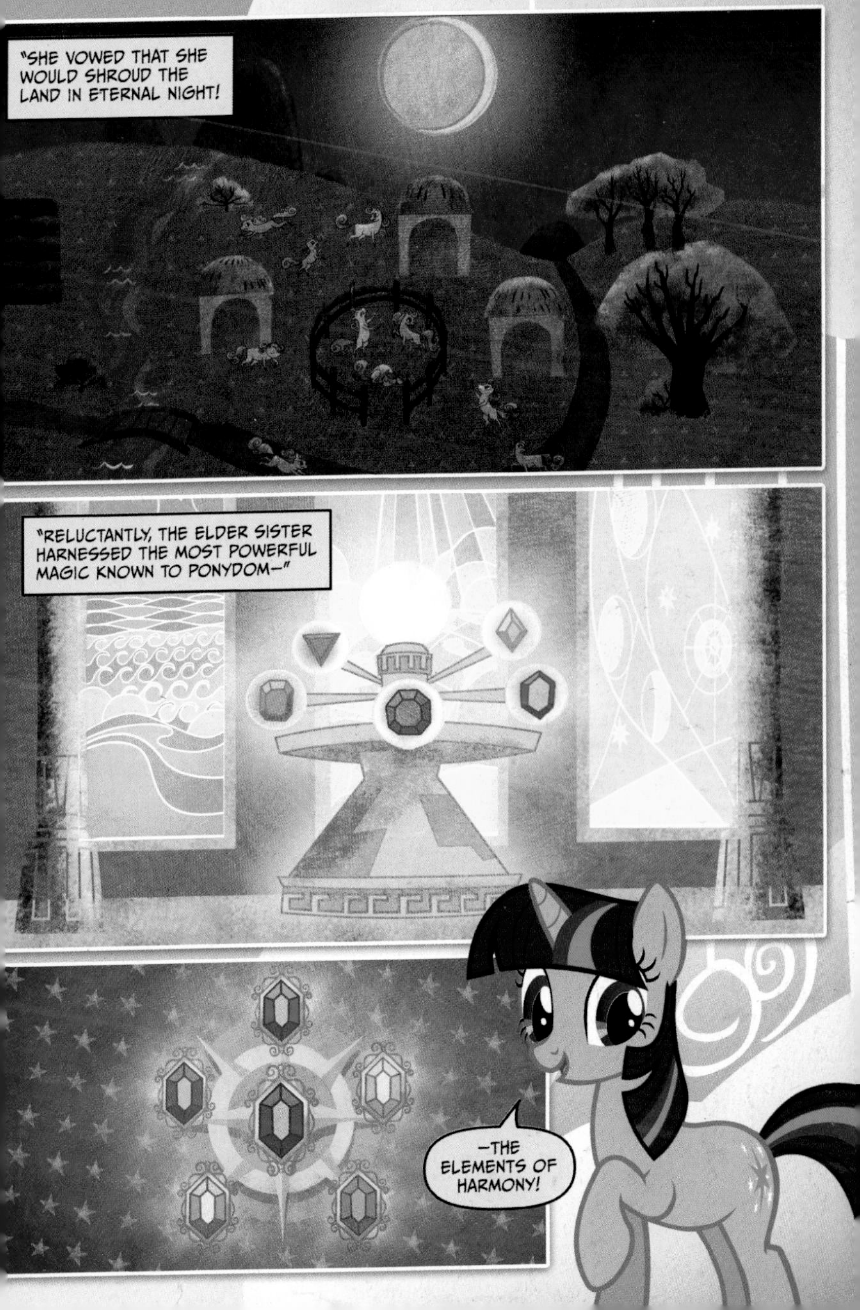
"SHE VOWED THAT SHE WOULD SHROUD THE LAND IN ETERNAL NIGHT!
"RELUCTANTLY, THE ELDER SISTER HARNESSED THE MOST POWERFUL MAGIC KNOWN TO PONYDOM—"
—THE ELEMENTS OF HARMONY!

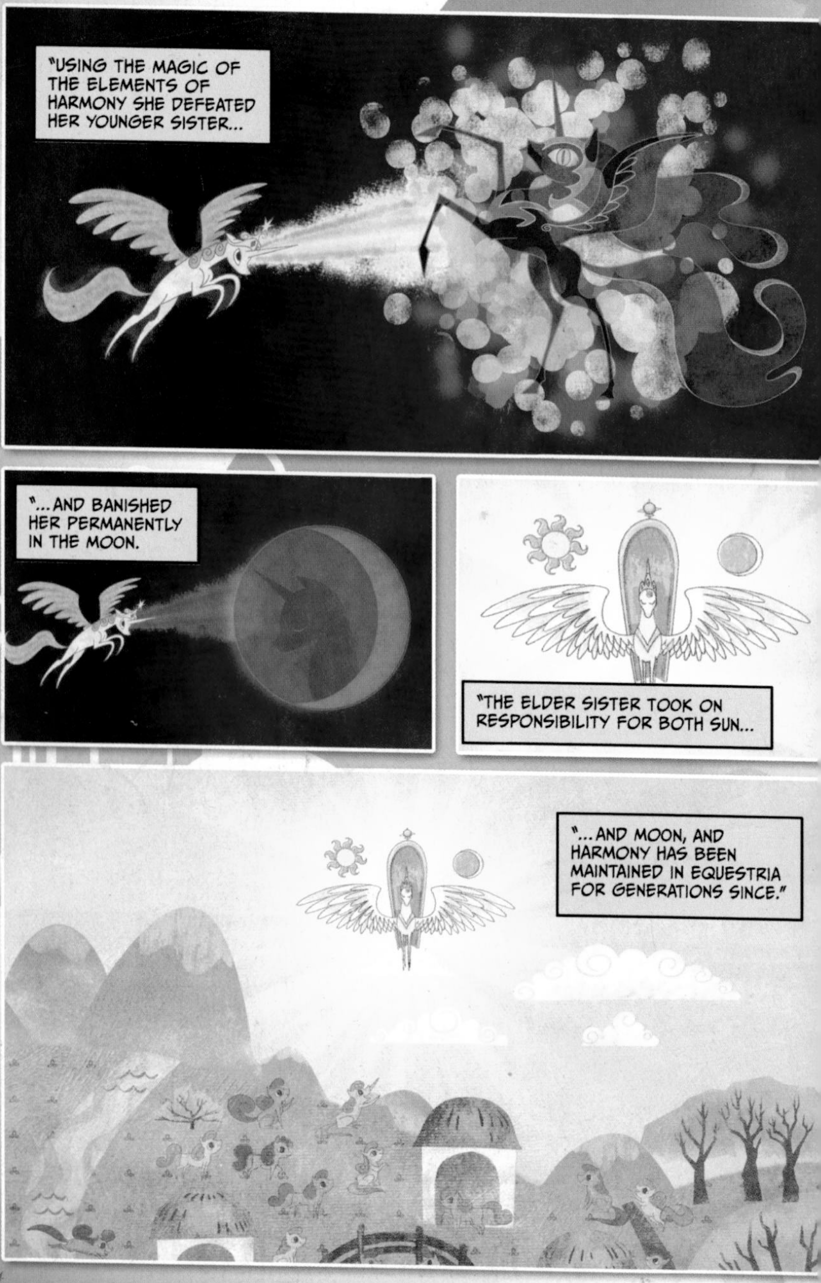
"USING THE MAGIC OF THE ELEMENTS OF HARMONY SHE DEFEATED HER YOUNGER SISTER...
"...AND BANISHED HER PERMANENTLY IN THE MOON.
"THE ELDER SISTER TOOK ON RESPONSIBILITY FOR BOTH SUN...
"...AND MOON, AND HARMONY HAS BEEN MAINTAINED IN EQUESTRIA FOR GENERATIONS SINCE."

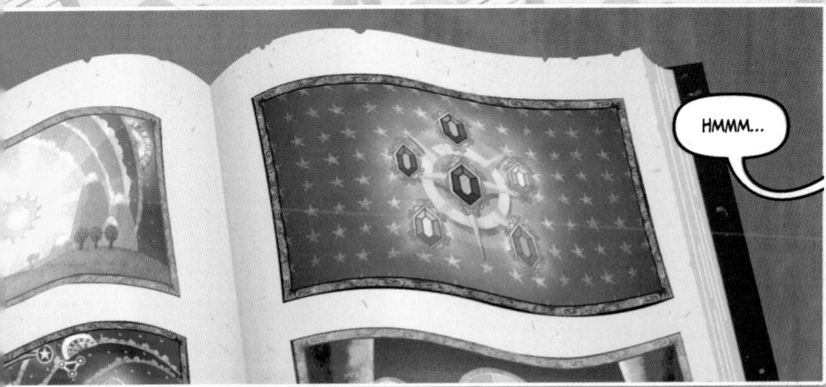
HMMM...

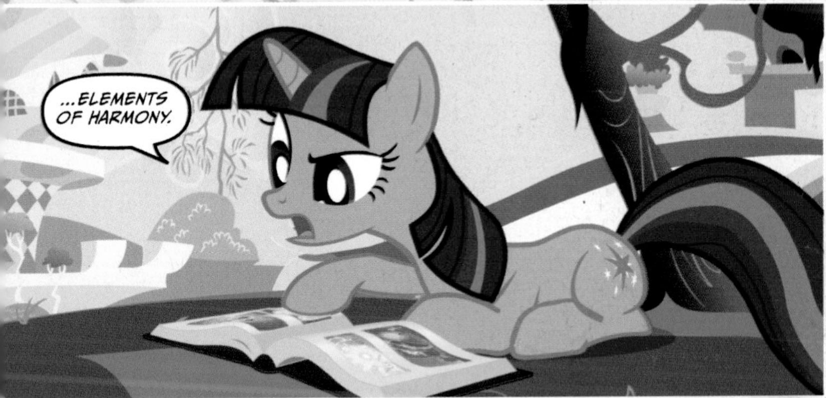
...ELEMENTS OF HARMONY.

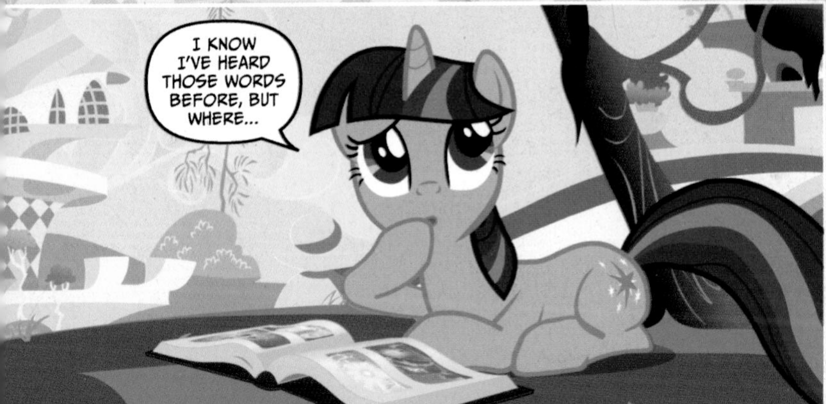
I KNOW I'VE HEARD THOSE WORDS BEFORE, BUT WHERE...

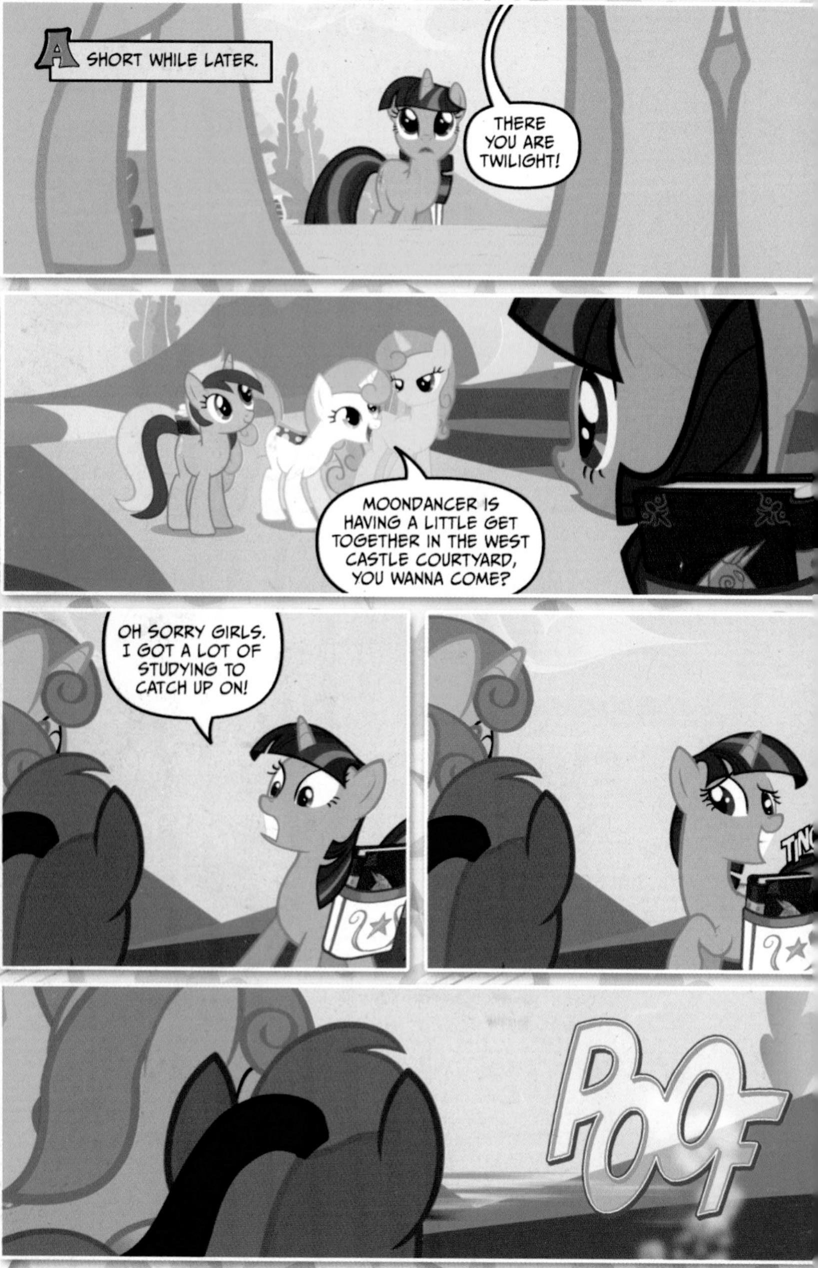
A SHORT WHILE LATER.
THERE YOU ARE TWILIGHT!
MOONDANCER IS HAVING A LITTLE GET TOGETHER IN THE WEST CASTLE COURTYARD, YOU WANNA COME?
OH SORRY GIRLS. I GOT A LOT OF STUDYING TO CATCH UP ON!
POOF

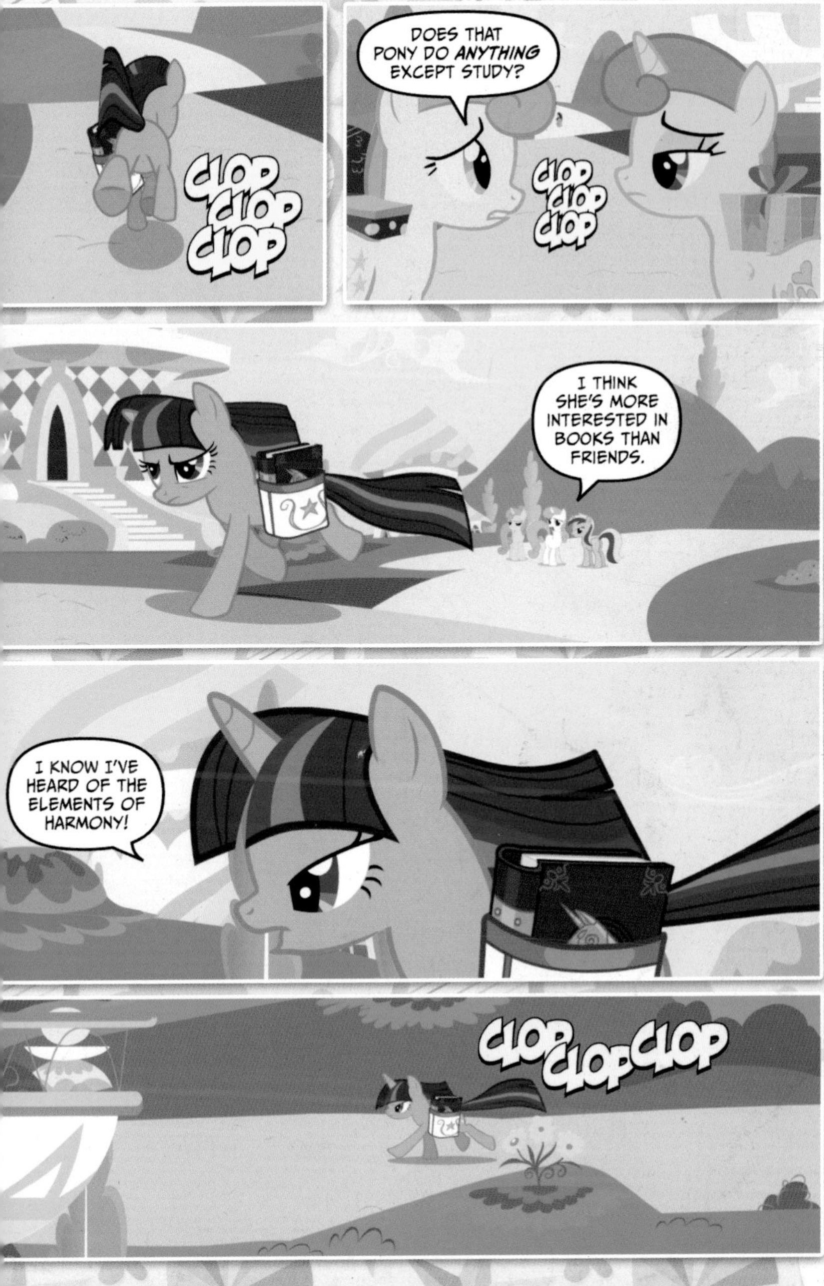
CLOP CLOP CLOP
DOES THAT PONY DO *ANYTHING* EXCEPT STUDY?
CLOP CLOP CLOP
I THINK SHE'S MORE INTERESTED IN BOOKS THAN FRIENDS.
I KNOW I'VE HEARD OF THE ELEMENTS OF HARMONY!
CLOP CLOP CLOP

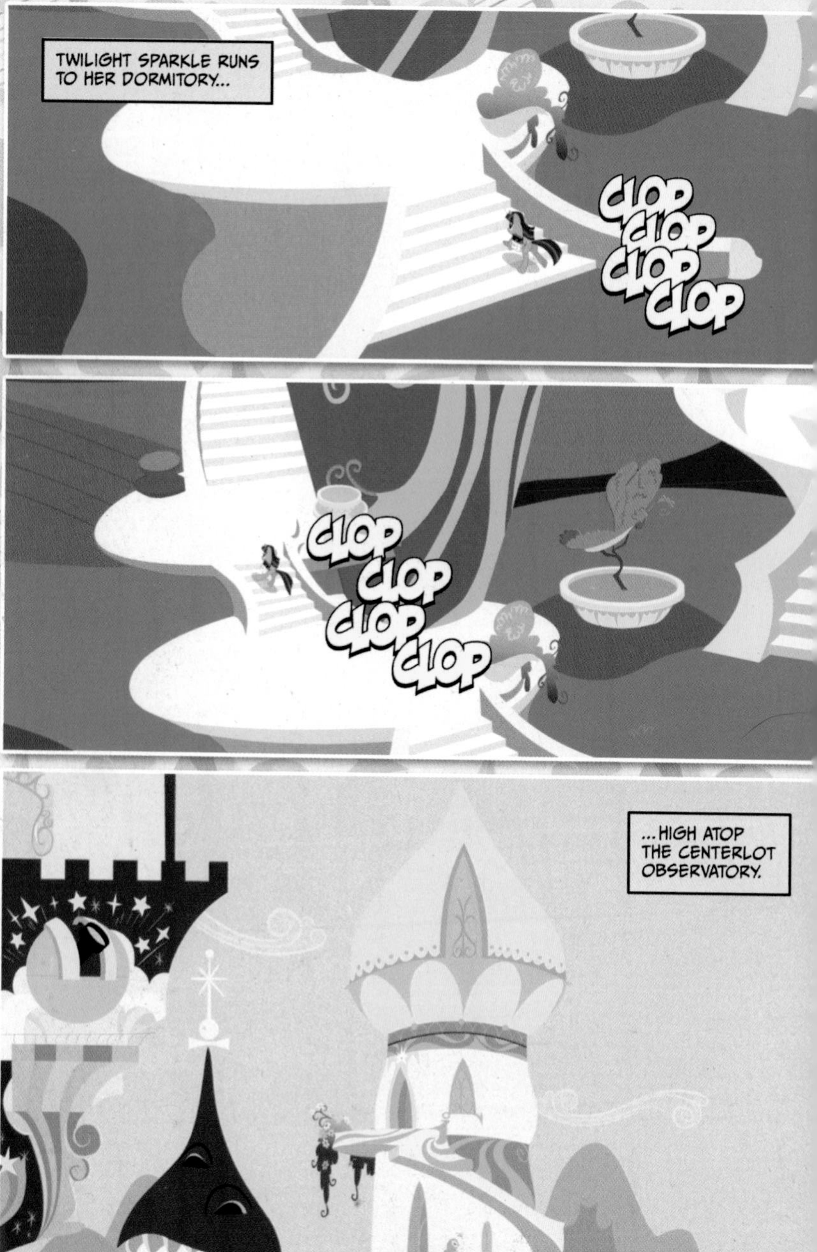
TWILIGHT SPARKLE RUNS TO HER DORMITORY...
CLOP CLOP CLOP CLOP
CLOP CLOP CLOP CLOP
...HIGH ATOP THE CENTERLOT OBSERVATORY.

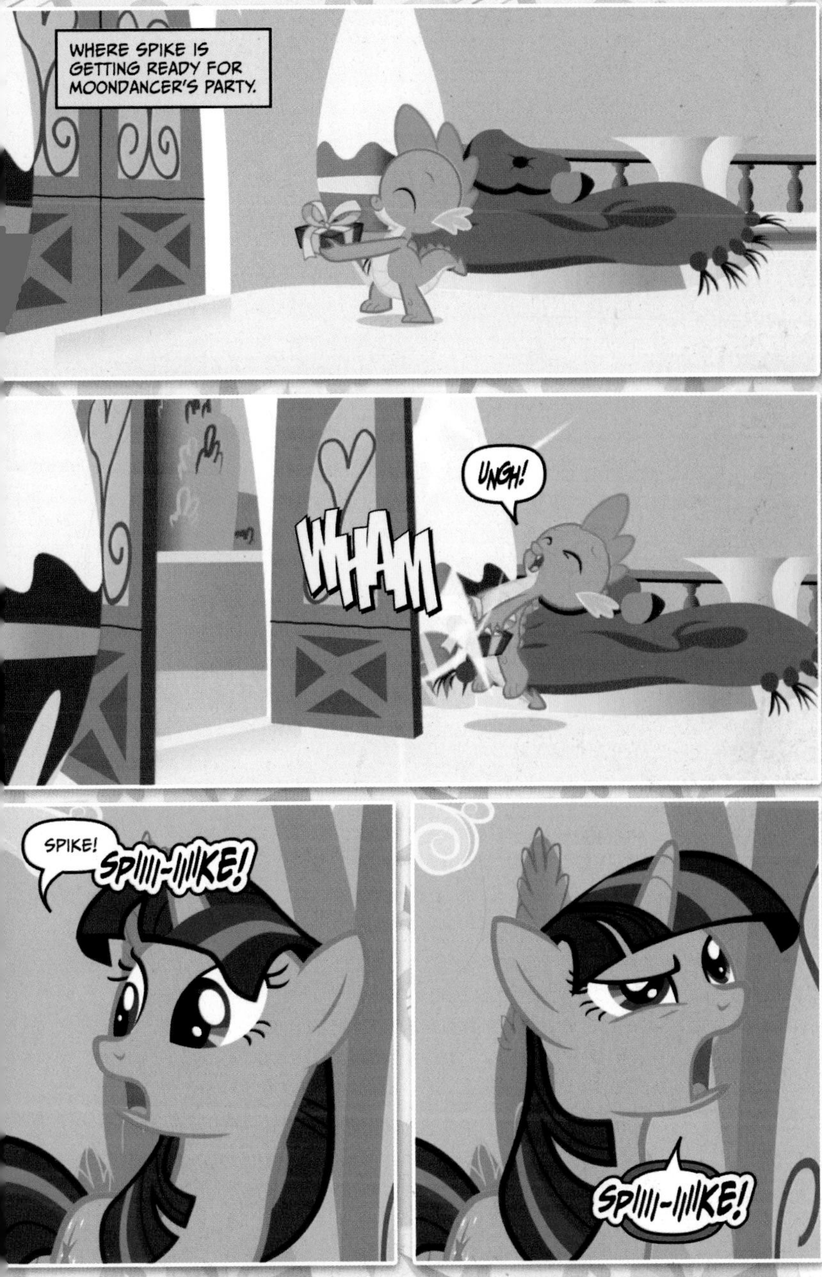
WHERE SPIKE IS GETTING READY FOR MOONDANCER'S PARTY.
UNGH!
WHAM
SPIKE!
SPIIIII-IIIIKE!
SPIIIII-IIIIKE!

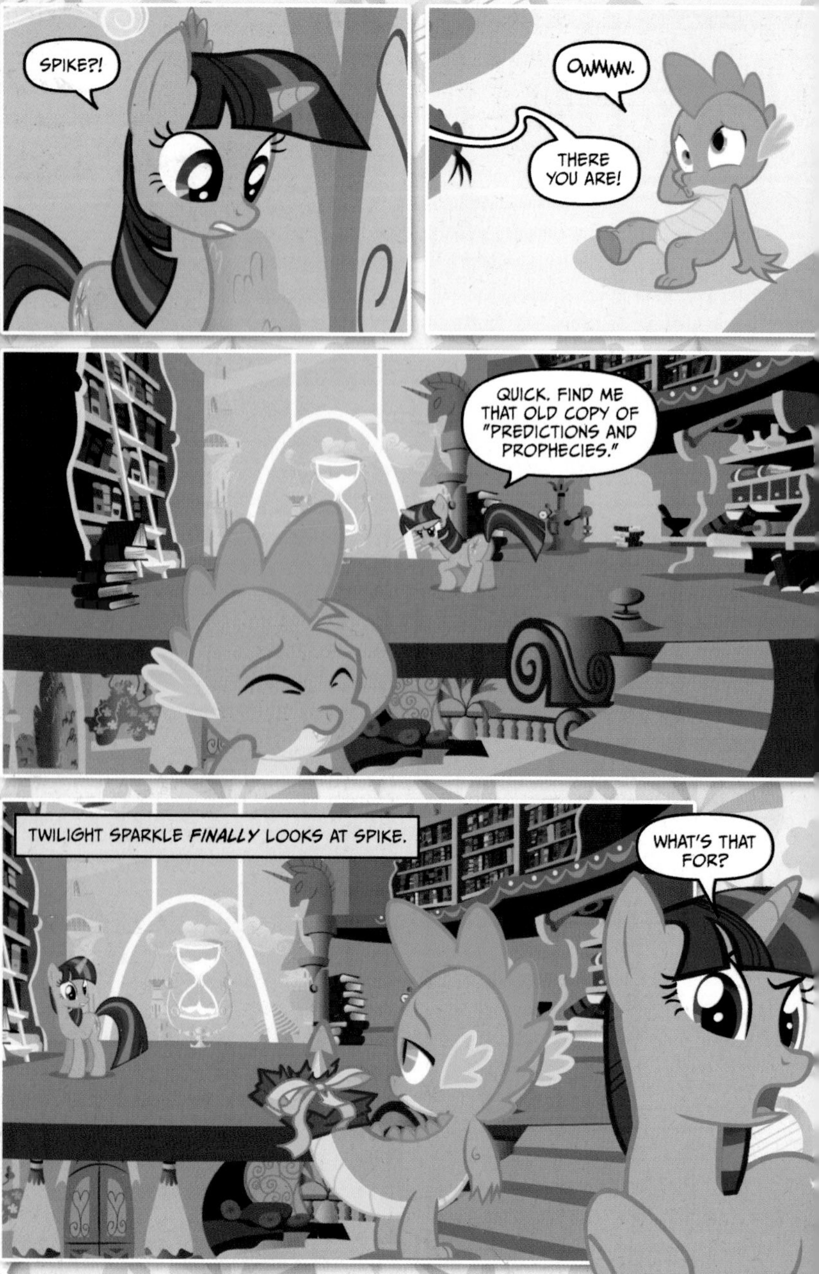
SPIKE?!
OWWWW.
THERE YOU ARE!
QUICK. FIND ME THAT OLD COPY OF "PREDICTIONS AND PROPHECIES."
TWILIGHT SPARKLE FINALLY LOOKS AT SPIKE.
WHAT'S THAT FOR?

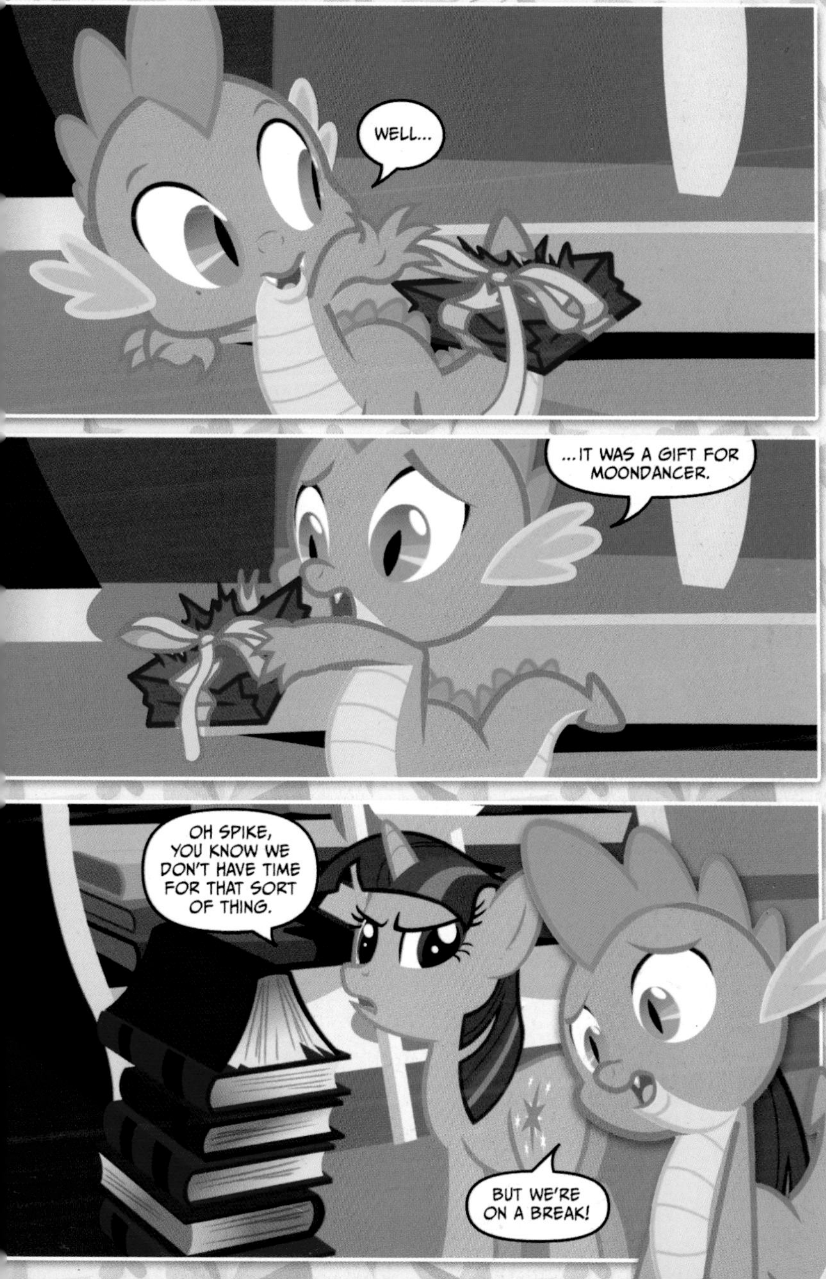
WELL...
...IT WAS A GIFT FOR MOONDANCER.
OH SPIKE, YOU KNOW WE DON'T HAVE TIME FOR THAT SORT OF THING.
BUT WE'RE ON A BREAK!

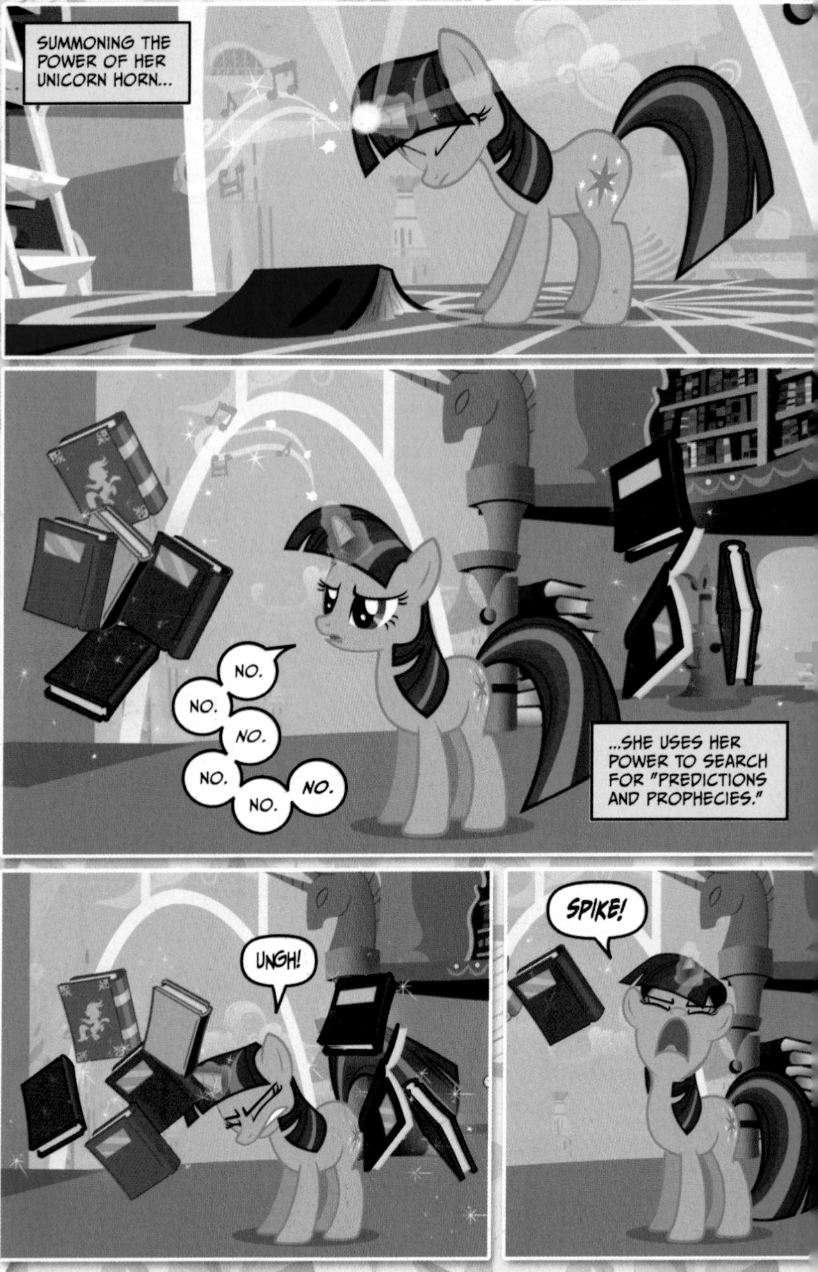
SUMMONING THE POWER OF HER UNICORN HORN...
NO.
NO.
NO.
NO.
NO.
NO.
...SHE USES HER POWER TO SEARCH FOR "PREDICTIONS AND PROPHECIES."
UNGH!
SPIKE!

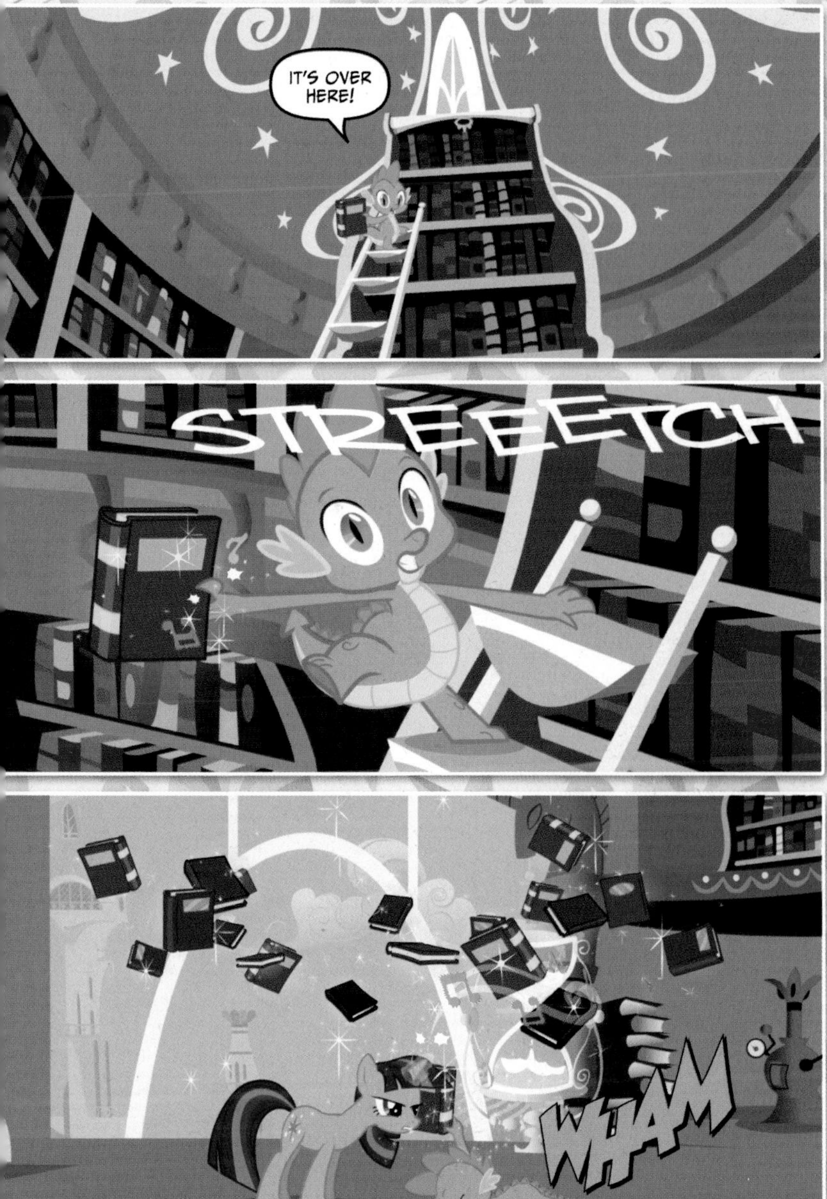
IT'S OVER HERE!
STREEETCH
WHAM

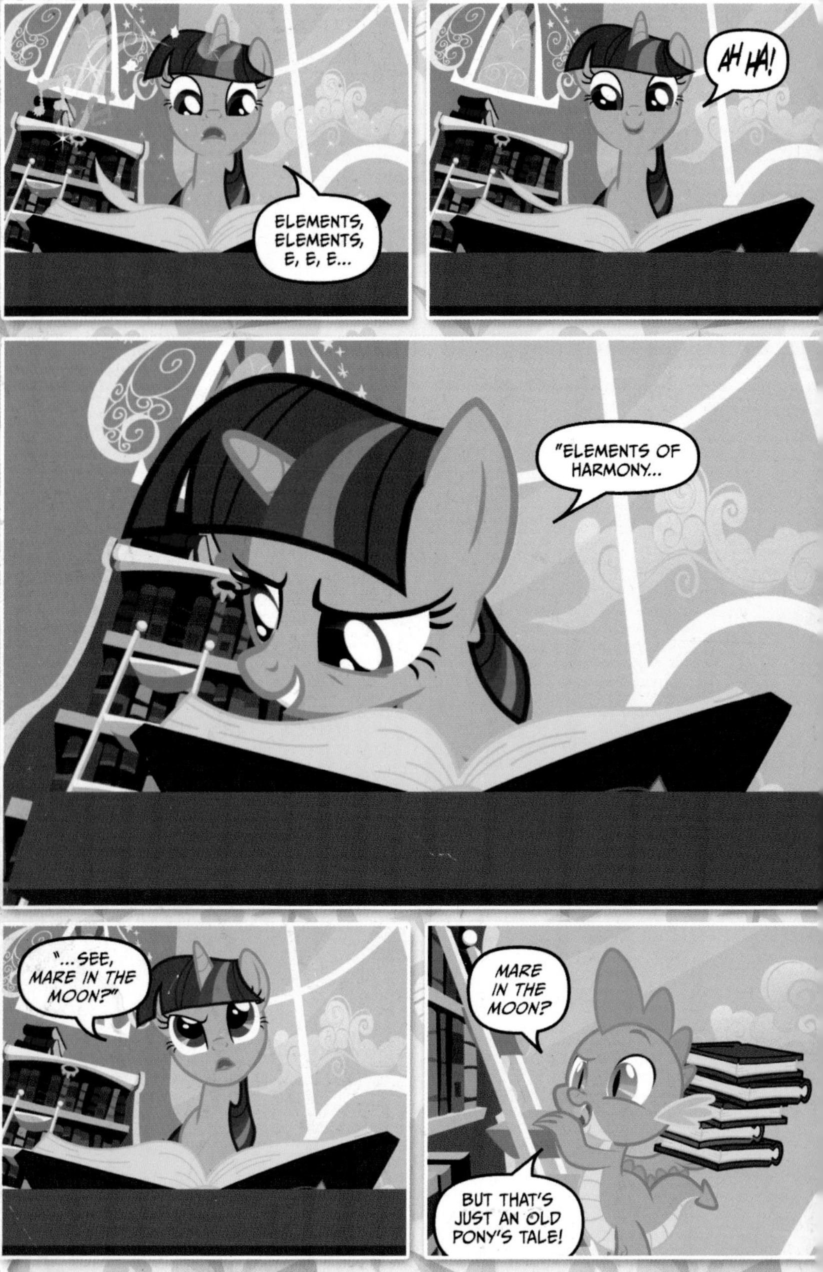
ELEMENTS, ELEMENTS, E, E, E...
AH HA!
"ELEMENTS OF HARMONY...
"...SEE, MARE IN THE MOON?"
MARE IN THE MOON?
BUT THAT'S JUST AN OLD PONY'S TALE!

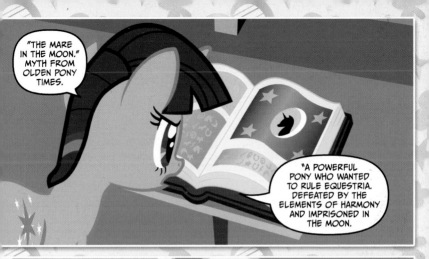

"THE MARE IN THE MOON." MYTH FROM OLDEN PONY TIMES.

"A POWERFUL PONY WHO WANTED TO RULE EQUESTRIA. DEFEATED BY THE ELEMENTS OF HARMONY AND IMPRISONED IN THE MOON.

"LEGEND HAS IT THAT ON THE LONGEST DAY OF THE THOUSANDTH YEAR, THE STARS WILL AID IN HER ESCAPE, AND SHE WILL BRING ABOUT NIGHT-TIME ETERNAL."

GASP!

SPIKE! DO YOU KNOW WHAT THIS MEANS?

NO... ?

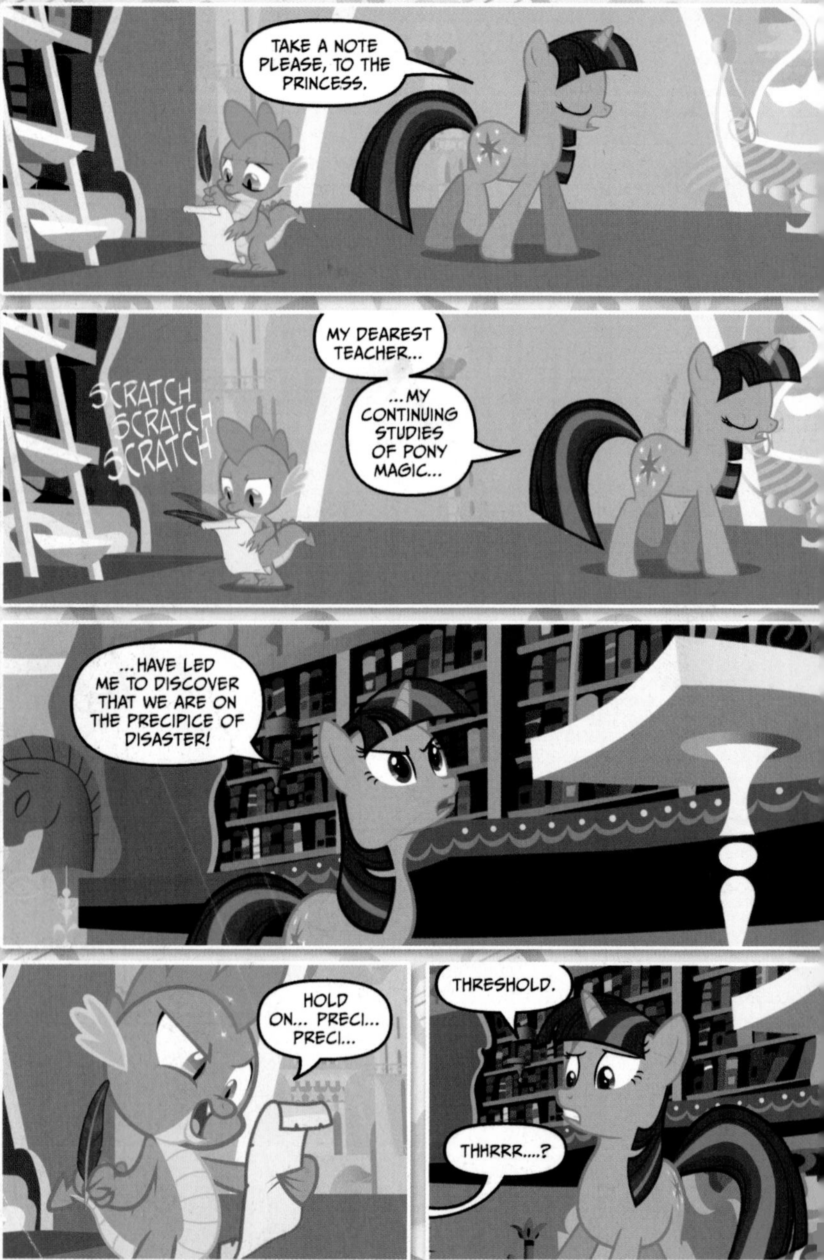
TAKE A NOTE PLEASE, TO THE PRINCESS.
MY DEAREST TEACHER...
SCRATCH SCRATCH SCRATCH
...MY CONTINUING STUDIES OF PONY MAGIC...
...HAVE LED ME TO DISCOVER THAT WE ARE ON THE PRECIPICE OF DISASTER!
HOLD ON... PRECI... PRECI...
THRESHOLD.
THHRRR....?

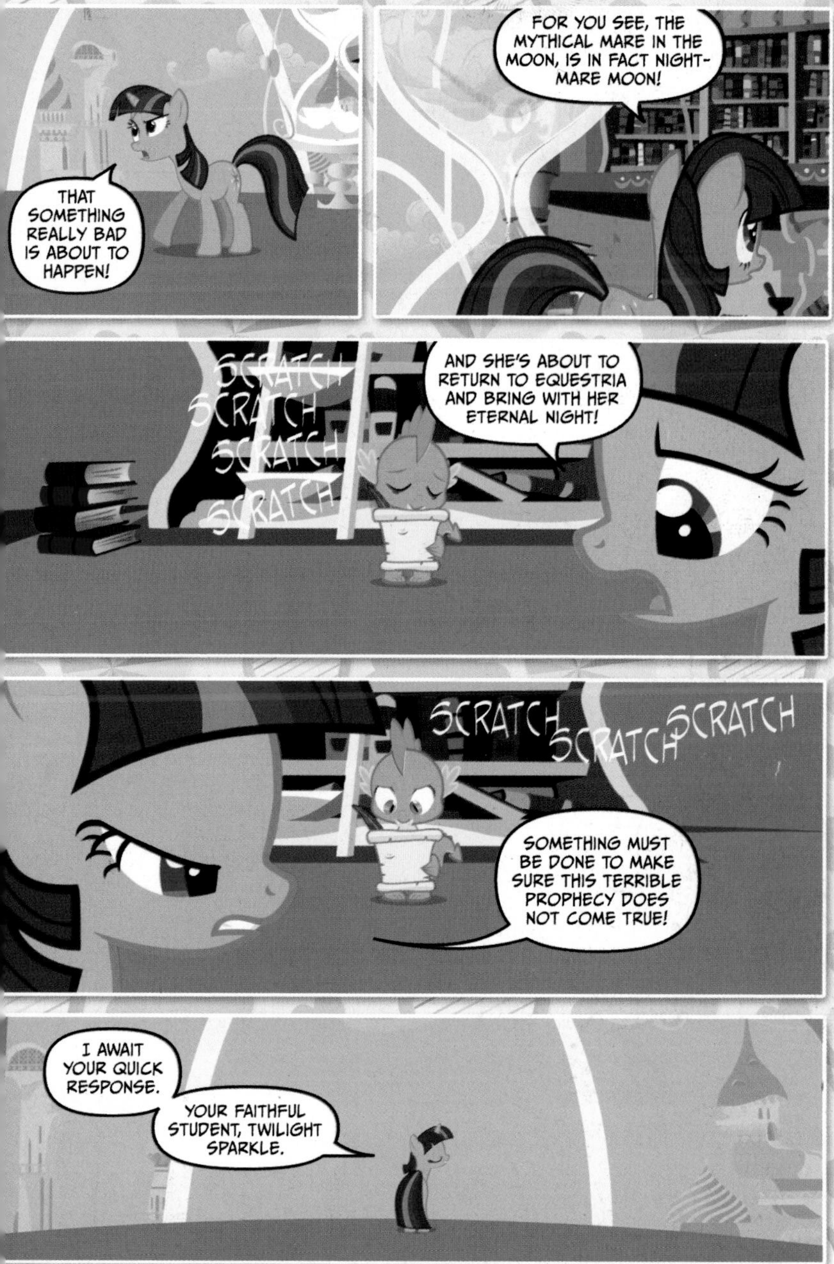
THAT SOMETHING REALLY BAD IS ABOUT TO HAPPEN!
FOR YOU SEE, THE MYTHICAL MARE IN THE MOON, IS IN FACT NIGHT-MARE MOON!
SCRATCH SCRATCH SCRATCH SCRATCH
AND SHE'S ABOUT TO RETURN TO EQUESTRIA AND BRING WITH HER ETERNAL NIGHT!
SCRATCH SCRATCH SCRATCH
SOMETHING MUST BE DONE TO MAKE SURE THIS TERRIBLE PROPHECY DOES NOT COME TRUE!
I AWAIT YOUR QUICK RESPONSE.
YOUR FAITHFUL STUDENT, TWILIGHT SPARKLE.

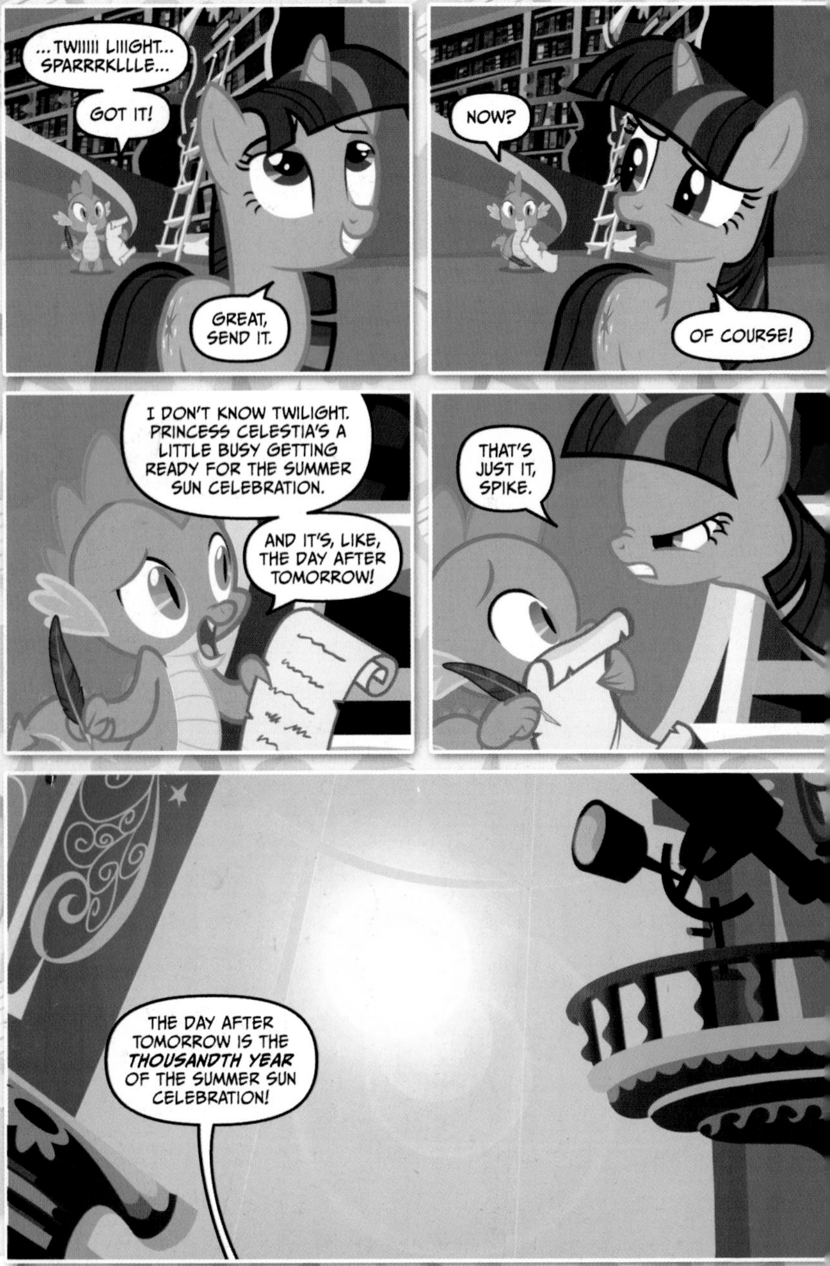
...TWIIIII LIIIGHT... SPARRRKLLLE...
GOT IT!
GREAT, SEND IT.
NOW?
OF COURSE!
I DON'T KNOW TWILIGHT. PRINCESS CELESTIA'S A LITTLE BUSY GETTING READY FOR THE SUMMER SUN CELEBRATION.
AND IT'S, LIKE, THE DAY AFTER TOMORROW!
THAT'S JUST IT, SPIKE.
THE DAY AFTER TOMORROW IS THE ***THOUSANDTH YEAR*** OF THE SUMMER SUN CELEBRATION!

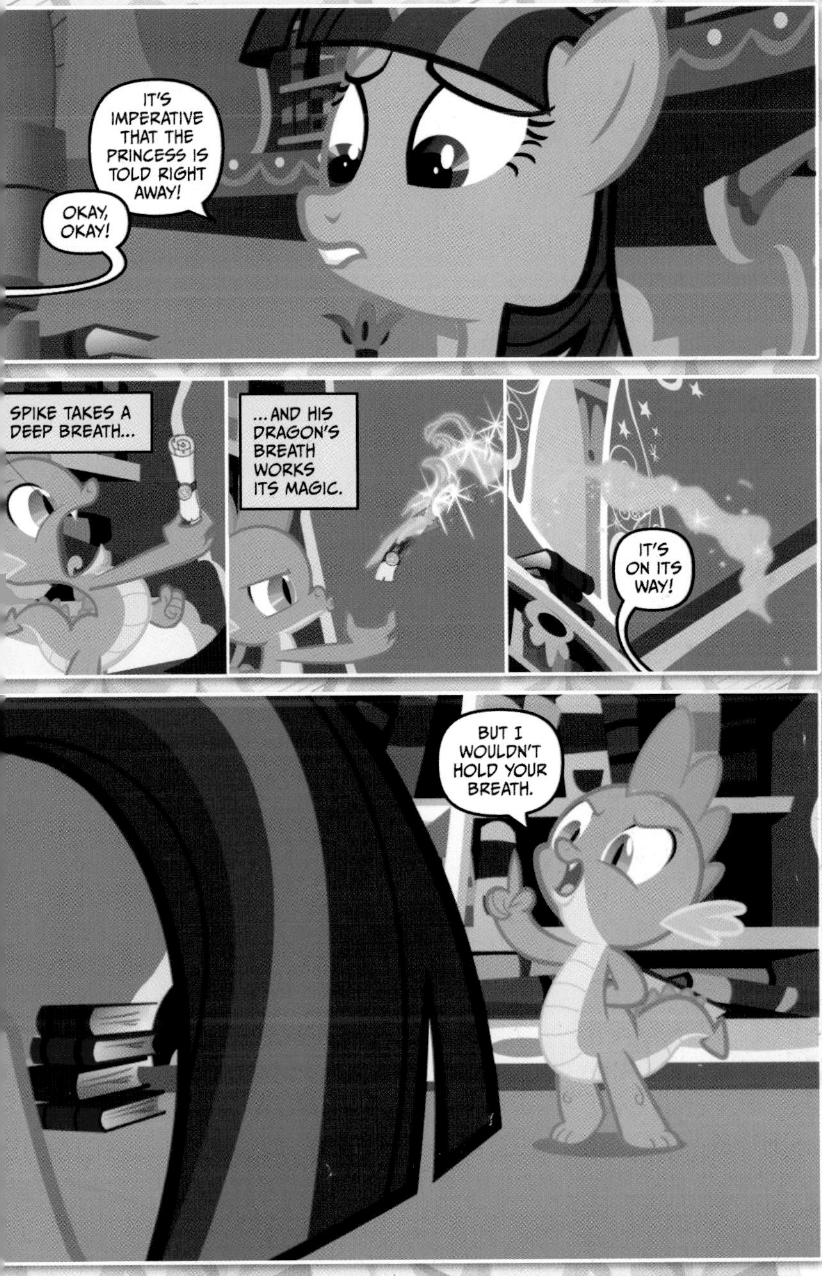
IT'S IMPERATIVE THAT THE PRINCESS IS TOLD RIGHT AWAY!
OKAY, OKAY!
SPIKE TAKES A DEEP BREATH...
...AND HIS DRAGON'S BREATH WORKS ITS MAGIC.
IT'S ON ITS WAY!
BUT I WOULDN'T HOLD YOUR BREATH.

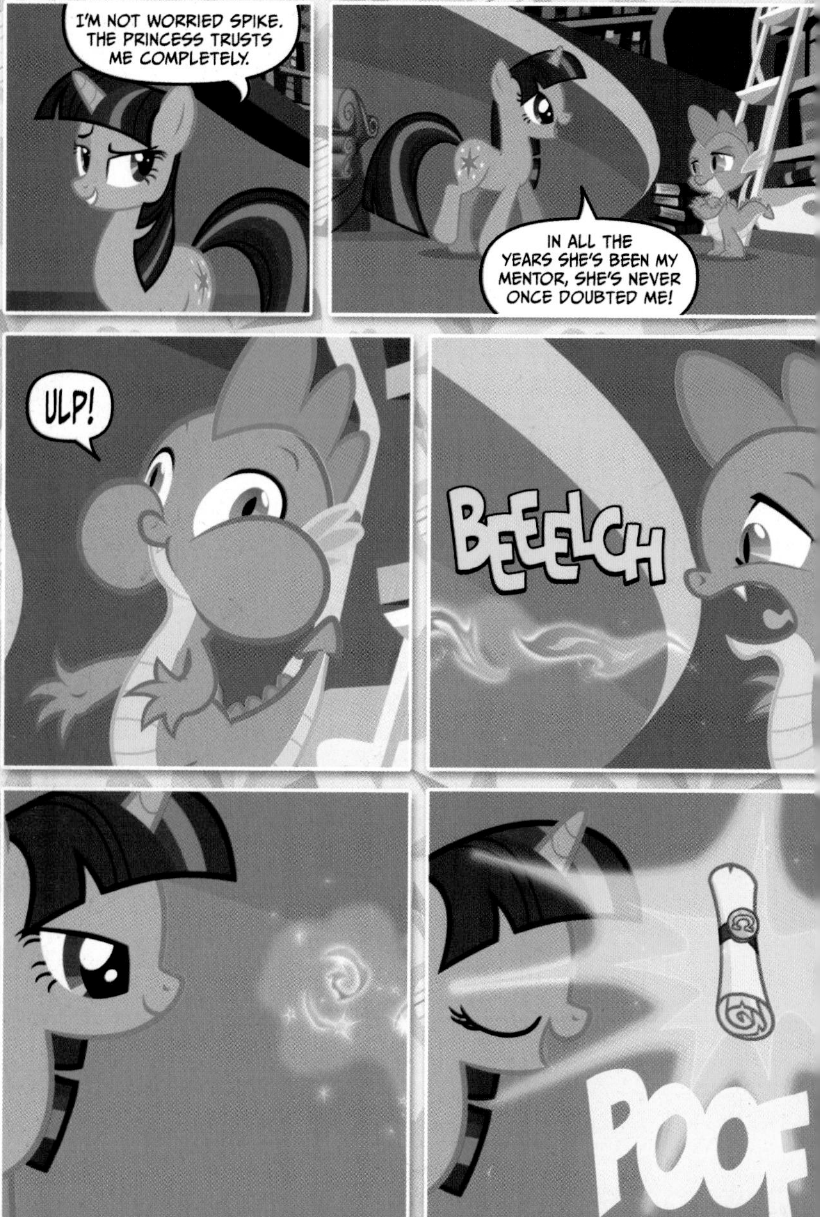
I'M NOT WORRIED SPIKE. THE PRINCESS TRUSTS ME COMPLETELY.
IN ALL THE YEARS SHE'S BEEN MY MENTOR, SHE'S NEVER ONCE DOUBTED ME!
ULP!
BEEELCH
POOF

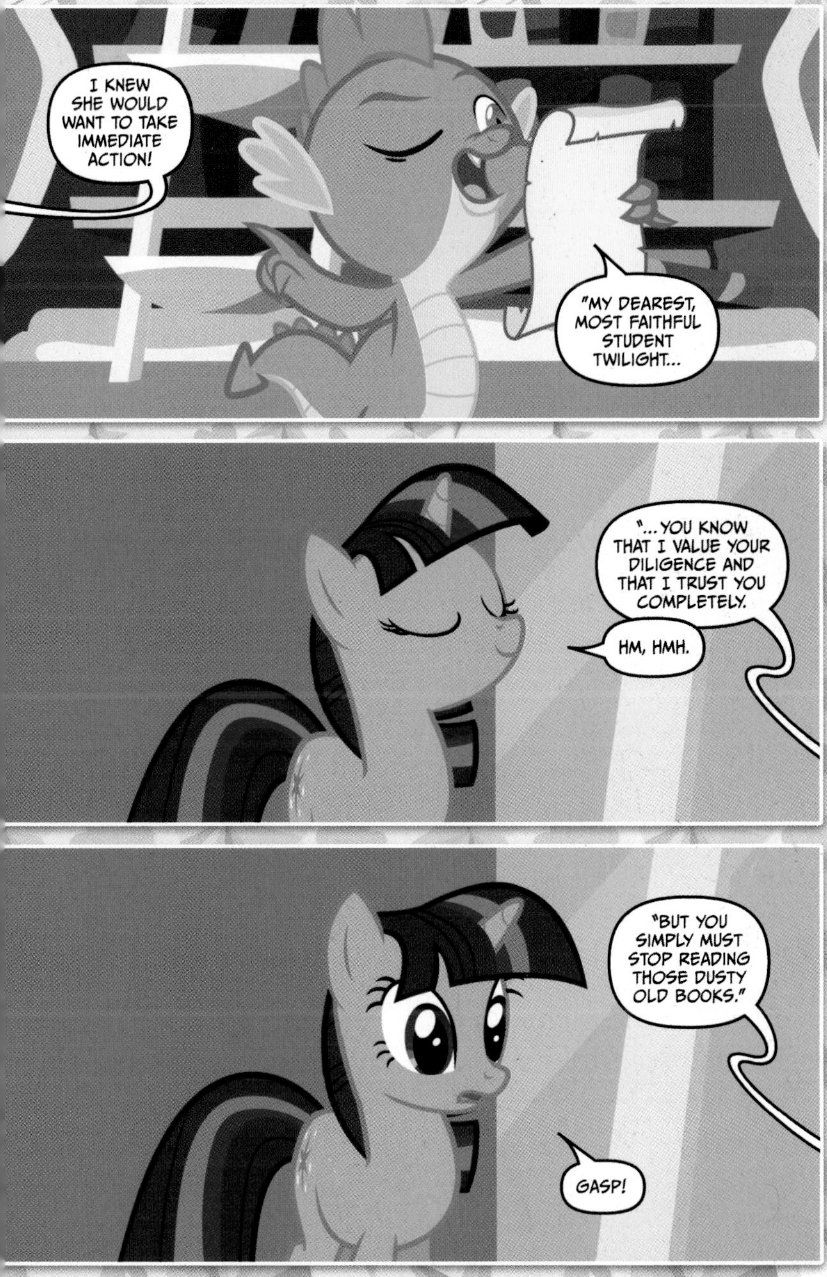

I KNEW SHE WOULD WANT TO TAKE IMMEDIATE ACTION!
"MY DEAREST, MOST FAITHFUL STUDENT TWILIGHT...
"...YOU KNOW THAT I VALUE YOUR DILIGENCE AND THAT I TRUST YOU COMPLETELY.
HM, HMH.
"BUT YOU SIMPLY MUST STOP READING THOSE DUSTY OLD BOOKS."
GASP!

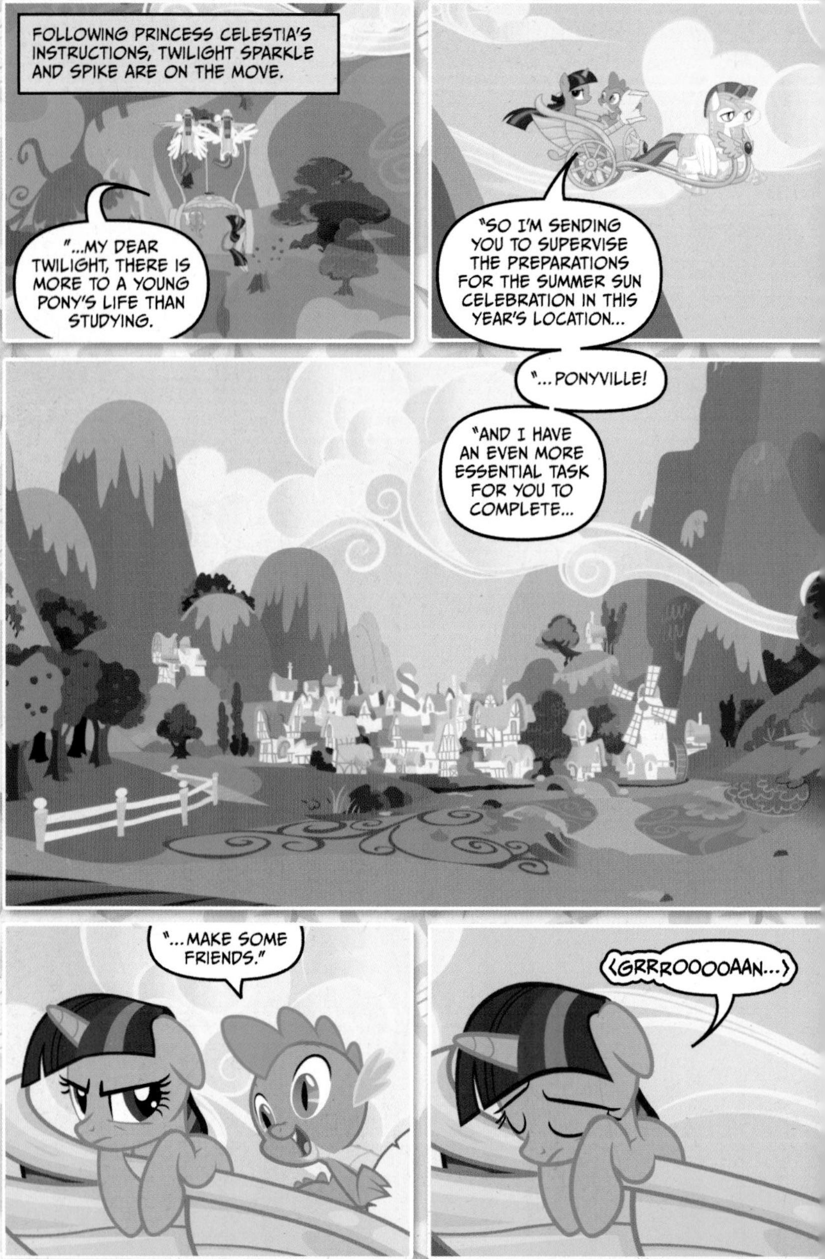
FOLLOWING PRINCESS CELESTIA'S INSTRUCTIONS, TWILIGHT SPARKLE AND SPIKE ARE ON THE MOVE.
"...MY DEAR TWILIGHT, THERE IS MORE TO A YOUNG PONY'S LIFE THAN STUDYING.
"SO I'M SENDING YOU TO SUPERVISE THE PREPARATIONS FOR THE SUMMER SUN CELEBRATION IN THIS YEAR'S LOCATION...
"...PONYVILLE!
"AND I HAVE AN EVEN MORE ESSENTIAL TASK FOR YOU TO COMPLETE...
"...MAKE SOME FRIENDS."
<GRRROOOOAAN...>

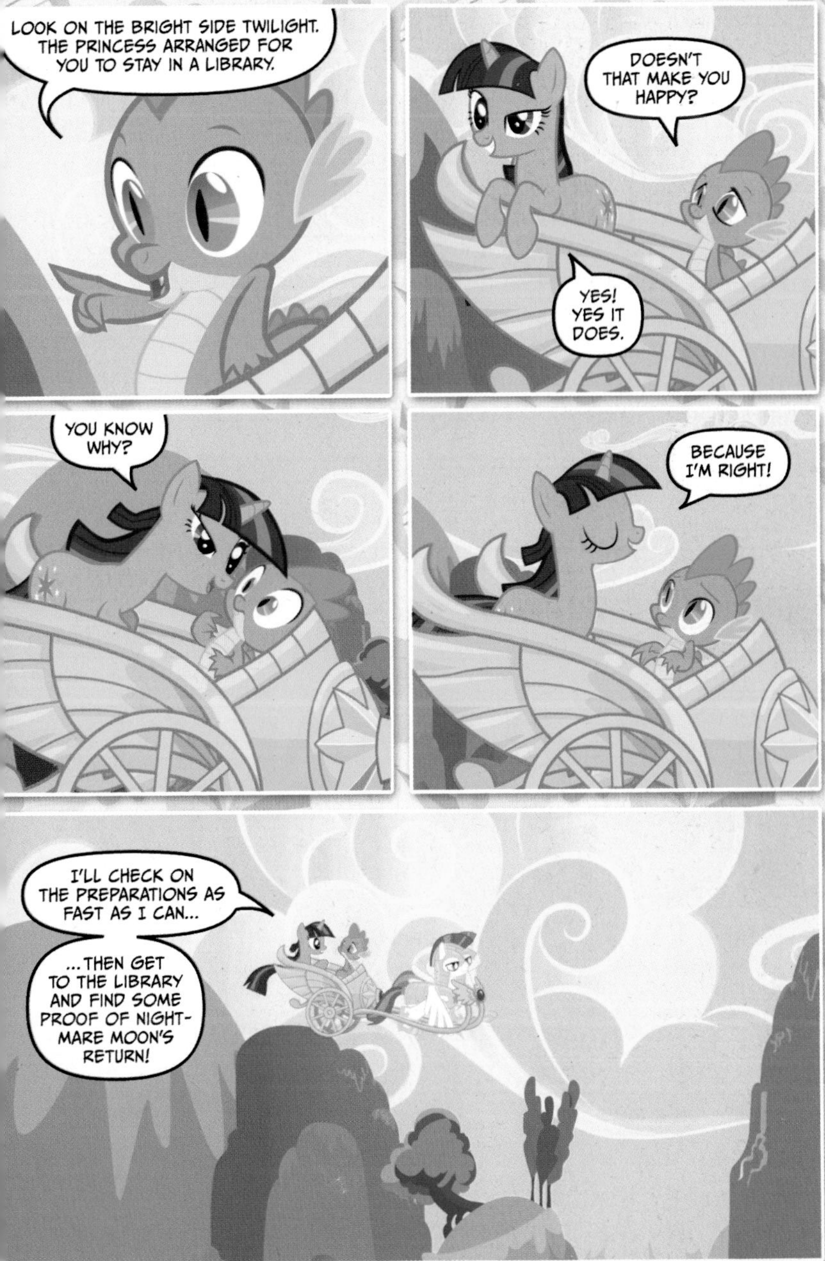
LOOK ON THE BRIGHT SIDE TWILIGHT. THE PRINCESS ARRANGED FOR YOU TO STAY IN A LIBRARY.
DOESN'T THAT MAKE YOU HAPPY?
YES! YES IT DOES.
YOU KNOW WHY?
BECAUSE I'M RIGHT!
I'LL CHECK ON THE PREPARATIONS AS FAST AS I CAN...
...THEN GET TO THE LIBRARY AND FIND SOME PROOF OF NIGHT-MARE MOON'S RETURN!

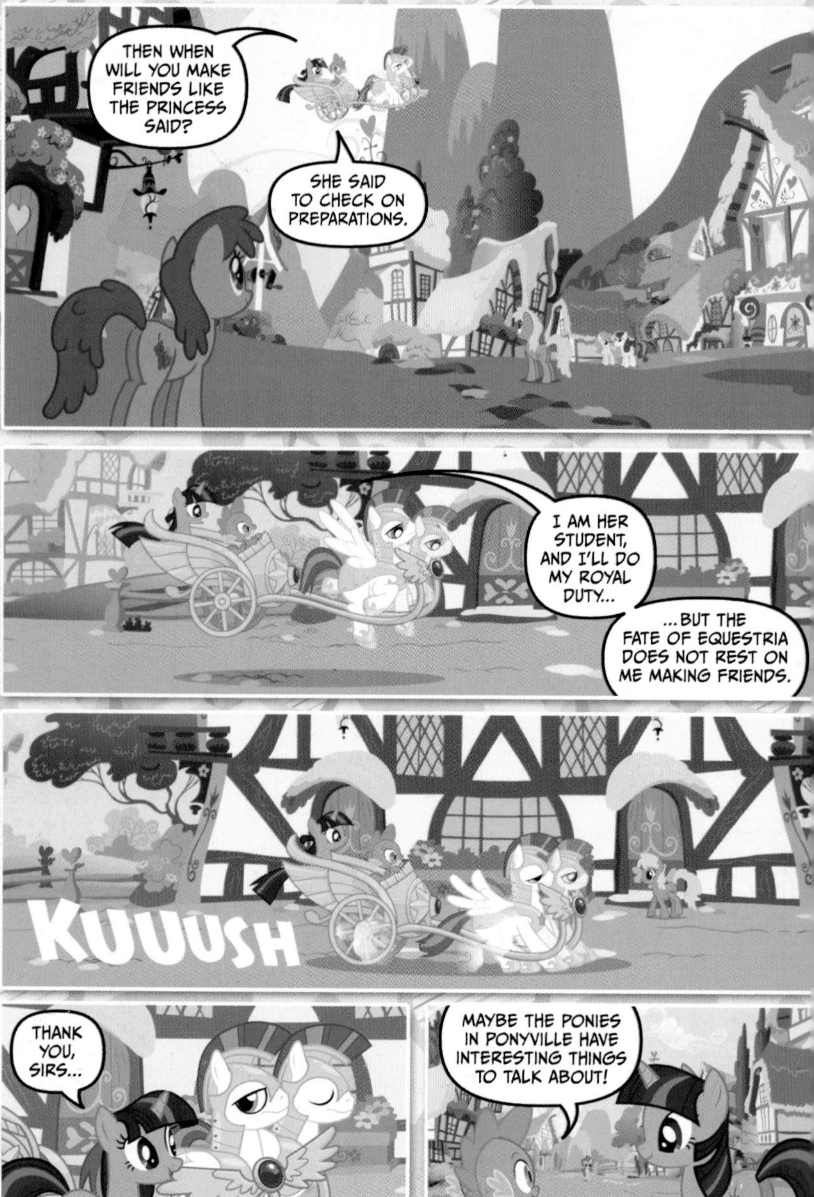

THEN WHEN WILL YOU MAKE FRIENDS LIKE THE PRINCESS SAID?
SHE SAID TO CHECK ON PREPARATIONS.
I AM HER STUDENT, AND I'LL DO MY ROYAL DUTY...
...BUT THE FATE OF EQUESTRIA DOES NOT REST ON ME MAKING FRIENDS.
KUUUSH
THANK YOU, SIRS...
MAYBE THE PONIES IN PONYVILLE HAVE INTERESTING THINGS TO TALK ABOUT!

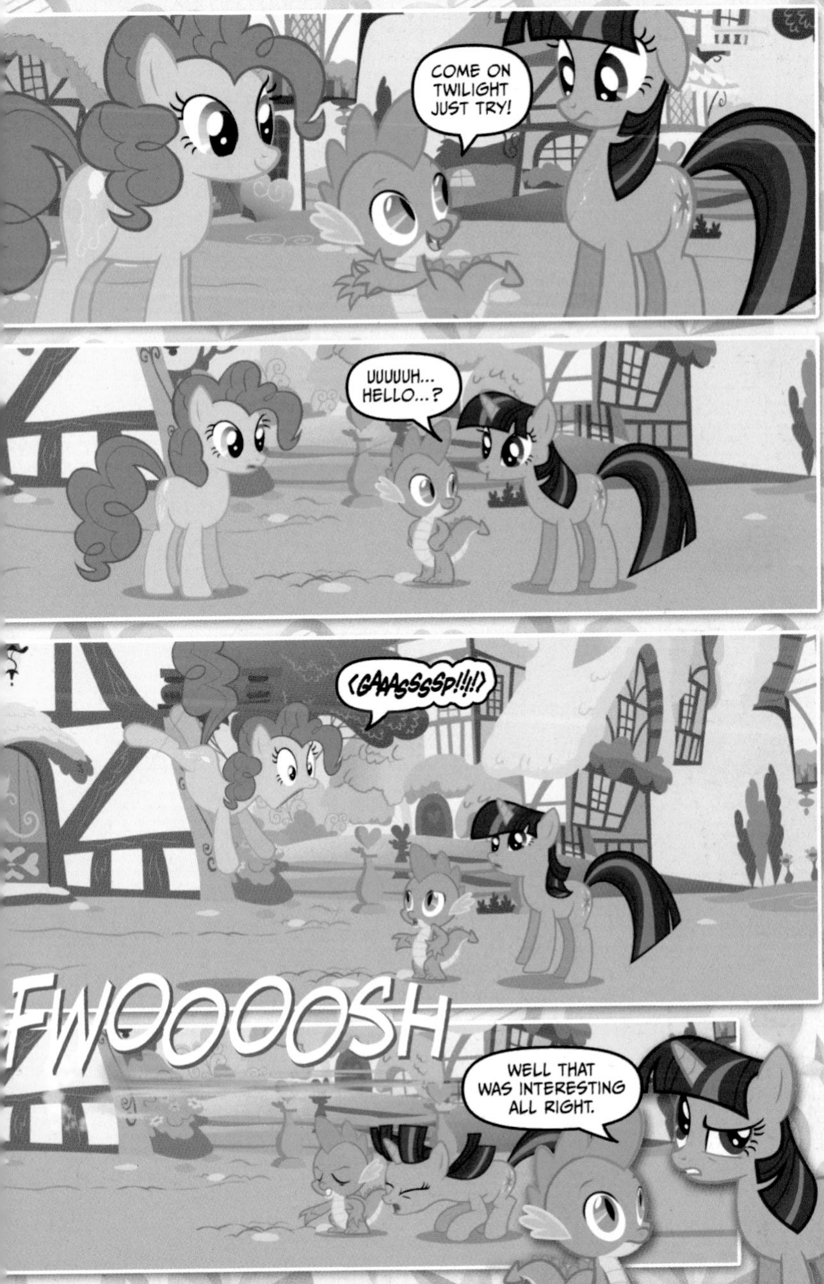
COME ON TWILIGHT JUST TRY!
UUUUUH... HELLO...?
<GAAASSSSP!!!!>
FWOOOOSH
WELL THAT WAS INTERESTING ALL RIGHT.

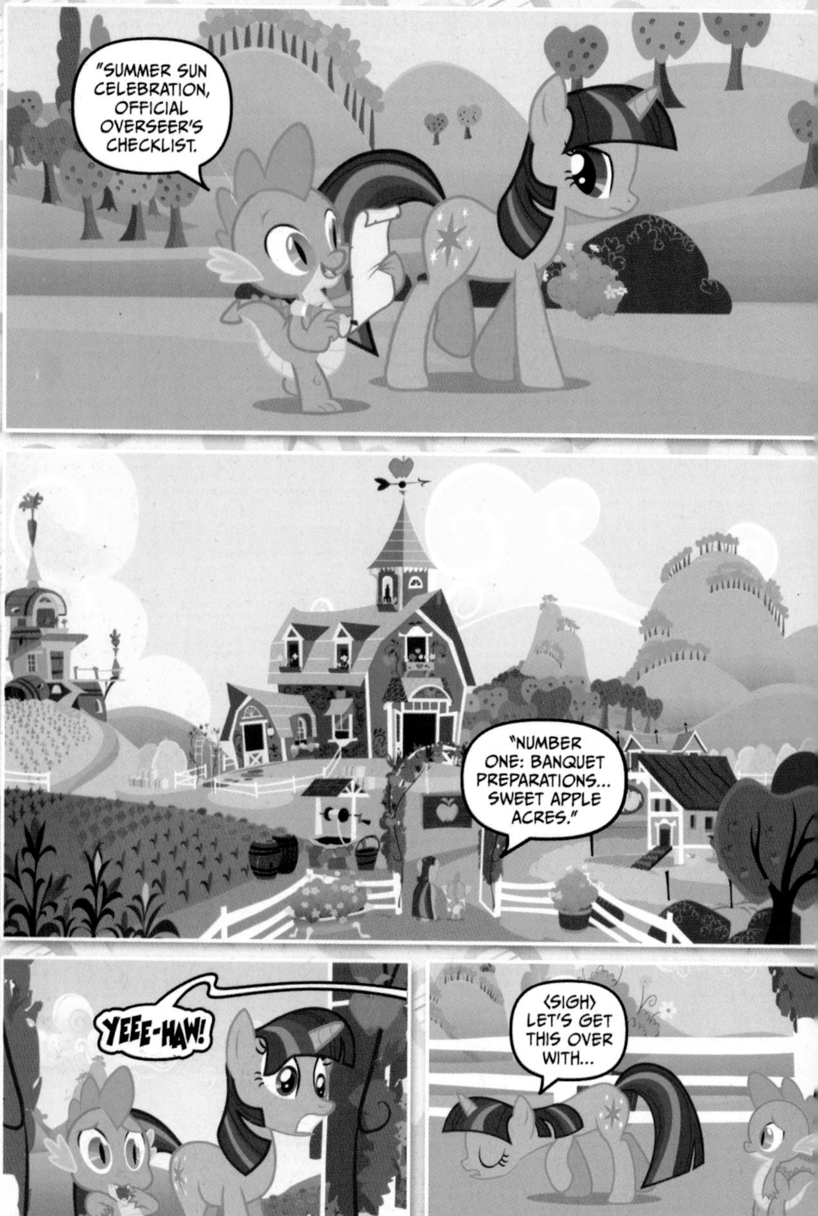
"SUMMER SUN CELEBRATION, OFFICIAL OVERSEER'S CHECKLIST.
"NUMBER ONE: BANQUET PREPARATIONS... SWEET APPLE ACRES."
YEEE-HAW!
(SIGH) LET'S GET THIS OVER WITH...

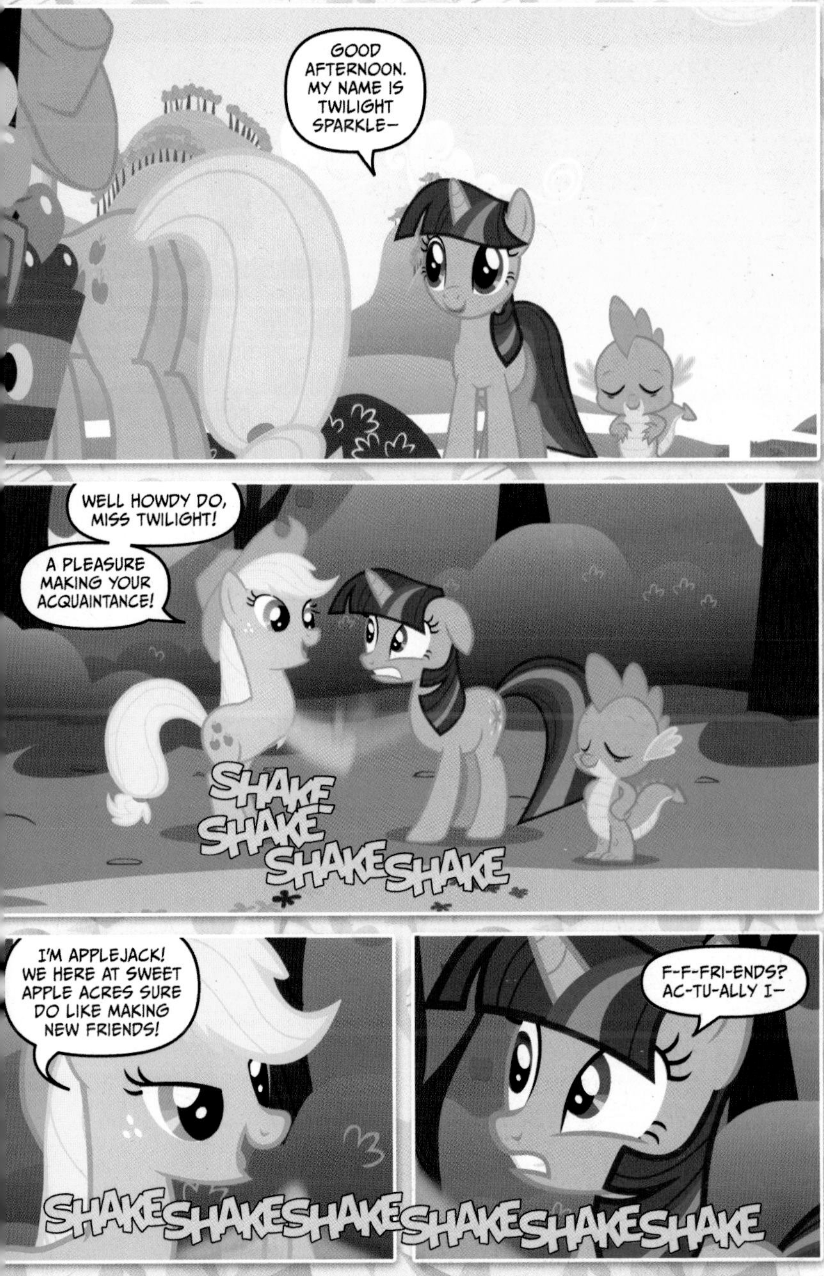
GOOD AFTERNOON. MY NAME IS TWILIGHT SPARKLE—
WELL HOWDY DO, MISS TWILIGHT!
A PLEASURE MAKING YOUR ACQUAINTANCE!
SHAKE SHAKE SHAKESHAKE
I'M APPLEJACK! WE HERE AT SWEET APPLE ACRES SURE DO LIKE MAKING NEW FRIENDS!
F-F-FRI-ENDS? AC-TU-ALLY I—
SHAKESHAKESHAKESHAKESHAKESHAKE

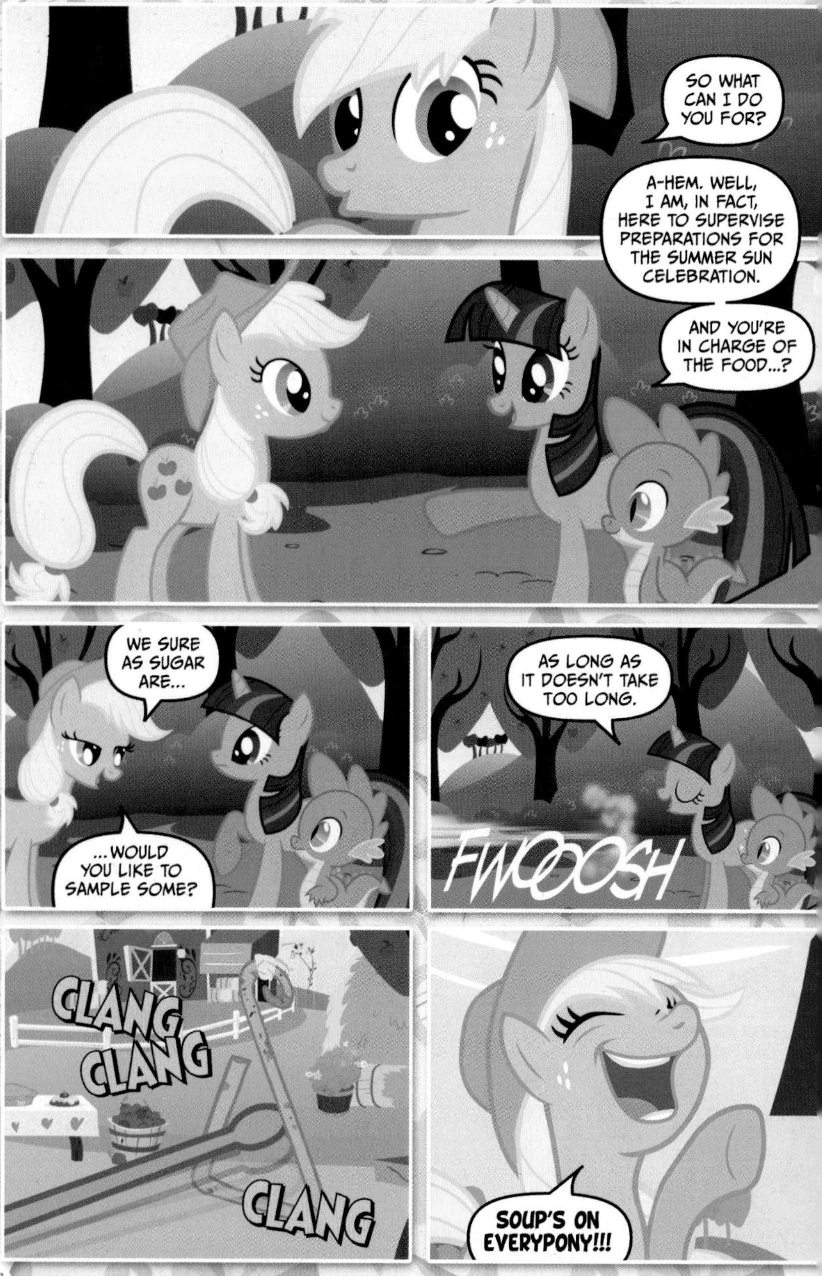
SO WHAT CAN I DO YOU FOR?
A-HEM. WELL, I AM, IN FACT, HERE TO SUPERVISE PREPARATIONS FOR THE SUMMER SUN CELEBRATION.
AND YOU'RE IN CHARGE OF THE FOOD...?
WE SURE AS SUGAR ARE...
...WOULD YOU LIKE TO SAMPLE SOME?
AS LONG AS IT DOESN'T TAKE TOO LONG.
FWOOSH
CLANG
CLANG
CLANG
SOUP'S ON EVERYPONY!!!

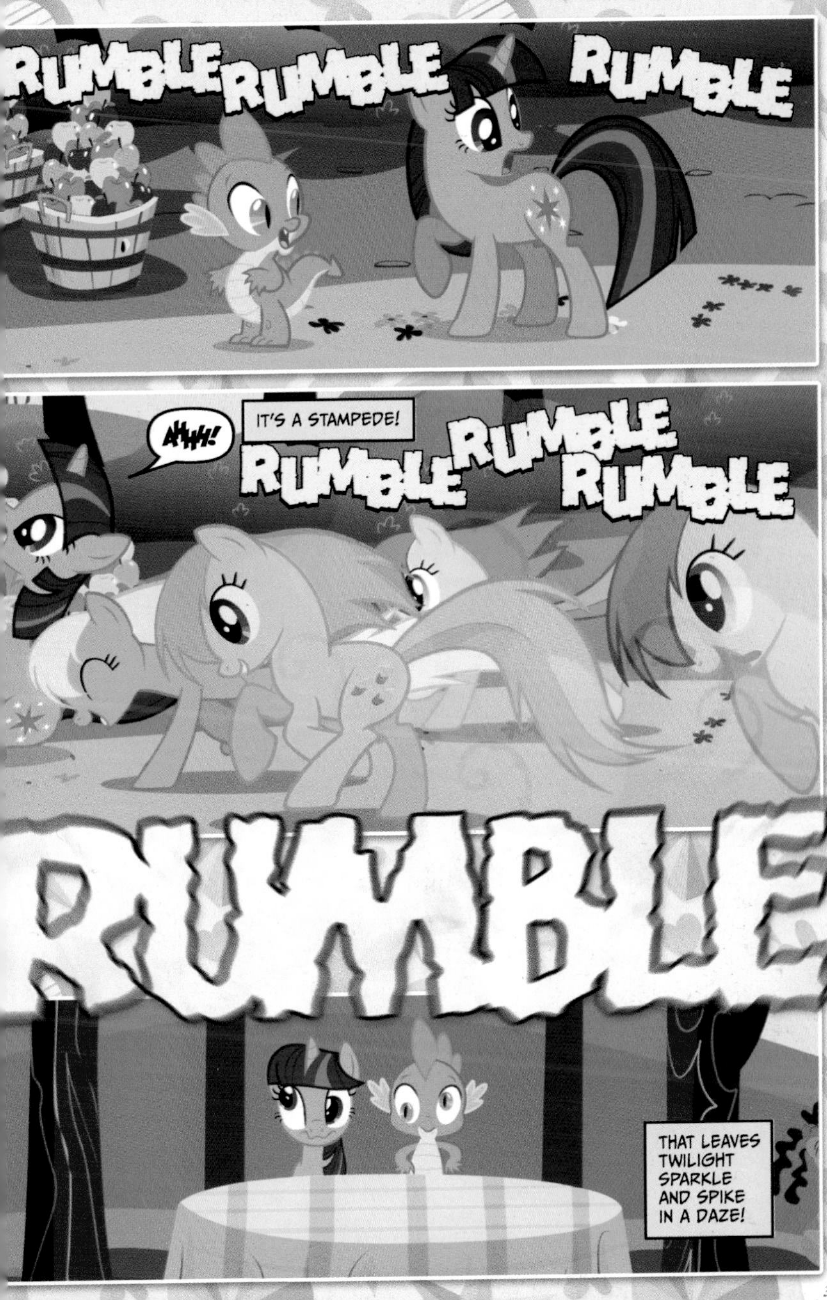
RUMBLE RUMBLE RUMBLE
AHHH!
IT'S A STAMPEDE!
RUMBLE RUMBLE RUMBLE
RUMBLE
THAT LEAVES TWILIGHT SPARKLE AND SPIKE IN A DAZE!

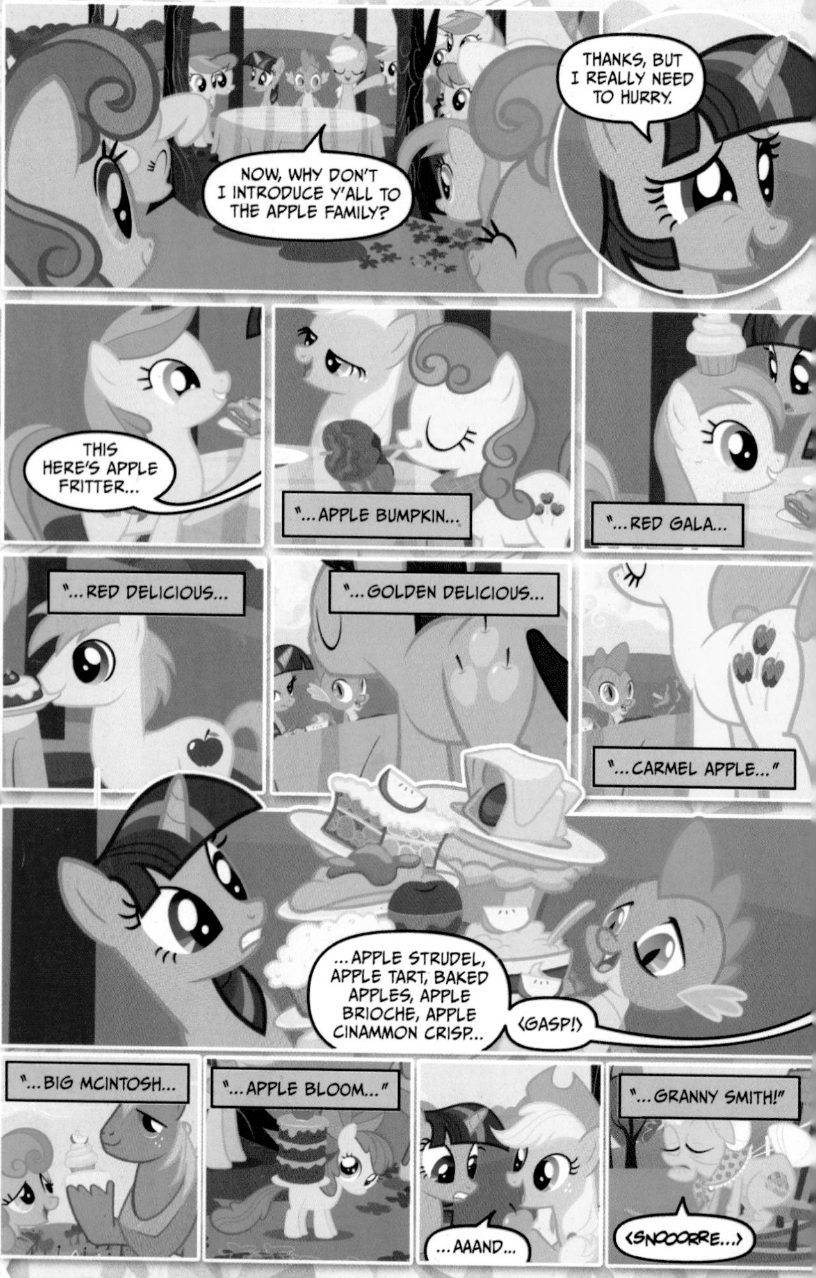
NOW, WHY DON'T I INTRODUCE Y'ALL TO THE APPLE FAMILY?
THANKS, BUT I REALLY NEED TO HURRY.
THIS HERE'S APPLE FRITTER...
"...APPLE BUMPKIN...
"...RED GALA...
"...RED DELICIOUS...
"...GOLDEN DELICIOUS...
"...CARMEL APPLE..."
...APPLE STRUDEL, APPLE TART, BAKED APPLES, APPLE BRIOCHE, APPLE CINAMMON CRISP...
<GASP!>
"...BIG MCINTOSH...
"...APPLE BLOOM..."
...AAAND...
"...GRANNY SMITH!"
<SNOOORRE...>

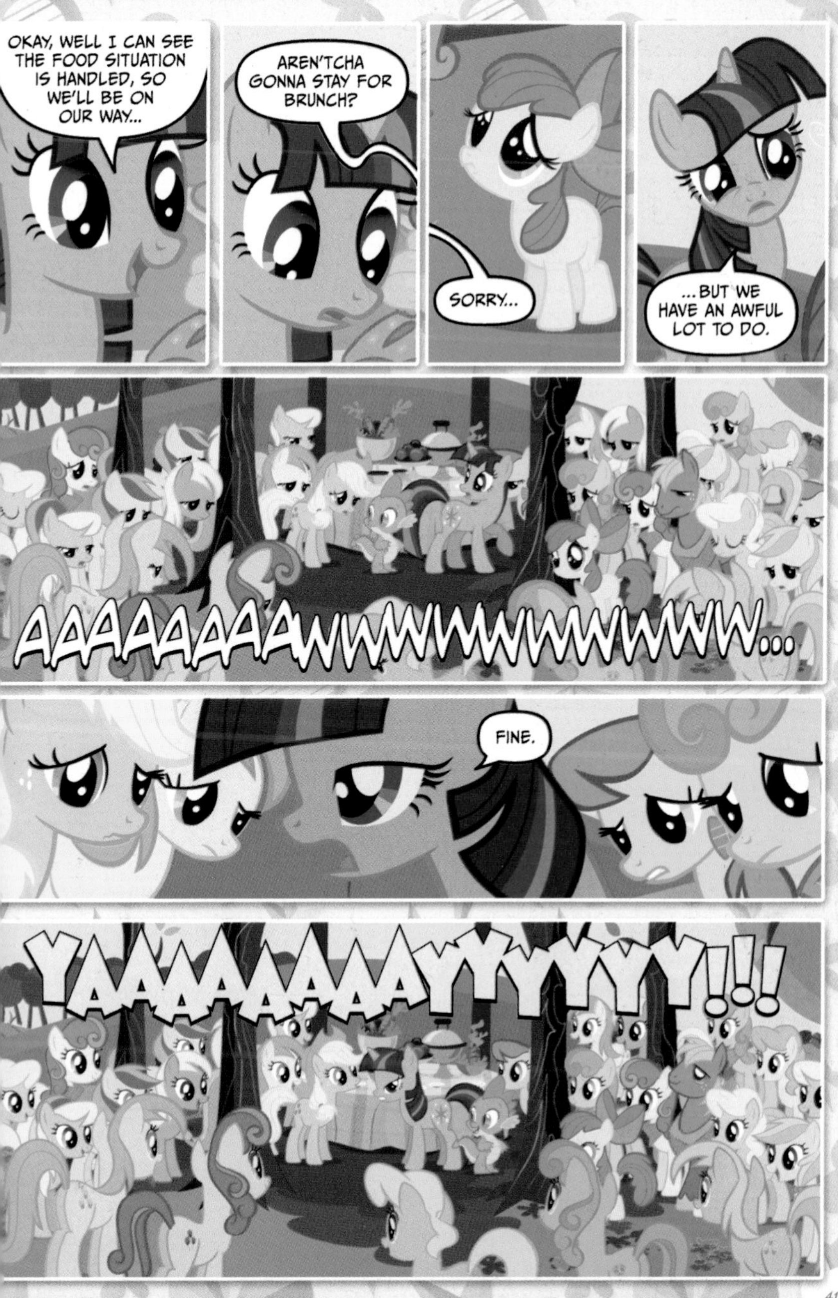
OKAY, WELL I CAN SEE THE FOOD SITUATION IS HANDLED, SO WE'LL BE ON OUR WAY...
AREN'TCHA GONNA STAY FOR BRUNCH?
SORRY...
...BUT WE HAVE AN AWFUL LOT TO DO.
AAAAAAAAWWWWWWWWWWW...
FINE.
YAAAAAAAYYYYY!!!

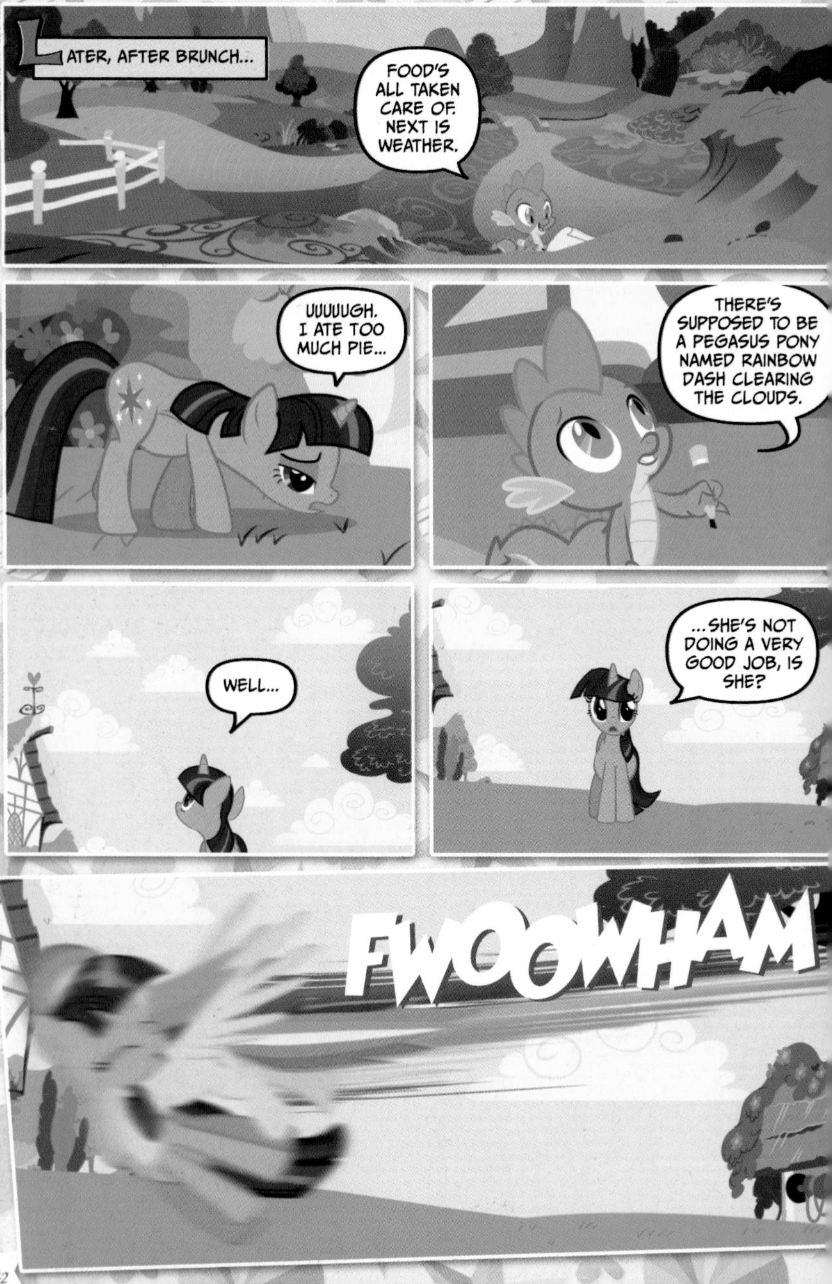
LATER, AFTER BRUNCH...
FOOD'S ALL TAKEN CARE OF. NEXT IS WEATHER.
UUUUUGH. I ATE TOO MUCH PIE...
THERE'S SUPPOSED TO BE A PEGASUS PONY NAMED RAINBOW DASH CLEARING THE CLOUDS.
WELL...
...SHE'S NOT DOING A VERY GOOD JOB, IS SHE?
FWOOWHAM

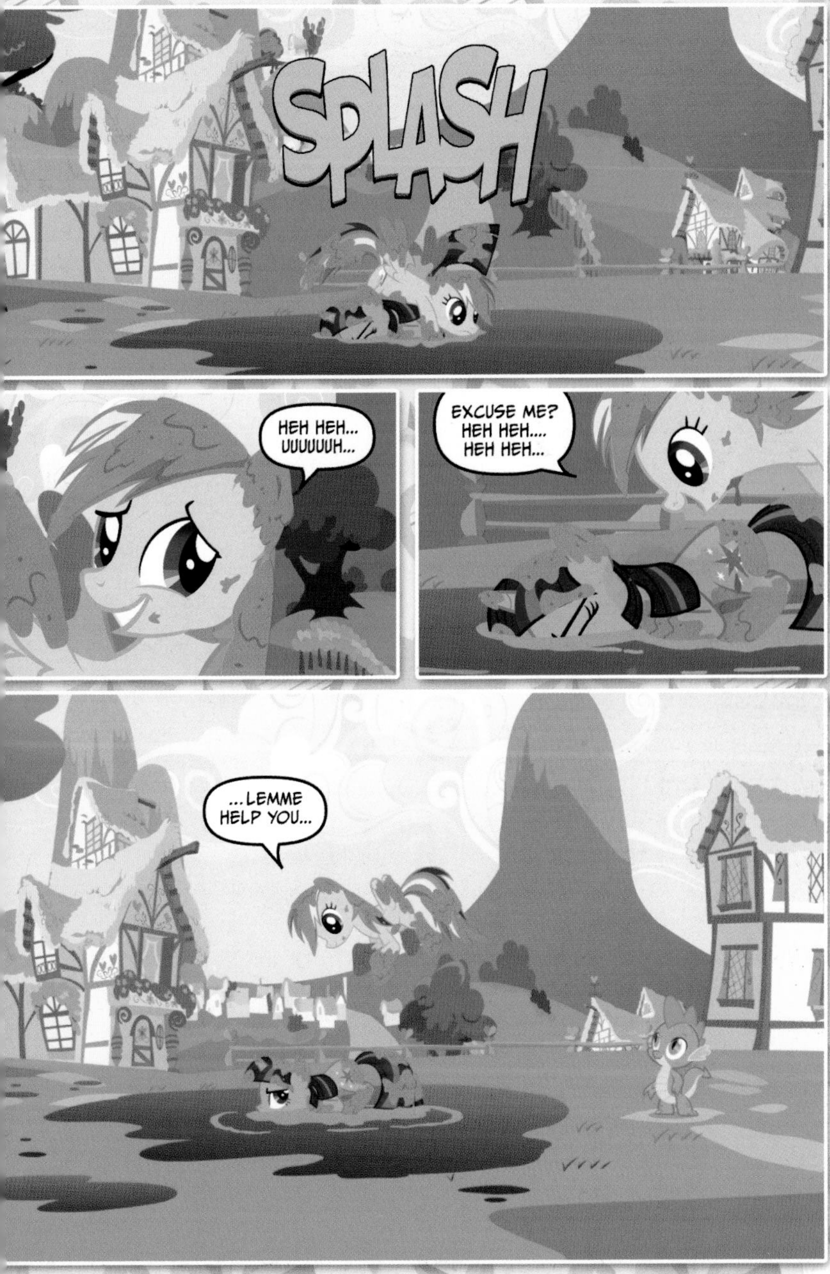
SPLASH
HEH HEH... UUUUUUH...
EXCUSE ME? HEH HEH.... HEH HEH...
...LEMME HELP YOU...

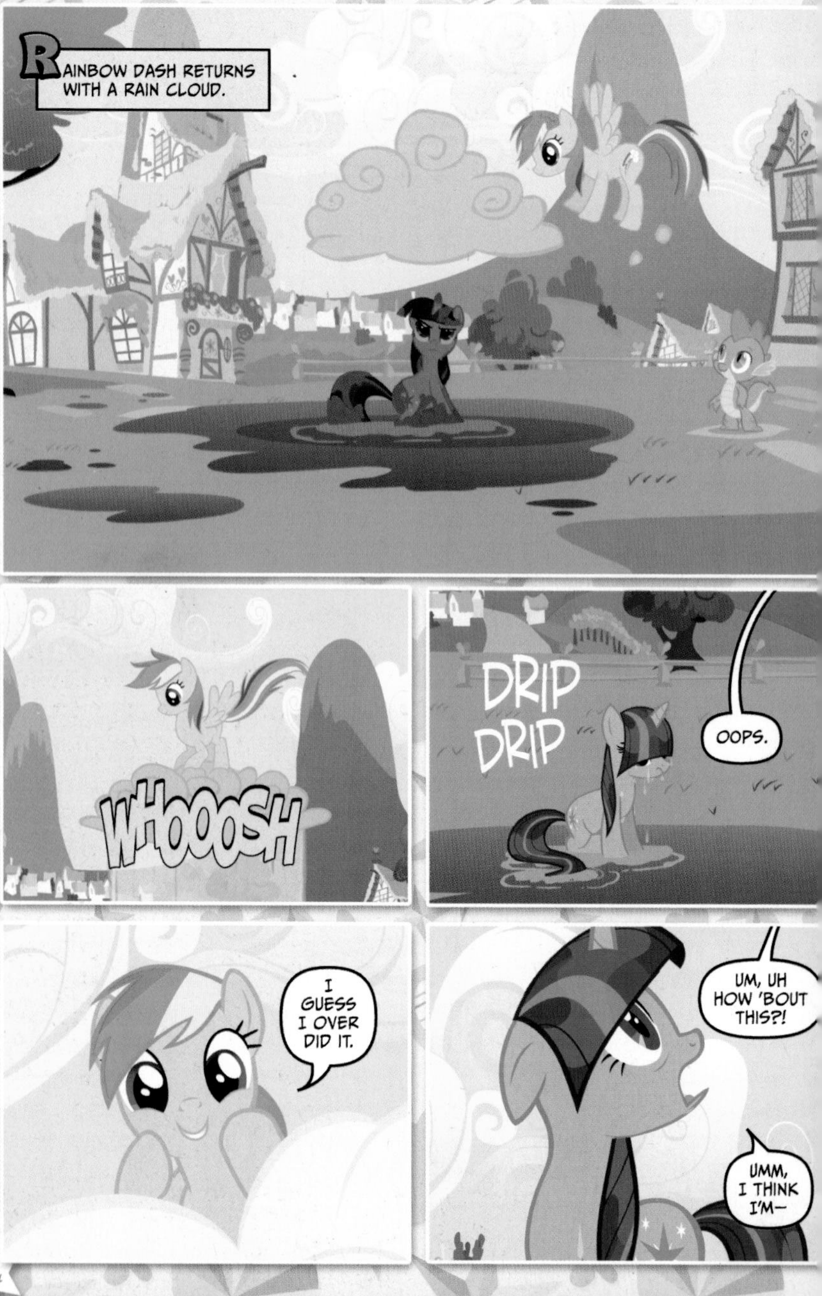
RAINBOW DASH RETURNS WITH A RAIN CLOUD.
WHOOOSH
DRIP DRIP
OOPS.
I GUESS I OVER DID IT.
UM, UH HOW 'BOUT THIS?!
UMM, I THINK I'M—

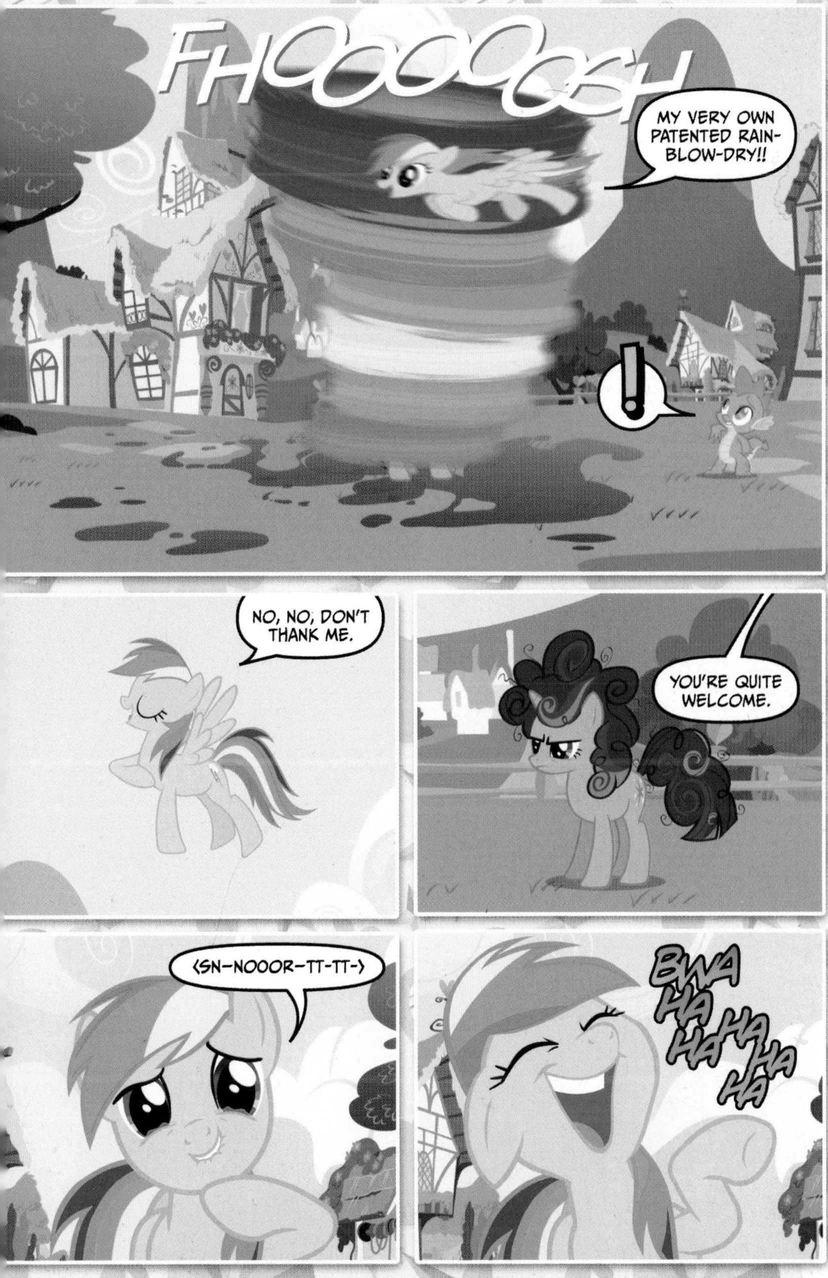
FHOOOOOOSH
MY VERY OWN PATENTED RAIN-BLOW-DRY!!
!
NO, NO, DON'T THANK ME.
YOU'RE QUITE WELCOME.
<SN-NOOOR-TT-TT->
BWA HA HA HA HA HA

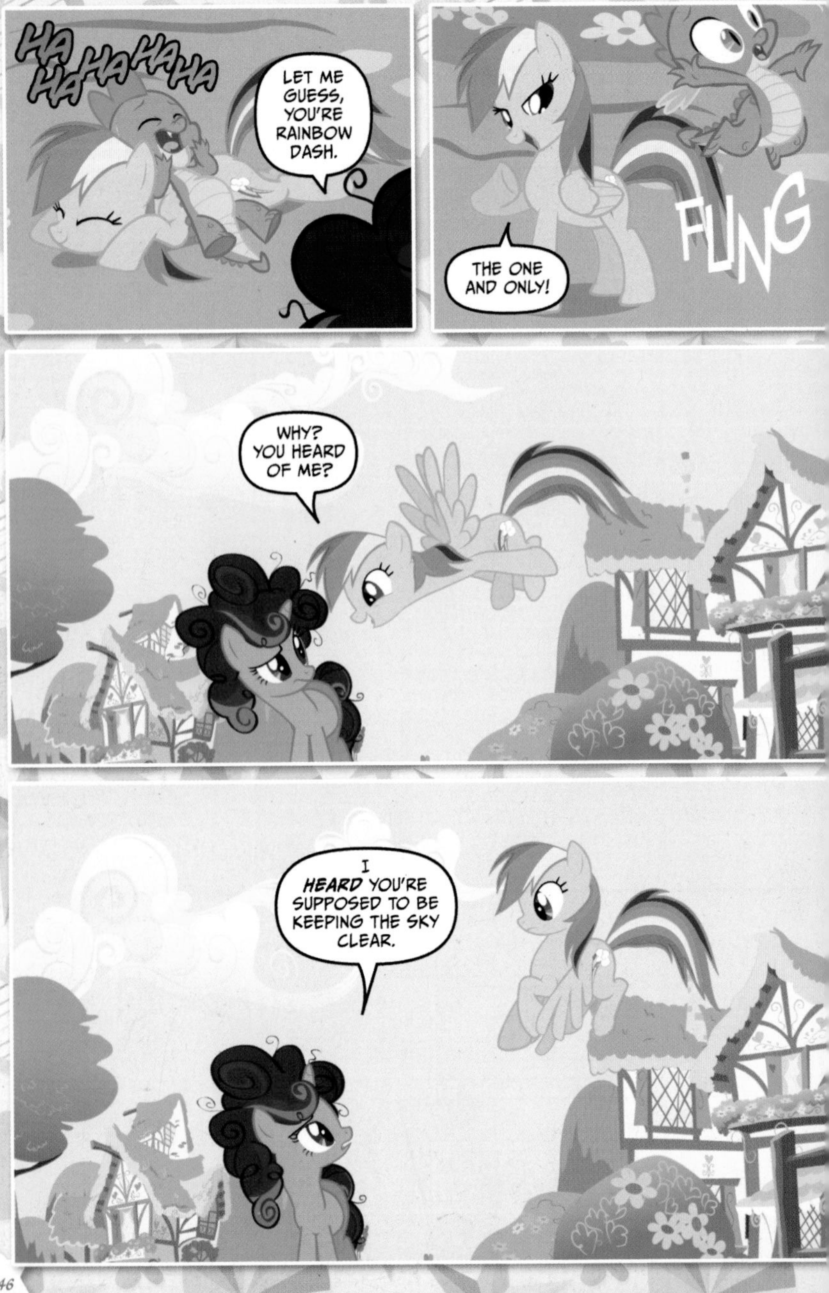
HA HA HA HA HA HA
LET ME GUESS, YOU'RE RAINBOW DASH.
THE ONE AND ONLY!
FLING
WHY? YOU HEARD OF ME?
I HEARD YOU'RE SUPPOSED TO BE KEEPING THE SKY CLEAR.

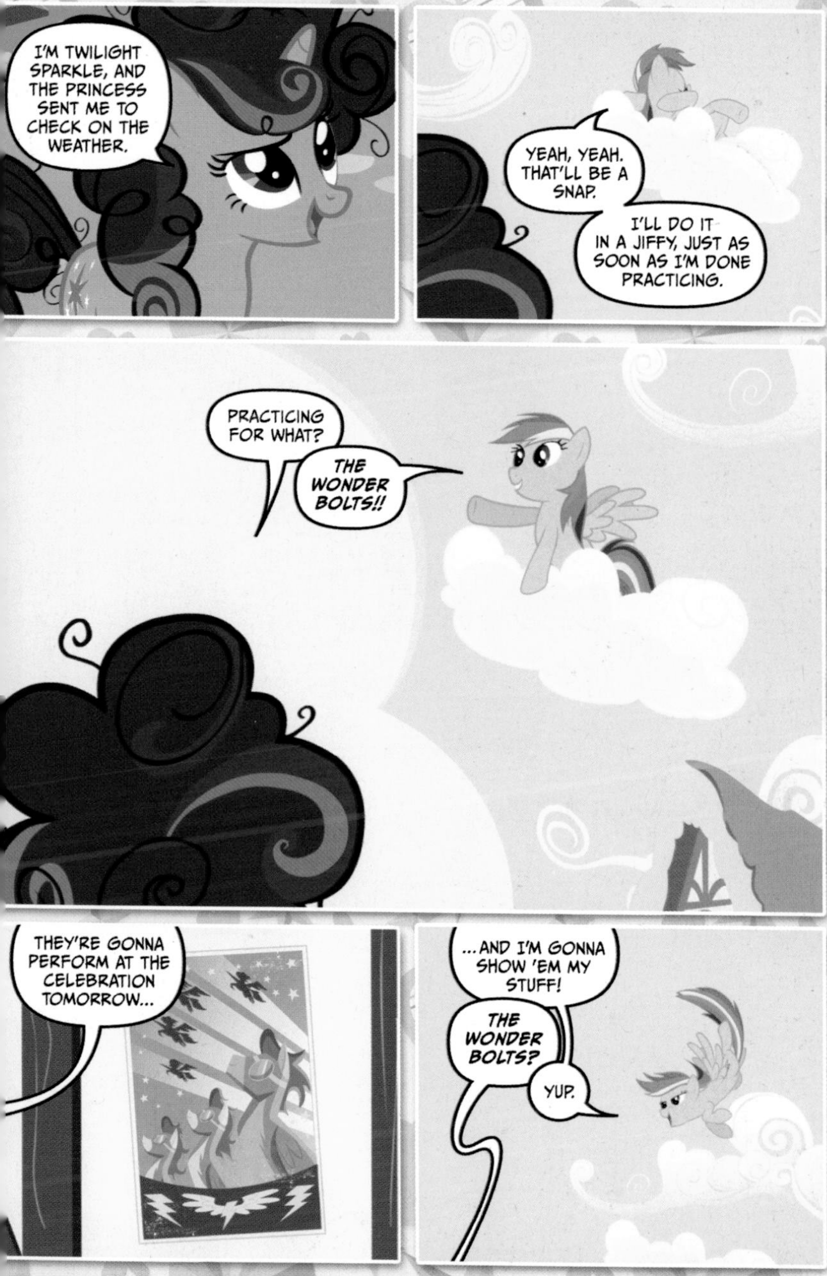
I'M TWILIGHT SPARKLE, AND THE PRINCESS SENT ME TO CHECK ON THE WEATHER.
YEAH, YEAH. THAT'LL BE A SNAP.
I'LL DO IT IN A JIFFY, JUST AS SOON AS I'M DONE PRACTICING.
PRACTICING FOR WHAT?
THE WONDER BOLTS!!
THEY'RE GONNA PERFORM AT THE CELEBRATION TOMORROW...
...AND I'M GONNA SHOW 'EM MY STUFF!
THE WONDER BOLTS?
YUP.

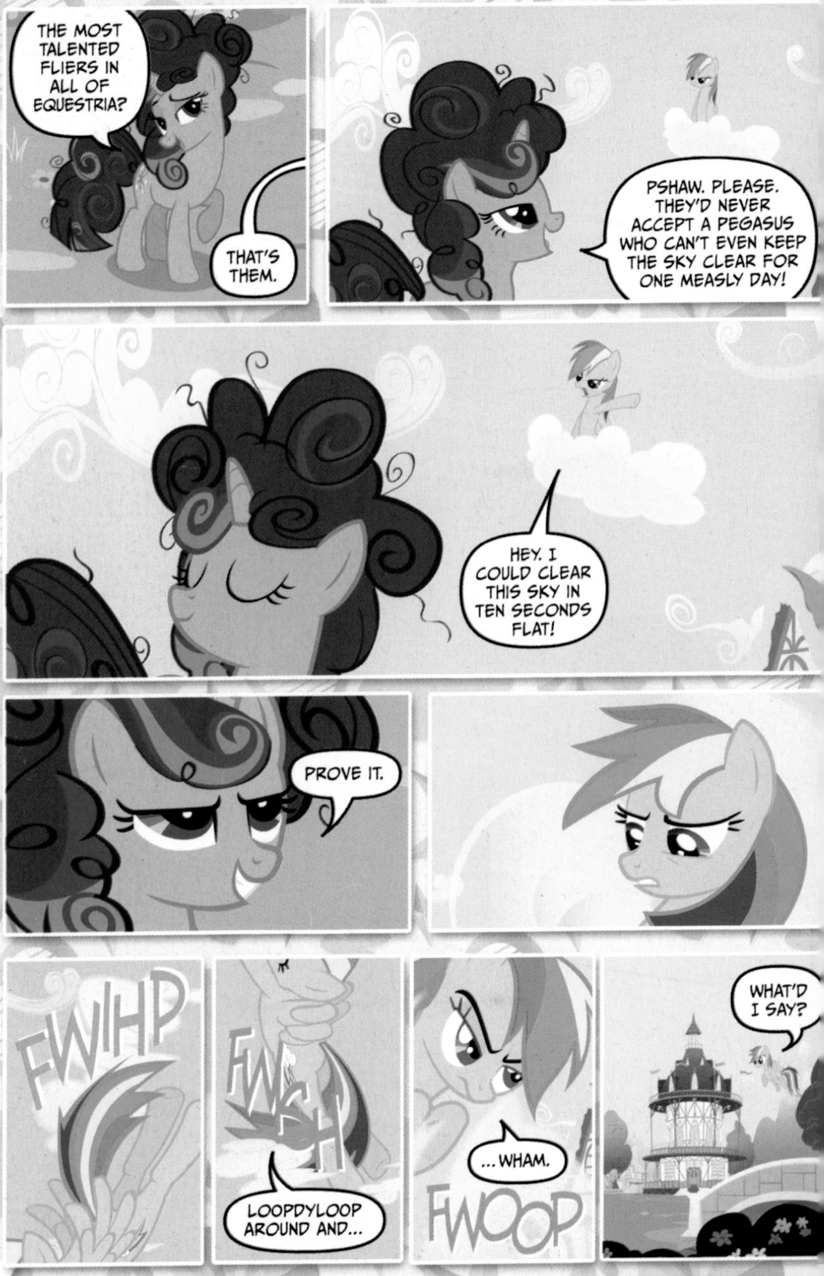
THE MOST TALENTED FLIERS IN ALL OF EQUESTRIA?
THAT'S THEM.
PSHAW. PLEASE. THEY'D NEVER ACCEPT A PEGASUS WHO CAN'T EVEN KEEP THE SKY CLEAR FOR ONE MEASLY DAY!
HEY. I COULD CLEAR THIS SKY IN TEN SECONDS FLAT!
PROVE IT.
FWIHP
FWSH
LOOPDYLOOP AROUND AND...
...WHAM.
FWOOP
WHAT'D I SAY?

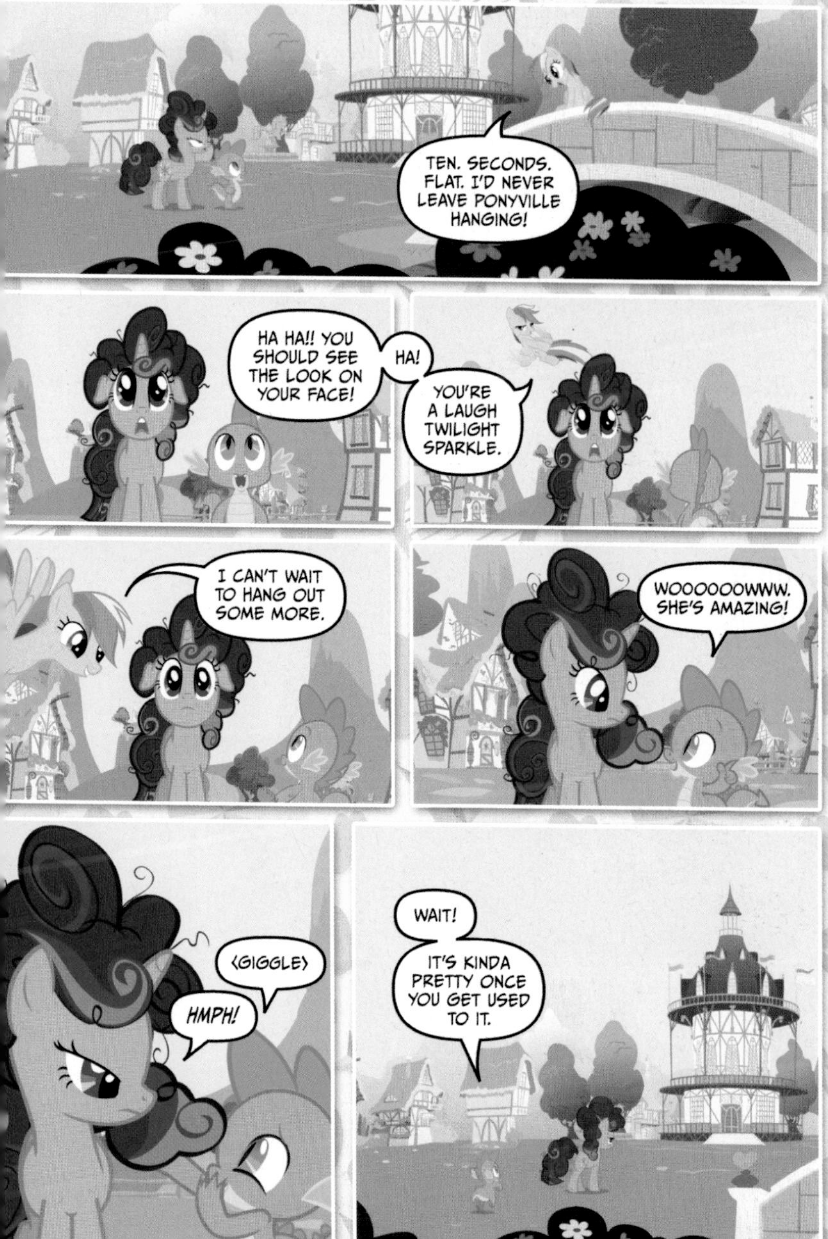
TEN. SECONDS. FLAT. I'D NEVER LEAVE PONYVILLE HANGING!
HA HA!! YOU SHOULD SEE THE LOOK ON YOUR FACE!
HA!
YOU'RE A LAUGH TWILIGHT SPARKLE.
I CAN'T WAIT TO HANG OUT SOME MORE.
WOOOOOOWWW. SHE'S AMAZING!
<GIGGLE>
HMPH!
WAIT!
IT'S KINDA PRETTY ONCE YOU GET USED TO IT.

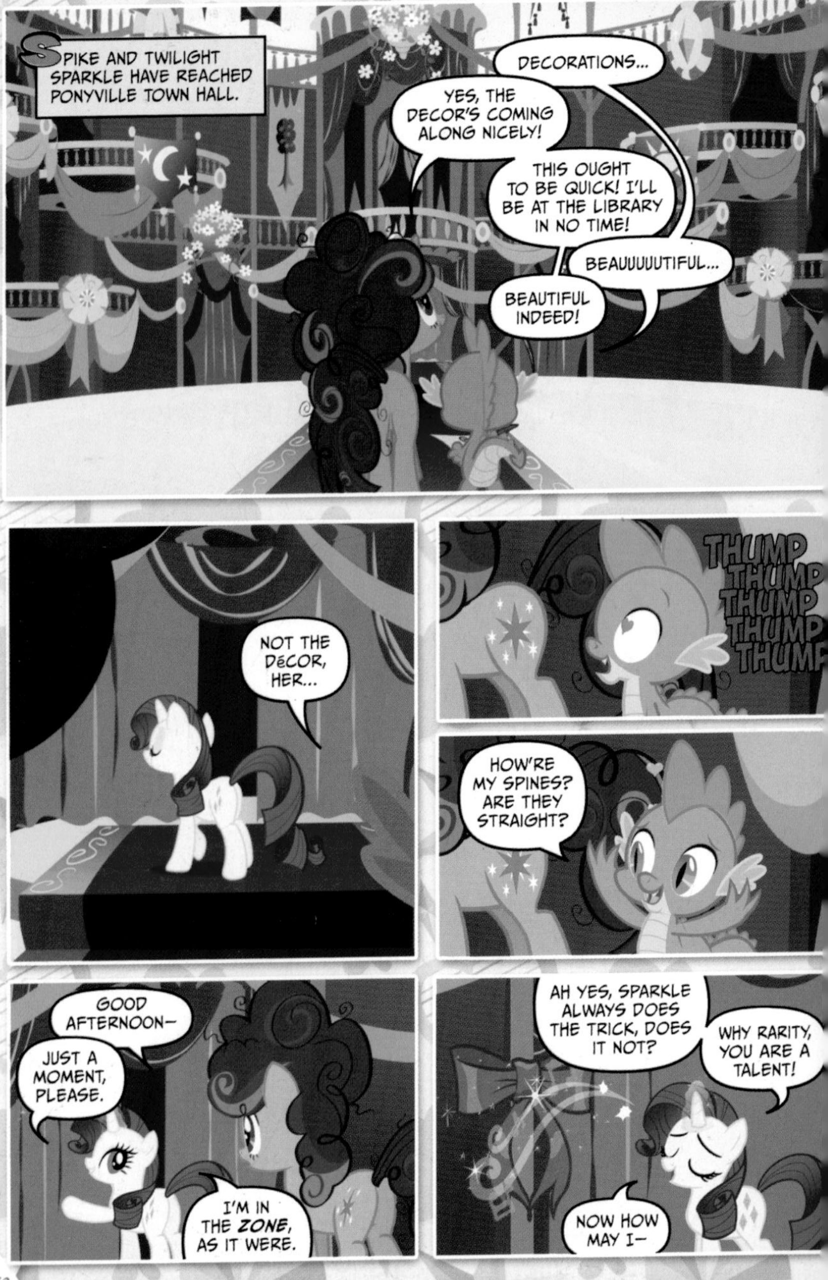
SPIKE AND TWILIGHT SPARKLE HAVE REACHED PONYVILLE TOWN HALL.
DECORATIONS...
YES, THE DECOR'S COMING ALONG NICELY!
THIS OUGHT TO BE QUICK! I'LL BE AT THE LIBRARY IN NO TIME!
BEAUUUUUTIFUL...
BEAUTIFUL INDEED!
NOT THE DéCOR, HER...
THUMP THUMP THUMP THUMP THUMP
HOW'RE MY SPINES? ARE THEY STRAIGHT?
GOOD AFTERNOON—
JUST A MOMENT, PLEASE.
I'M IN THE *ZONE*, AS IT WERE.
AH YES, SPARKLE ALWAYS DOES THE TRICK, DOES IT NOT?
WHY RARITY, YOU ARE A TALENT!
NOW HOW MAY I—

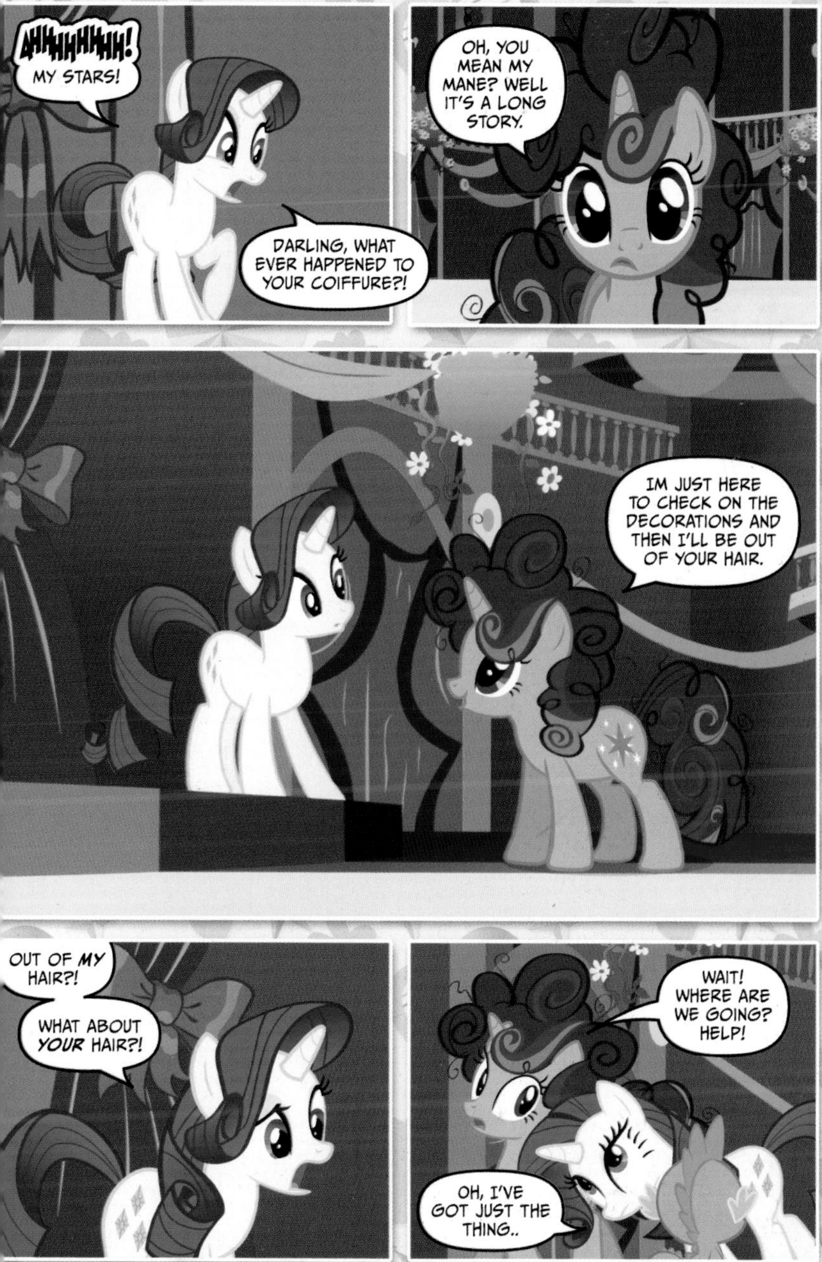
AHHHHHHHH!
MY STARS!
DARLING, WHAT EVER HAPPENED TO YOUR COIFFURE?!
OH, YOU MEAN MY MANE? WELL IT'S A LONG STORY.
IM JUST HERE TO CHECK ON THE DECORATIONS AND THEN I'LL BE OUT OF YOUR HAIR.
OUT OF *MY* HAIR?!
WHAT ABOUT *YOUR* HAIR?!
WAIT! WHERE ARE WE GOING? HELP!
OH, I'VE GOT JUST THE THING..

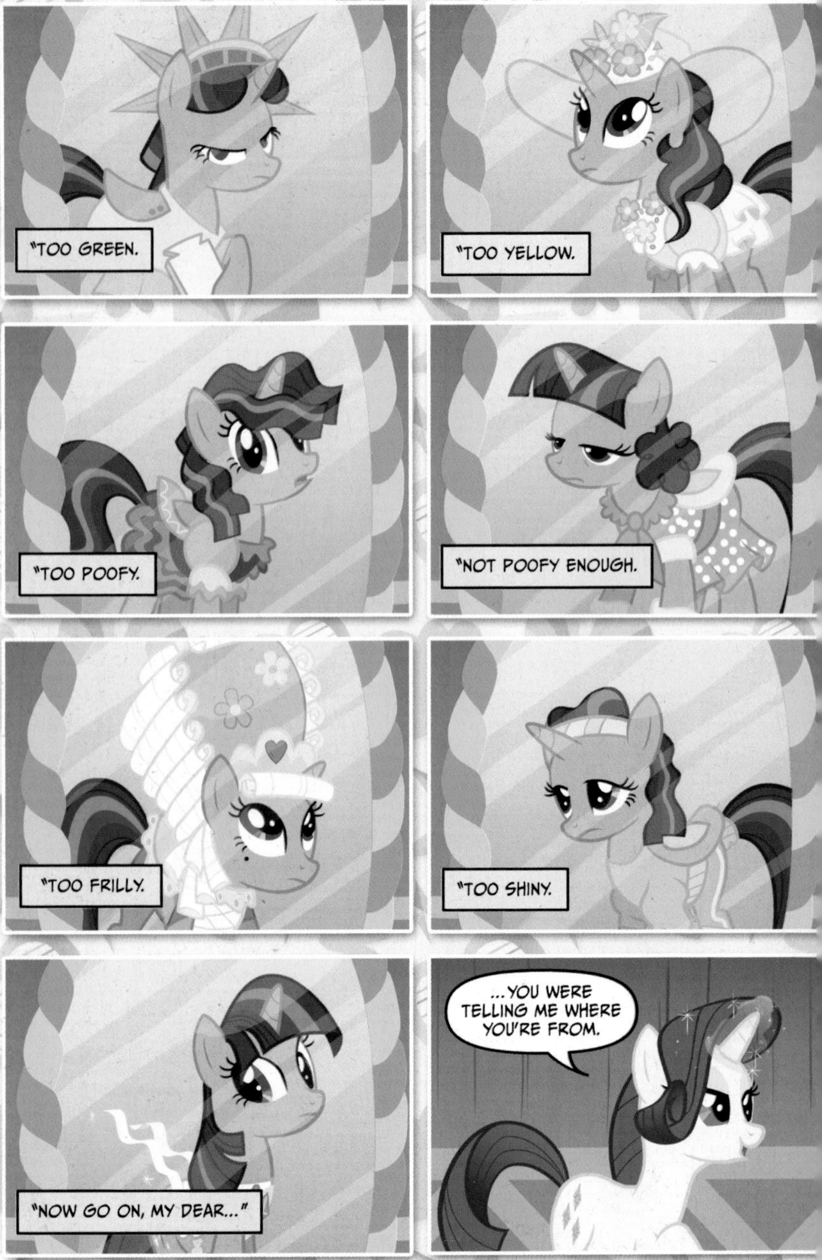
"TOO GREEN.
"TOO YELLOW.
"TOO POOFY.
"NOT POOFY ENOUGH.
"TOO FRILLY.
"TOO SHINY.
"NOW GO ON, MY DEAR..."
...YOU WERE TELLING ME WHERE YOU'RE FROM.

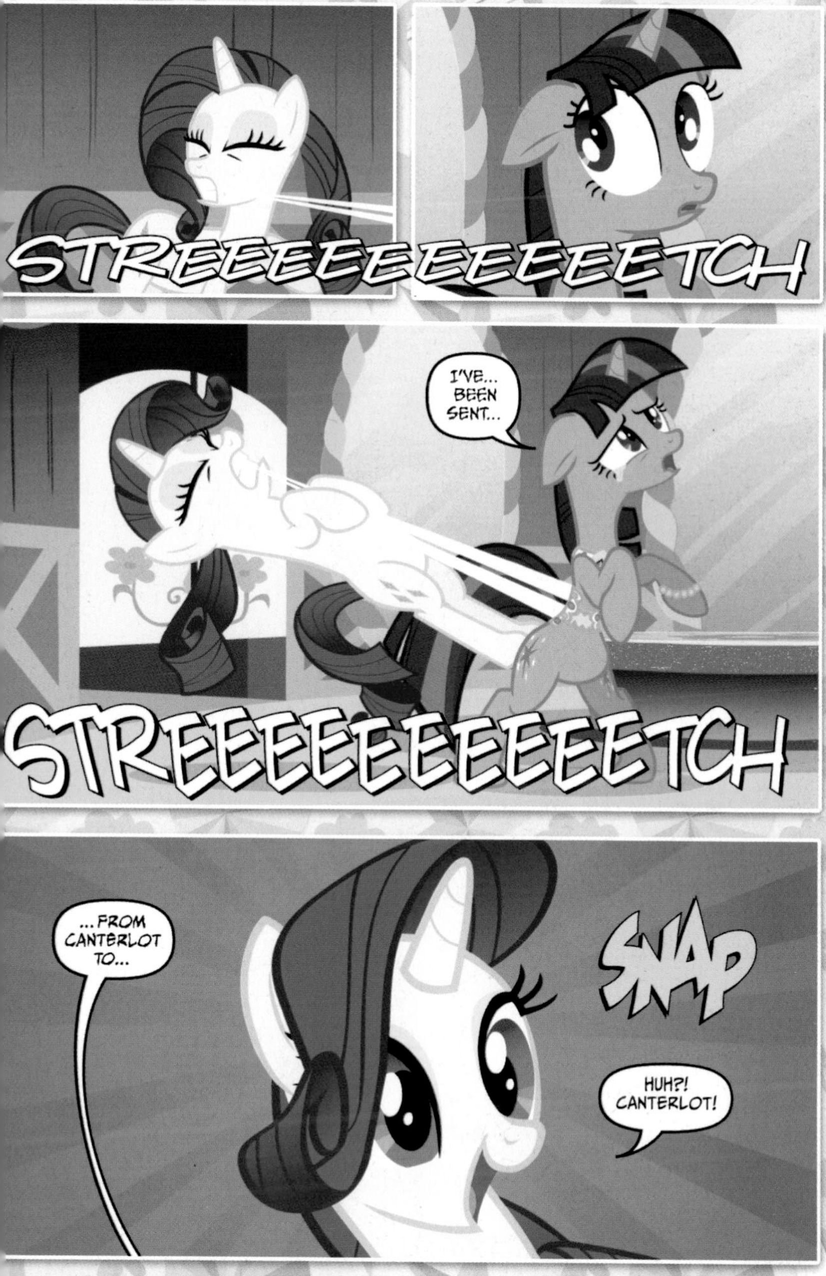
STREEEEEEEEEEEETCH
I'VE... BEEN SENT...
STREEEEEEEEEEEETCH
...FROM CANTERLOT TO...
SNAP
HUH?! CANTERLOT!

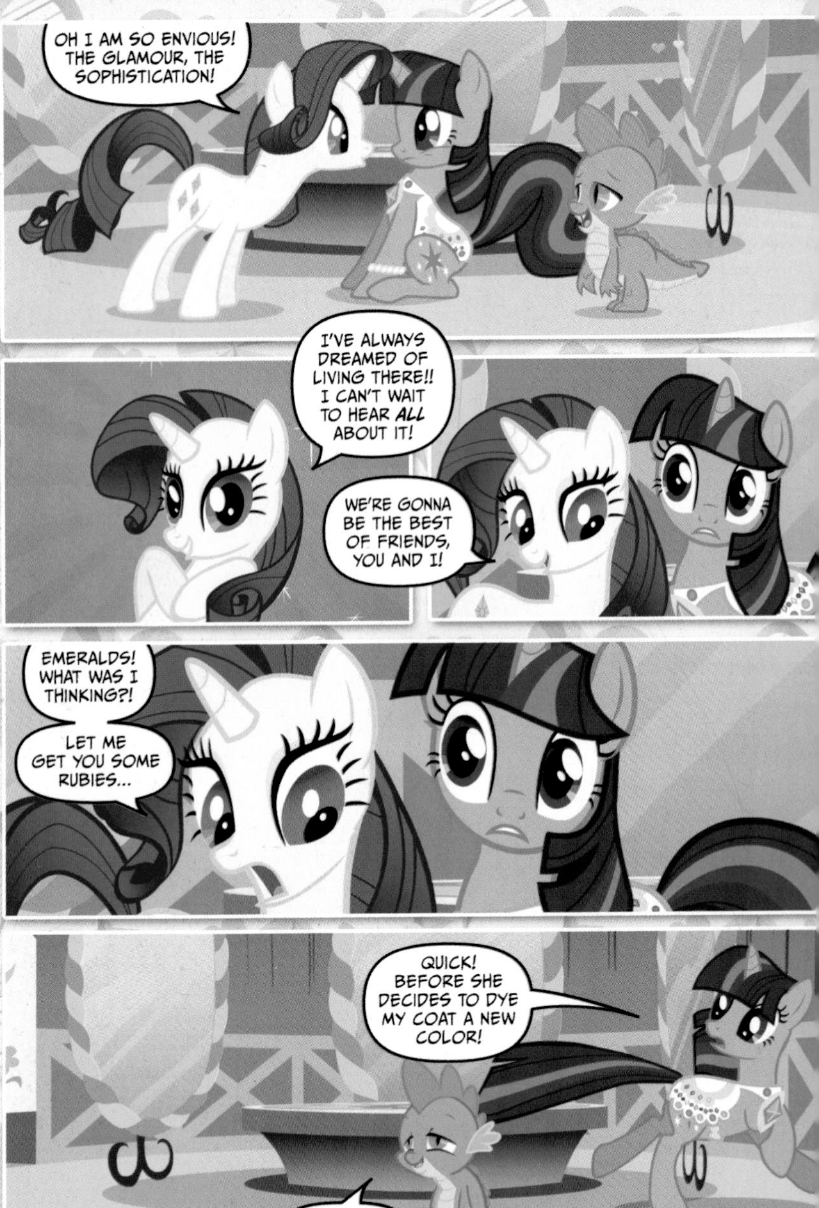
OH I AM SO ENVIOUS! THE GLAMOUR, THE SOPHISTICATION!
I'VE ALWAYS DREAMED OF LIVING THERE!! I CAN'T WAIT TO HEAR ALL ABOUT IT!
WE'RE GONNA BE THE BEST OF FRIENDS, YOU AND I!
EMERALDS! WHAT WAS I THINKING?!
LET ME GET YOU SOME RUBIES...
QUICK! BEFORE SHE DECIDES TO DYE MY COAT A NEW COLOR!
‹SIIIIIIIIIGH›

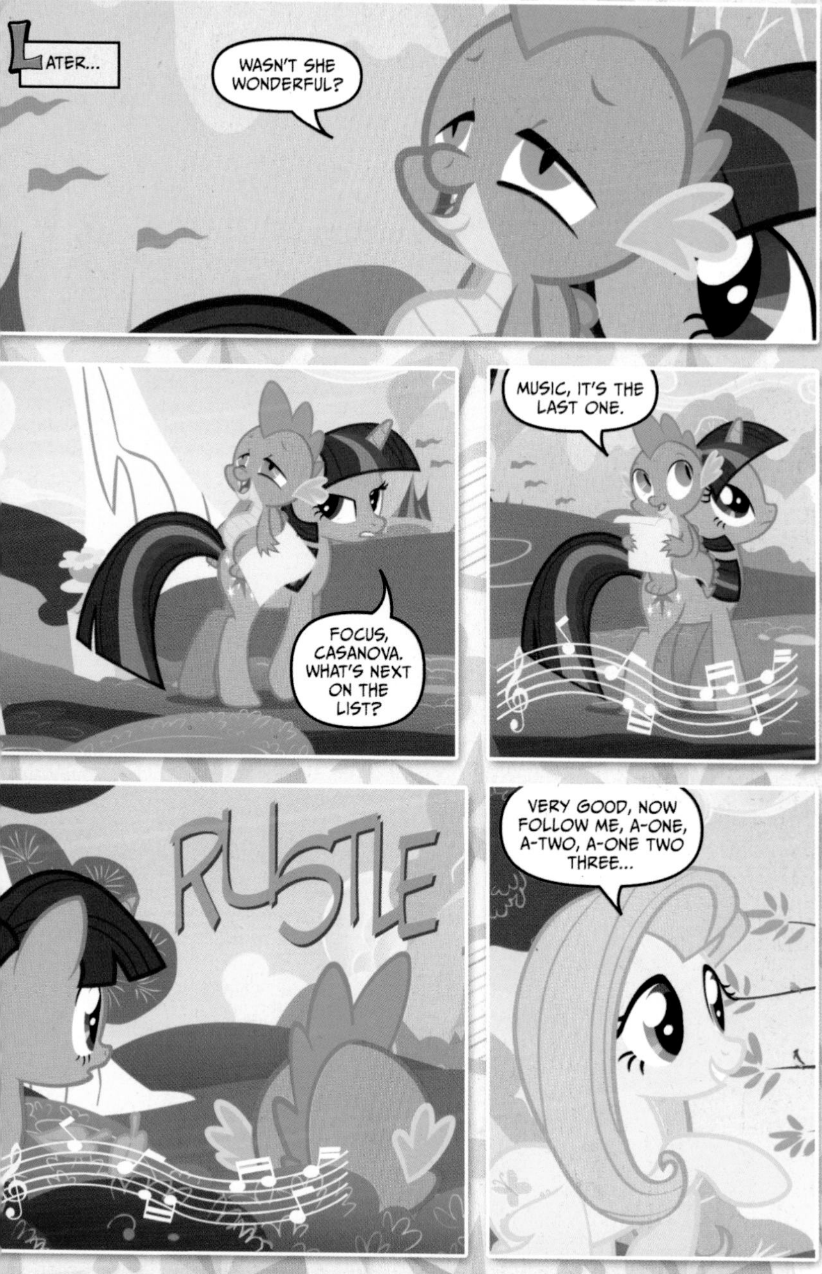
LATER...
WASN'T SHE WONDERFUL?
FOCUS, CASANOVA. WHAT'S NEXT ON THE LIST?
MUSIC, IT'S THE LAST ONE.
RUSTLE
VERY GOOD, NOW FOLLOW ME, A-ONE, A-TWO, A-ONE TWO THREE...

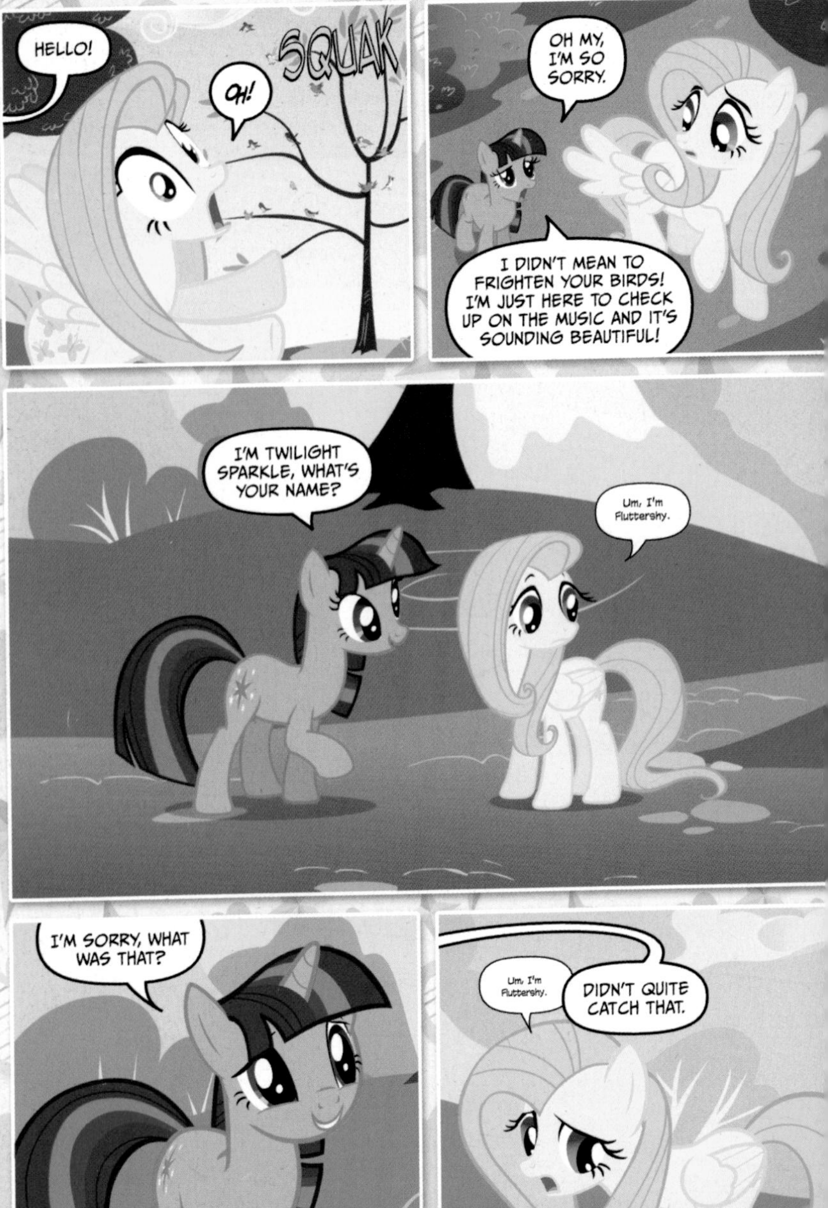

HELLO!
OH!
SQUAK
OH MY, I'M SO SORRY.
I DIDN'T MEAN TO FRIGHTEN YOUR BIRDS! I'M JUST HERE TO CHECK UP ON THE MUSIC AND IT'S SOUNDING BEAUTIFUL!
I'M TWILIGHT SPARKLE, WHAT'S YOUR NAME?
Um, I'm Fluttershy.
I'M SORRY, WHAT WAS THAT?
Um, I'm Fluttershy.
DIDN'T QUITE CATCH THAT.

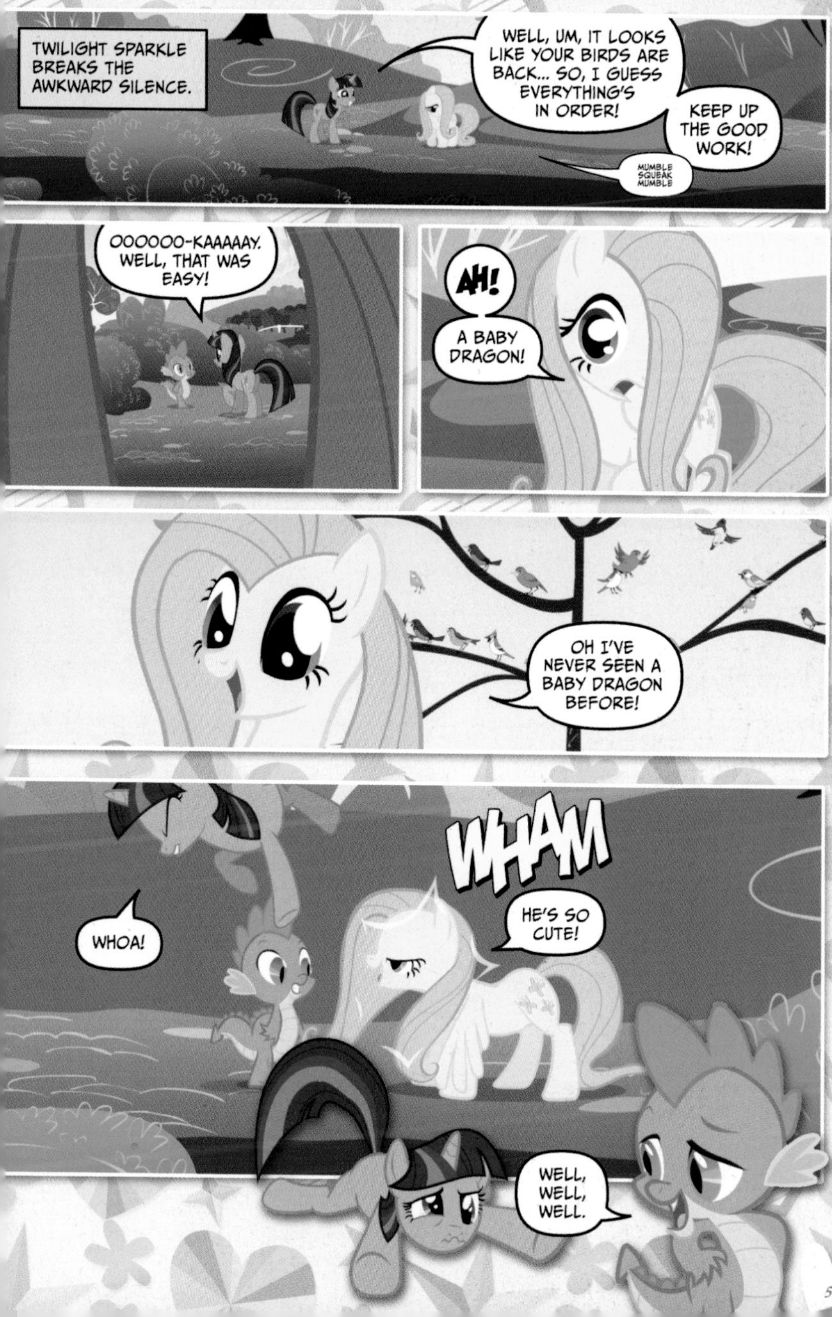
TWILIGHT SPARKLE BREAKS THE AWKWARD SILENCE.
WELL, UM, IT LOOKS LIKE YOUR BIRDS ARE BACK... SO, I GUESS EVERYTHING'S IN ORDER!
KEEP UP THE GOOD WORK!
MUMBLE SQUEAK MUMBLE
OOOOOO-KAAAAAY. WELL, THAT WAS EASY!
AH!
A BABY DRAGON!
OH I'VE NEVER SEEN A BABY DRAGON BEFORE!
WHAM
WHOA!
HE'S SO CUTE!
WELL, WELL, WELL.

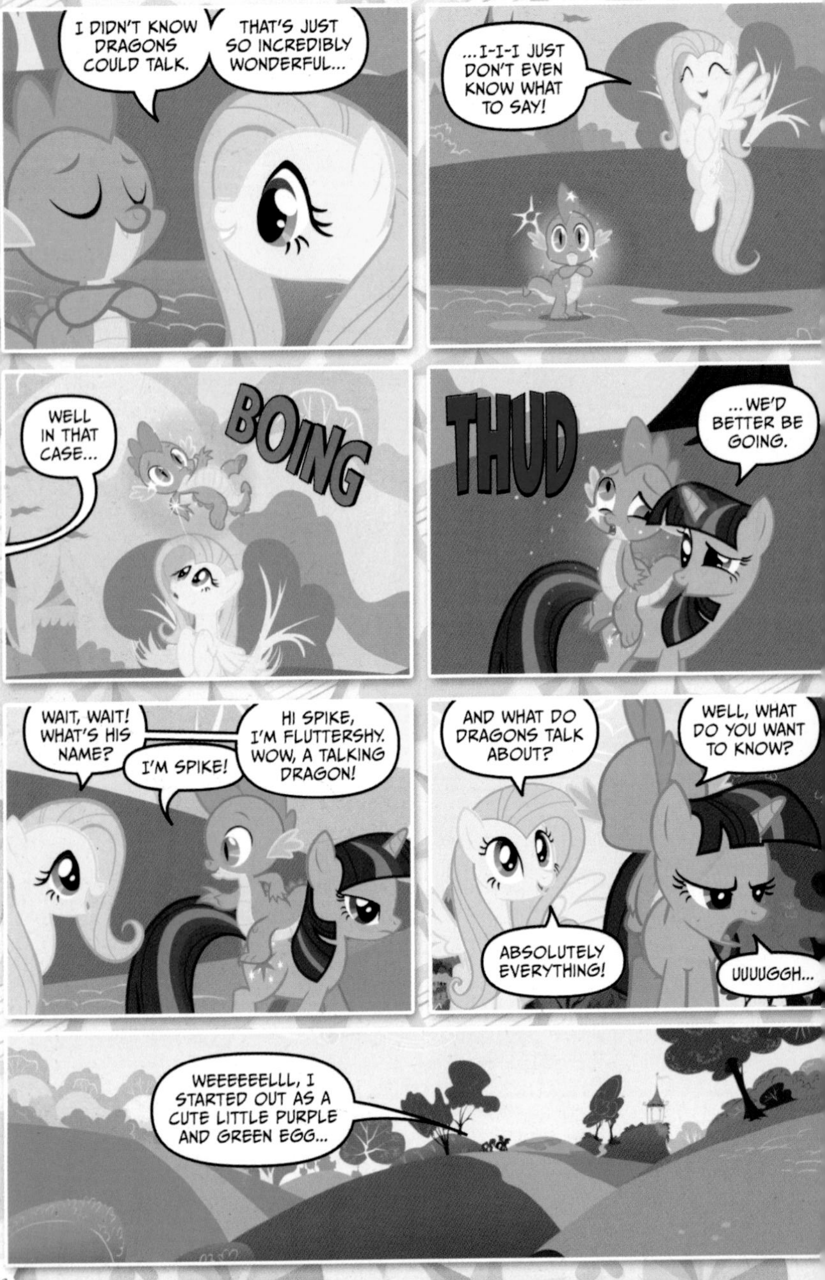
I DIDN'T KNOW DRAGONS COULD TALK.
THAT'S JUST SO INCREDIBLY WONDERFUL...
...I-I-I JUST DON'T EVEN KNOW WHAT TO SAY!
WELL IN THAT CASE...
BOING
THUD
...WE'D BETTER BE GOING.
WAIT, WAIT! WHAT'S HIS NAME?
I'M SPIKE!
HI SPIKE, I'M FLUTTERSHY. WOW, A TALKING DRAGON!
AND WHAT DO DRAGONS TALK ABOUT?
WELL, WHAT DO YOU WANT TO KNOW?
ABSOLUTELY EVERYTHING!
UUUUGGH...
WEEEEEELLL, I STARTED OUT AS A CUTE LITTLE PURPLE AND GREEN EGG...

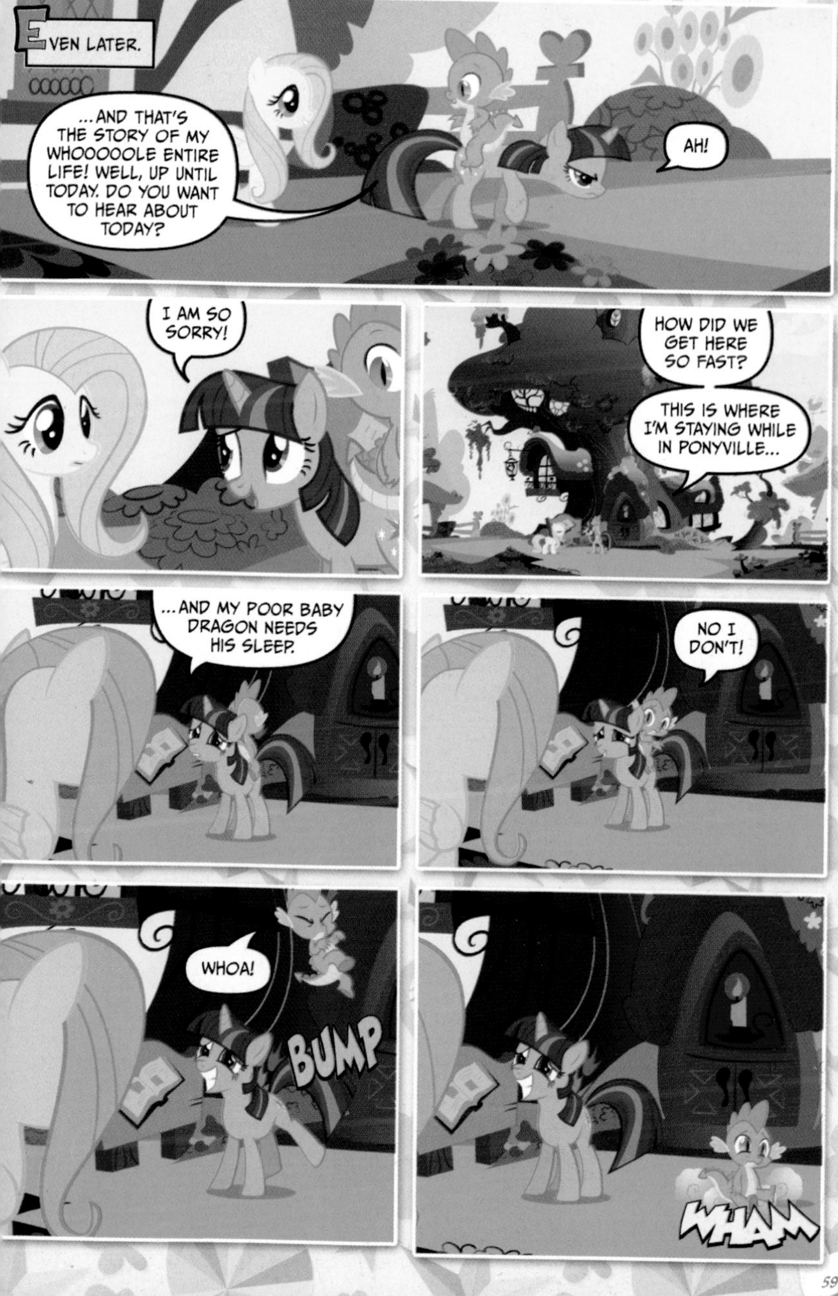
EVEN LATER.
...AND THAT'S THE STORY OF MY WHOOOOOLE ENTIRE LIFE! WELL, UP UNTIL TODAY. DO YOU WANT TO HEAR ABOUT TODAY?
AH!
I AM SO SORRY!
HOW DID WE GET HERE SO FAST?
THIS IS WHERE I'M STAYING WHILE IN PONYVILLE...
...AND MY POOR BABY DRAGON NEEDS HIS SLEEP.
NO I DON'T!
WHOA!
BUMP
WHAM

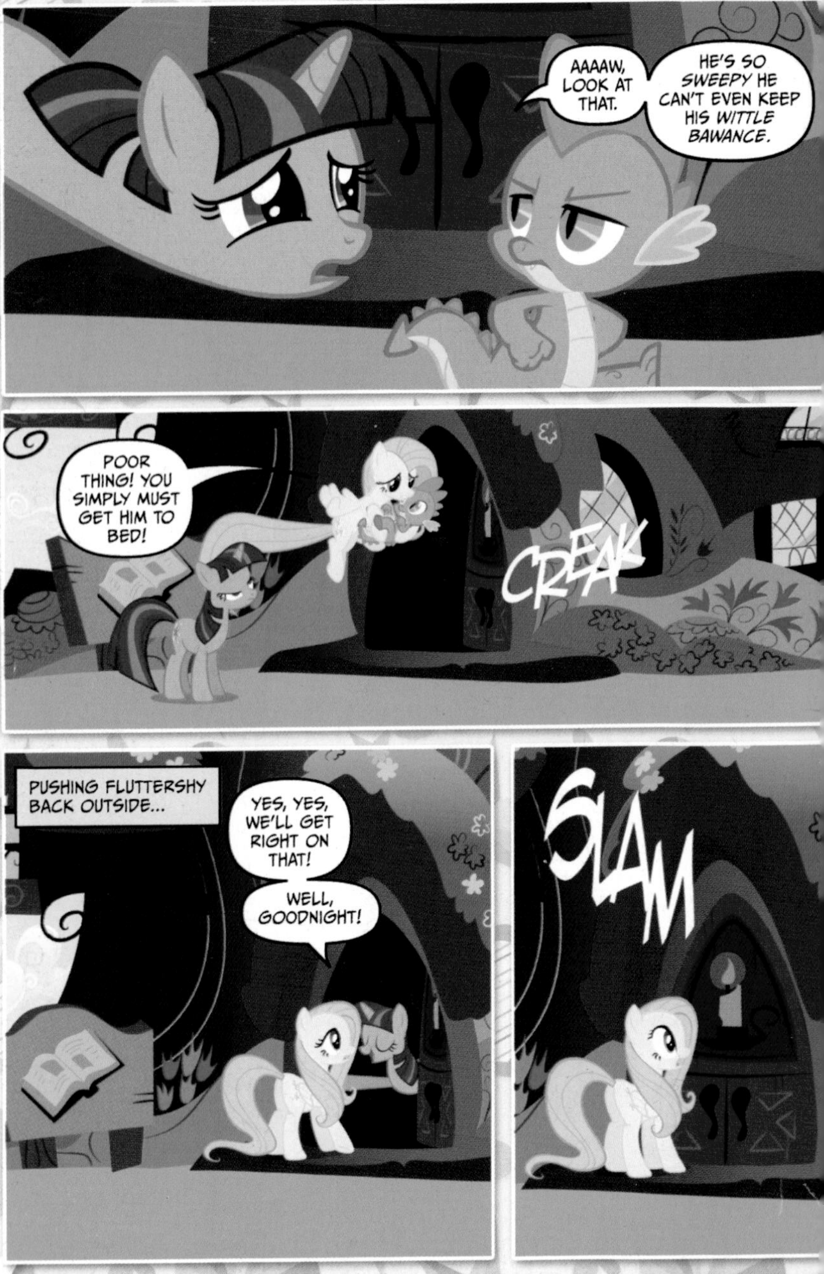
AAAAW, LOOK AT THAT.
HE'S SO SWEEPY HE CAN'T EVEN KEEP HIS WITTLE BAWANCE.
POOR THING! YOU SIMPLY MUST GET HIM TO BED!
CREAK
PUSHING FLUTTERSHY BACK OUTSIDE...
YES, YES, WE'LL GET RIGHT ON THAT!
WELL, GOODNIGHT!
SLAM

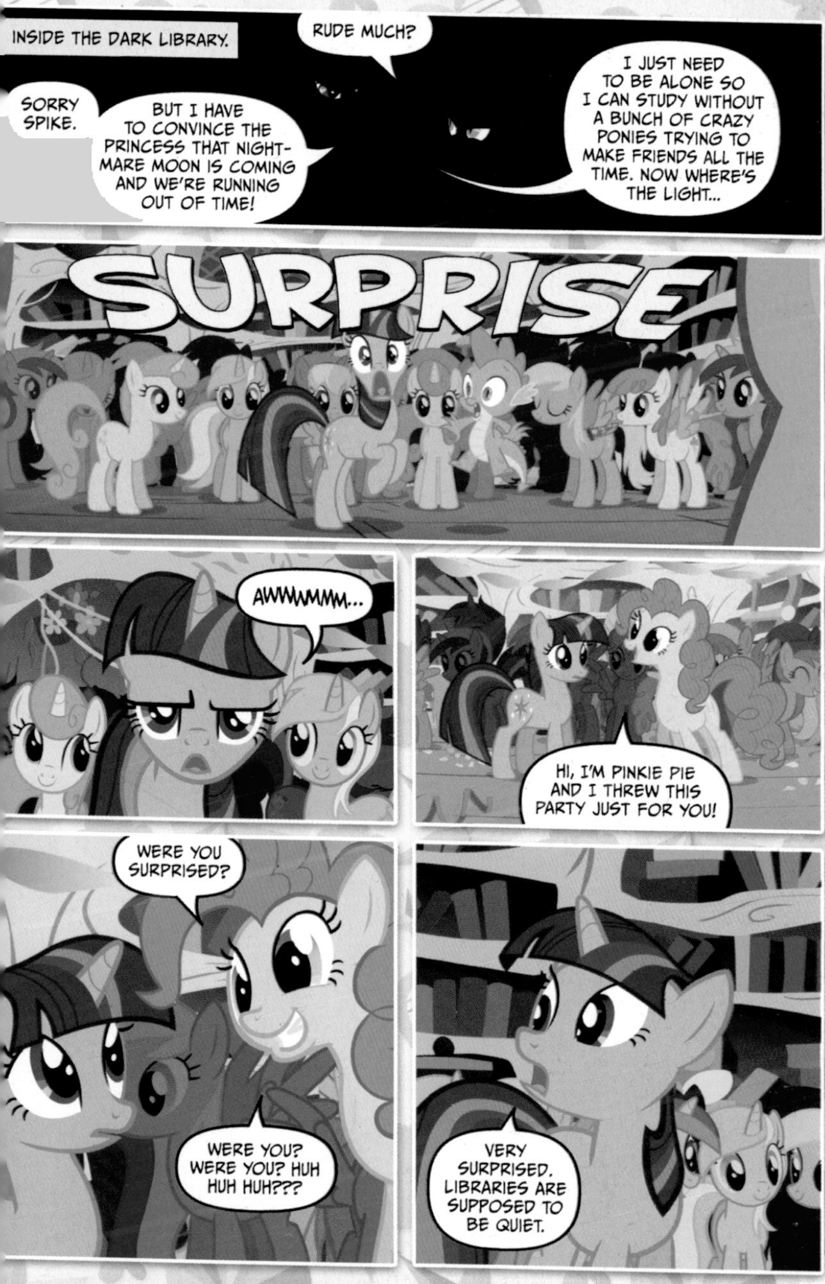
INSIDE THE DARK LIBRARY.
RUDE MUCH?
SORRY SPIKE.
BUT I HAVE TO CONVINCE THE PRINCESS THAT NIGHT-MARE MOON IS COMING AND WE'RE RUNNING OUT OF TIME!
I JUST NEED TO BE ALONE SO I CAN STUDY WITHOUT A BUNCH OF CRAZY PONIES TRYING TO MAKE FRIENDS ALL THE TIME. NOW WHERE'S THE LIGHT...
SURPRISE
AWWWMMM...
HI, I'M PINKIE PIE AND I THREW THIS PARTY JUST FOR YOU!
WERE YOU SURPRISED?
WERE YOU? WERE YOU? HUH HUH HUH???
VERY SURPRISED. LIBRARIES ARE SUPPOSED TO BE QUIET.

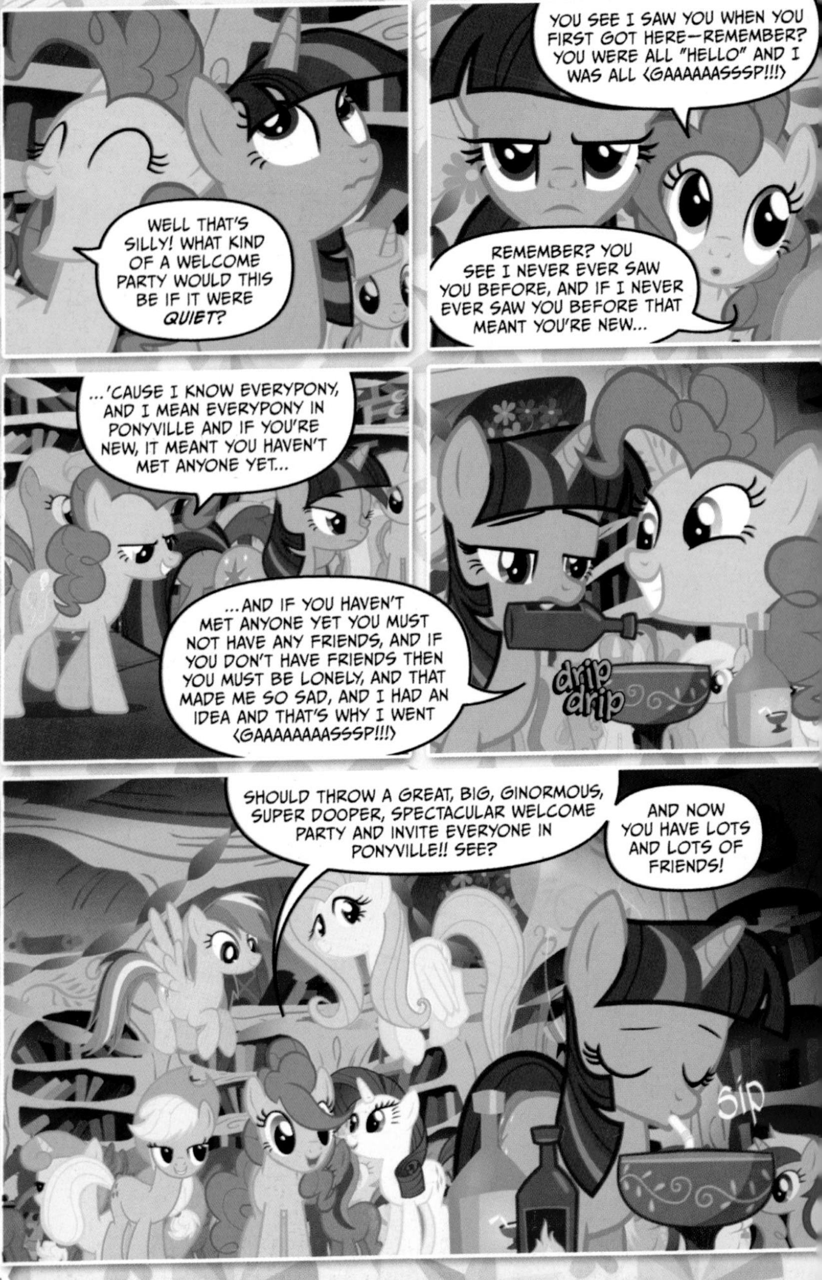

WELL THAT'S SILLY! WHAT KIND OF A WELCOME PARTY WOULD THIS BE IF IT WERE *QUIET*?
YOU SEE I SAW YOU WHEN YOU FIRST GOT HERE—REMEMBER? YOU WERE ALL "HELLO" AND I WAS ALL <GAAAAAAASSSP!!!>
REMEMBER? YOU SEE I NEVER EVER SAW YOU BEFORE, AND IF I NEVER EVER SAW YOU BEFORE THAT MEANT YOU'RE NEW...
...'CAUSE I KNOW EVERYPONY, AND I MEAN EVERYPONY IN PONYVILLE AND IF YOU'RE NEW, IT MEANT YOU HAVEN'T MET ANYONE YET...
...AND IF YOU HAVEN'T MET ANYONE YET YOU MUST NOT HAVE ANY FRIENDS, AND IF YOU DON'T HAVE FRIENDS THEN YOU MUST BE LONELY, AND THAT MADE ME SO SAD, AND I HAD AN IDEA AND THAT'S WHY I WENT <GAAAAAAAAASSSP!!!>
drip drip
SHOULD THROW A GREAT, BIG, GINORMOUS, SUPER DOOPER, SPECTACULAR WELCOME PARTY AND INVITE EVERYONE IN PONYVILLE!! SEE?
AND NOW YOU HAVE LOTS AND LOTS OF FRIENDS!
sip

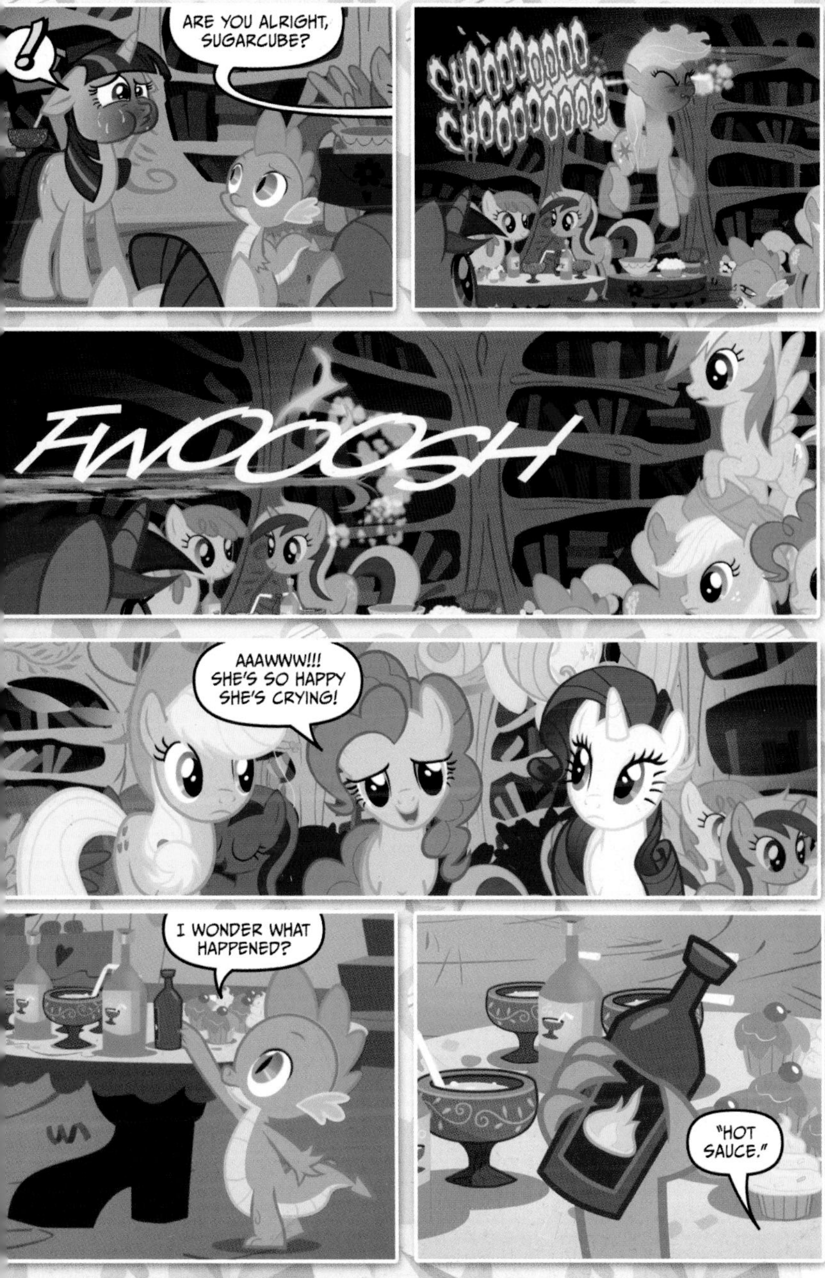

!
ARE YOU ALRIGHT, SUGARCUBE?
CHOOOOOOOO CHOOOOOOOO
FWOOOSH
AAAWWW!!! SHE'S SO HAPPY SHE'S CRYING!
I WONDER WHAT HAPPENED?
"HOT SAUCE."

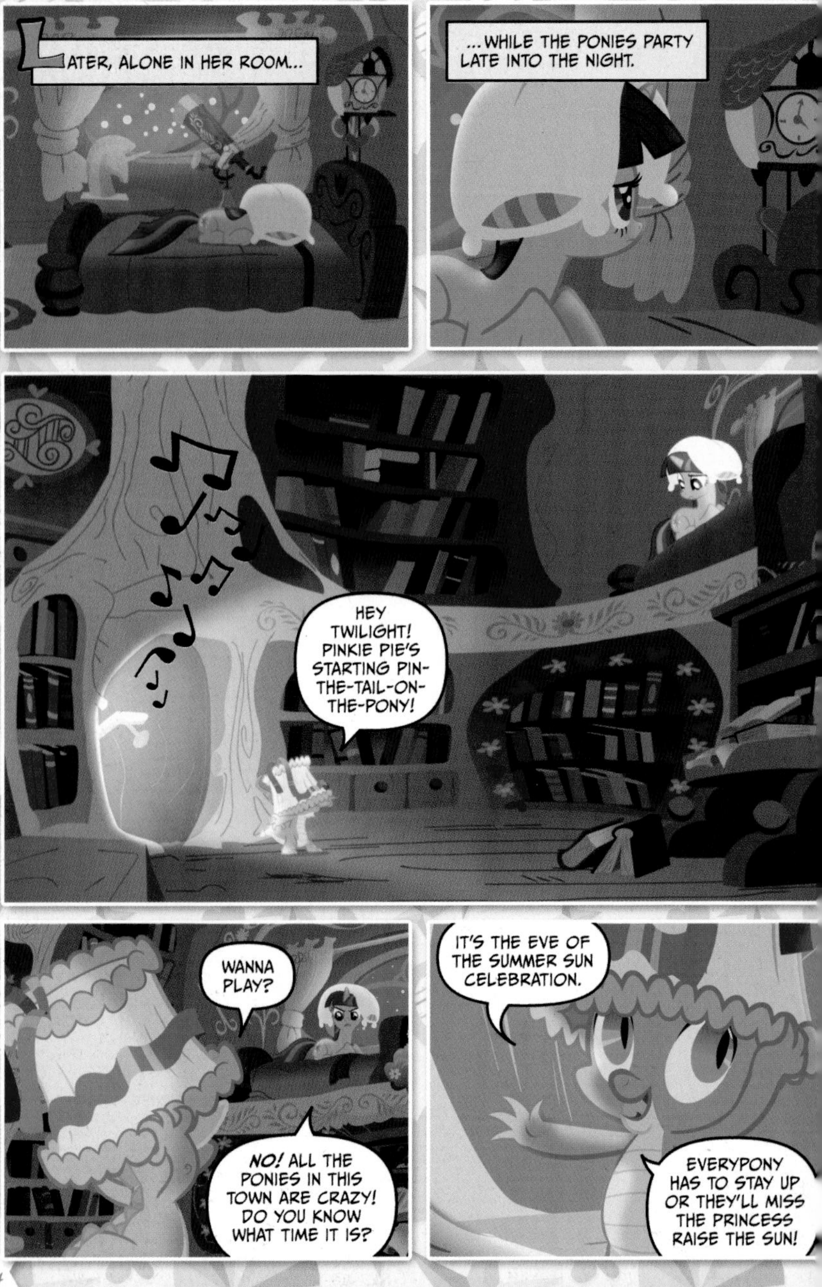
LATER, ALONE IN HER ROOM...
...WHILE THE PONIES PARTY LATE INTO THE NIGHT.
HEY TWILIGHT! PINKIE PIE'S STARTING PIN-THE-TAIL-ON-THE-PONY!
WANNA PLAY?
NO! ALL THE PONIES IN THIS TOWN ARE CRAZY! DO YOU KNOW WHAT TIME IT IS?
IT'S THE EVE OF THE SUMMER SUN CELEBRATION.
EVERYPONY HAS TO STAY UP OR THEY'LL MISS THE PRINCESS RAISE THE SUN!

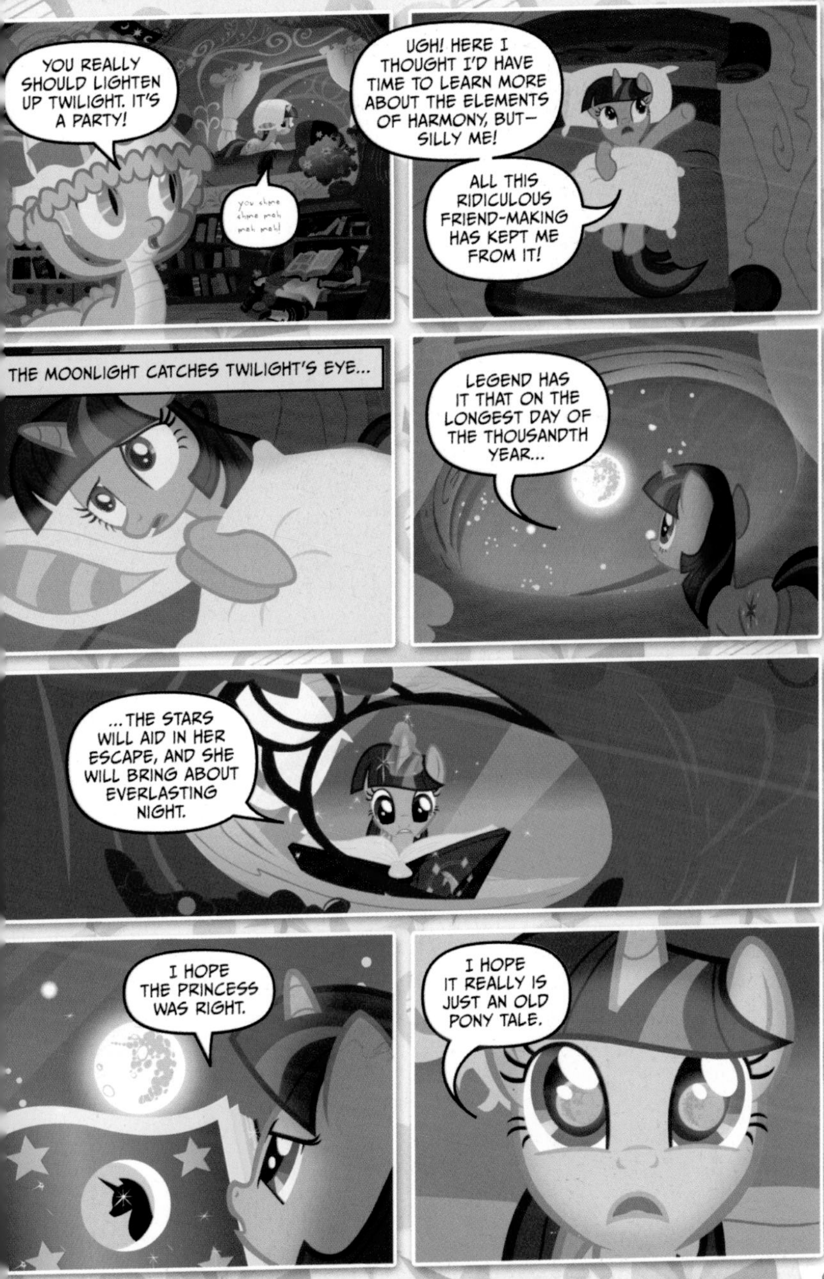
YOU REALLY SHOULD LIGHTEN UP TWILIGHT. IT'S A PARTY!
you shine shine meh meh meh!
UGH! HERE I THOUGHT I'D HAVE TIME TO LEARN MORE ABOUT THE ELEMENTS OF HARMONY, BUT— SILLY ME!
ALL THIS RIDICULOUS FRIEND-MAKING HAS KEPT ME FROM IT!
THE MOONLIGHT CATCHES TWILIGHT'S EYE...
LEGEND HAS IT THAT ON THE LONGEST DAY OF THE THOUSANDTH YEAR...
...THE STARS WILL AID IN HER ESCAPE, AND SHE WILL BRING ABOUT EVERLASTING NIGHT.
I HOPE THE PRINCESS WAS RIGHT.
I HOPE IT REALLY IS JUST AN OLD PONY TALE.

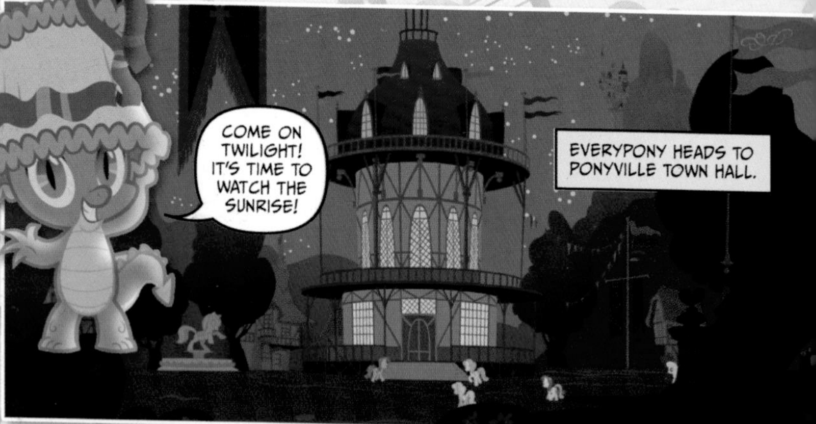
COME ON TWILIGHT! IT'S TIME TO WATCH THE SUNRISE!
EVERYPONY HEADS TO PONYVILLE TOWN HALL.

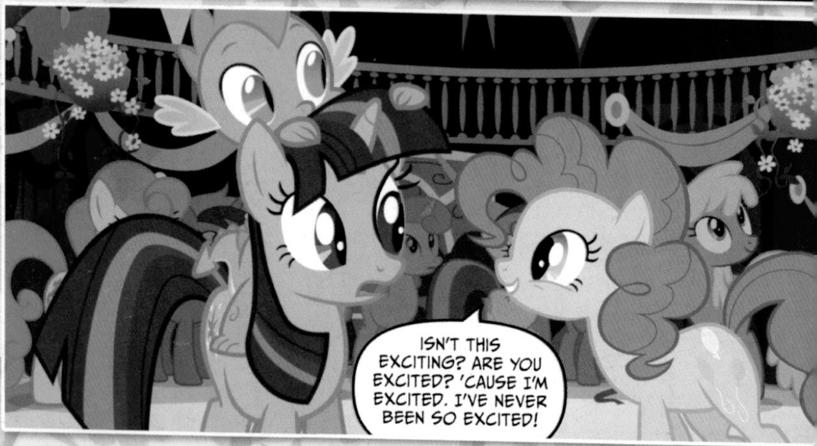
ISN'T THIS EXCITING? ARE YOU EXCITED? 'CAUSE I'M EXCITED. I'VE NEVER BEEN SO EXCITED!

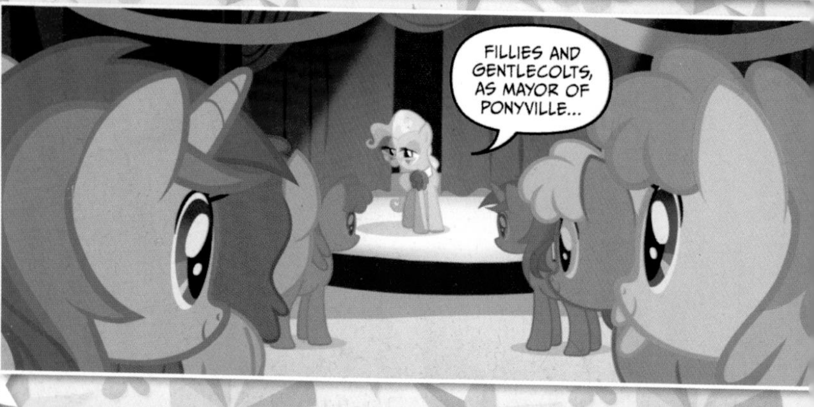
FILLIES AND GENTLECOLTS, AS MAYOR OF PONYVILLE...

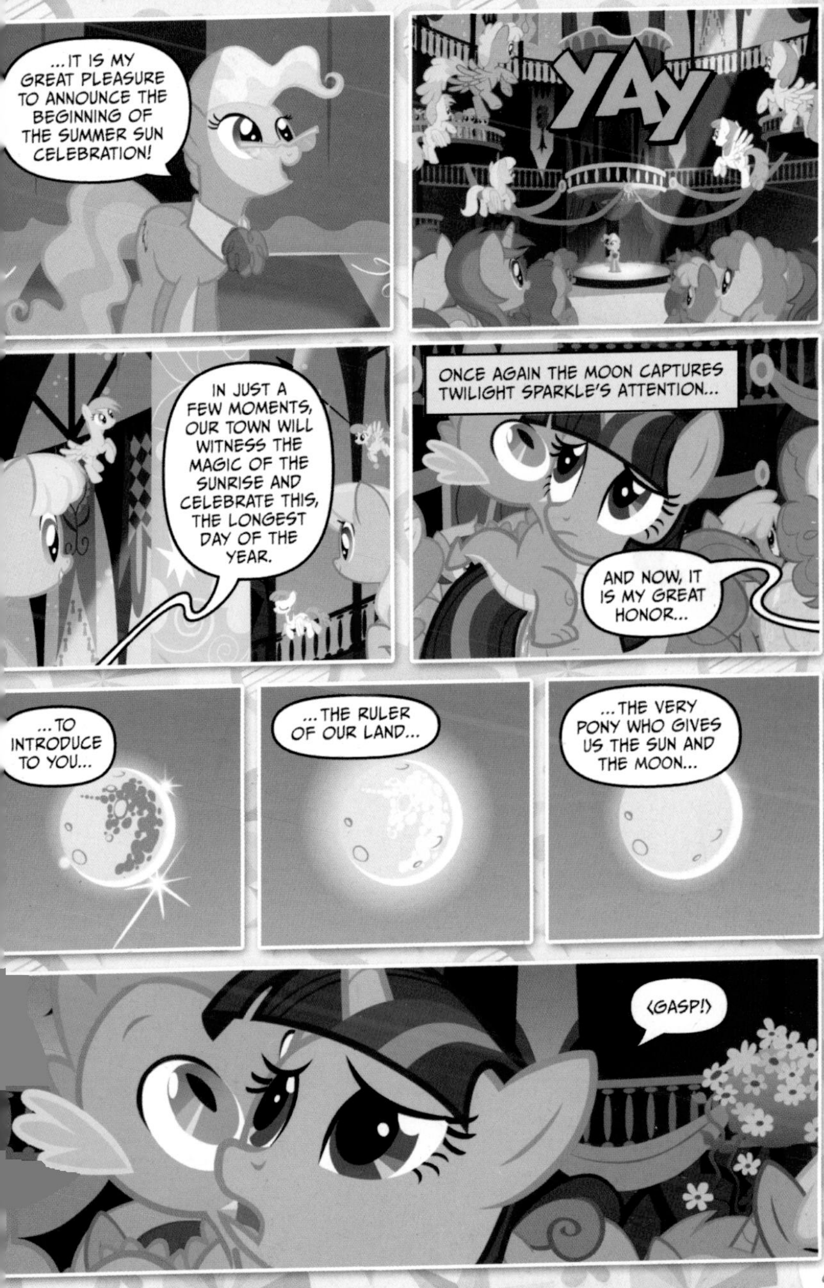
...IT IS MY GREAT PLEASURE TO ANNOUNCE THE BEGINNING OF THE SUMMER SUN CELEBRATION!
YAY
IN JUST A FEW MOMENTS, OUR TOWN WILL WITNESS THE MAGIC OF THE SUNRISE AND CELEBRATE THIS, THE LONGEST DAY OF THE YEAR.
ONCE AGAIN THE MOON CAPTURES TWILIGHT SPARKLE'S ATTENTION...
AND NOW, IT IS MY GREAT HONOR...
...TO INTRODUCE TO YOU...
...THE RULER OF OUR LAND...
...THE VERY PONY WHO GIVES US THE SUN AND THE MOON...
(GASP!)

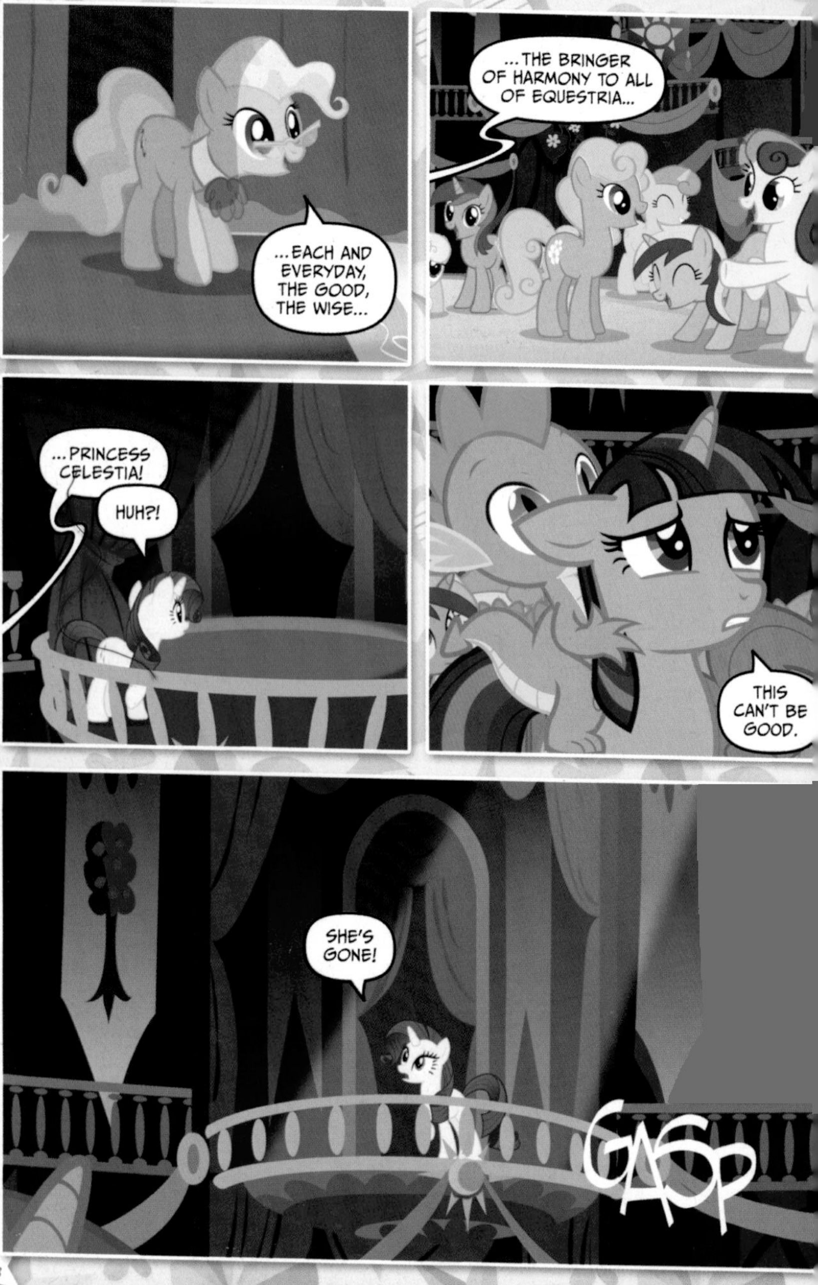
...EACH AND EVERYDAY, THE GOOD, THE WISE...
...THE BRINGER OF HARMONY TO ALL OF EQUESTRIA...
...PRINCESS CELESTIA!
HUH?!
THIS CAN'T BE GOOD.
SHE'S GONE!
GASP

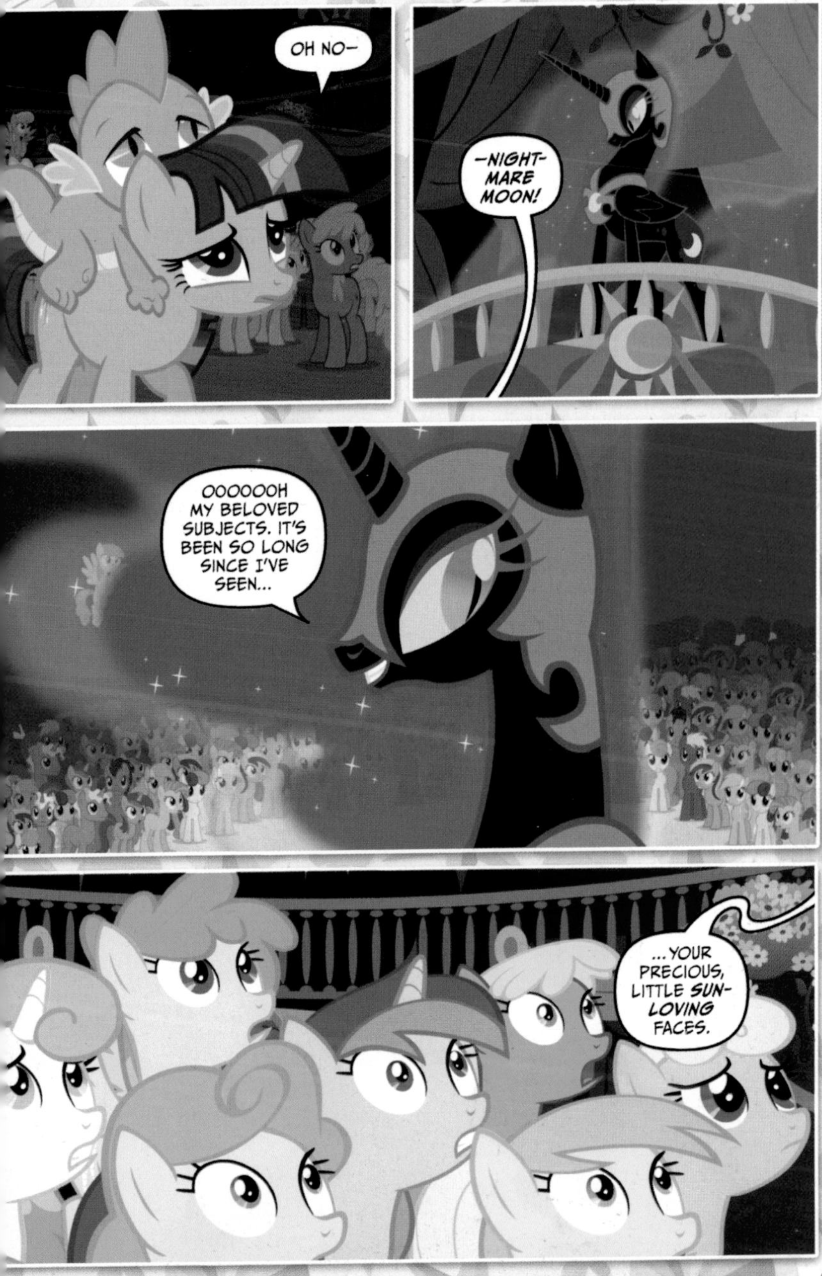
OH NO—
—NIGHT-MARE MOON!
OOOOOOH MY BELOVED SUBJECTS. IT'S BEEN SO LONG SINCE I'VE SEEN...
...YOUR PRECIOUS, LITTLE SUN-LOVING FACES.

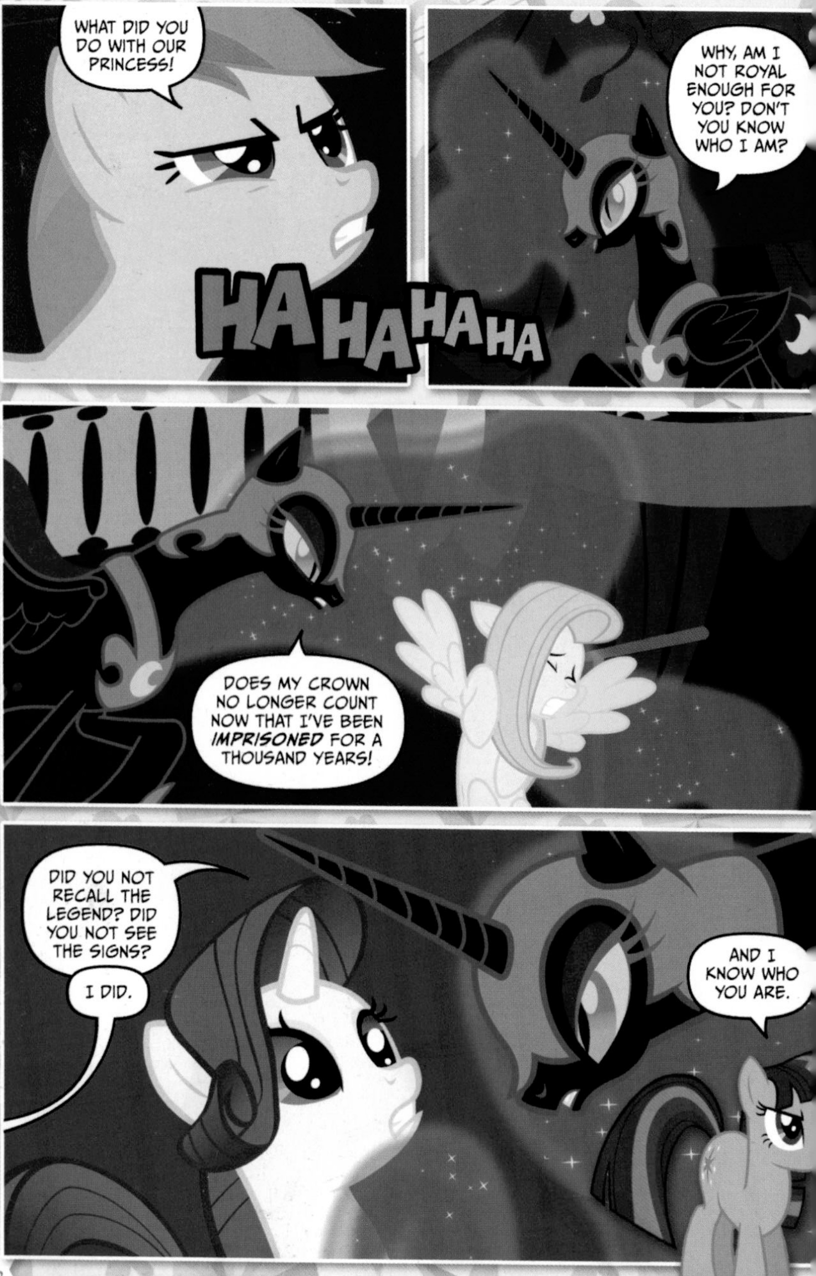
WHAT DID YOU DO WITH OUR PRINCESS!
WHY, AM I NOT ROYAL ENOUGH FOR YOU? DON'T YOU KNOW WHO I AM?
HAHAHAHAHA
DOES MY CROWN NO LONGER COUNT NOW THAT I'VE BEEN IMPRISONED FOR A THOUSAND YEARS!
DID YOU NOT RECALL THE LEGEND? DID YOU NOT SEE THE SIGNS?
I DID.
AND I KNOW WHO YOU ARE.

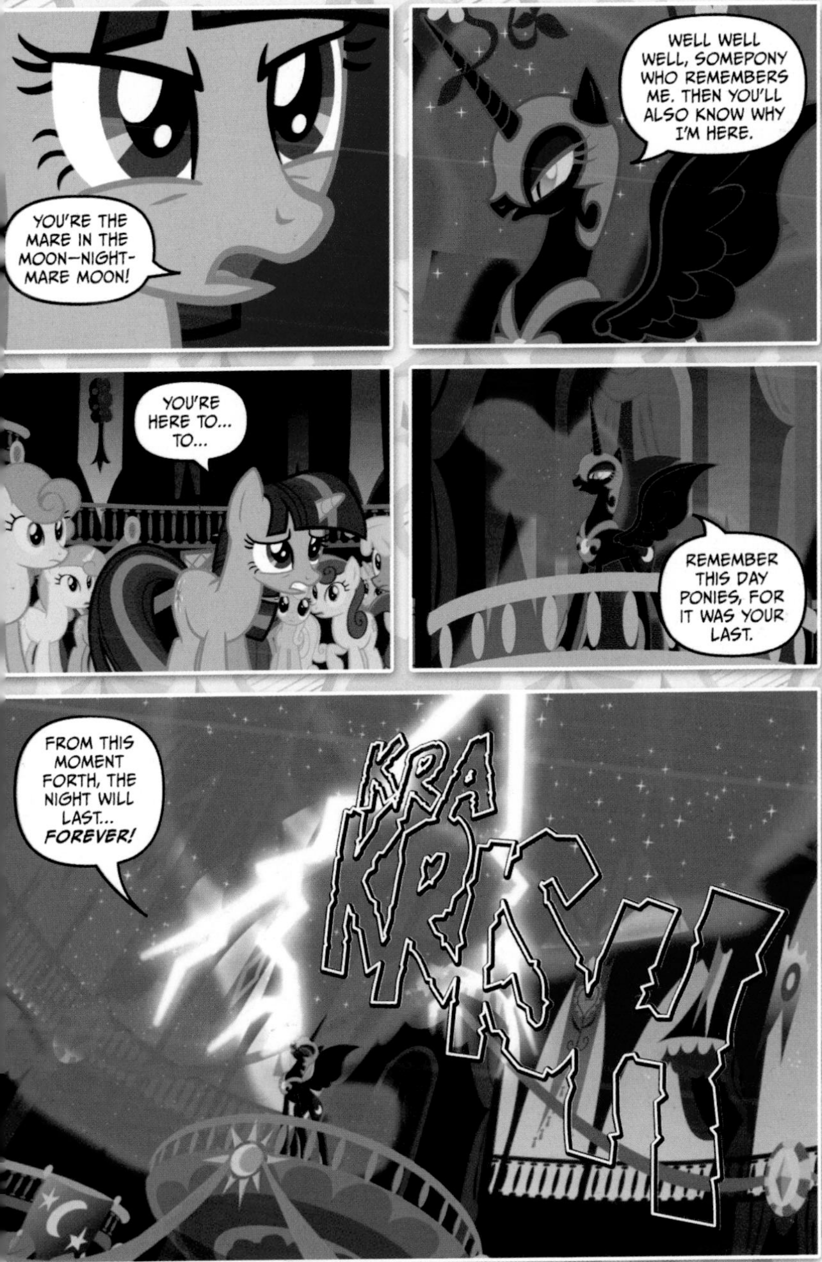
YOU'RE THE MARE IN THE MOON—NIGHT-MARE MOON!
WELL WELL WELL, SOMEPONY WHO REMEMBERS ME. THEN YOU'LL ALSO KNOW WHY I'M HERE.
YOU'RE HERE TO... TO...
REMEMBER THIS DAY PONIES, FOR IT WAS YOUR LAST.
FROM THIS MOMENT FORTH, THE NIGHT WILL LAST... *FOREVER!*
KRA KRASH!!

SEIZE HER!

ONLY SHE KNOWS WHERE THE PRINCESS IS!

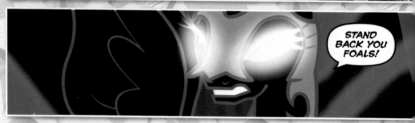

STAND BACK YOU FOALS!

ZAP

ZAP

HA HA HA HA HA

HA HA HA HA HA

WHOOSH

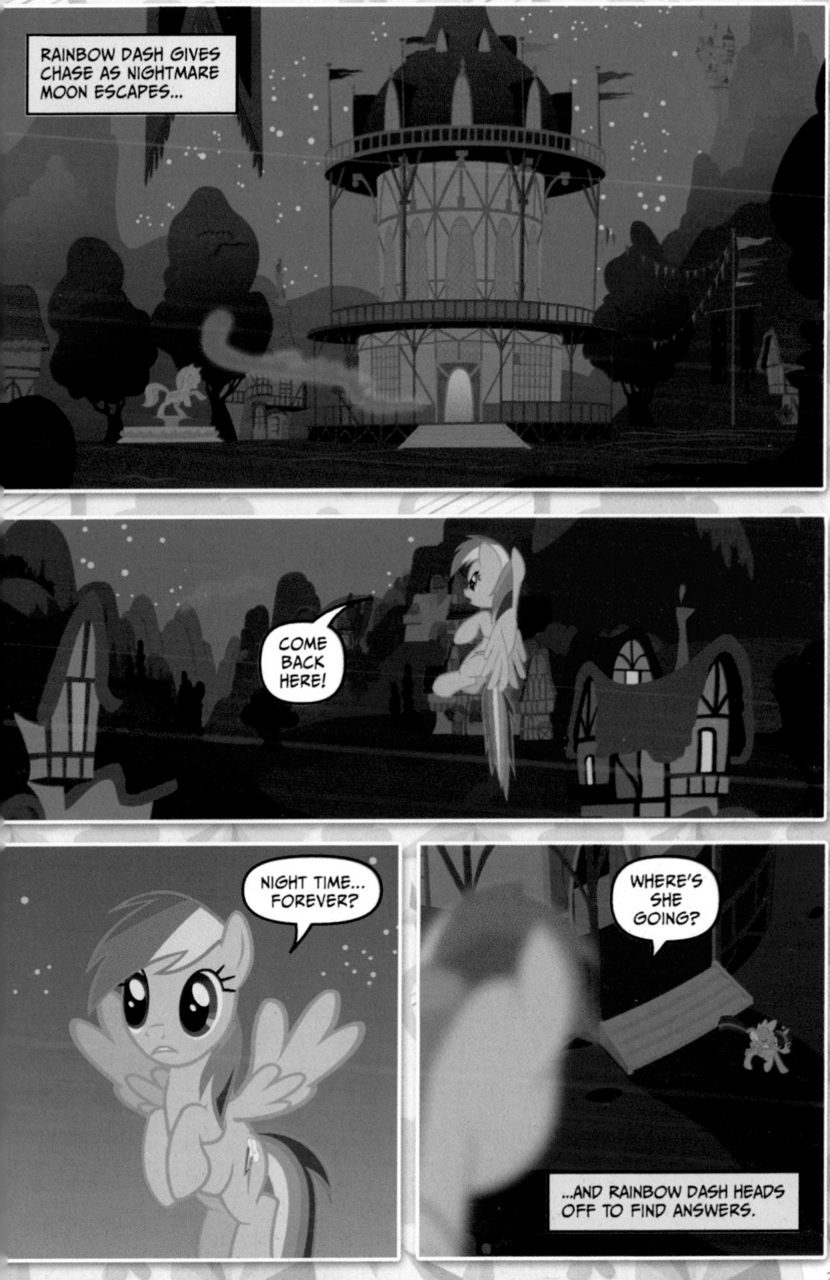
RAINBOW DASH GIVES CHASE AS NIGHTMARE MOON ESCAPES...
COME BACK HERE!
NIGHT TIME... FOREVER?
WHERE'S SHE GOING?
...AND RAINBOW DASH HEADS OFF TO FIND ANSWERS.

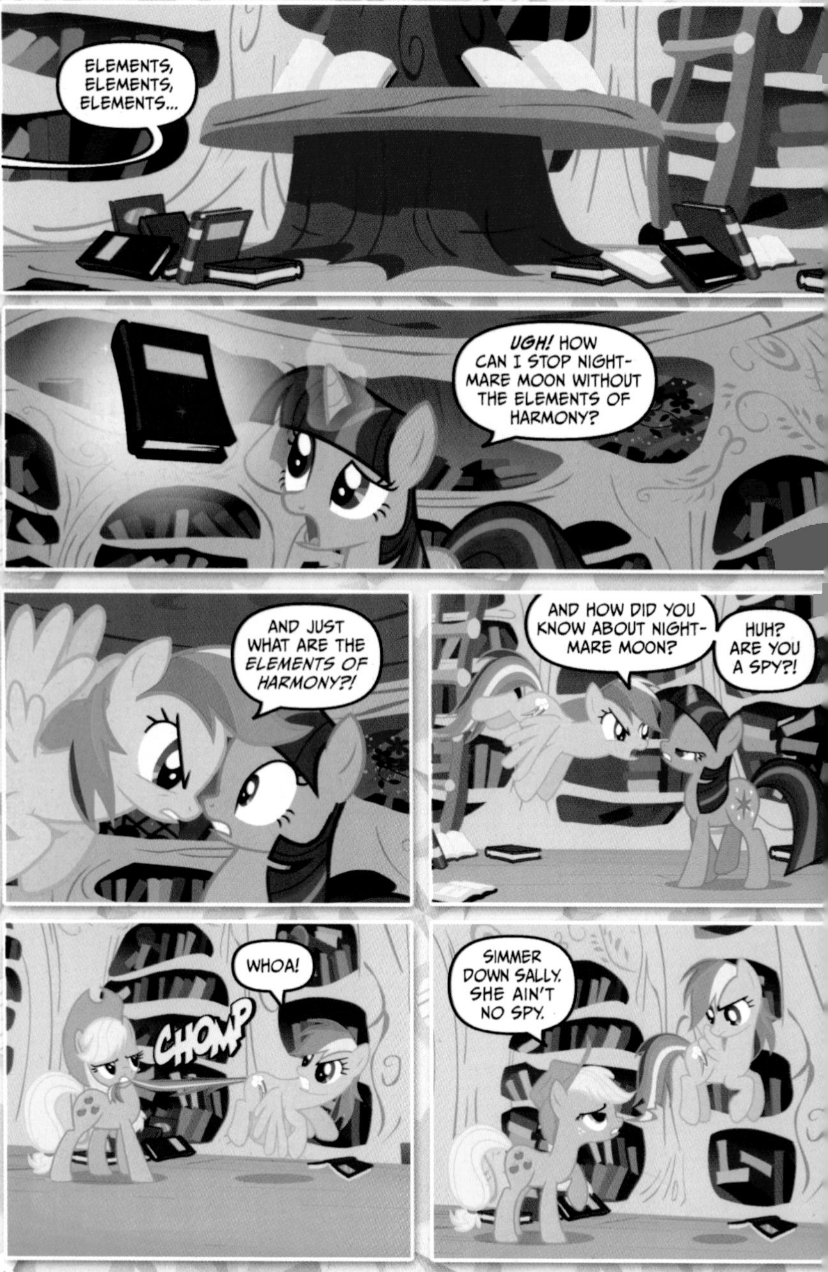
ELEMENTS, ELEMENTS, ELEMENTS...
UGH! HOW CAN I STOP NIGHT-MARE MOON WITHOUT THE ELEMENTS OF HARMONY?
AND JUST WHAT ARE THE ELEMENTS OF HARMONY?!
AND HOW DID YOU KNOW ABOUT NIGHT-MARE MOON?
HUH? ARE YOU A SPY?!
WHOA!
CHOMP
SIMMER DOWN SALLY. SHE AIN'T NO SPY.

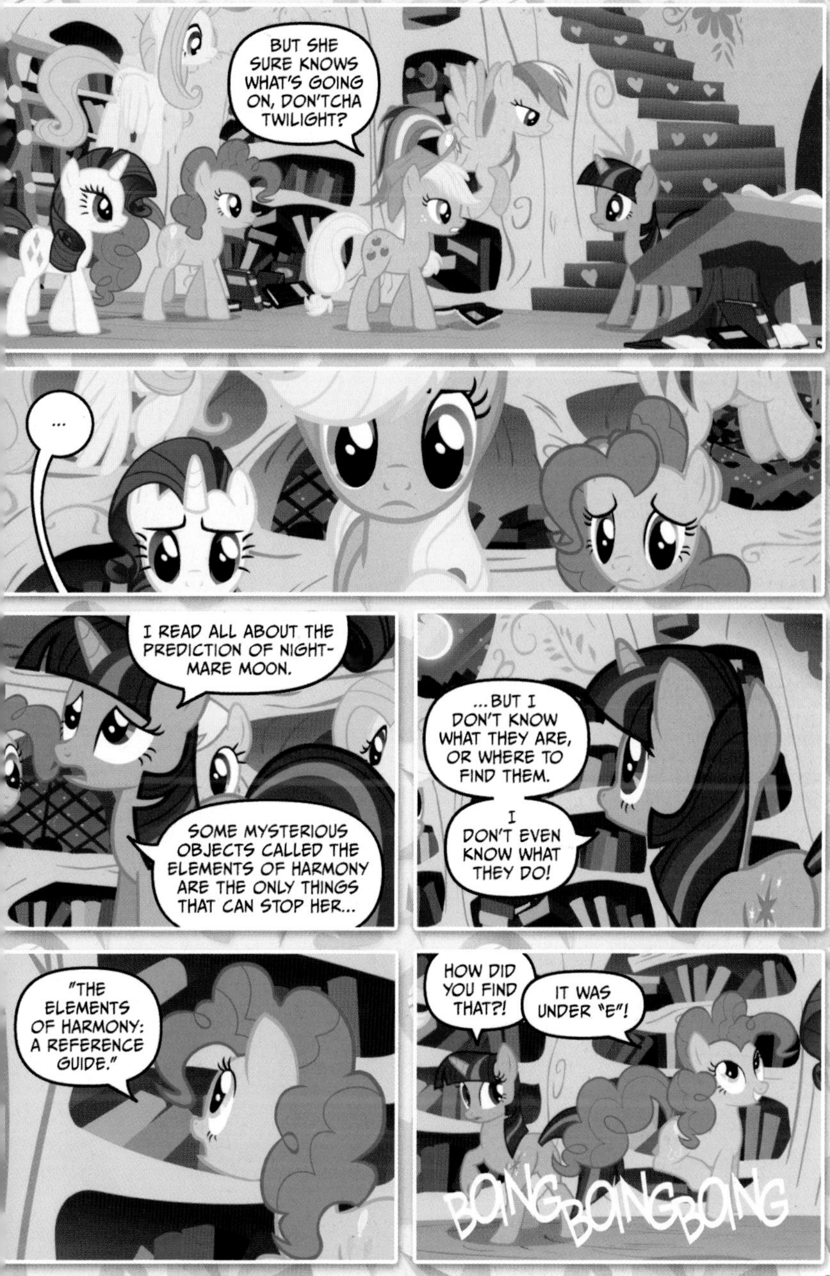

BUT SHE SURE KNOWS WHAT'S GOING ON, DON'TCHA TWILIGHT?
...
I READ ALL ABOUT THE PREDICTION OF NIGHT-MARE MOON.
SOME MYSTERIOUS OBJECTS CALLED THE ELEMENTS OF HARMONY ARE THE ONLY THINGS THAT CAN STOP HER...
...BUT I DON'T KNOW WHAT THEY ARE, OR WHERE TO FIND THEM.
I DON'T EVEN KNOW WHAT THEY DO!
"THE ELEMENTS OF HARMONY: A REFERENCE GUIDE."
HOW DID YOU FIND THAT?!
IT WAS UNDER "E"!
BOING BOING BOING

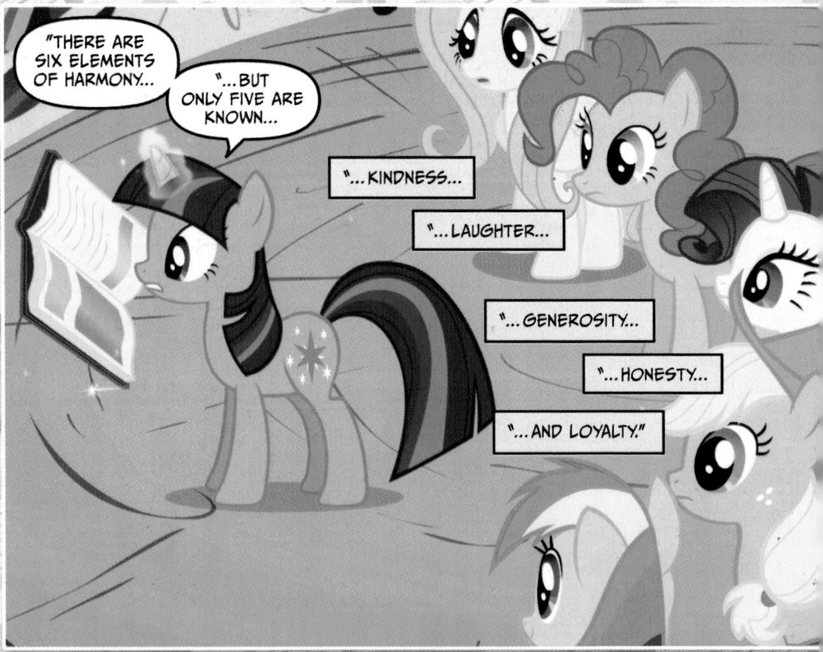
"THERE ARE SIX ELEMENTS OF HARMONY...
"...BUT ONLY FIVE ARE KNOWN...
"...KINDNESS...
"...LAUGHTER...
"...GENEROSITY...
"...HONESTY...
"...AND LOYALTY."

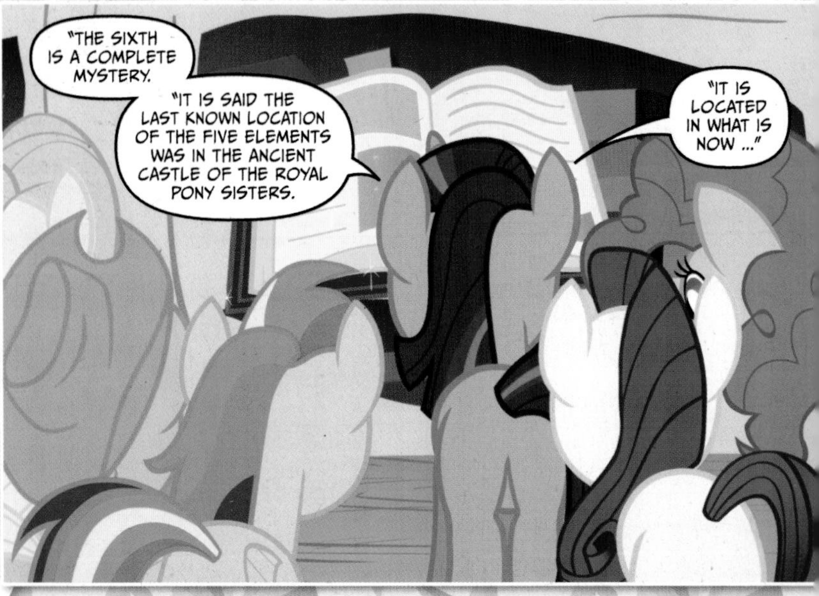
"THE SIXTH IS A COMPLETE MYSTERY.
"IT IS SAID THE LAST KNOWN LOCATION OF THE FIVE ELEMENTS WAS IN THE ANCIENT CASTLE OF THE ROYAL PONY SISTERS.
"IT IS LOCATED IN WHAT IS NOW ..."

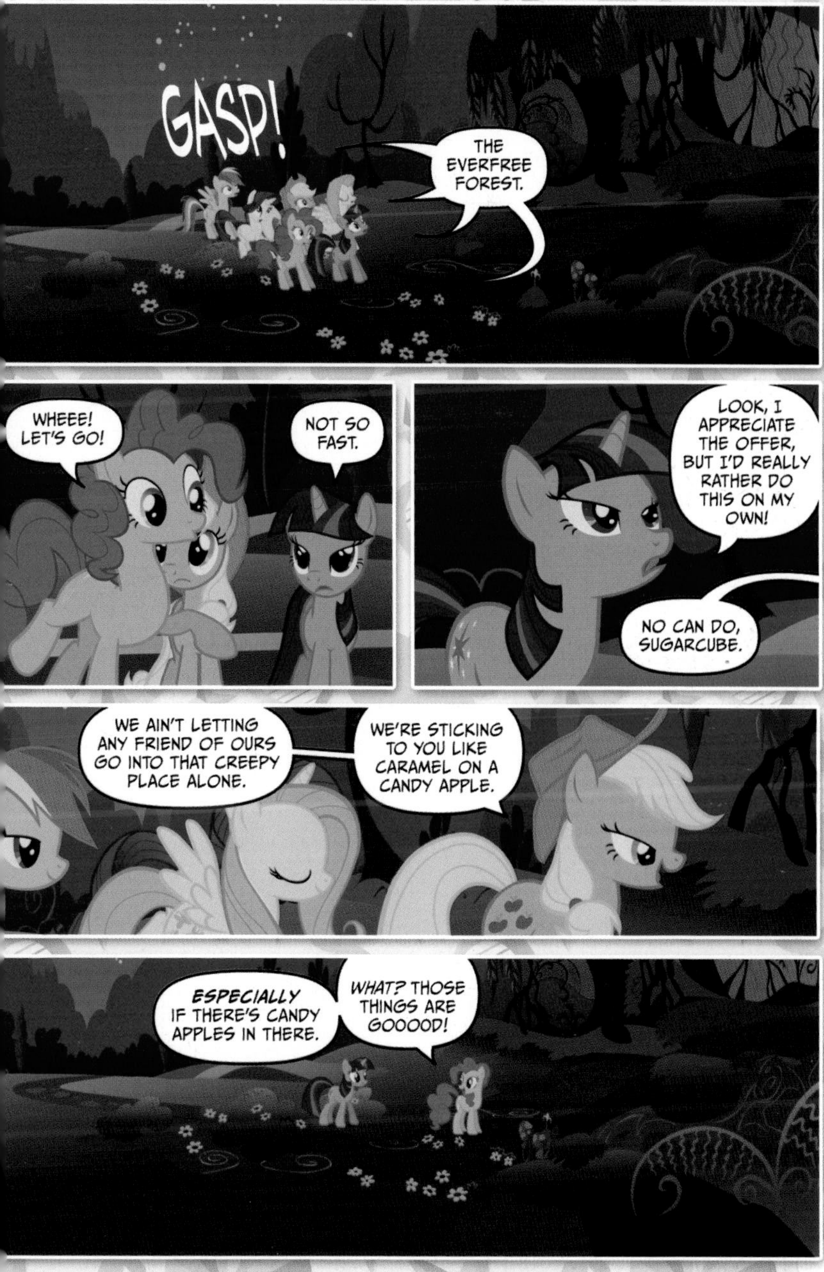
GASP!
THE EVERFREE FOREST.
WHEEE! LET'S GO!
NOT SO FAST.
LOOK, I APPRECIATE THE OFFER, BUT I'D REALLY RATHER DO THIS ON MY OWN!
NO CAN DO, SUGARCUBE.
WE AIN'T LETTING ANY FRIEND OF OURS GO INTO THAT CREEPY PLACE ALONE.
WE'RE STICKING TO YOU LIKE CARAMEL ON A CANDY APPLE.
ESPECIALLY IF THERE'S CANDY APPLES IN THERE.
WHAT? THOSE THINGS ARE GOOOOD!

S-SO NONE OF YOU HAVE BEEN IN HERE BEFORE?

HEAVENS NO! J-JUST LOOK AT IT! IT'S DREADFUL!

AND IT AIN'T NATURAL! FOLKS SAY IT DON'T WORK THE SAME AS EQUESTRIA...

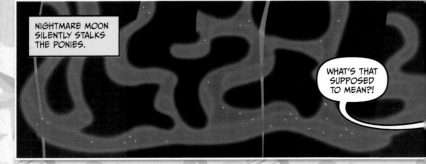

NIGHTMARE MOON SILENTLY STALKS THE PONIES.

WHAT'S THAT SUPPOSED TO MEAN?!

NOOOOOPONY KNOOOOOOWS!

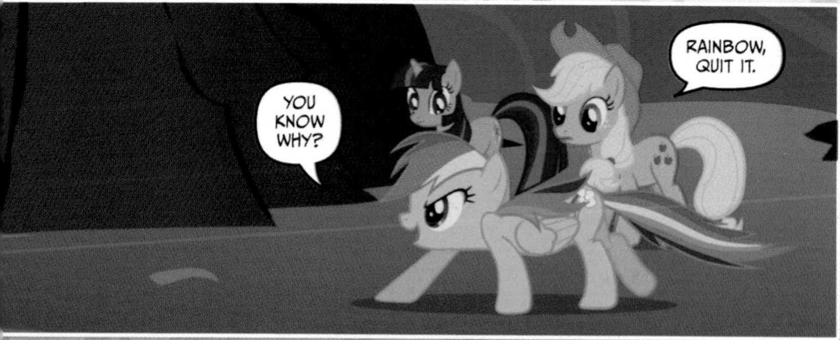
YOU KNOW WHY?
RAINBOW, QUIT IT.

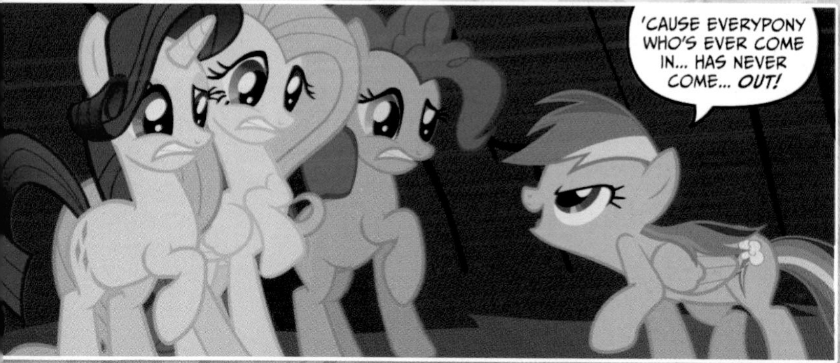
'CAUSE EVERYPONY WHO'S EVER COME IN... HAS NEVER COME... *OUT!*

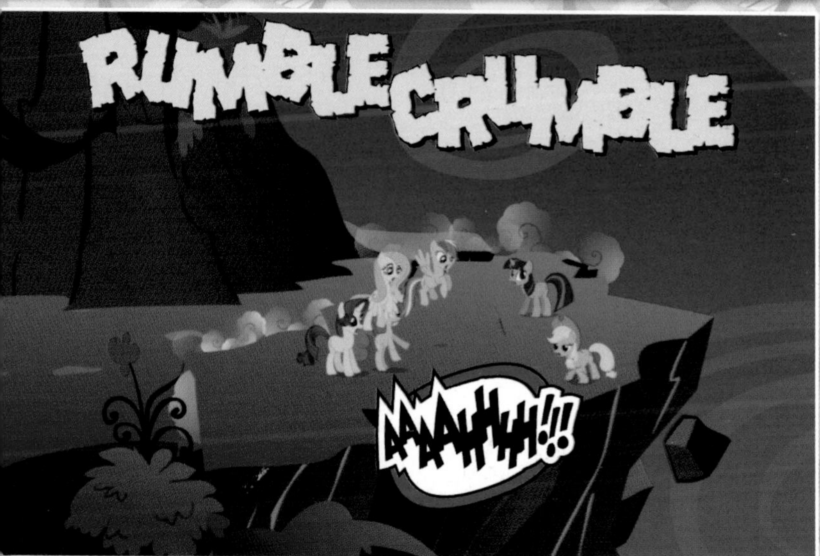
RUMBLE CRUMBLE
AAAAHHHH!!!

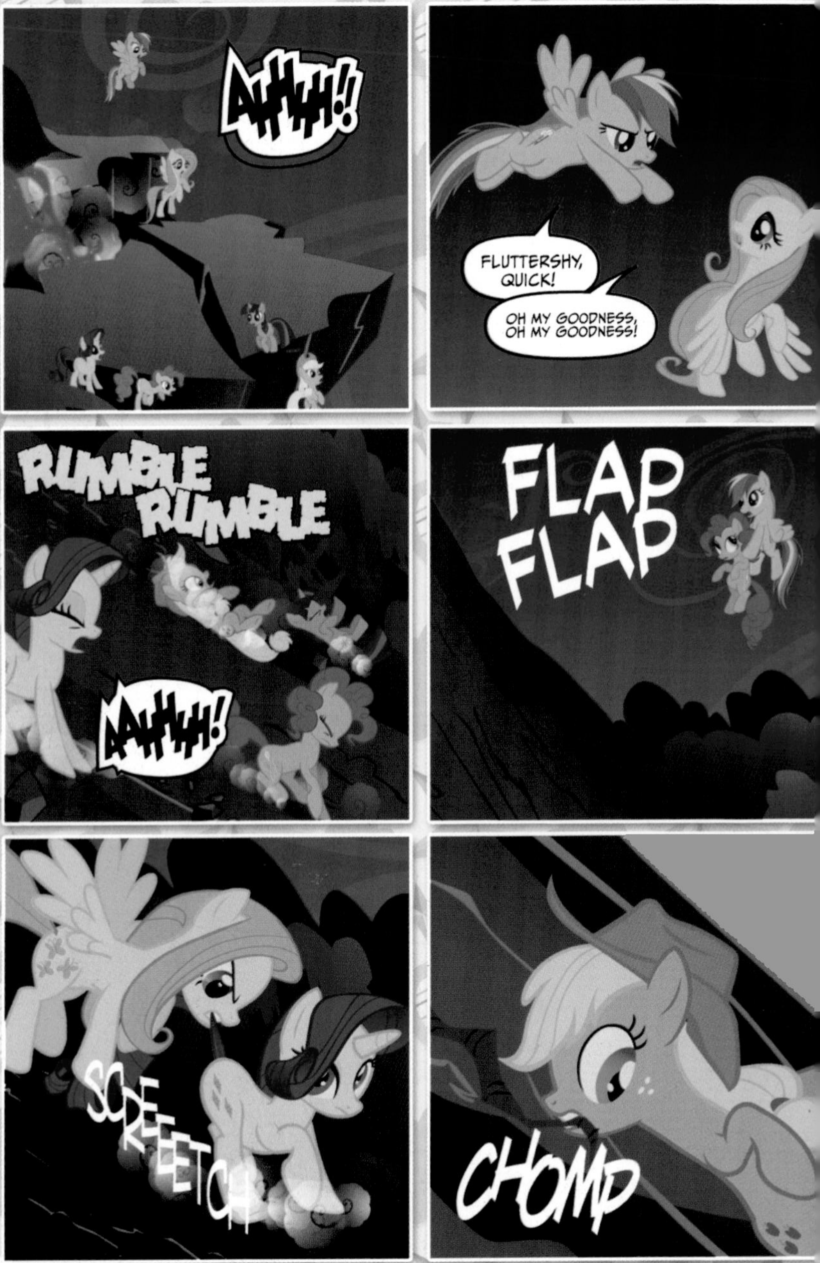
AHHHH!!
FLUTTERSHY, QUICK!
OH MY GOODNESS, OH MY GOODNESS!
RUMBLE RUMBLE
AAHHHH!
FLAP FLAP
SCREEEETCH
CHOMP

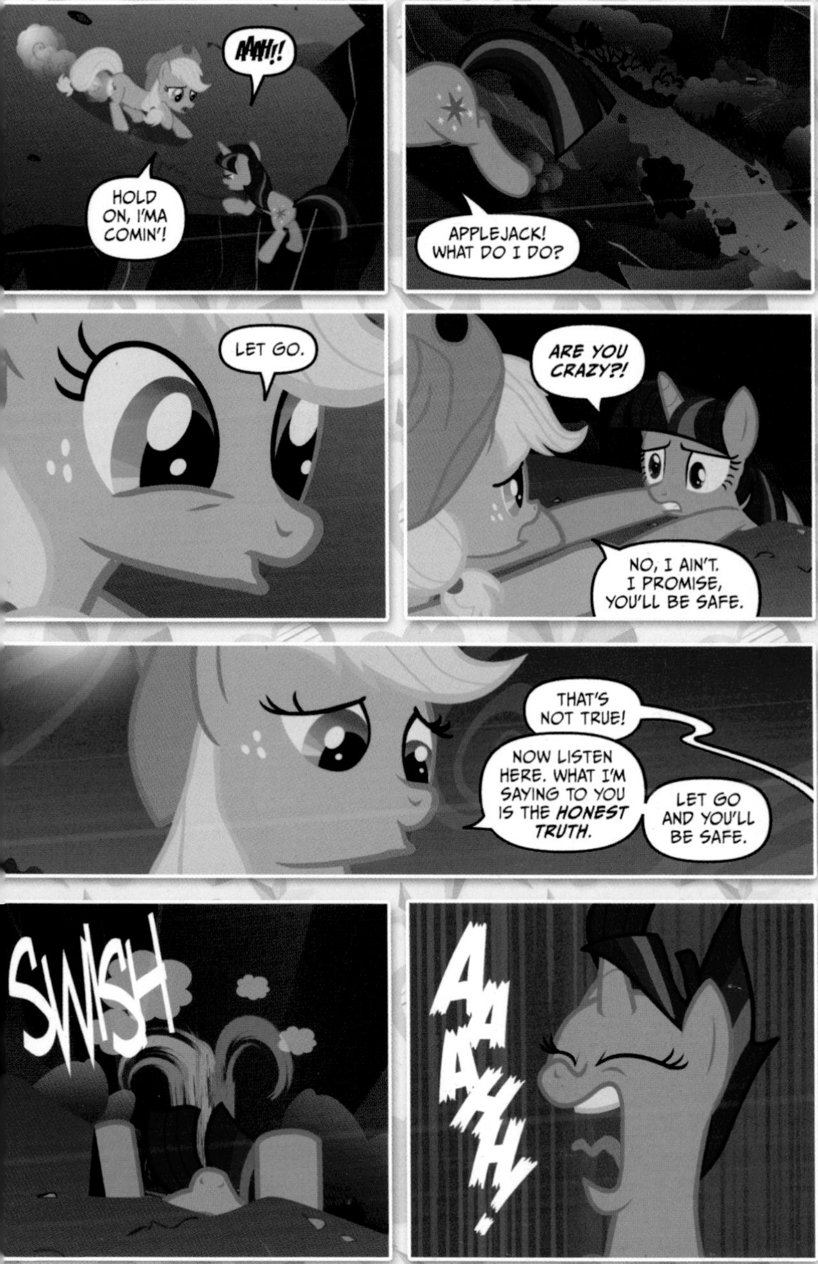
AAAH!!
HOLD ON, I'MA COMIN'!
APPLEJACK! WHAT DO I DO?
LET GO.
ARE YOU CRAZY?!
NO, I AIN'T. I PROMISE, YOU'LL BE SAFE.
NOW LISTEN HERE. WHAT I'M SAYING TO YOU IS THE *HONEST TRUTH*.
THAT'S NOT TRUE!
LET GO AND YOU'LL BE SAFE.
SWISH
AAAHH!

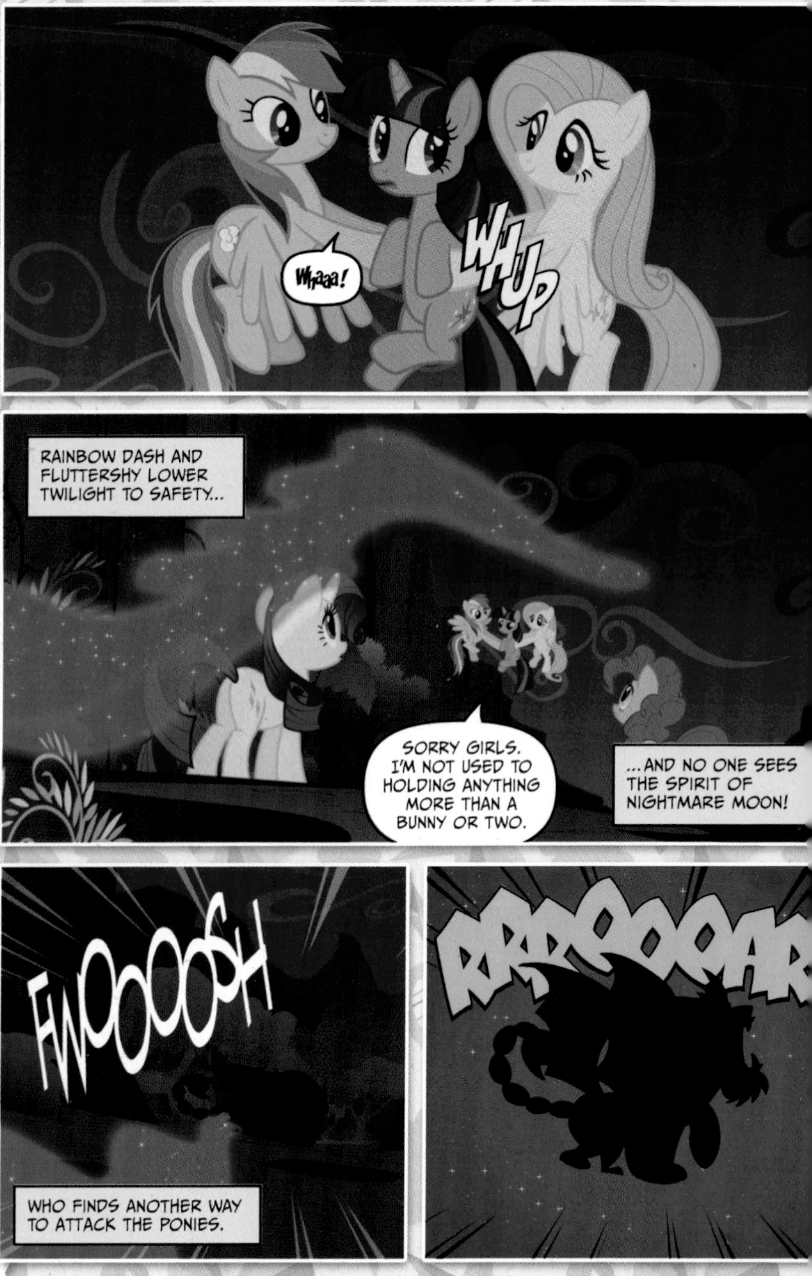

Whaaa!
WHUP
RAINBOW DASH AND FLUTTERSHY LOWER TWILIGHT TO SAFETY...
SORRY GIRLS. I'M NOT USED TO HOLDING ANYTHING MORE THAN A BUNNY OR TWO.
...AND NO ONE SEES THE SPIRIT OF NIGHTMARE MOON!
FWOOOSH
WHO FINDS ANOTHER WAY TO ATTACK THE PONIES.
RRROOOAR

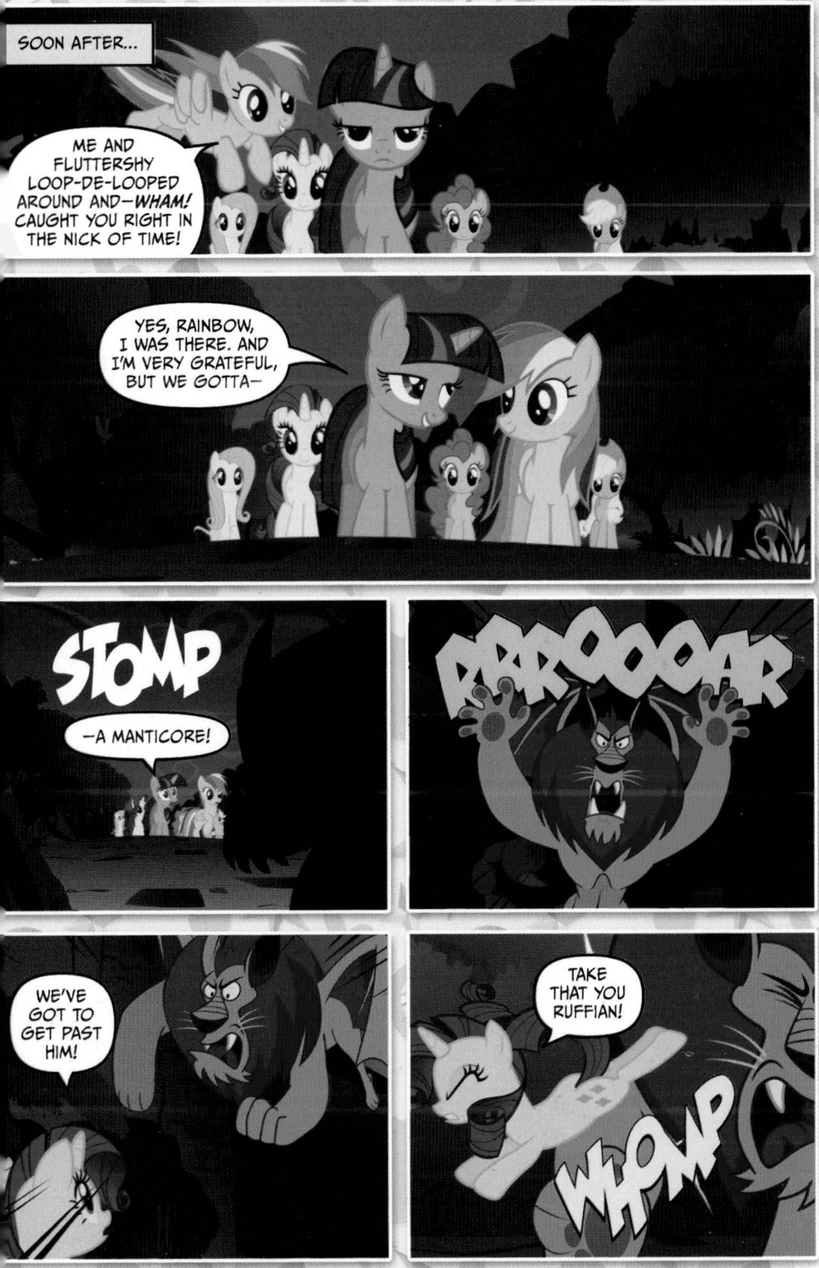
SOON AFTER...
ME AND FLUTTERSHY LOOP-DE-LOOPED AROUND AND—WHAM! CAUGHT YOU RIGHT IN THE NICK OF TIME!
YES, RAINBOW, I WAS THERE. AND I'M VERY GRATEFUL, BUT WE GOTTA—
STOMP
—A MANTICORE!
RRROOOAR
WE'VE GOT TO GET PAST HIM!
TAKE THAT YOU RUFFIAN!
WHOMP

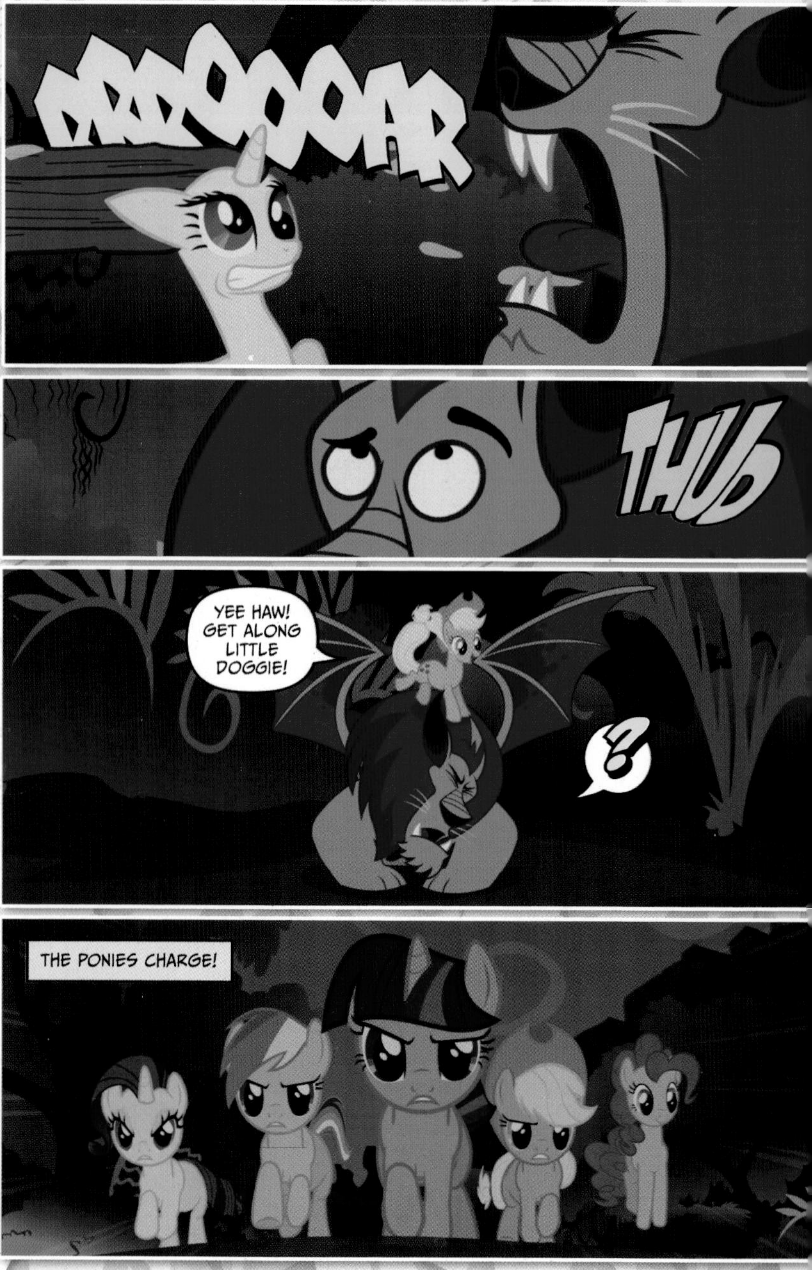
RRROOOOAR
THUD
YEE HAW! GET ALONG LITTLE DOGGIE!
?
THE PONIES CHARGE!

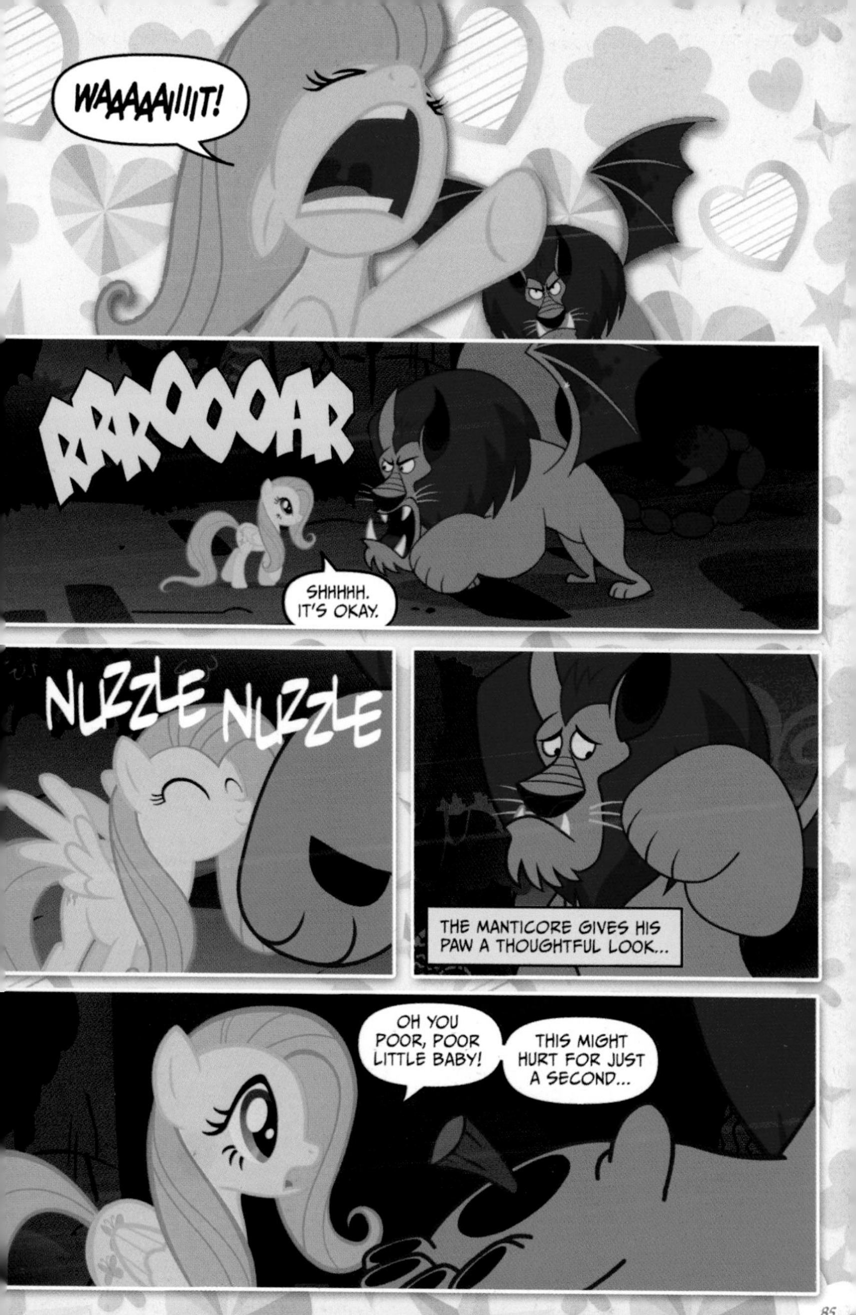
WAAAAAIIIIT!
RRROOOAR
SHHHHH. IT'S OKAY.
NUZZLE NUZZLE
THE MANTICORE GIVES HIS PAW A THOUGHTFUL LOOK...
OH YOU POOR, POOR LITTLE BABY!
THIS MIGHT HURT FOR JUST A SECOND...

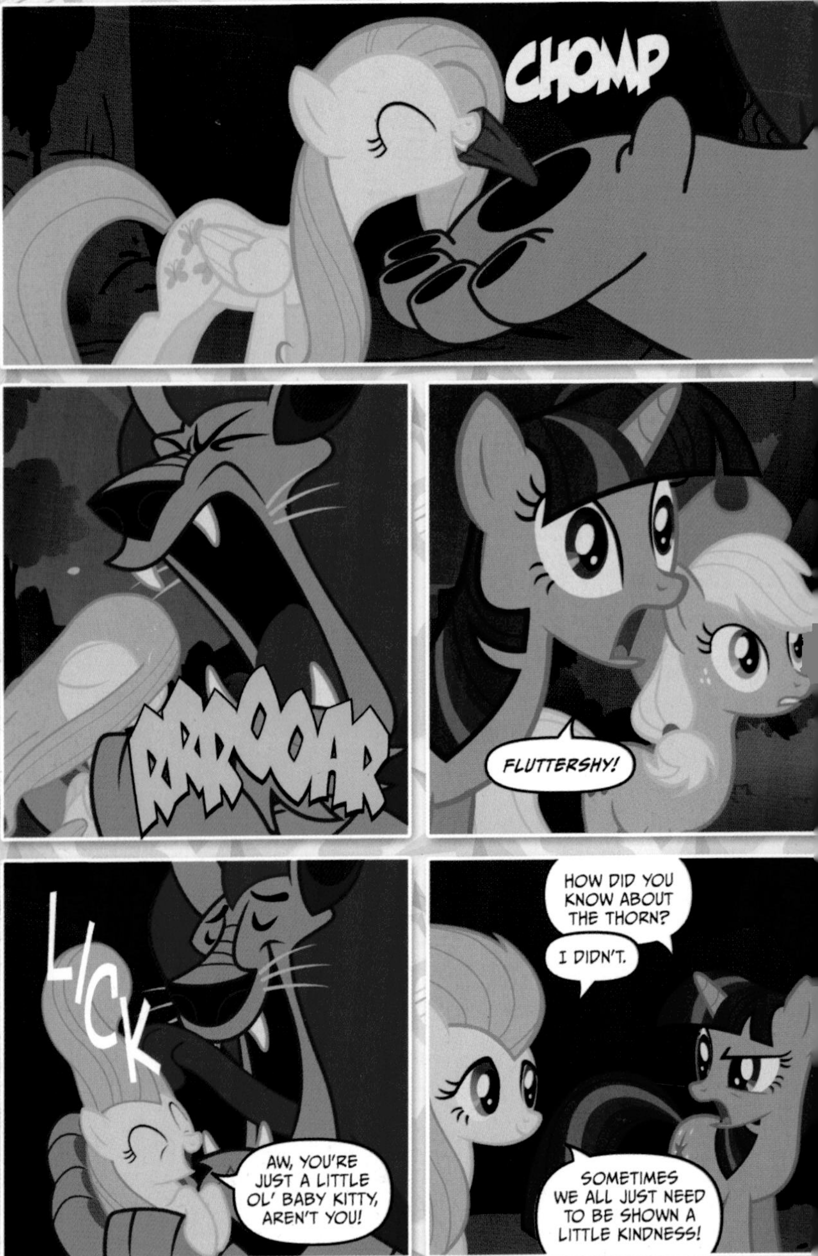
CHOMP
RRROOAR
FLUTTERSHY!
LICK
AW, YOU'RE JUST A LITTLE OL' BABY KITTY, AREN'T YOU!
HOW DID YOU KNOW ABOUT THE THORN?
I DIDN'T.
SOMETIMES WE ALL JUST NEED TO BE SHOWN A LITTLE KINDNESS!

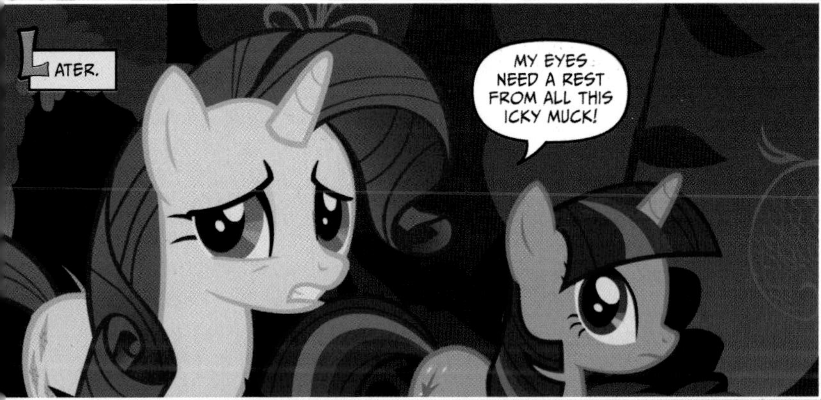
LATER.
MY EYES NEED A REST FROM ALL THIS ICKY MUCK!

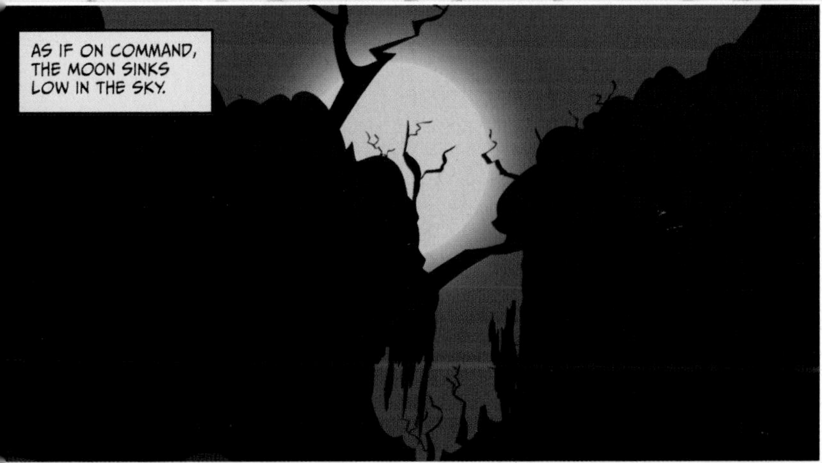
AS IF ON COMMAND, THE MOON SINKS LOW IN THE SKY.

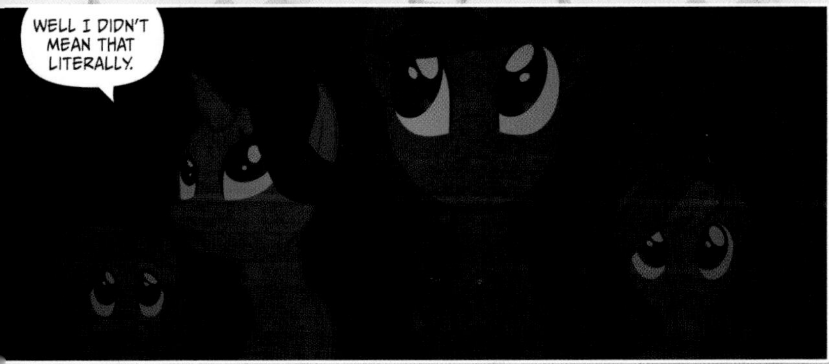
WELL I DIDN'T MEAN THAT LITERALLY.

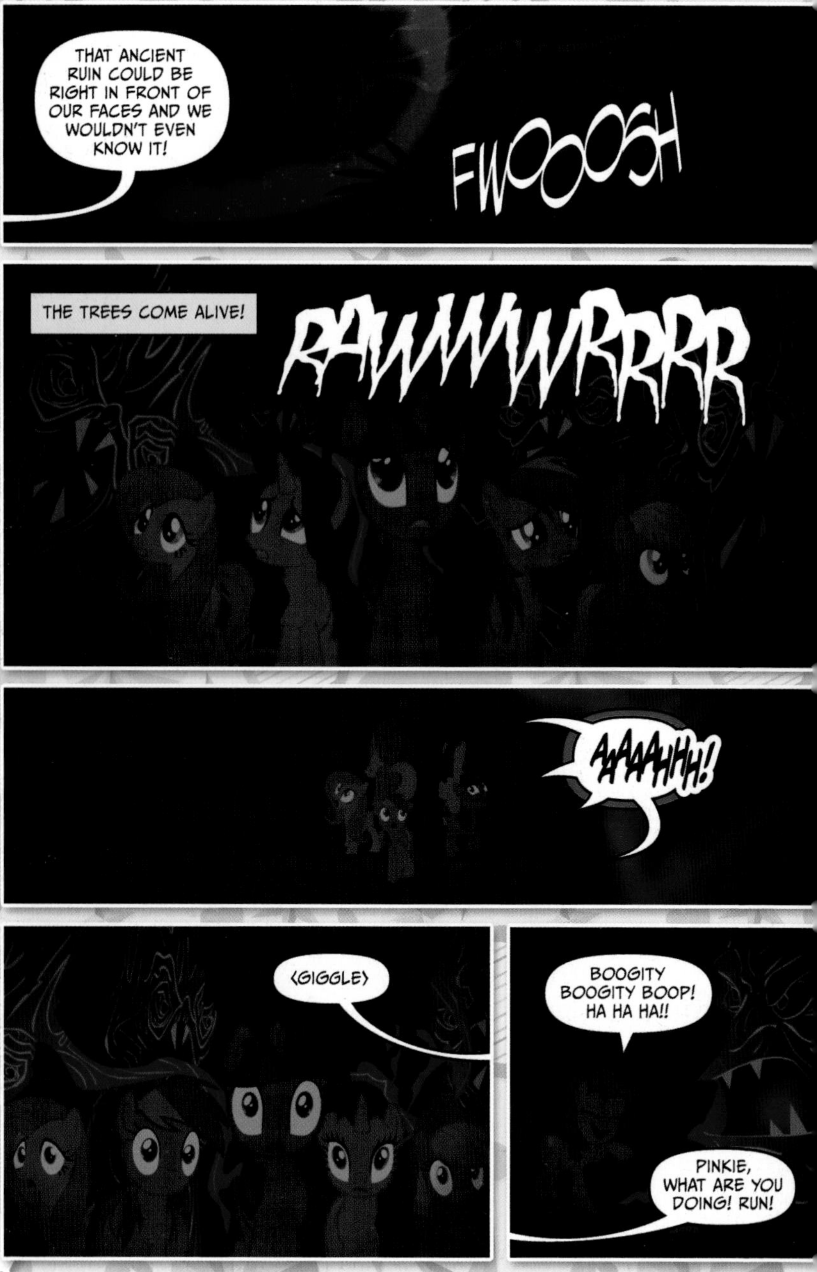
THAT ANCIENT RUIN COULD BE RIGHT IN FRONT OF OUR FACES AND WE WOULDN'T EVEN KNOW IT!
FWOOOSH
THE TREES COME ALIVE!
RAWWWRRRR
AAAAHHH!
‹GIGGLE›
BOOGITY BOOGITY BOOP! HA HA HA!!
PINKIE, WHAT ARE YOU DOING! RUN!

OH GIRLS, DON'T YOU SEE?

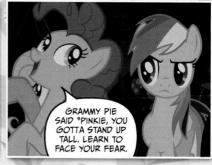

GRAMMY PIE SAID "PINKIE, YOU GOTTA STAND UP TALL. LEARN TO FACE YOUR FEAR.

"YOU'LL SEE THAT THEY CAN'T HURT YOU...

"JUST LAUGHING CAN MAKE THEM—

"—DISAPPEAR!"

POP

HA! HA! HA!

HA HA POP POP POP HA HA

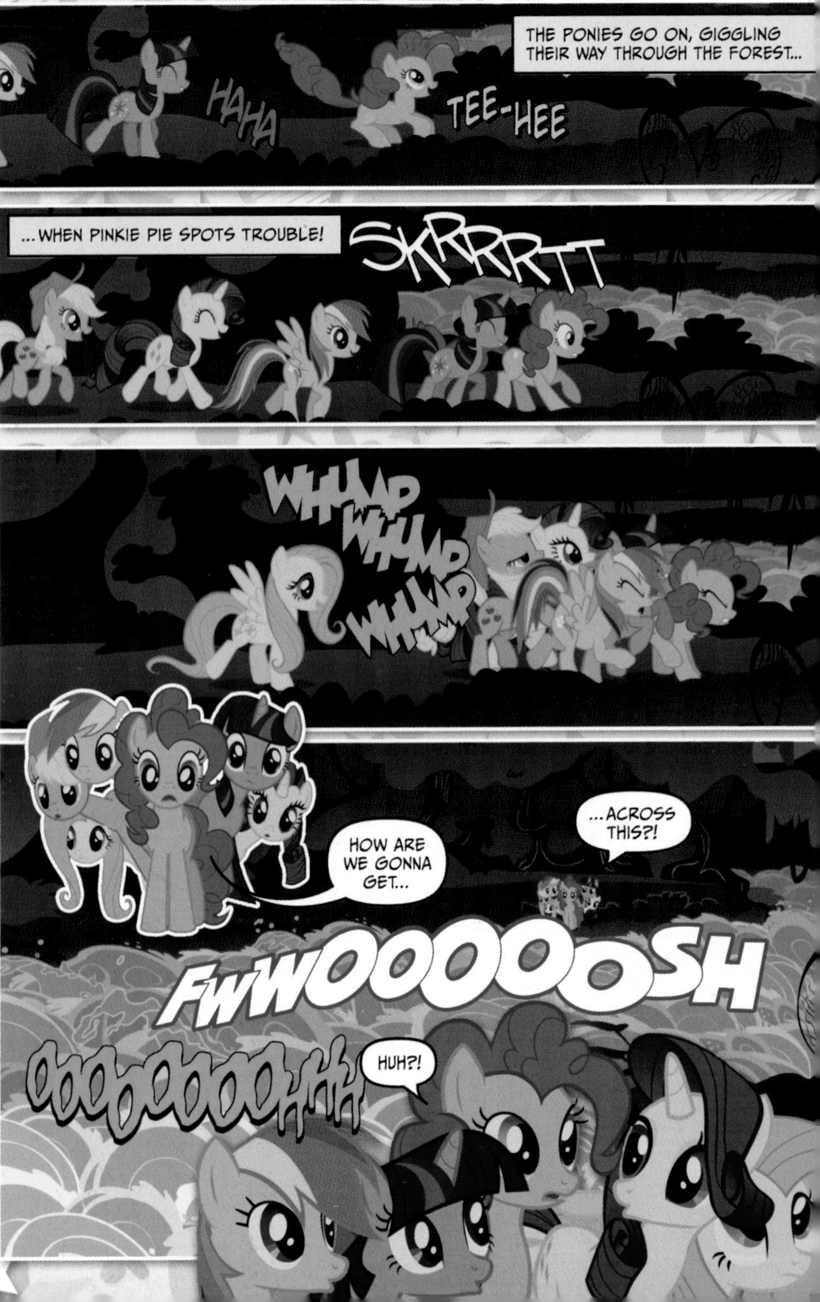
THE PONIES GO ON, GIGGLING THEIR WAY THROUGH THE FOREST...
HAHA
TEE-HEE
...WHEN PINKIE PIE SPOTS TROUBLE!
SKRRRRTT
WHUMP
WHUMP
WHUMP
HOW ARE WE GONNA GET...
...ACROSS THIS?!
FWWOOOOOOSH
OOOOOOOOHHH
HUH?!

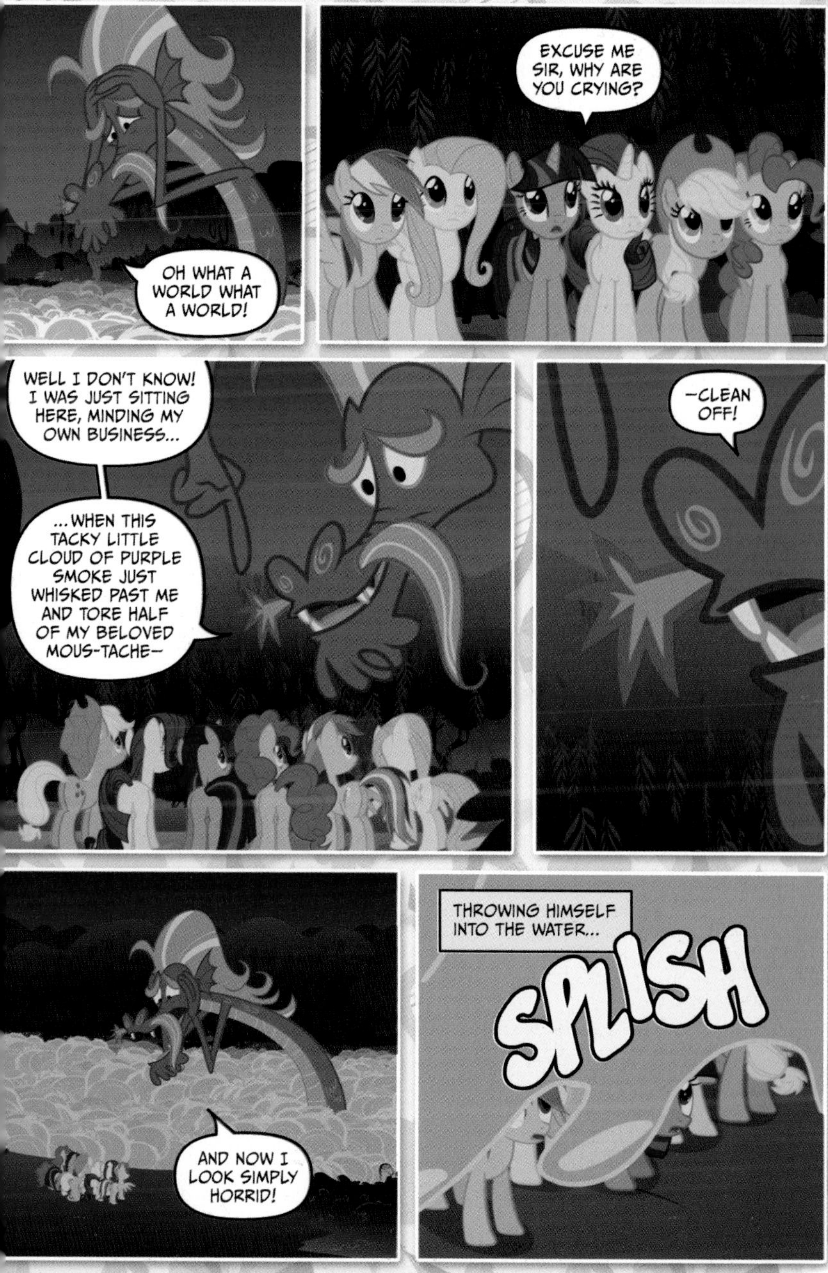
OH WHAT A WORLD WHAT A WORLD!
EXCUSE ME SIR, WHY ARE YOU CRYING?
WELL I DON'T KNOW! I WAS JUST SITTING HERE, MINDING MY OWN BUSINESS...
...WHEN THIS TACKY LITTLE CLOUD OF PURPLE SMOKE JUST WHISKED PAST ME AND TORE HALF OF MY BELOVED MOUS-TACHE–
–CLEAN OFF!
AND NOW I LOOK SIMPLY HORRID!
THROWING HIMSELF INTO THE WATER...
SPLISH

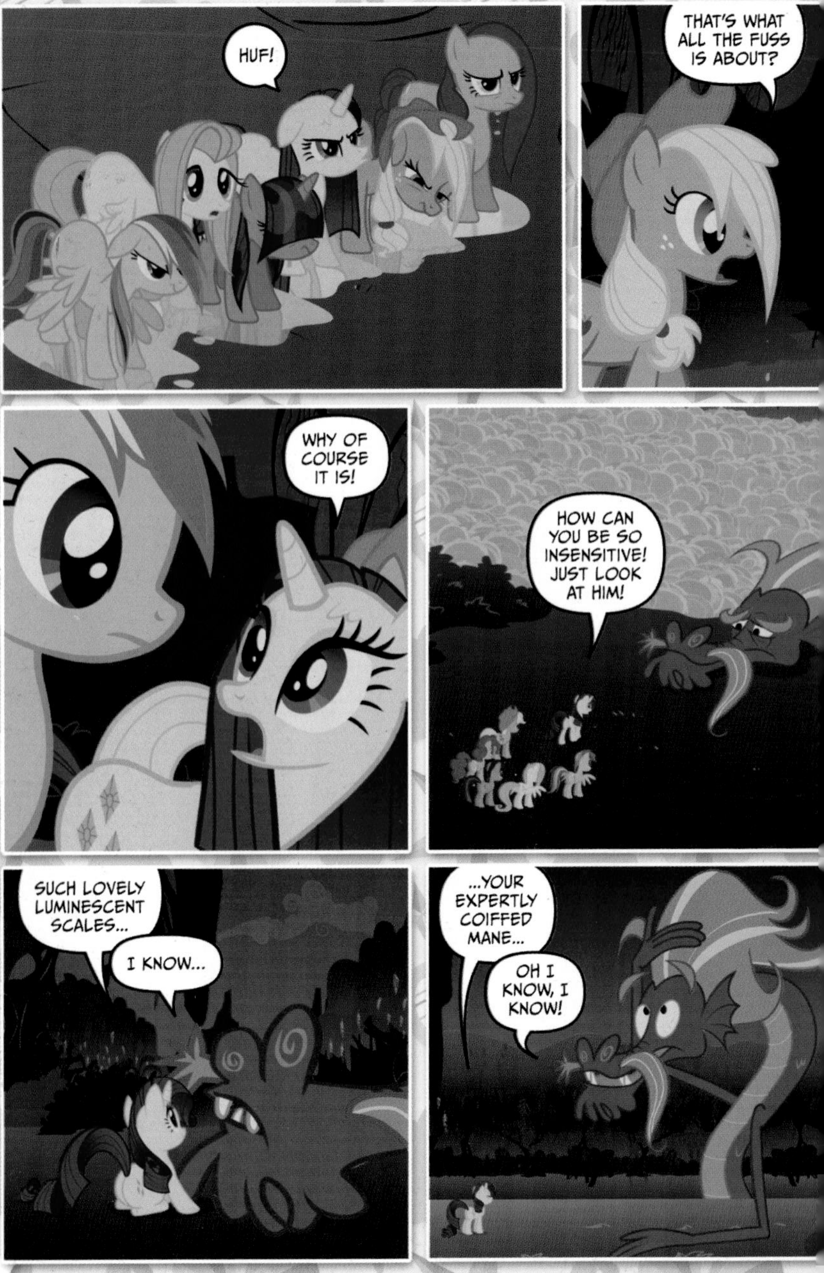
HUF!
THAT'S WHAT ALL THE FUSS IS ABOUT?
WHY OF COURSE IT IS!
HOW CAN YOU BE SO INSENSITIVE! JUST LOOK AT HIM!
SUCH LOVELY LUMINESCENT SCALES...
I KNOW...
...YOUR EXPERTLY COIFFED MANE...
OH I KNOW, I KNOW!

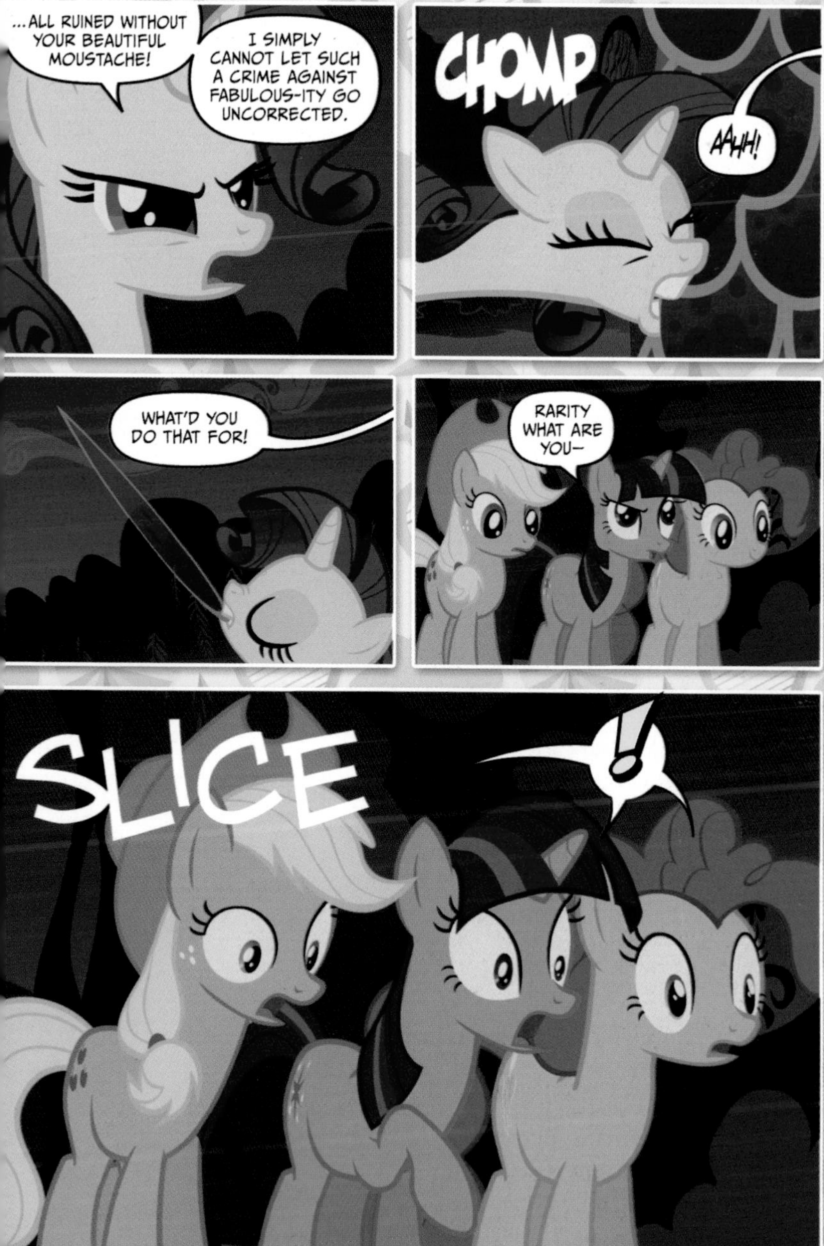

...ALL RUINED WITHOUT YOUR BEAUTIFUL MOUSTACHE!
I SIMPLY CANNOT LET SUCH A CRIME AGAINST FABULOUS-ITY GO UNCORRECTED.
CHOMP
AAHH!
WHAT'D YOU DO THAT FOR!
RARITY WHAT ARE YOU—
SLICE
!

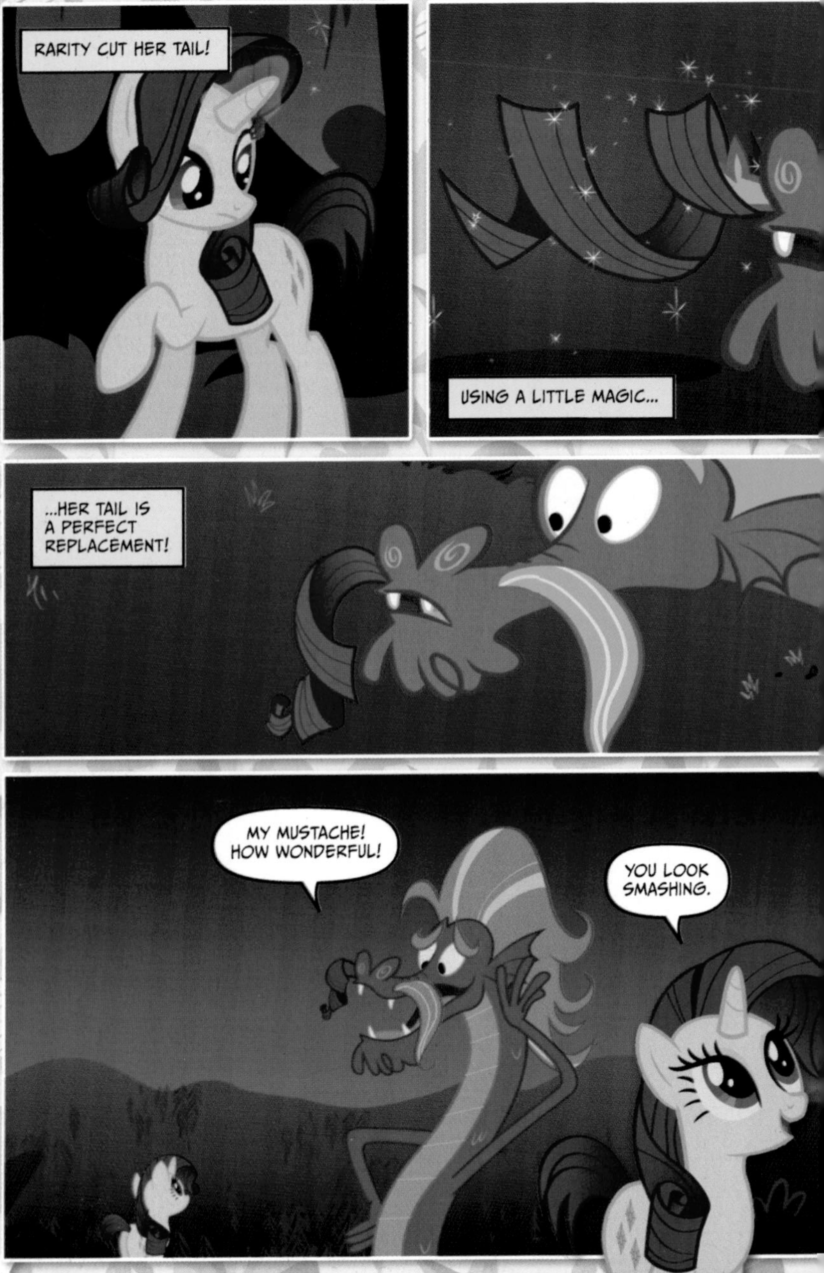
RARITY CUT HER TAIL!
USING A LITTLE MAGIC...
...HER TAIL IS A PERFECT REPLACEMENT!
MY MUSTACHE! HOW WONDERFUL!
YOU LOOK SMASHING.

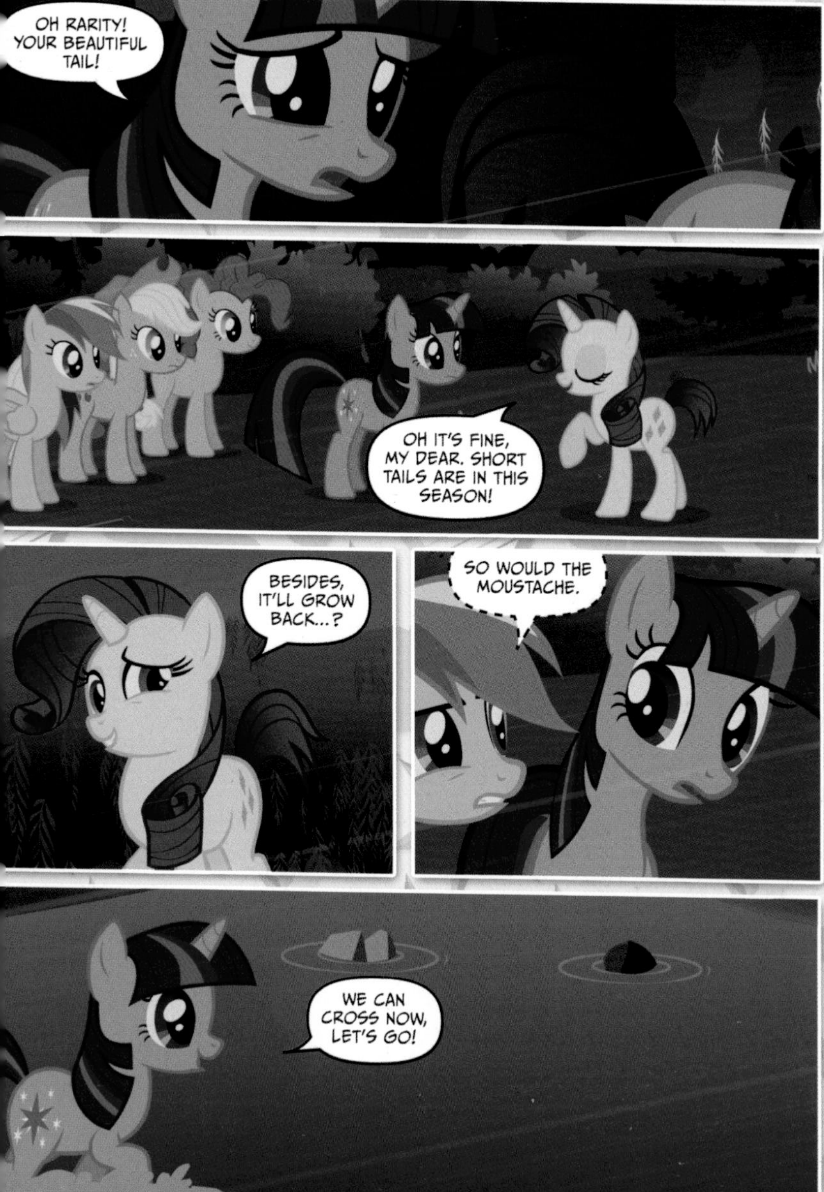

OH RARITY! YOUR BEAUTIFUL TAIL!
OH IT'S FINE, MY DEAR. SHORT TAILS ARE IN THIS SEASON!
BESIDES, IT'LL GROW BACK...?
SO WOULD THE MOUSTACHE.
WE CAN CROSS NOW, LET'S GO!

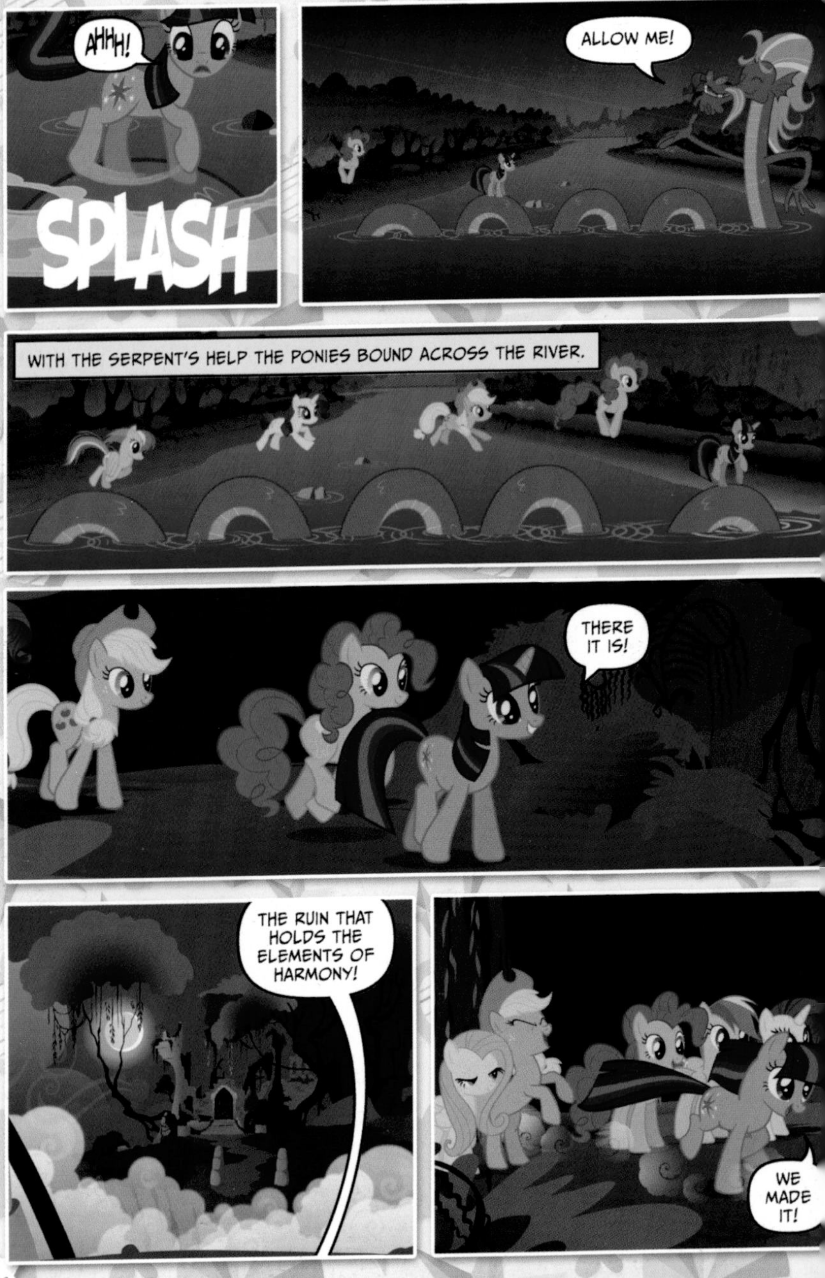
AHHH!
SPLASH
ALLOW ME!
WITH THE SERPENT'S HELP THE PONIES BOUND ACROSS THE RIVER.
THERE IT IS!
THE RUIN THAT HOLDS THE ELEMENTS OF HARMONY!
WE MADE IT!

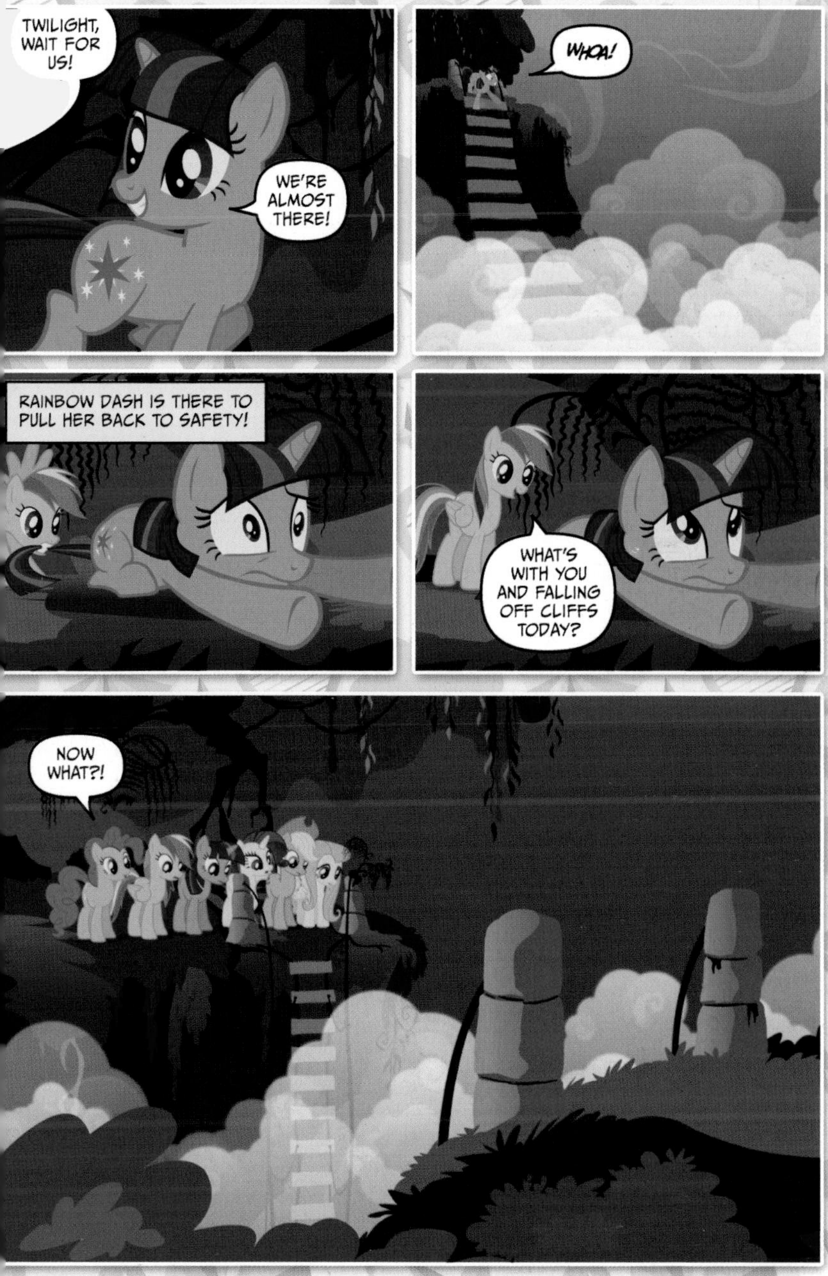
TWILIGHT, WAIT FOR US!
WE'RE ALMOST THERE!
WHOA!
RAINBOW DASH IS THERE TO PULL HER BACK TO SAFETY!
WHAT'S WITH YOU AND FALLING OFF CLIFFS TODAY?
NOW WHAT?!

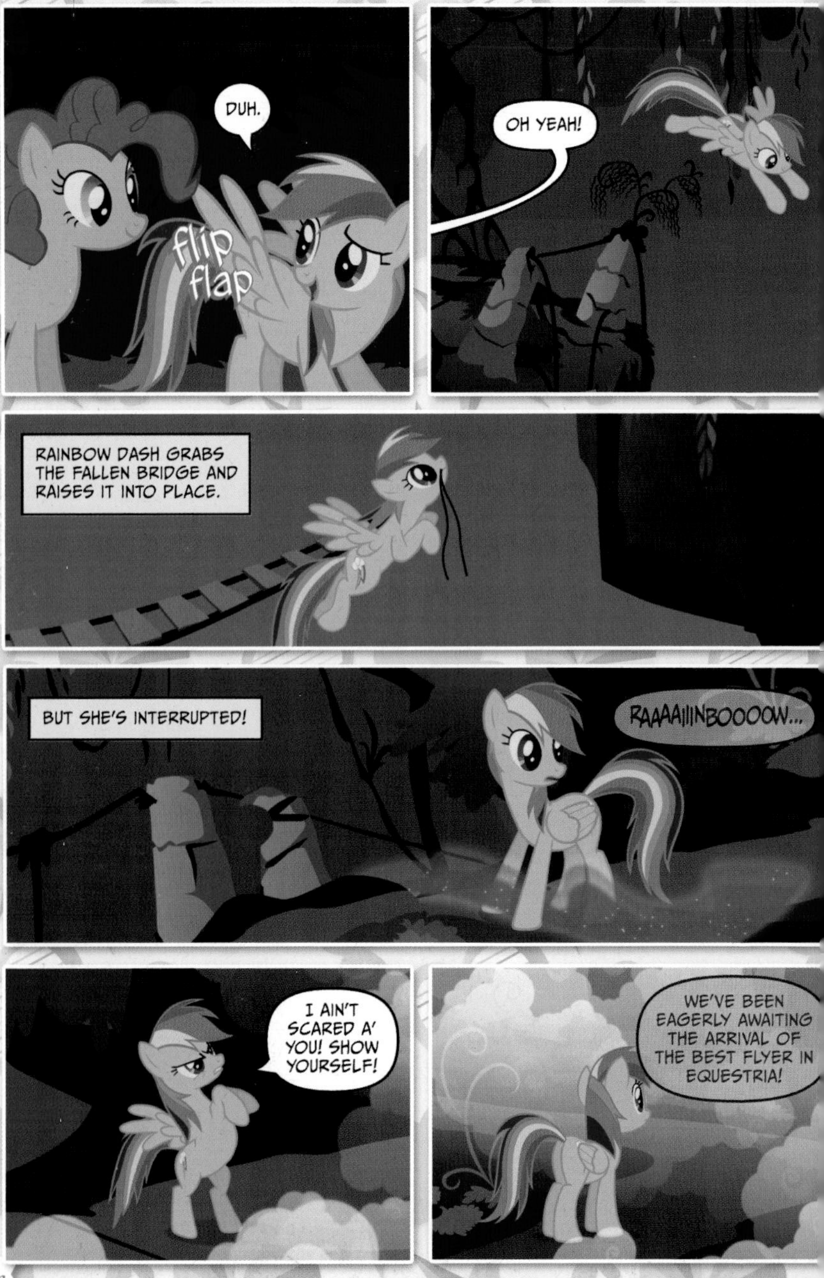
DUH.
flip flap
OH YEAH!
RAINBOW DASH GRABS THE FALLEN BRIDGE AND RAISES IT INTO PLACE.
BUT SHE'S INTERRUPTED!
RAAAAIIIINBOOOOW...
I AIN'T SCARED A' YOU! SHOW YOURSELF!
WE'VE BEEN EAGERLY AWAITING THE ARRIVAL OF THE BEST FLYER IN EQUESTRIA!

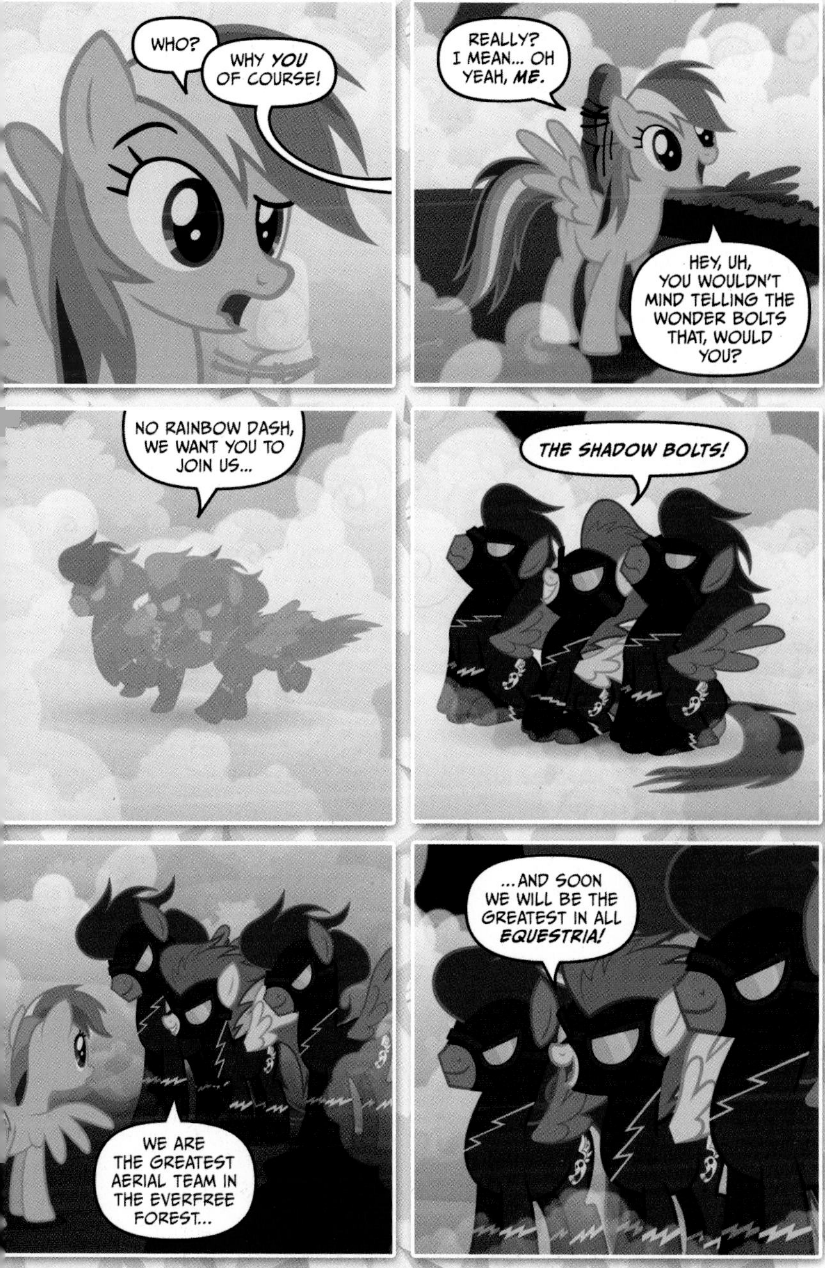
WHO?
WHY *YOU* OF COURSE!
REALLY? I MEAN... OH YEAH, *ME.*
HEY, UH, YOU WOULDN'T MIND TELLING THE WONDER BOLTS THAT, WOULD YOU?
NO RAINBOW DASH, WE WANT YOU TO JOIN US...
THE SHADOW BOLTS!
WE ARE THE GREATEST AERIAL TEAM IN THE EVERFREE FOREST...
...AND SOON WE WILL BE THE GREATEST IN ALL *EQUESTRIA!*

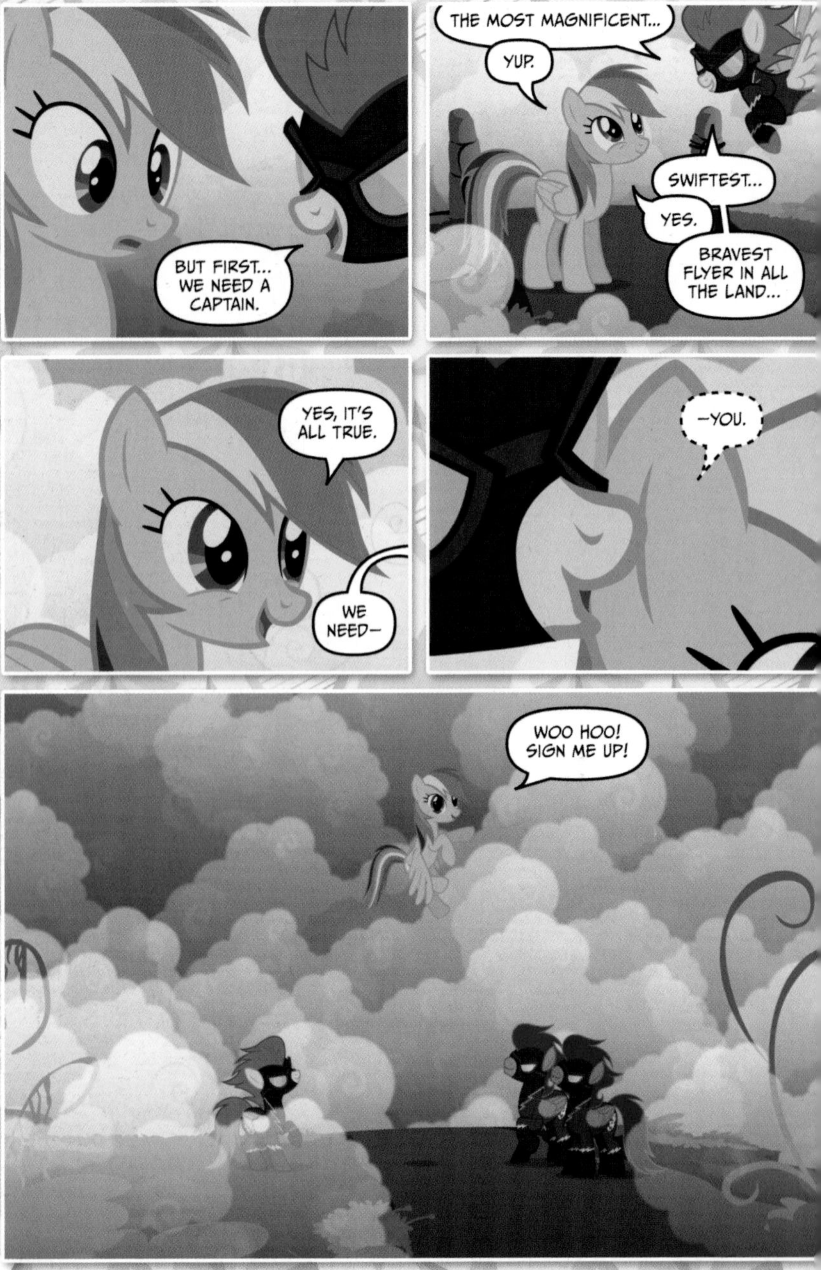
BUT FIRST... WE NEED A CAPTAIN.
THE MOST MAGNIFICENT...
YUP.
SWIFTEST...
YES.
BRAVEST FLYER IN ALL THE LAND...
YES, IT'S ALL TRUE.
WE NEED—
—YOU.
WOO HOO! SIGN ME UP!

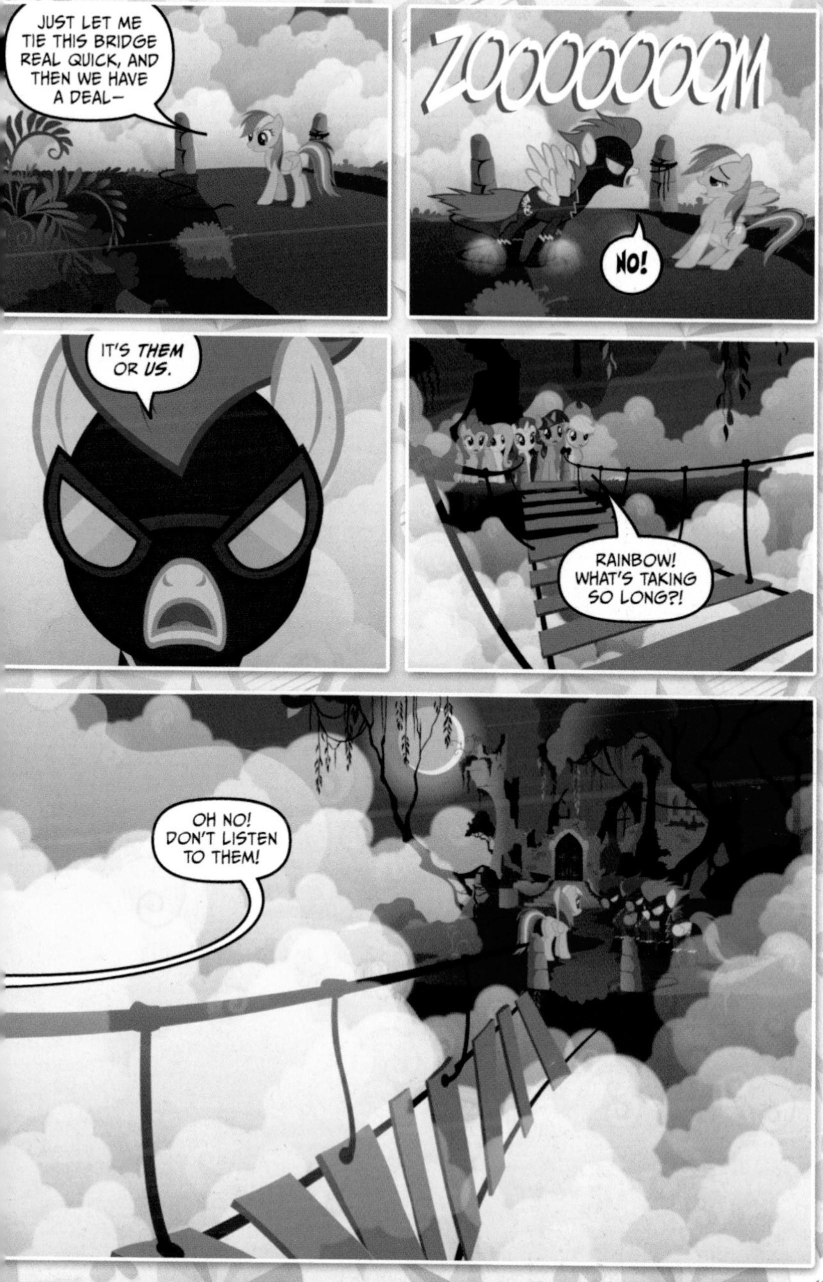
JUST LET ME TIE THIS BRIDGE REAL QUICK, AND THEN WE HAVE A DEAL—
ZOOOOOOOM
NO!
IT'S *THEM* OR *US*.
RAINBOW! WHAT'S TAKING SO LONG?!
OH NO! DON'T LISTEN TO THEM!

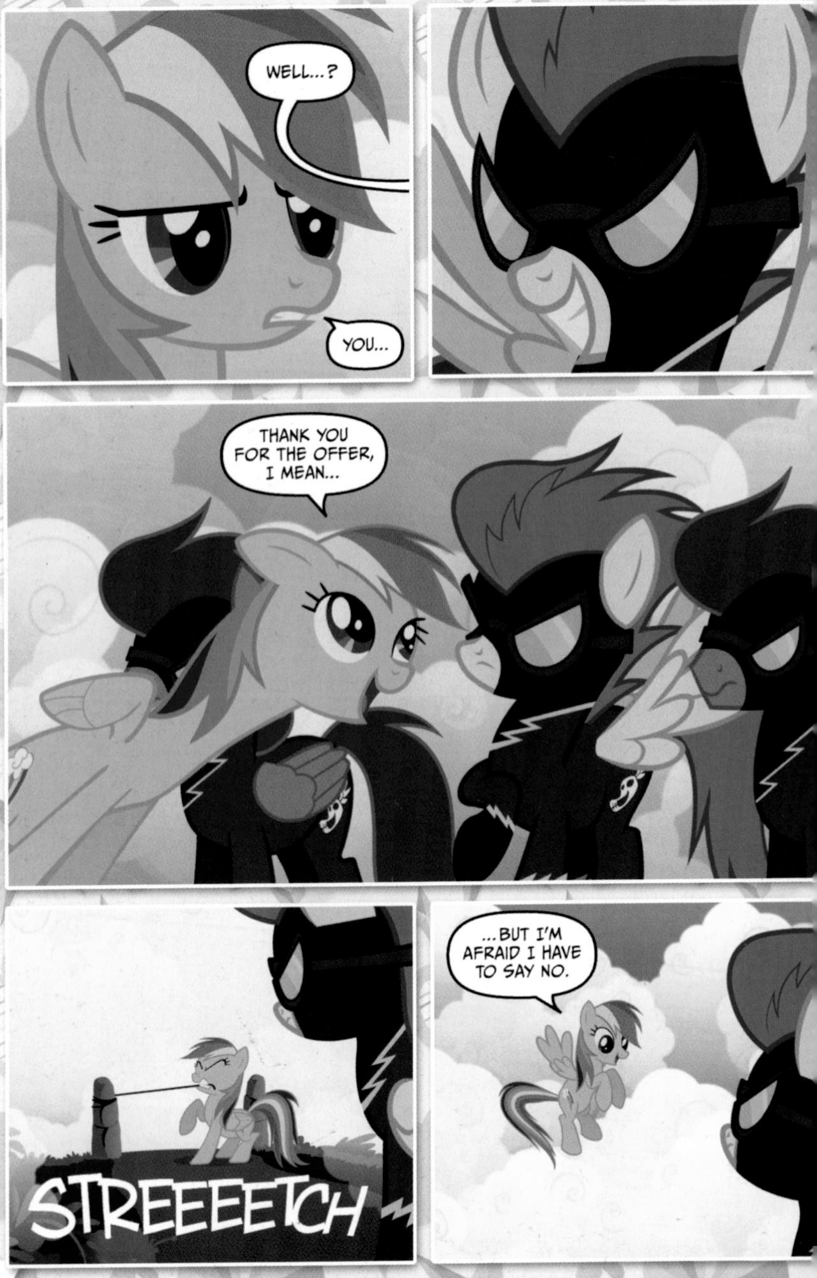
WELL...?
YOU...
THANK YOU FOR THE OFFER, I MEAN...
STREEEEETCH
...BUT I'M AFRAID I HAVE TO SAY NO.

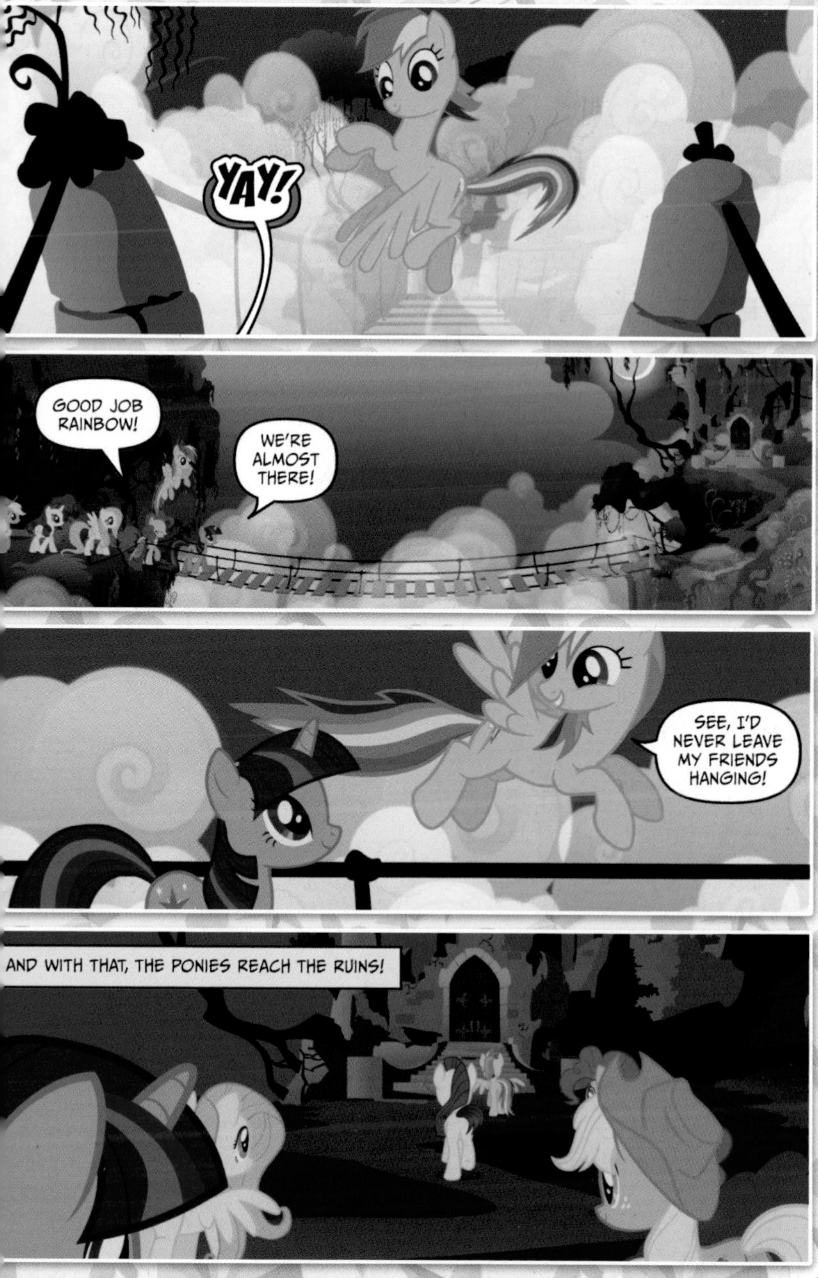
YAY!
GOOD JOB RAINBOW!
WE'RE ALMOST THERE!
SEE, I'D NEVER LEAVE MY FRIENDS HANGING!
AND WITH THAT, THE PONIES REACH THE RUINS!

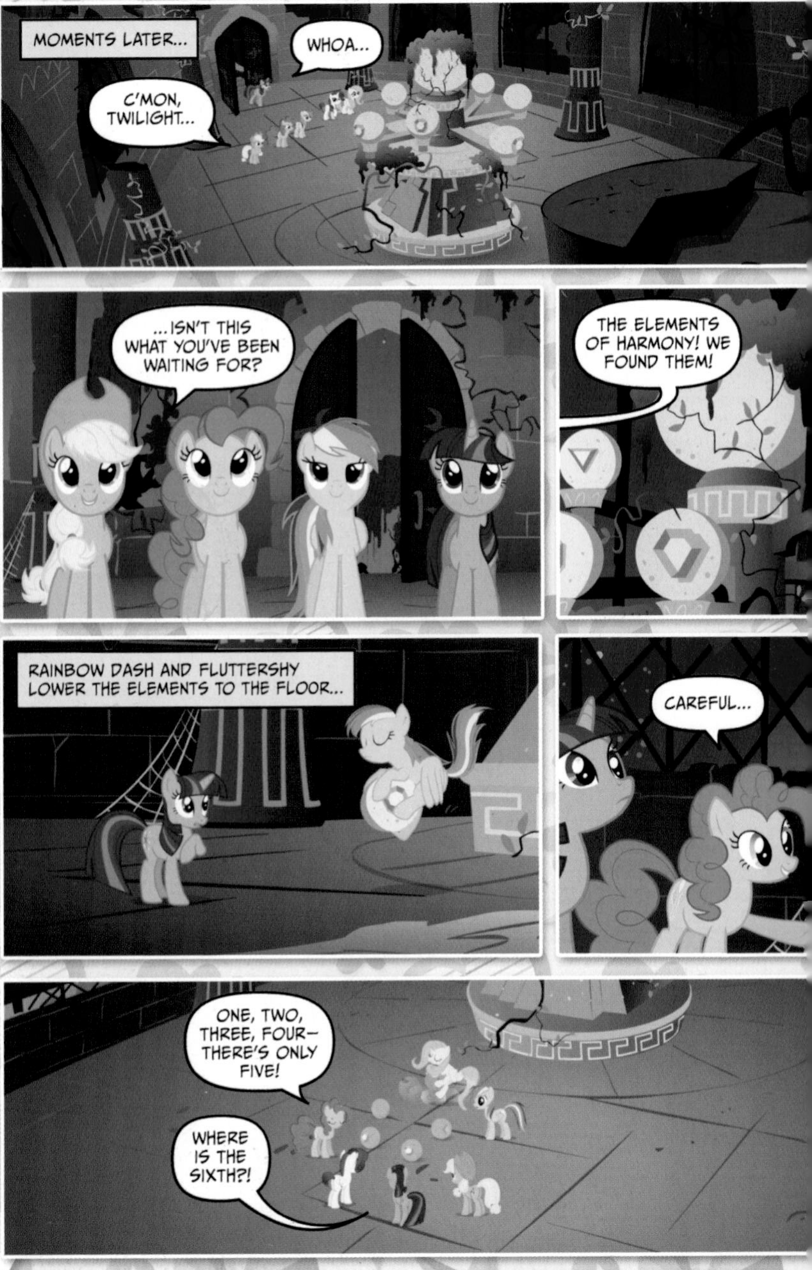
MOMENTS LATER...
C'MON, TWILIGHT...
WHOA...
...ISN'T THIS WHAT YOU'VE BEEN WAITING FOR?
THE ELEMENTS OF HARMONY! WE FOUND THEM!
RAINBOW DASH AND FLUTTERSHY LOWER THE ELEMENTS TO THE FLOOR...
CAREFUL...
ONE, TWO, THREE, FOUR— THERE'S ONLY FIVE!
WHERE IS THE SIXTH?!

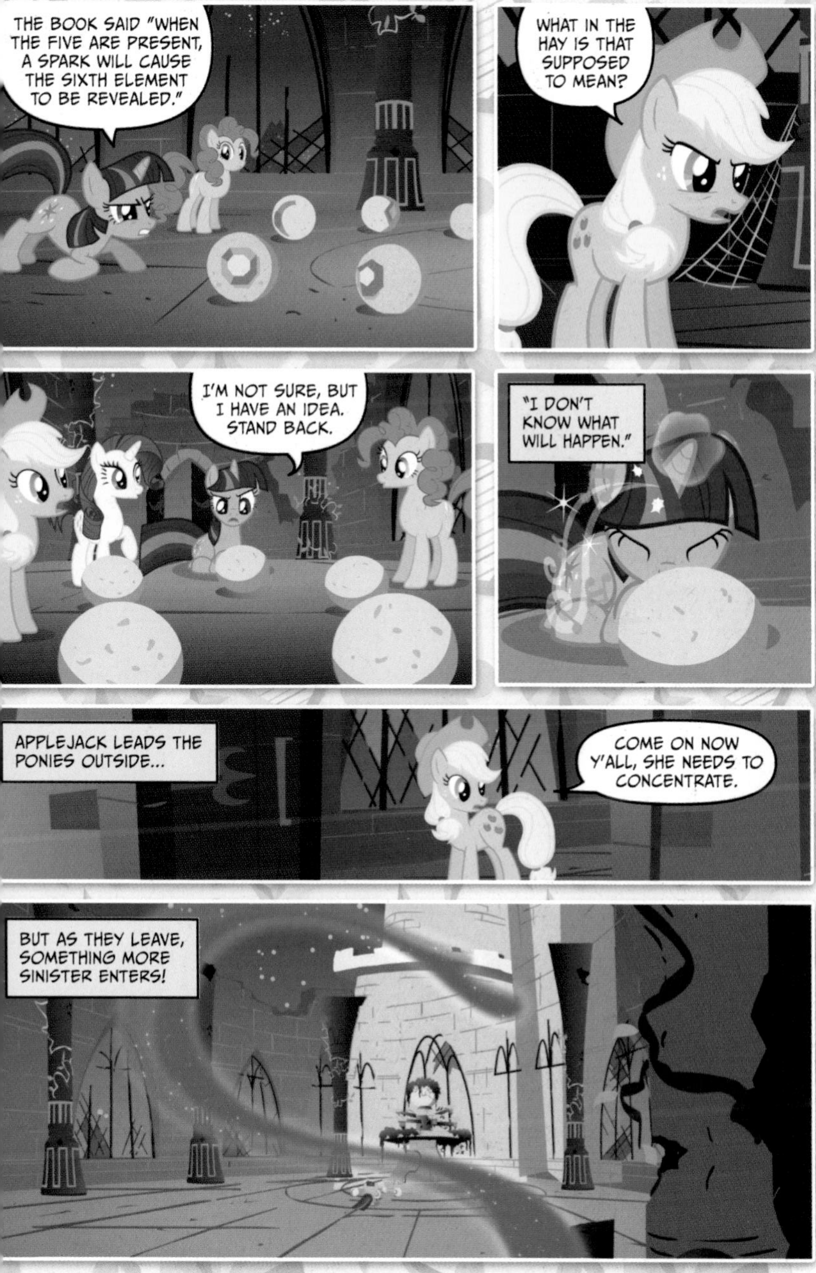
THE BOOK SAID "WHEN THE FIVE ARE PRESENT, A SPARK WILL CAUSE THE SIXTH ELEMENT TO BE REVEALED."
WHAT IN THE HAY IS THAT SUPPOSED TO MEAN?
I'M NOT SURE, BUT I HAVE AN IDEA. STAND BACK.
"I DON'T KNOW WHAT WILL HAPPEN."
APPLEJACK LEADS THE PONIES OUTSIDE...
COME ON NOW Y'ALL, SHE NEEDS TO CONCENTRATE.
BUT AS THEY LEAVE, SOMETHING MORE SINISTER ENTERS!

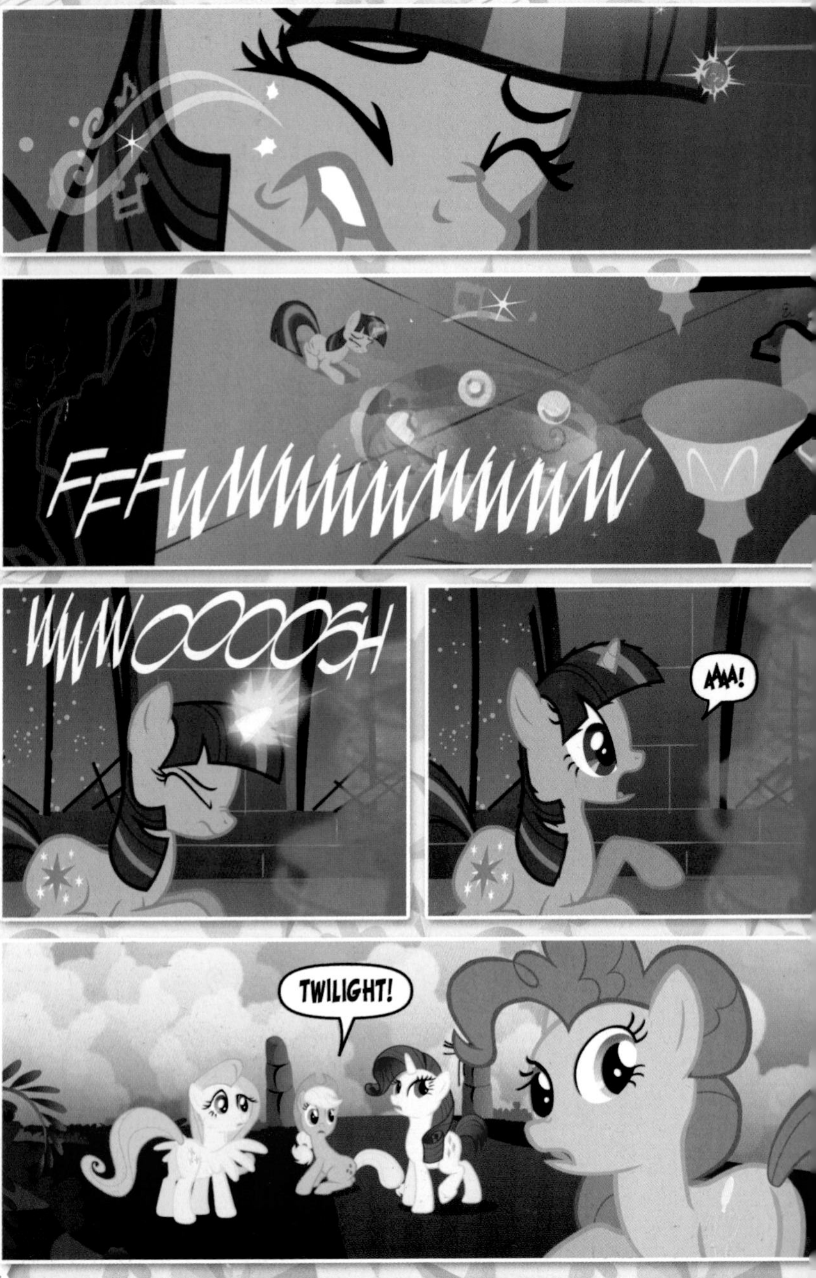
FFFUUUUUUUUUUUUU
WWWOOOOOSH
AAAA!
TWILIGHT!

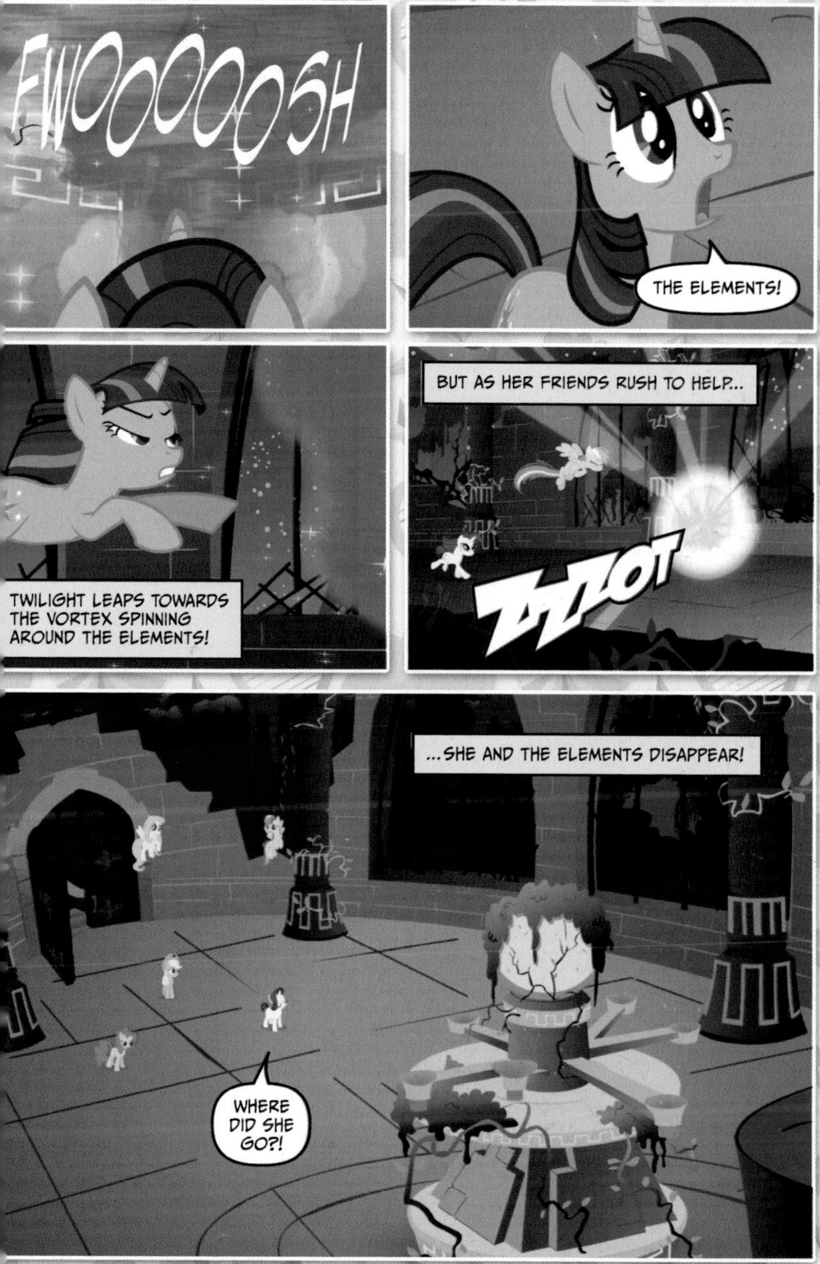
FWOOOOOSH
THE ELEMENTS!
TWILIGHT LEAPS TOWARDS THE VORTEX SPINNING AROUND THE ELEMENTS!
BUT AS HER FRIENDS RUSH TO HELP...
ZZZOT
...SHE AND THE ELEMENTS DISAPPEAR!
WHERE DID SHE GO?!

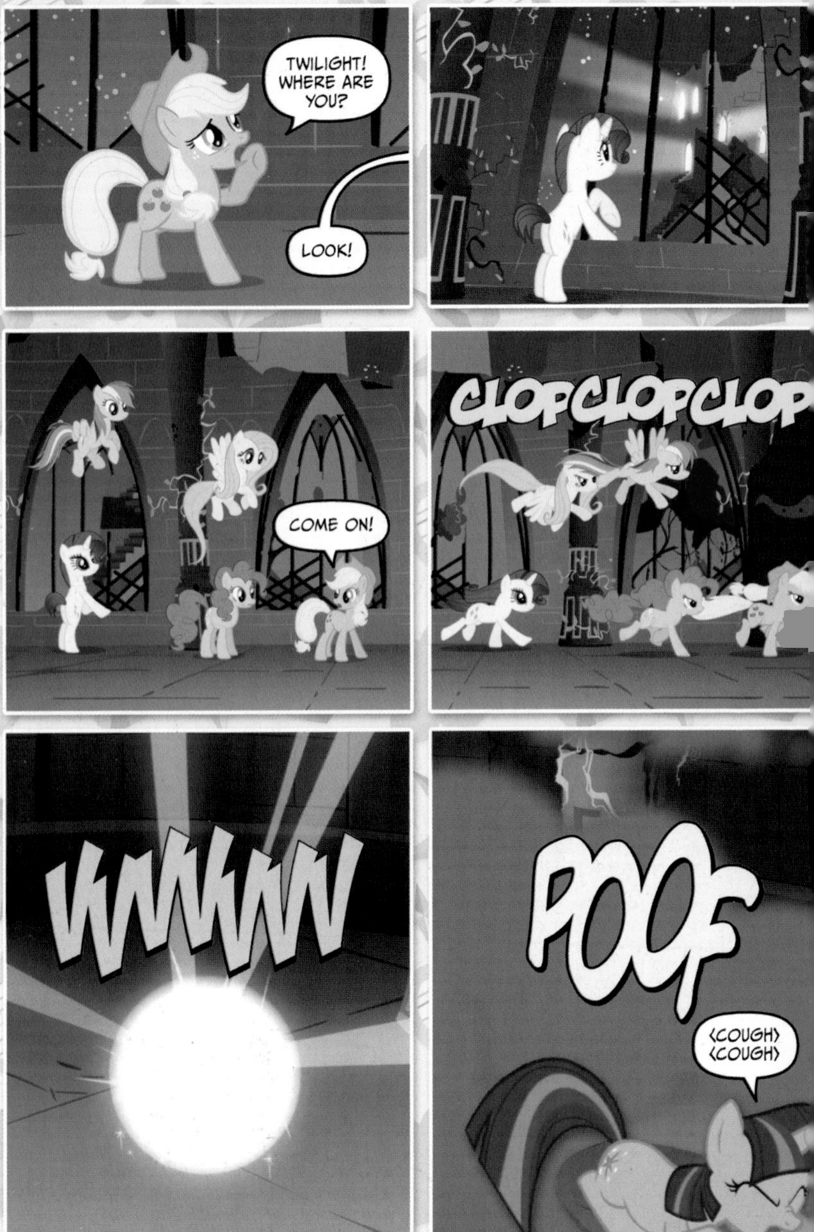
TWILIGHT! WHERE ARE YOU?
LOOK!
COME ON!
CLOPCLOPCLOP
POOF
<COUGH> <COUGH>

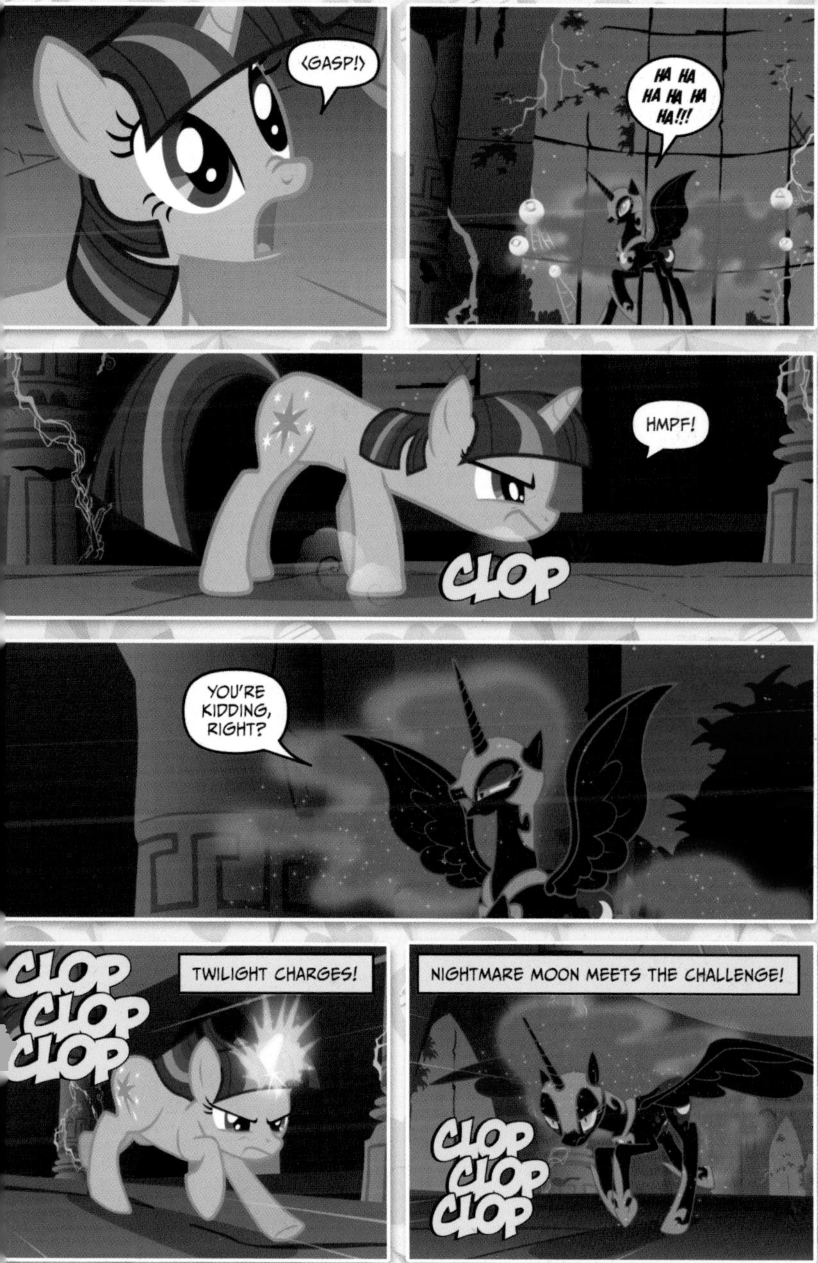

‹GASP!›
HA HA HA HA HA HA!!!
HMPF!
CLOP
YOU'RE KIDDING, RIGHT?
CLOP CLOP CLOP
TWILIGHT CHARGES!
NIGHTMARE MOON MEETS THE CHALLENGE!
CLOP CLOP CLOP

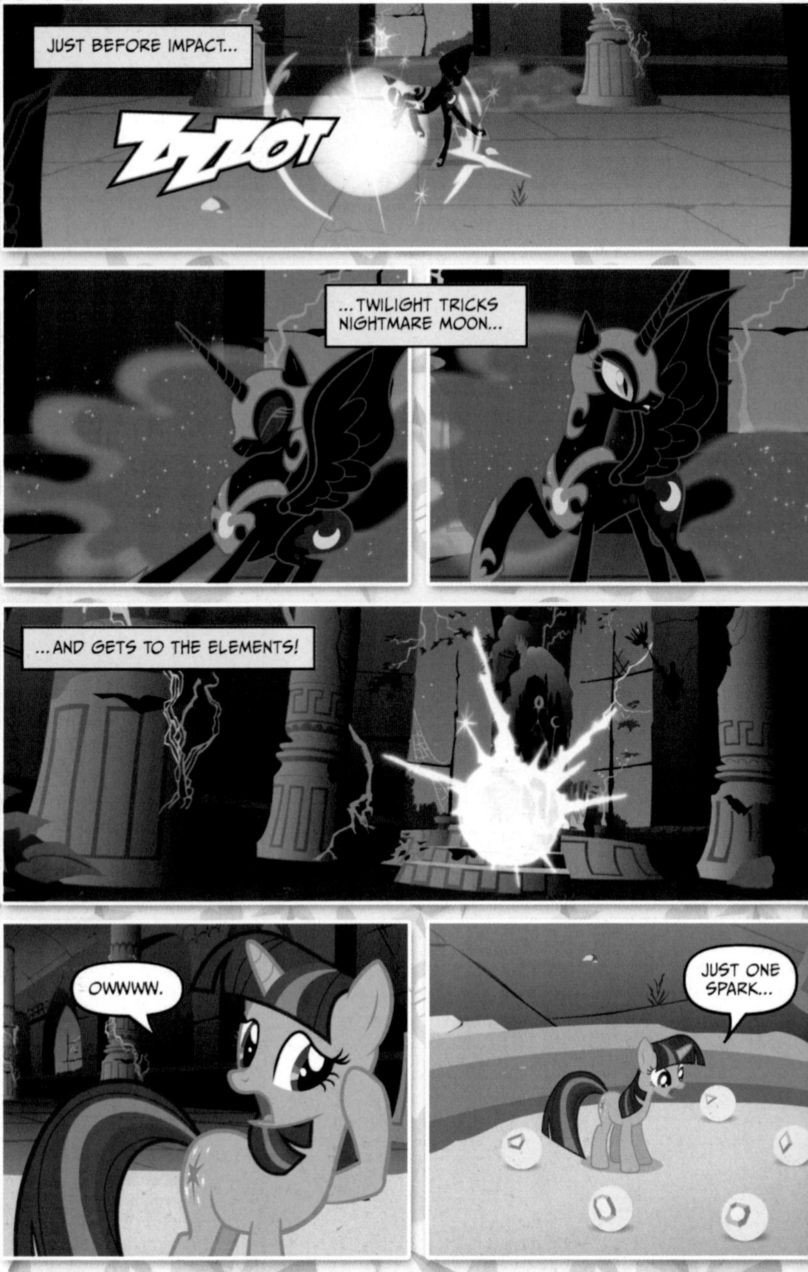
JUST BEFORE IMPACT...
ZZZOT
...TWILIGHT TRICKS NIGHTMARE MOON...
...AND GETS TO THE ELEMENTS!
OWWWW.
JUST ONE SPARK...

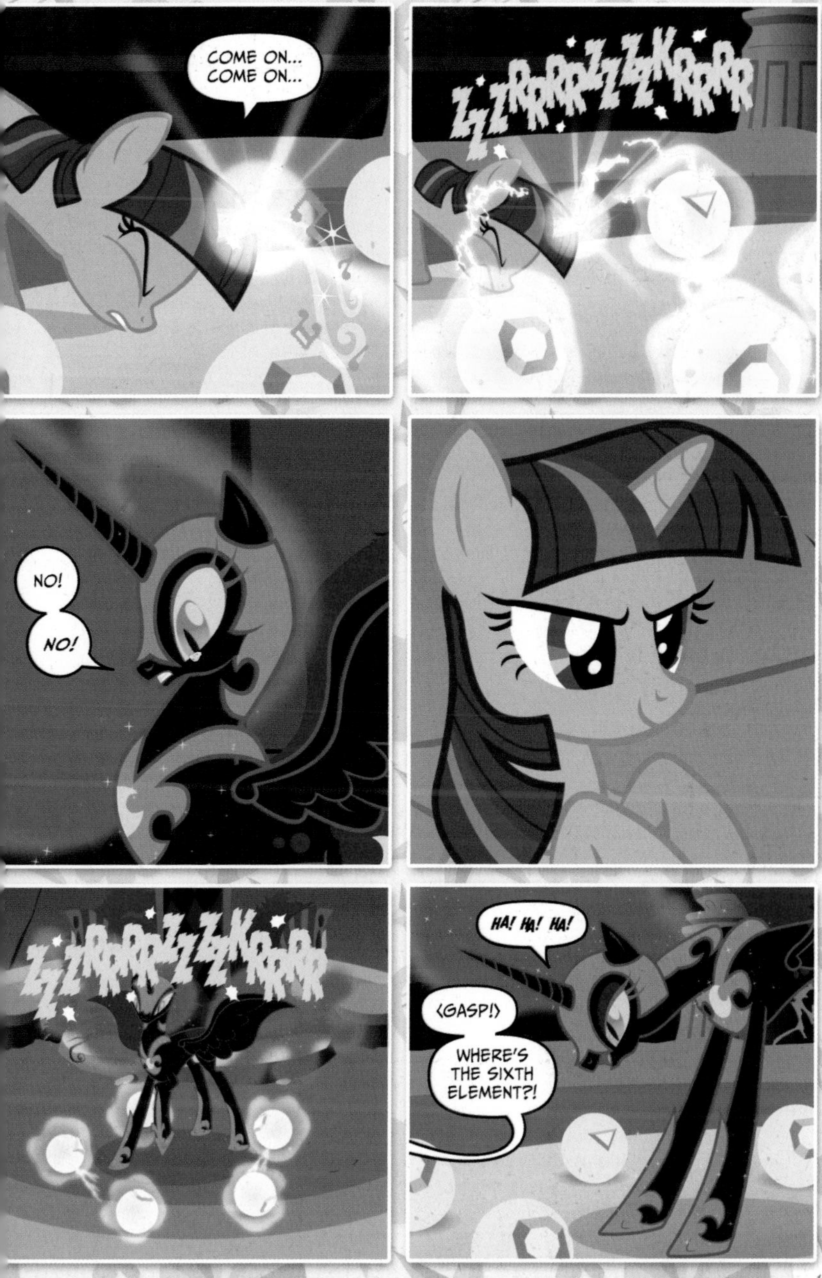
COME ON... COME ON...
ZZZRRRRZZZZKRRRR
NO!
NO!
ZZZRRRRZZZZKRRRR
HA! HA! HA!
(GASP!)
WHERE'S THE SIXTH ELEMENT?!

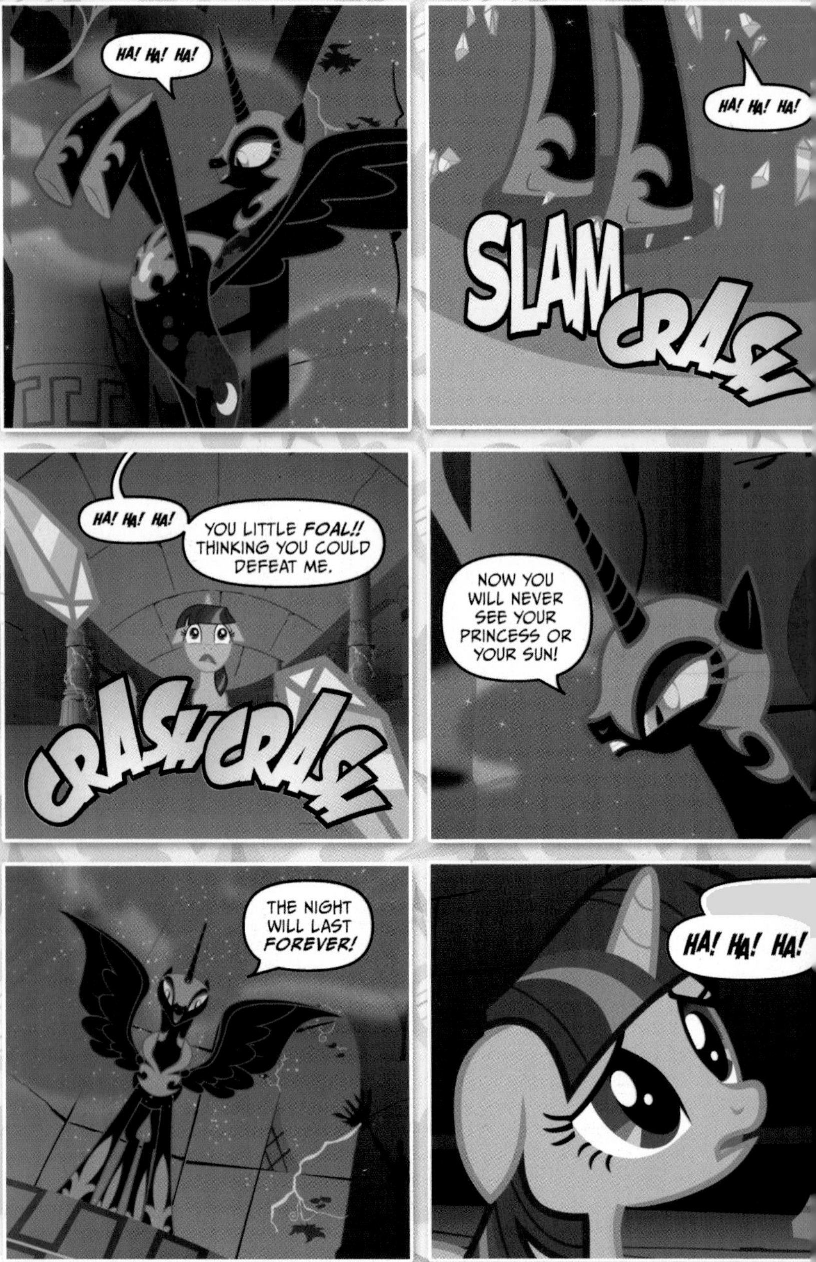
HA! HA! HA!
HA! HA! HA!
SLAM
CRASH
HA! HA! HA!
YOU LITTLE *FOAL!!* THINKING YOU COULD DEFEAT ME.
CRASH CRASH
NOW YOU WILL NEVER SEE YOUR PRINCESS OR YOUR SUN!
THE NIGHT WILL LAST *FOREVER!*
HA! HA! HA!

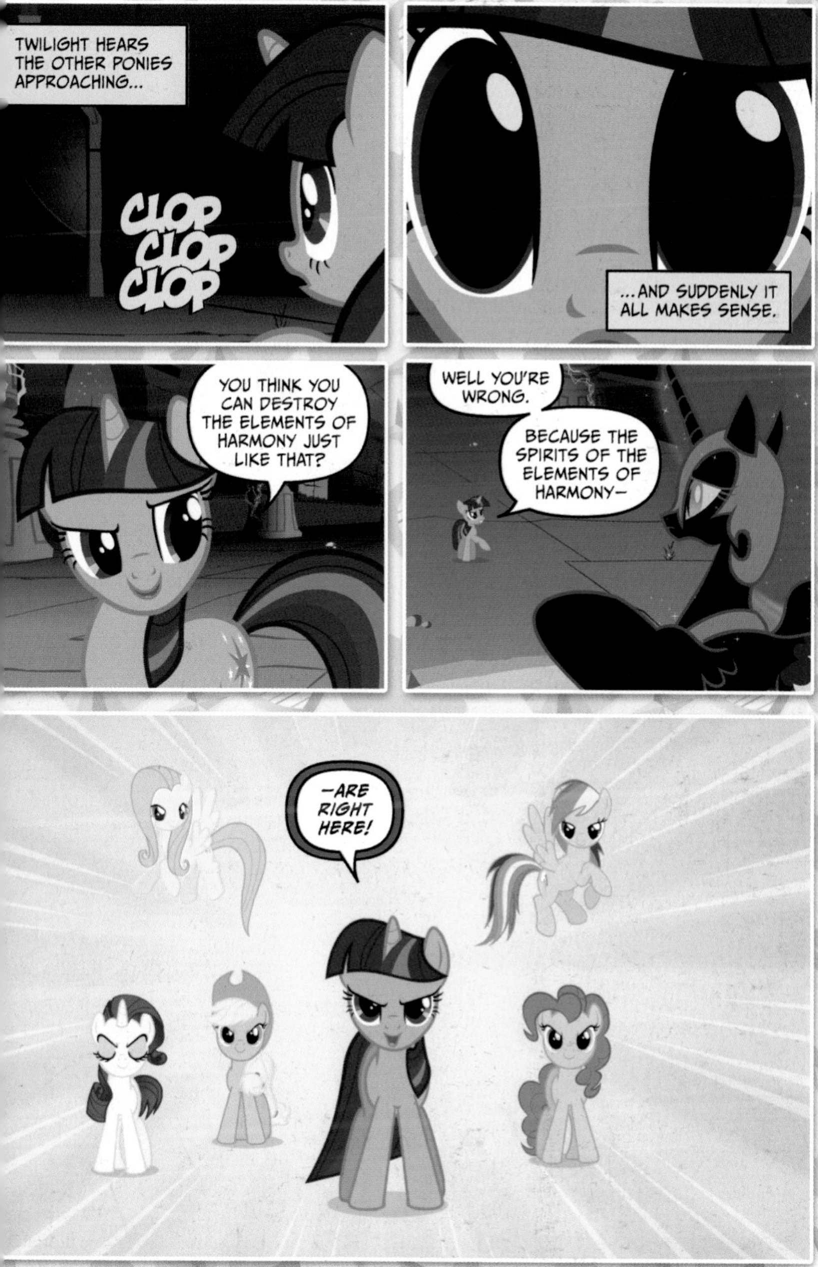
TWILIGHT HEARS THE OTHER PONIES APPROACHING...
CLOP CLOP CLOP
...AND SUDDENLY IT ALL MAKES SENSE.
YOU THINK YOU CAN DESTROY THE ELEMENTS OF HARMONY JUST LIKE THAT?
WELL YOU'RE WRONG.
BECAUSE THE SPIRITS OF THE ELEMENTS OF HARMONY—
—ARE RIGHT HERE!

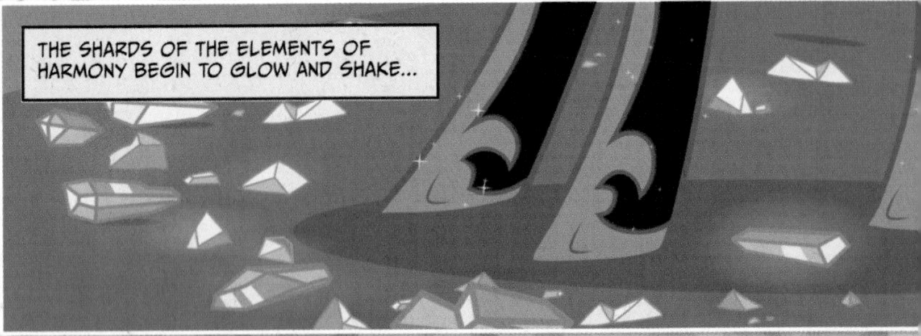
THE SHARDS OF THE ELEMENTS OF HARMONY BEGIN TO GLOW AND SHAKE...

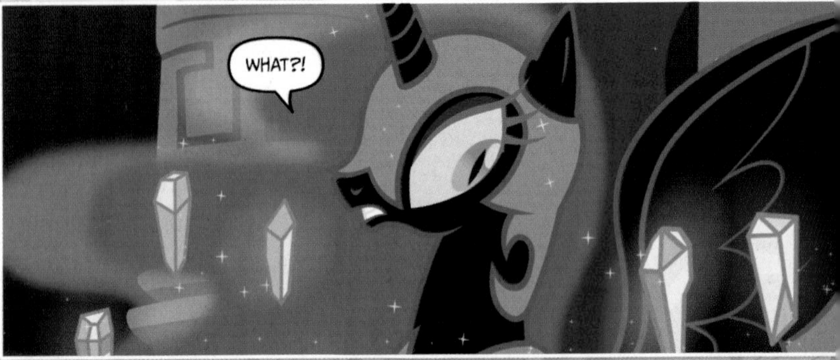
WHAT?!

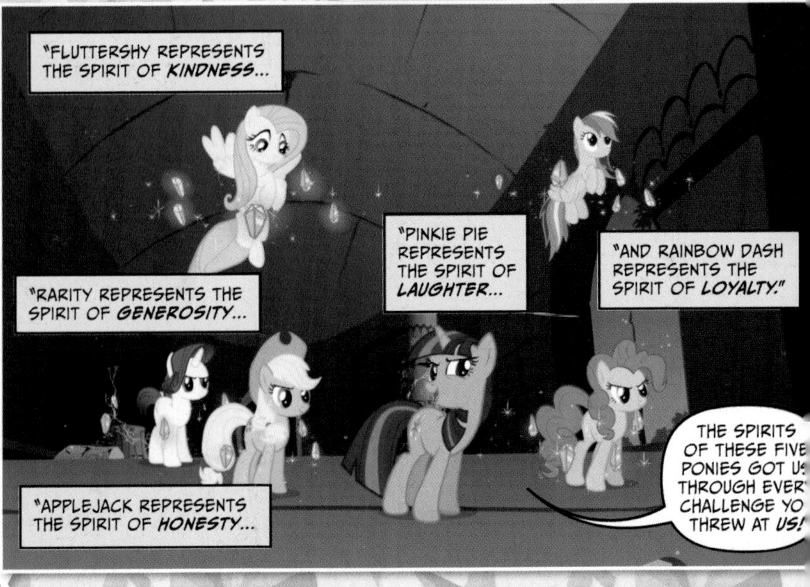
"FLUTTERSHY REPRESENTS THE SPIRIT OF *KINDNESS*...
"RARITY REPRESENTS THE SPIRIT OF *GENEROSITY*...
"PINKIE PIE REPRESENTS THE SPIRIT OF *LAUGHTER*...
"AND RAINBOW DASH REPRESENTS THE SPIRIT OF *LOYALTY*."
"APPLEJACK REPRESENTS THE SPIRIT OF *HONESTY*...
THE SPIRITS OF THESE FIVE PONIES GOT U THROUGH EVER CHALLENGE YO THREW AT *US!*

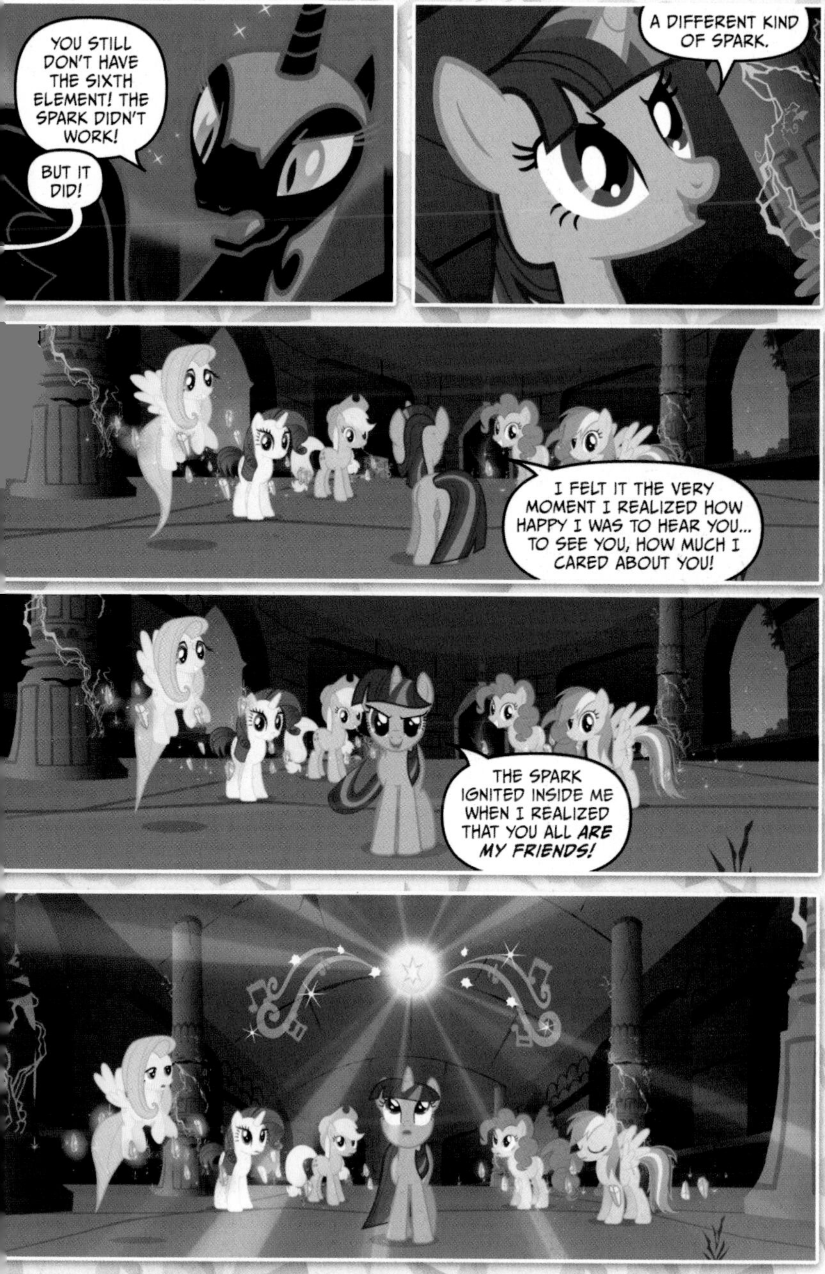
YOU STILL DON'T HAVE THE SIXTH ELEMENT! THE SPARK DIDN'T WORK!
BUT IT DID!
A DIFFERENT KIND OF SPARK.
I FELT IT THE VERY MOMENT I REALIZED HOW HAPPY I WAS TO HEAR YOU... TO SEE YOU, HOW MUCH I CARED ABOUT YOU!
THE SPARK IGNITED INSIDE ME WHEN I REALIZED THAT YOU ALL ***ARE MY FRIENDS!***

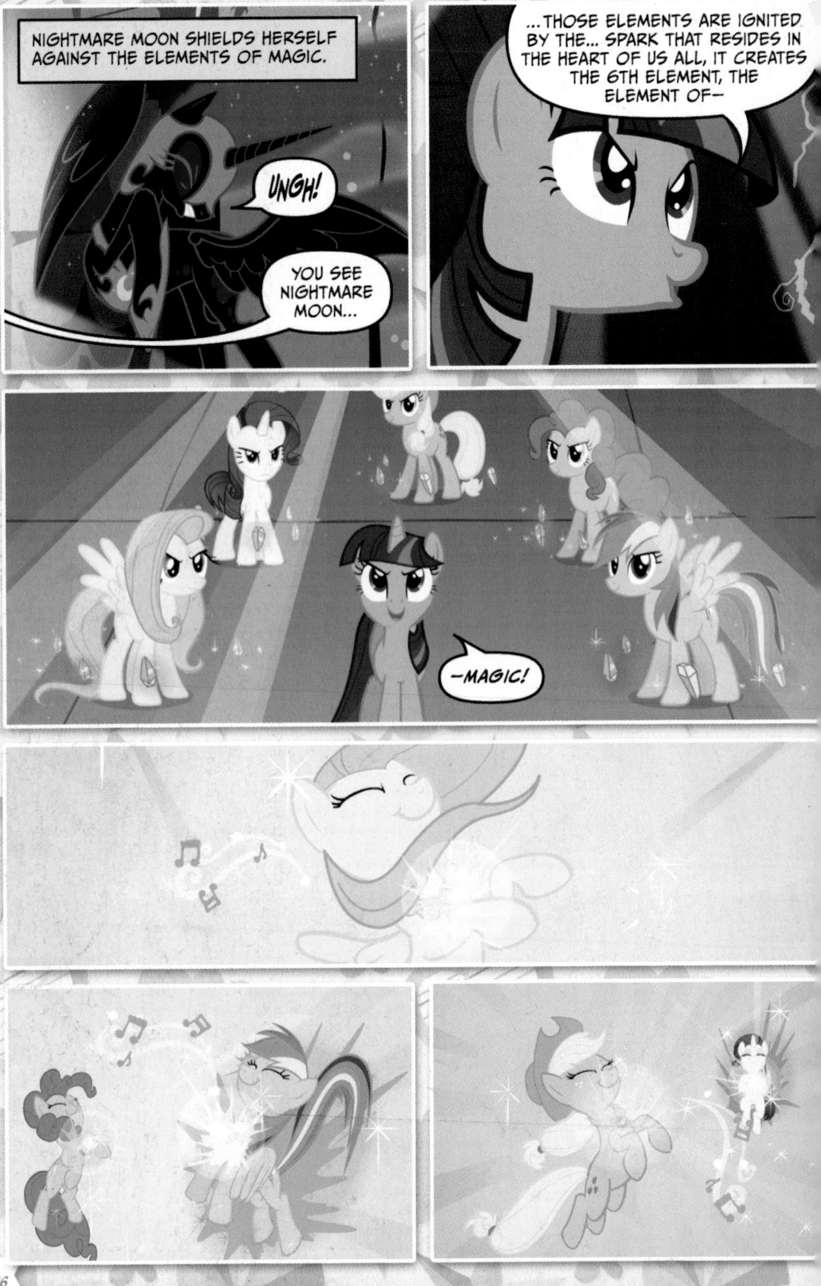
NIGHTMARE MOON SHIELDS HERSELF AGAINST THE ELEMENTS OF MAGIC.
UNGH!
YOU SEE NIGHTMARE MOON...
...THOSE ELEMENTS ARE IGNITED BY THE... SPARK THAT RESIDES IN THE HEART OF US ALL, IT CREATES THE 6TH ELEMENT, THE ELEMENT OF–
–MAGIC!

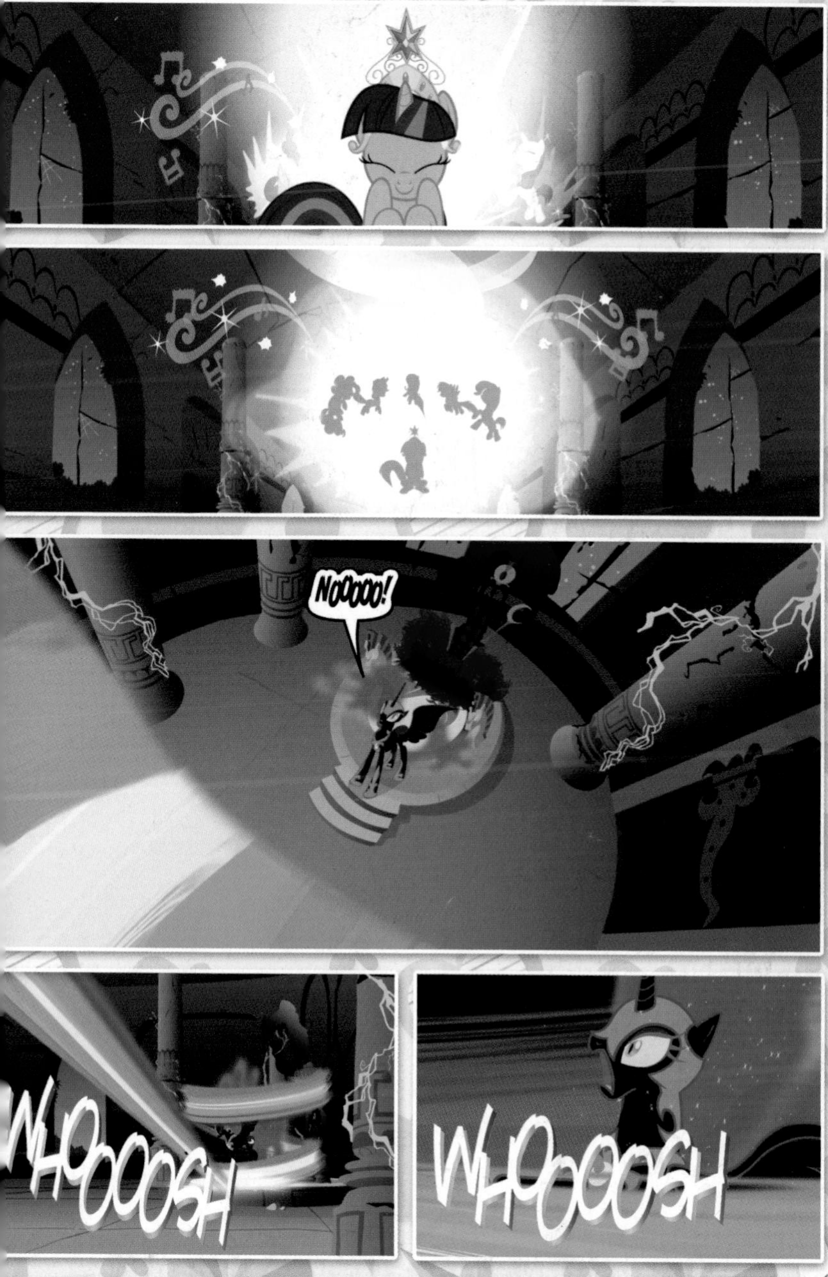
NOOOOO!
WHOOOOSH
WHOOOOSH

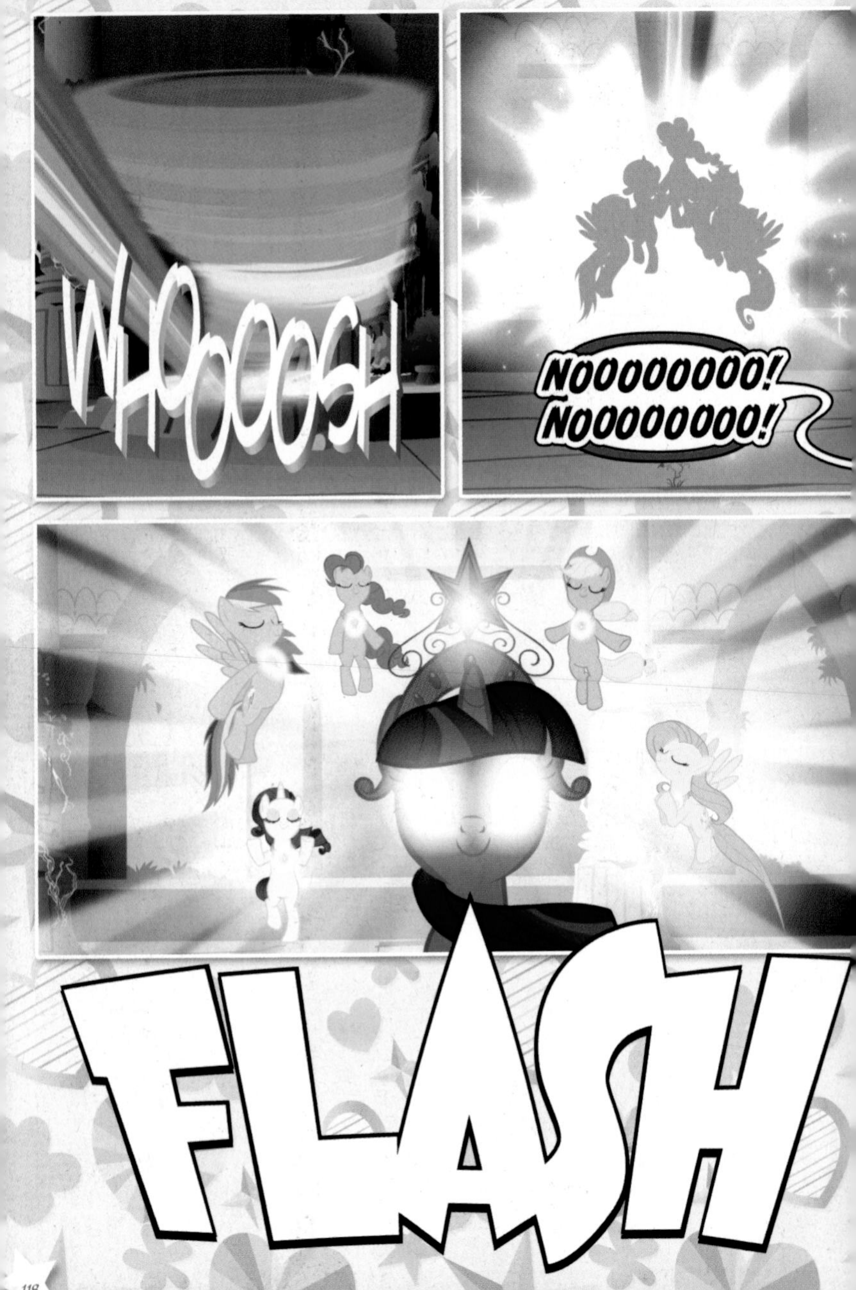
WHOOOOSH
NOOOOOOOO! NOOOOOOOO!
FLASH

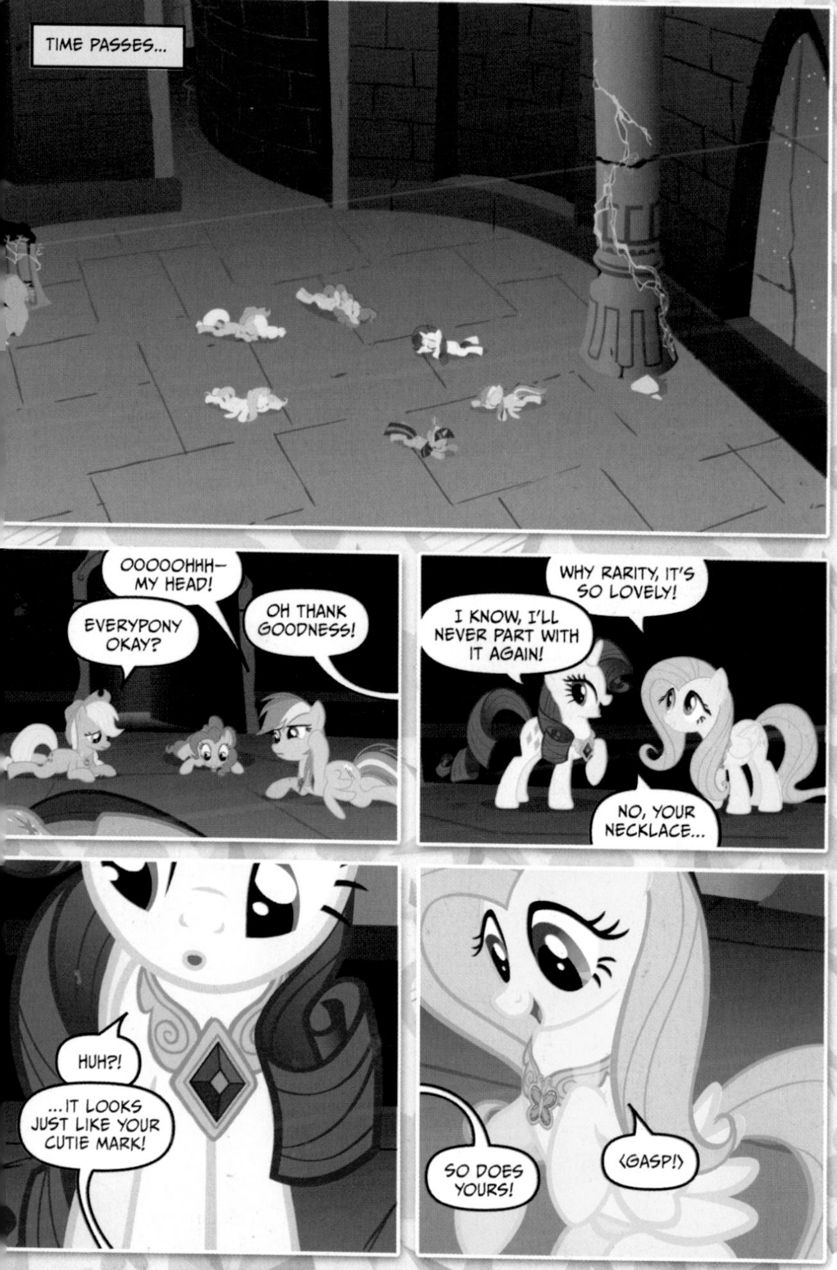
TIME PASSES...
OOOOOHHH— MY HEAD!
EVERYPONY OKAY?
OH THANK GOODNESS!
WHY RARITY, IT'S SO LOVELY!
I KNOW, I'LL NEVER PART WITH IT AGAIN!
NO, YOUR NECKLACE...
HUH?!
...IT LOOKS JUST LIKE YOUR CUTIE MARK!
SO DOES YOURS!
<GASP!>

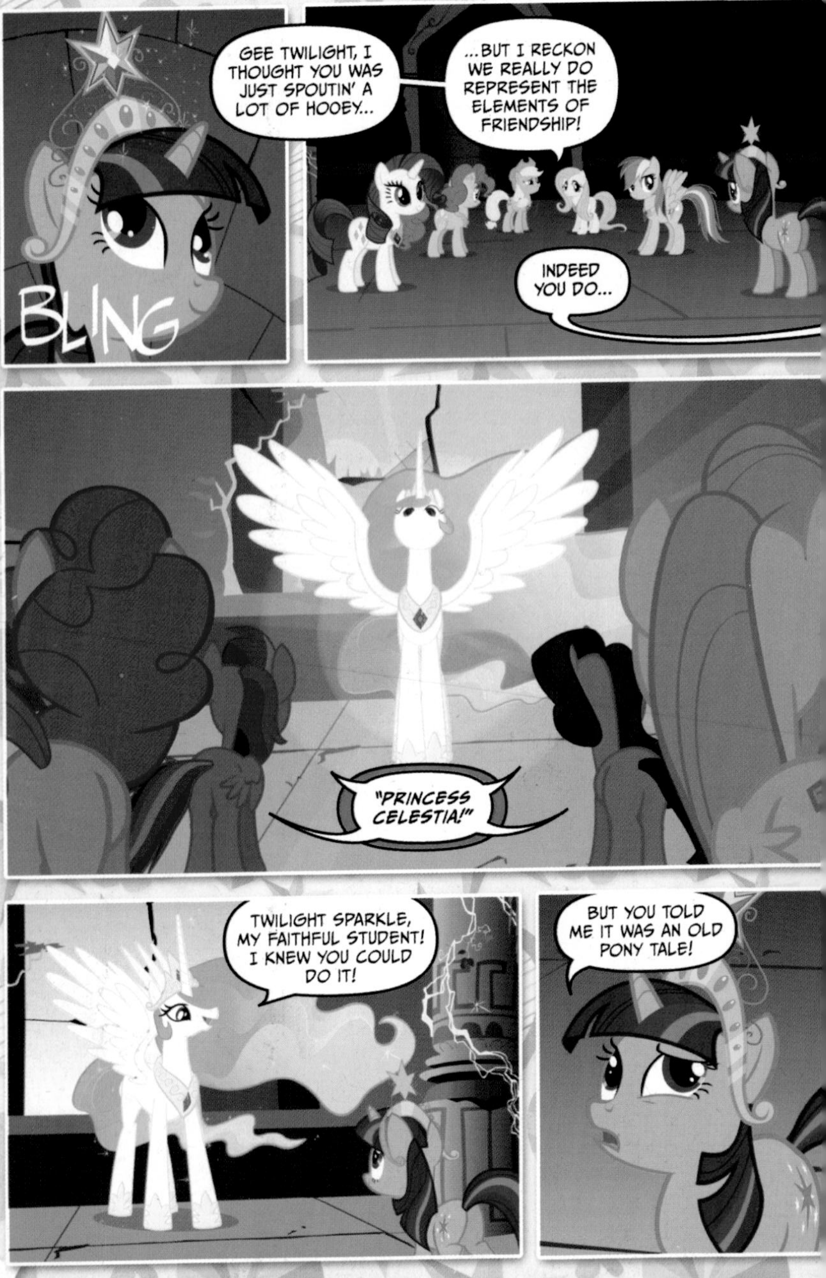
BLING
GEE TWILIGHT, I THOUGHT YOU WAS JUST SPOUTIN' A LOT OF HOOEY...
...BUT I RECKON WE REALLY DO REPRESENT THE ELEMENTS OF FRIENDSHIP!
INDEED YOU DO...
"PRINCESS CELESTIA!"
TWILIGHT SPARKLE, MY FAITHFUL STUDENT! I KNEW YOU COULD DO IT!
BUT YOU TOLD ME IT WAS AN OLD PONY TALE!

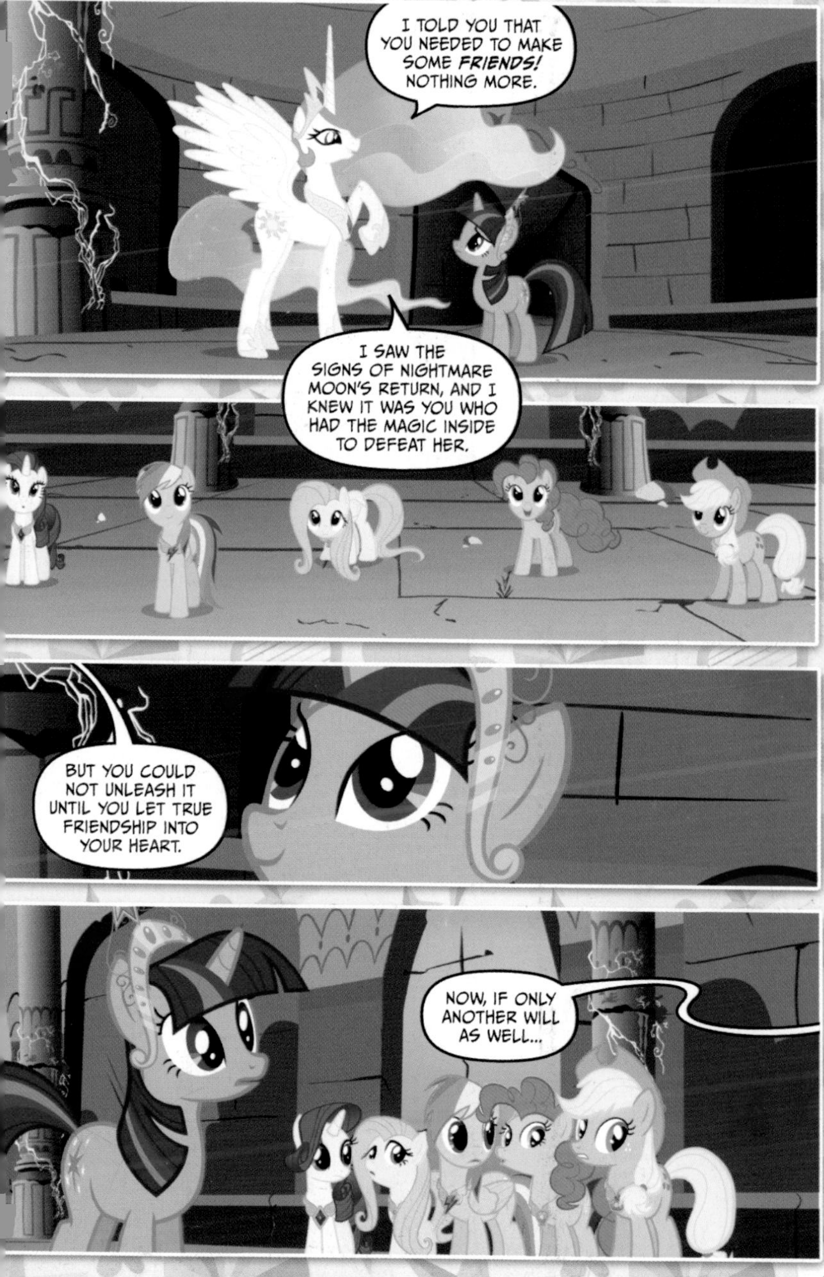
I TOLD YOU THAT YOU NEEDED TO MAKE SOME *FRIENDS!* NOTHING MORE.
I SAW THE SIGNS OF NIGHTMARE MOON'S RETURN, AND I KNEW IT WAS YOU WHO HAD THE MAGIC INSIDE TO DEFEAT HER.
BUT YOU COULD NOT UNLEASH IT UNTIL YOU LET TRUE FRIENDSHIP INTO YOUR HEART.
NOW, IF ONLY ANOTHER WILL AS WELL...

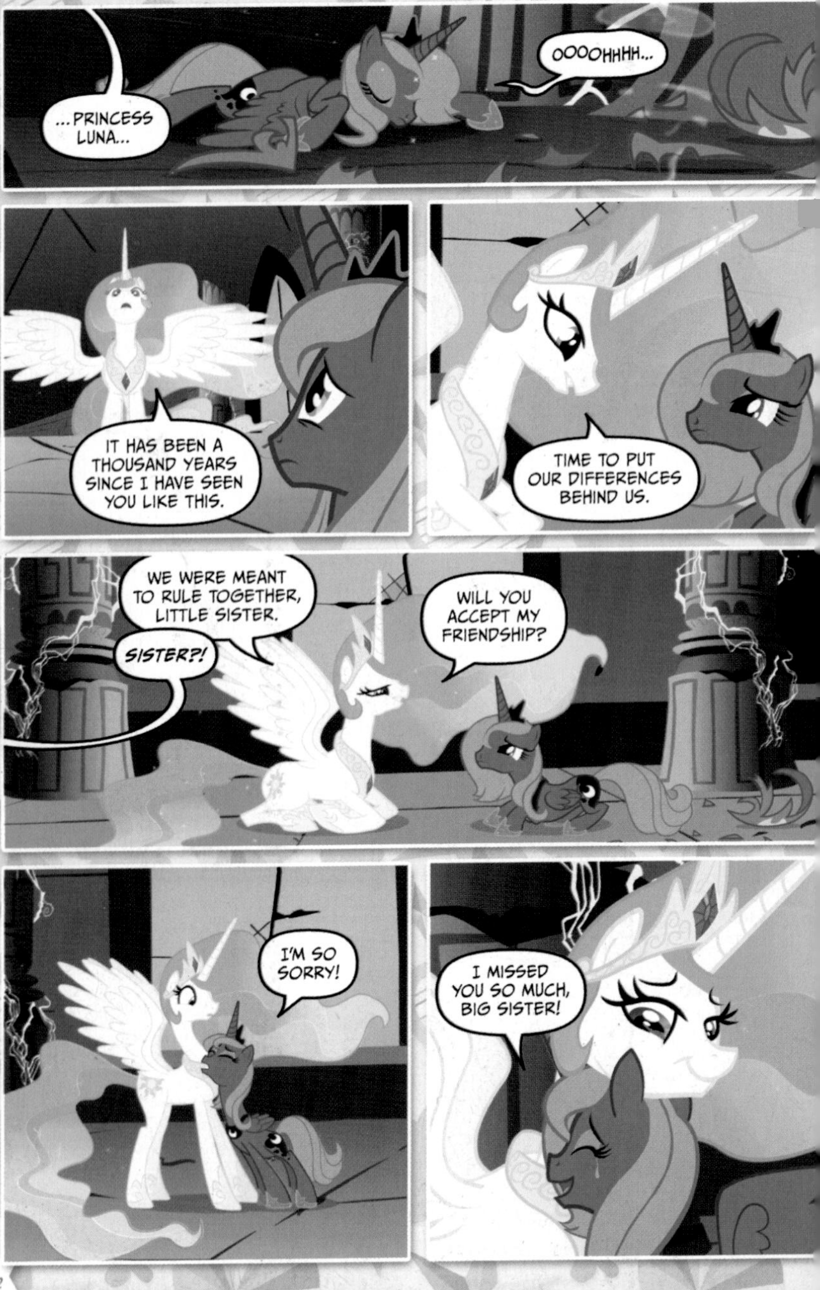
...PRINCESS LUNA...
OOOOHHHH...
IT HAS BEEN A THOUSAND YEARS SINCE I HAVE SEEN YOU LIKE THIS.
TIME TO PUT OUR DIFFERENCES BEHIND US.
WE WERE MEANT TO RULE TOGETHER, LITTLE SISTER.
SISTER?!
WILL YOU ACCEPT MY FRIENDSHIP?
I'M SO SORRY!
I MISSED YOU SO MUCH, BIG SISTER!

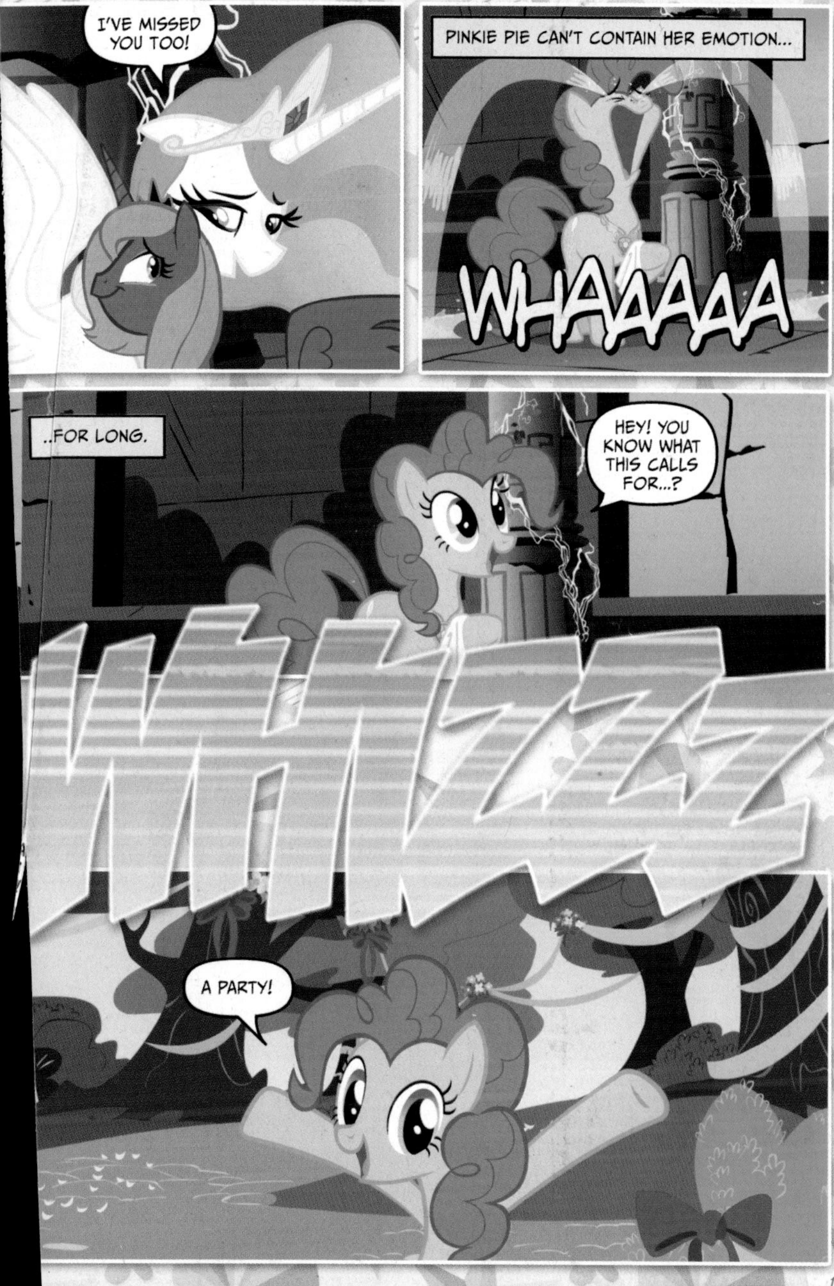
I'VE MISSED YOU TOO!
PINKIE PIE CAN'T CONTAIN HER EMOTION...
WHAAAAA
..FOR LONG.
HEY! YOU KNOW WHAT THIS CALLS FOR...?
WHIZZZ
A PARTY!

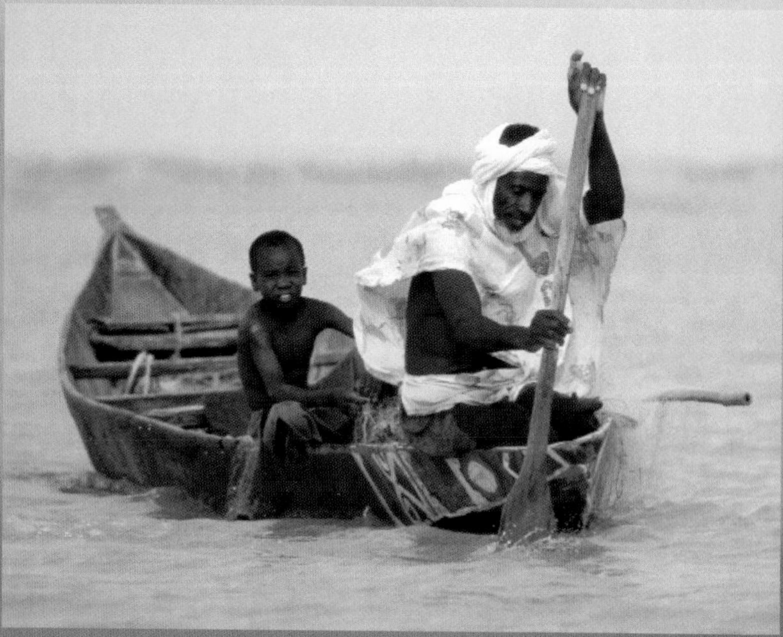

Above: Songhai man with his son. Men do all the paddling in Mali.

Below: As early-morning storms loom ominously to the north,
I prepare for another day of paddling.

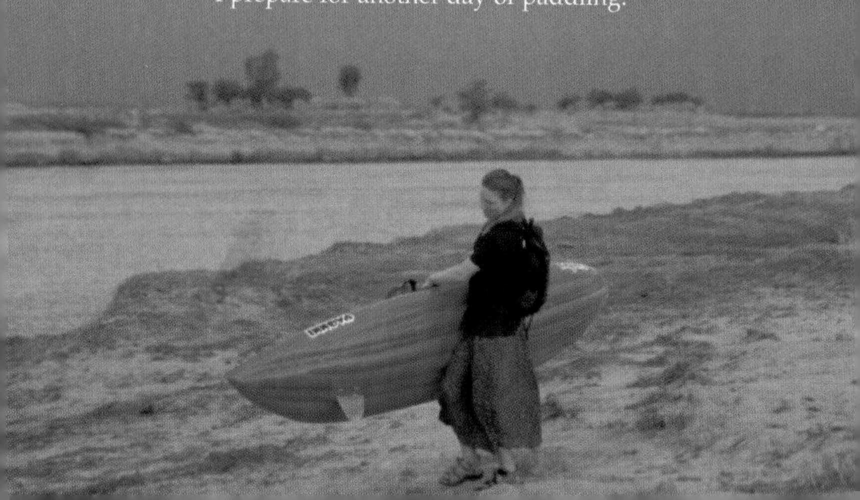

Halfway through my trip,
I depart from the city of Mopti.

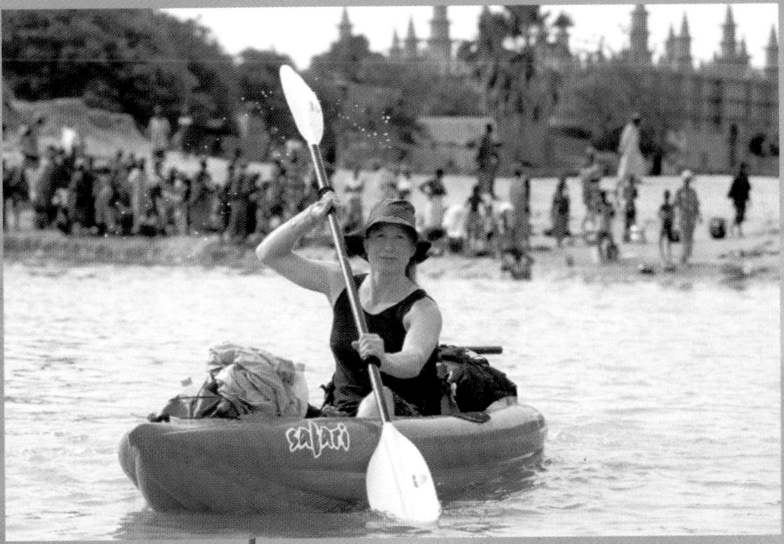
safari

Bozo fishermen cast their nets before the
high dunes of the Sahara.

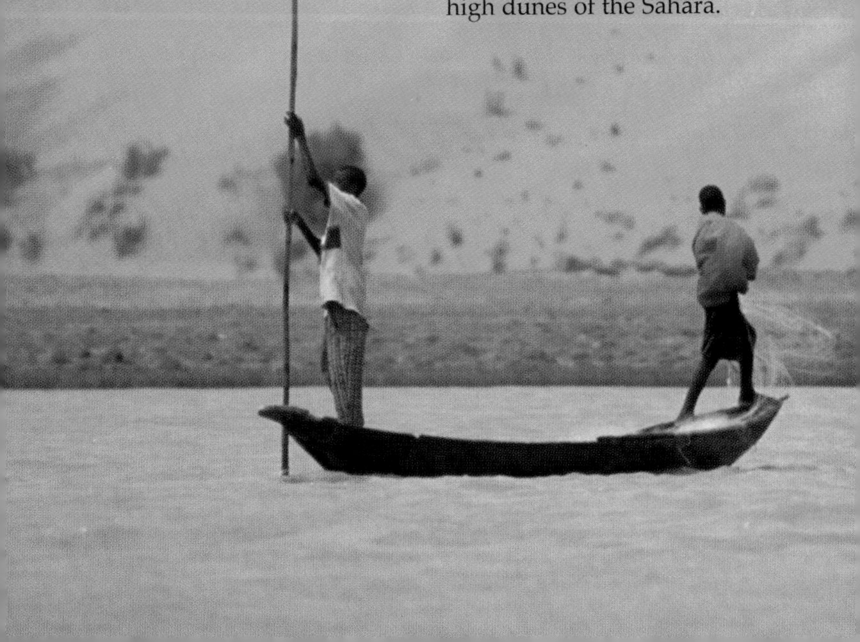

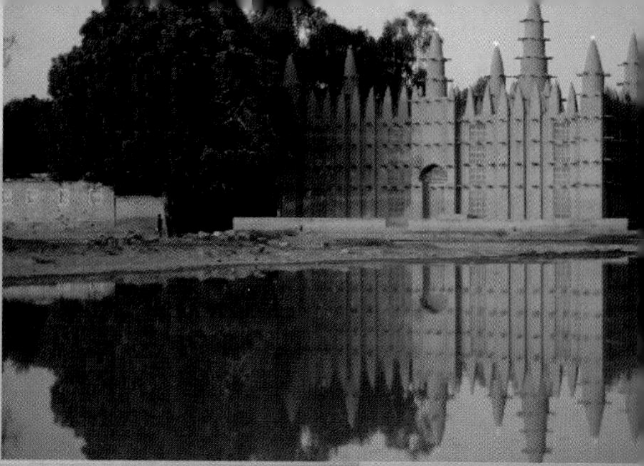

Adobe mosques were a common sight in Niger River towns.

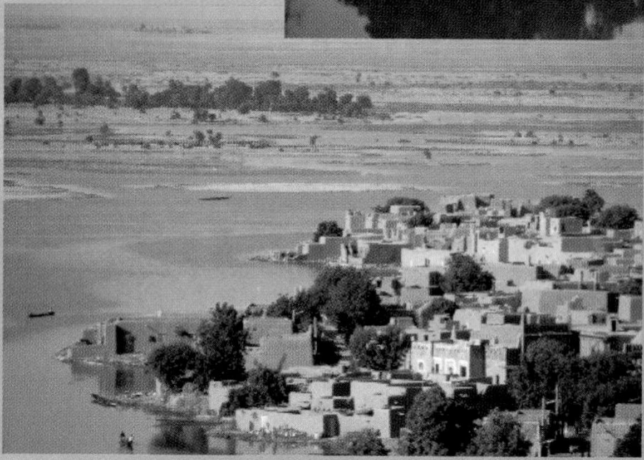

The Niger River widens into a floodplain as it flows into the enormous Lake Debo.

In Aka village, I am overrun by a swarm of curious children. This kind of feverish welcome was typical.

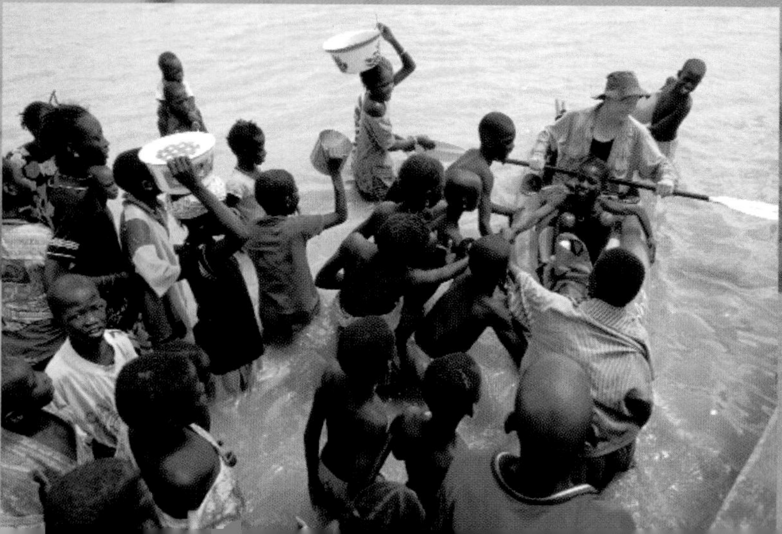

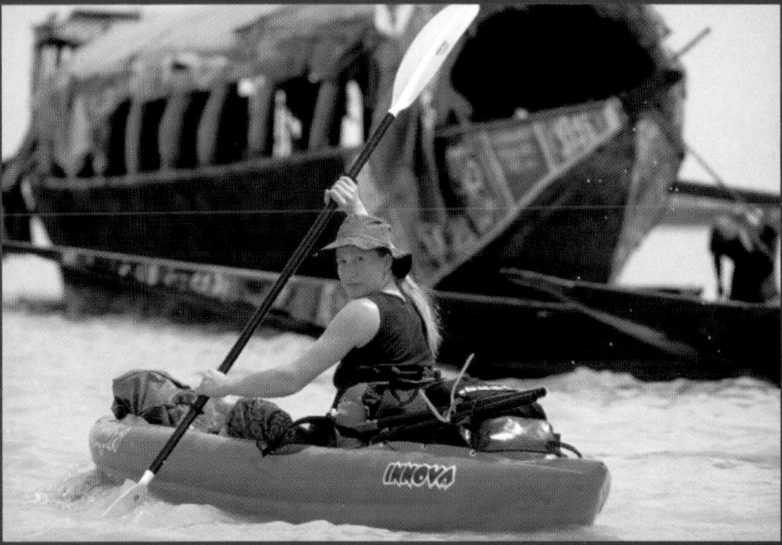
INNOVA

My kayak was dwarfed by the large 'pinasses', or river boats, that frequently plied the Niger.

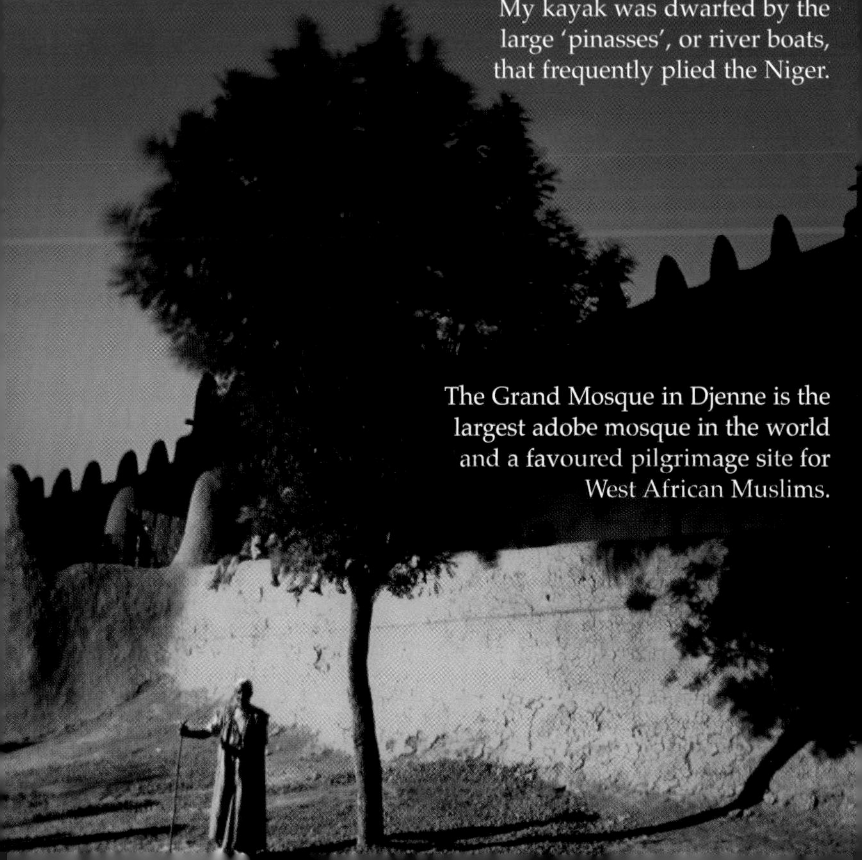

The Grand Mosque in Djenne is the largest adobe mosque in the world and a favoured pilgrimage site for West African Muslims.

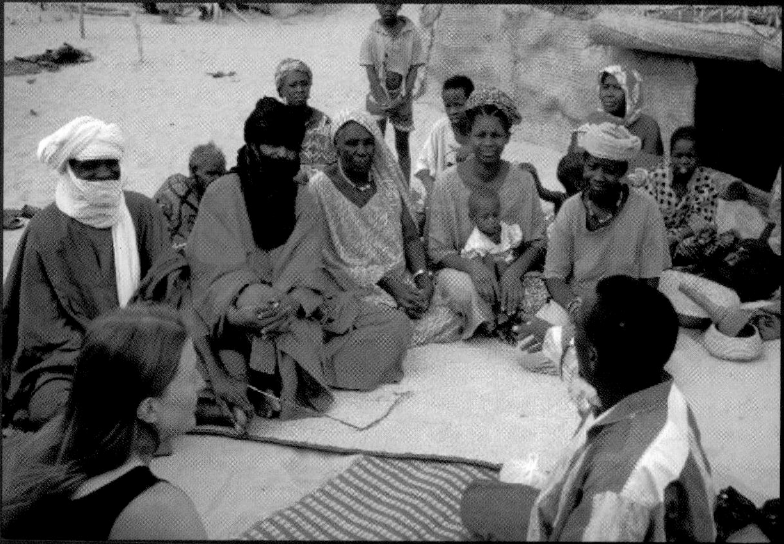

The Bella slaves owned by Zengi, their Tuareg master (*second from left*). I am sitting with Assou in the foreground, negotiating the freedom of two women, Fadimata and Akina (*sitting to the far right of Zengi*). Fadimata holds her baby, whose freedom Zengi refused to sell to me.

Saying goodbye to Fadimata and Akina, having purchased their freedom. I gave each woman enough money to start her own business and become self-sufficient.

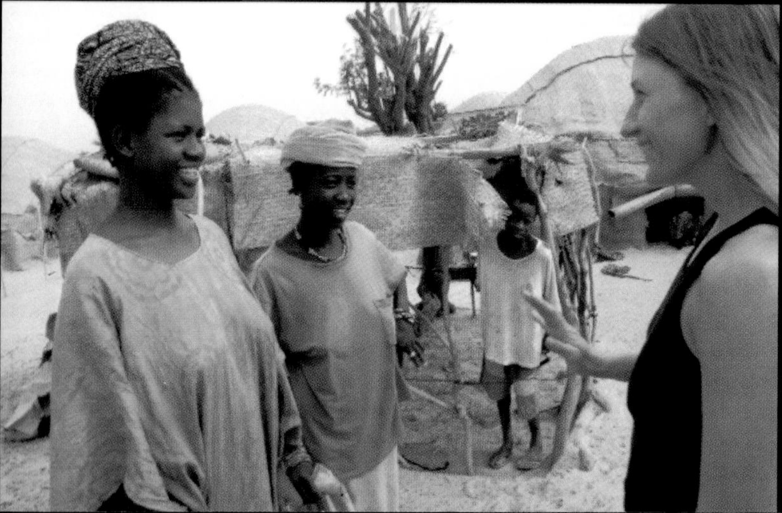

'The journey will tell you when it's over . . .'
I say goodbye to Mungo Park's 'majestic Niger'.

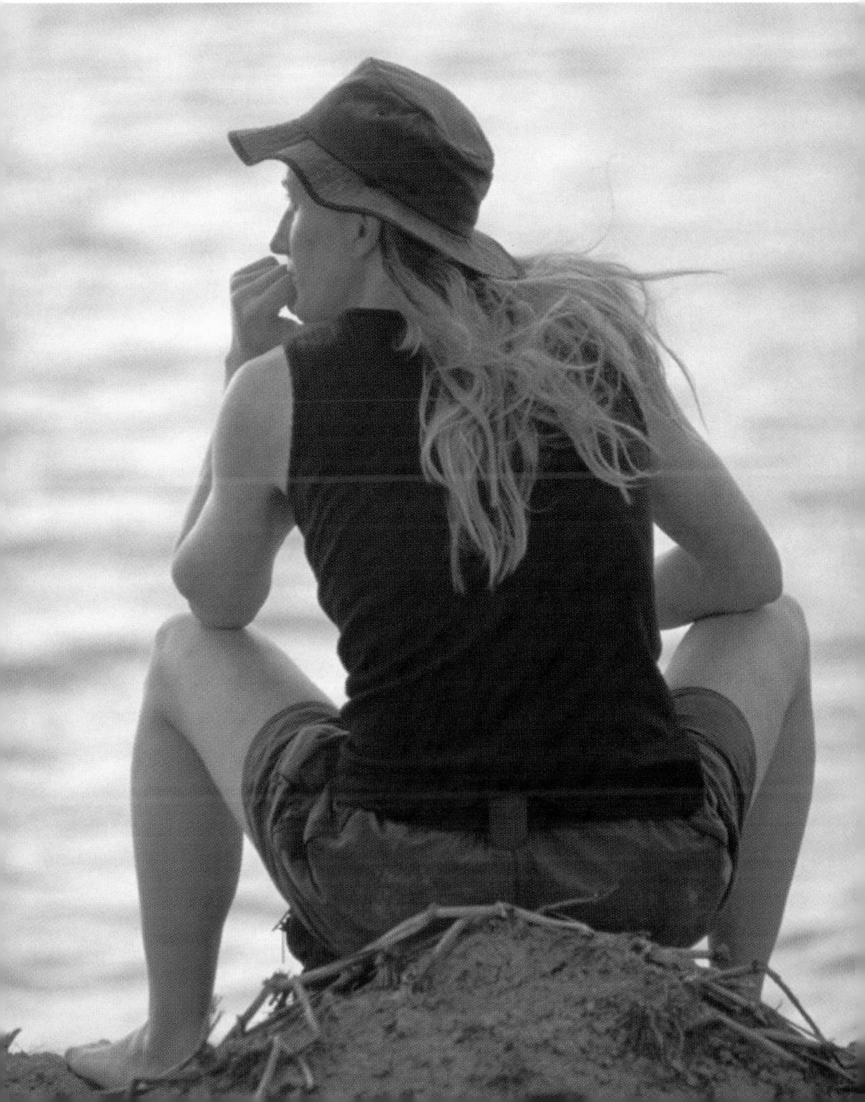

me of how, for hundreds of years (including the time when Park was here), foreigners were charged a duty to travel through each part of the country, and were completely barred entry into Djenné. Only Westerners in disguise had the chance of viewing the city and its mosque, as it was considered a holy Islamic city and off-limits to non-Muslims.

Djenné has been around for centuries; it was founded as early as AD 800 and is the oldest known city in sub-Saharan Africa. For a long time it had been as important as Timbuktu, sitting at the crossroads of all the major Saharan trade routes. Gold, salt and ivory passed through its gates, not to mention one of its most prized and lucrative commodities: slaves. Even today, there are families in Djenné who tacitly own slaves, passed down to them from the previous generation. But what makes Djenné unique is its anachronistic charm: little has changed in this town for hundreds of years. Goat herders chase their flocks down narrow alleyways lined with ancient, double-floored adobe-brick houses. Fulani women, their mouths tattooed dark blue and a gold band placed through the septum of their noses, stroll quietly through town. The focal point of everything is the Great Mosque, its three spiky mud turrets reaching above the skyline and topped with ostrich eggs (symbols of fertility and chastity). It's an enormous structure built on a platform of adobe bricks and covering what must be the size of an entire football field. I walk around its base, admiring the sheer breadth and elegance of its construction. Every year, African Muslims make a

pilgrimage here to pray within the mosque's walls or to study in the surrounding *madrasas*, or Koranic schools. It's the next best thing to Mecca.

While the Great Mosque at its current size was completed in 1907, it replaced another that was originally built in the thirteenth century by Djenné's first Muslim ruler, the sultan Koy Konboro. I walk up to the adobe walls and run a hand over them. Their two-foot thickness supports the building's bulky weight and provides insulation from the sun's heat. Each year, torrential rains collude to wash away some of the mosque's walls; each spring, everyone in town gathers together to replaster the outside with mud, occasioning a great local festival.

I'm not able to go inside because non-Muslims have been banned from entering since 1996. People have given me several different reasons for this, but the story I've pieced together tells of a European fashion photographer taking pictures of bikini models inside. Some Djenné residents suggest it went further than that, however, and that a porn movie was actually made; others mention only that foreigners filmed the inside without permission. Regardless, a large sign rests before the mosque, explaining that non-Muslims are *interdit* from entering.

I sit in the market area, eating a mango and trying to imagine this city as it would have been back in Park's time. Undoubtedly, aside from the upgrade of the mosque in 1907, the town would have looked nearly the same. Park himself had wanted to come here but finally deemed it too dangerous. The fact that the city was controlled by

Moroccan kings and had a large population of Moors convinced him to give up his first river trip and return to England in 1797. Even the idea of passing the Bani River's confluence at what is now Mopti made him nervous, as Djenné and the Niger were linked by waterways. Park had valid reason for his trepidation: he'd just barely escaped with his life from brutal imprisonment by the Moors in the Sahara; his journal was riddled with references to the terror he felt at the prospect of being recaptured. 'I had but little hope,' he wrote,

> of subsisting by charity in a country where the Moors have such influence. But above all, I perceived that I was advancing, more and more, within the power of those merciless fanatics; and from my reception both at Sego and Sansanding, I was apprehensive that, in attempting to even reach Djenné (unless under the protection of some man of consequence amongst them, which I had no means of obtaining), I should sacrifice my life to no purpose; for my discoveries would perish with me. I saw inevitable destruction in attempting to proceed to the eastward.

Back in Mopti, I meet Assou so we can visit his sorcerer of choice, a man named Salla, who will supposedly be able to tell me how to appease the genies of the Niger and reach Timbuktu. With divination and voodoo such an integral part of West African society, I'm infinitely curious to find out what it is about the fortune tellers and their

spells that makes them such an indispensable part of Malian life.

I walk with Assou down a muddy alleyway in downtown Mopti. We enter a courtyard, crossing a dark room lit only by a television set. Salla's extended family lounges on foam mattresses spread on the floor, and they barely glance at us as we enter, their eyes fixed on the television screen, on an African music video. We pass by without a word, ascending old, winding adobe stairs to the second floor. Salla is in a back room, asleep, and Assou nudges him awake with his foot. He sits up, scratching his chest through his stained *grand bubu* robe, and straightens the white skullcap he is wearing. He lights a kerosene lamp in the dim room and invites us to sit on a carpet on the floor.

I don't know what I expected a sorcerer to look like. Maybe some old, wizened man with a silver beard and some sort of magical implement he waves around. Salla is the first sorcerer I've ever met, and I'm not particularly impressed. He rubs the sleep from his eyes, yawns and mumbles wearily to Assou.

'He needs money,' Assou explains to me.

'Right.' I place some bills in Salla's extended hand. The man's countenance brightens and he speaks.

'He needs your name,' Assou says.

I tell him, and he writes down characters in Arabic to fit the pronunciation. Assou tells me that Salla will be making what is called a *turaboo beradela* in Bambarra – a consultation using both cowrie shells and the Koran,

illustrative of a confluence of animist and Islamic traditions. This technique – one of numerous varieties of divination available in West Africa – uses a kind of automatic writing technique to read the future and obtain answers to questions. Salla throws the shells into a shallow basket, studies them, then crouches over a notebook and begins writing furiously in Arabic.

'He didn't ask me what I wanted to know,' I whisper to Assou.

'We don't need to tell him. He knows your questions when he writes your name.'

'You're sure about this?'

Assou rolls his eyes at me. 'Of course. This man is the best sorcerer in Mopti.'

In the car coming over here, Assou had been especially cocky about Salla's abilities, so I say nothing now and watch and wait. The Arabic writing increases in speed, until Salla reaches a frenzy of impassioned scribbling. At last he stops, dropping the pen with dramatic finality and looking up at me with pursed lips. Assou has enormous respect for Salla, maintaining that he has correctly read his future each and every time he's come in for a consultation – which is now up to three times a week. Based on all of Assou's praise, I have great expectations for this man.

'Your name, "Kira", is interesting,' Salla says, Assou translating his tribal language. 'In Bambarra, it means "prophet". You will sit on the power chair and have a long life.'

I'm starting to like this consultation.

'I have seen that you have something in mind about a man,' Salla adds, staring at the Arabic scribbles, 'but that might not work.'

'I don't know what he means,' I say to Assou.

'What you have in mind about this man,' Salla emphasizes, 'could come to trouble.'

'But I don't *have* anything in my mind about a man.'

Salla continues solemnly: 'You will have four children in the future.'

'Never, ever, never,' I tell him.

Piqued, Salla replies in French, 'I am never wrong, miss.' He glares at me and looks to Assou for guidance. Assou shrugs.

Salla stares at his scribbles. 'This man you're thinking about,' he tells me, wagging his finger at me impatiently. 'If you want him, this is the sacrifice you must make: you must buy three guinea fowls. Then you must kill them, cook them, and eat only the wings and necks. In this way, you will have him.' He closes his notebook and folds his hands.

'So I can't eat the drumsticks?' I say to Assou.

Assou shrugs. Salla speaks, telling us that the consultation is over. There's nothing about my river trip. Nothing about my getting to Timbuktu.

'I think your guy needs a refresher course,' I tell Assou.

'If you would like,' Assou offers apologetically, 'we can buy guinea fowls in the market.'

I tell Assou that I'd like to see the real thing next time. An honest-to-God, first-rate sorcerer type. Assou, wanting to

win my faith in such people, takes me to see Binta, a Dogon witch living on the outskirts of Mopti in a village called Wailirde. Along the way, we pick up Assou's friend Barou, who happens to be Peace Corps Baba's younger brother. Barou, a local guide, is also a Dogon by birth and can understand the language. He is quiet and timid, so Assou gladly does the talking for all of us on the way to the village. When we finally arrive in Wailirde, it's after sunset, only a faint orange light colouring the western horizon. Darkness settles on the land, shutting out what light remains and obscuring the shapes of the mud huts. Nothing is lit up in the village, not even a cooking fire. Strangely, the village appears empty, a lone donkey neighing like a banshee into the night.

'Where is everyone?' I ask.

'I don't know,' Barou says. 'This place scares me.'

I follow Assou and Barou into a round adobe hut – Binta's hut. We can barely see where we're going, and we sit down on a wooden bench that faces a dark doorway. A young girl appears out of nowhere, and without saying a word she lights a kerosene lamp, hangs it on a nail nearby, and leaves. It lets out a sickly, scratchy light that barely touches the darkness.

'Where's Binta?' I ask Barou. A Dogon himself, I'm assuming he knows something about these matters. But he doesn't. He shakes his head and gazes around with apprehension.

Assou smiles nervously and cracks a joke in Bambarra to Barou. They laugh. Their laughing stops all at once, however, as a woman creeps inside the hut.

'Binta,' Assou whispers to me.

She appears as just a dark form. I can barely see her at all, except for her hand which reaches out from the darkness. Her voice comes at us, and Barou tells me that she wants payment for her divinatory services. We all drop bills in her hand, and she retreats into the dark room before us. Inside, Barou tells me, are carved ancestor figures – objects so sacred and imbued with magic that no-one except Binta and her apprentices are ever allowed to see them.

We hear a gourd rattle being shaken. Binta chants in Dogon in a loud, monotone voice, repeating the same phrase over and over. The effect is hypnotic and powerful. I look to Assou and then to Barou.

'What's she doing now?' I ask them.

Barou tells me he thinks she's contacting the spirit world. Assou is smiling nervously and fingering the sunglasses in his lap.

The sound of the rattle stops. Suddenly, from out of the darkness, comes a screeching voice. It is so angry and high-pitched that Assou and I jump up, terrified. Barou motions for us to calm down. He explains that we're hearing the voice of the *binu*, or spirit. It won't hurt us. It's telling Binta what we need to do in order to dispel evil spirits from our lives and have good fortune. Apparently, a whole slew of evil spirits might bother you at any given time. They build up around a person, so it's important to rid yourself of them periodically, almost like getting an oil change.

It would seem as if we all have quite a number working against us, from the way this *binu* is screeching at us. I'm

struck by how the staccato voice is wholly unlike Binta's, as if a completely different person had materialized in the room. Binta starts asking this *binu* questions in her own voice, and it responds in a shrieking, impatient way, the words fired out. I keep straining my eyes to see into the dark room before us, to get some glimpse of what's happening inside. I feel as if I'm trapped in some scene from a horror movie, caught as I am in this thick darkness, with frantic, demonic voices screaming at me.

Now a deep male voice booms out – a new *binu* – its baritone pitch resonating across the hut. This voice, like the other, sounds entirely autonomous from Binta's. It rages and bellows in Bambarra, and Binta interrupts it to ask questions. It fumes back at her with such a loud, ornery list of objections that my ears ring in its wake.

'Which *binu* is this?' I ask Barou.

He shakes his head. His mouth is open. We three stare at the source of the voices, Binta cajoling them to tell her things, her voice calm yet persistent, while they yell and scold.

It's interesting how the earlier *binu* spoke in Dogon, and this one speaks in Bambarra. Binta responds in whichever language they prefer to communicate with, and Barou translates the Dogon words for us. The spirits, he says, are still complaining about the three of us.

Finally, the voices subside. Binta, still in her dark room, tells us what they said: We must all make a 'sacrifice'. Usually this doesn't have anything to do with killing animals, but rather with 'sacrificing' something of value by

giving it to someone else. The size of the sacrifice is dependent on the degree of problems that you have and the number of spirits that you've offended. Barou must give away ten kola nuts. Assou must buy some cow's milk and pour it on an active termite mound.

Me – well, apparently I've got some work to do. Binta speaks to Barou for a while, and when he finally translates, I feel like I've lost a Monopoly game. I must buy fifty dates and a hundred fried rice cakes, and I must give them away to young children or beggars. *Only* to young children or beggars; the children should be under the age of twelve.

I ask Barou if Binta will take questions, but he shakes his head. She doesn't field questions to the *binu*. They tell *us* what we need to know, explaining how we can offset angry spirits and evil spells. If I want to get some real answers, I'll have to see a celebrated Muslim marabout, a holy man with prophetic powers, whom Barou calls Big Father.

Big Father lives in Manako, east of Mopti. Manako is a typical village of adobe huts sitting in the midst of a dusty savannah of scrub brush and wilted trees. Rain has come later and less often to this region in recent years, so the Sahel, or South Sahara, is trespassing upon once-fertile farmland, turning it quickly and irrevocably to desert. Prices in Mopti for basic food items have sky-rocketed as a result, a single chicken doubling in price, rice tripling, the people here wondering how long they can survive the inflation and drought.

Assou is unable to join us today, so I go with Barou in his

car. Manako is in the midst of its weekly market when we arrive. Donkey carts crowd the dirt track, loaded with vegetables, fruit, rice. Manako appears fairly prosperous compared to many of the villages we've passed while driving out here, as its huts are intact, and kids don't run around wearing ratty clothes. Still, the pastureland around the village has become a dustbowl.

A man walks by wearing a T-shirt that shows Osama bin Laden's face looking at George W. Bush's; it reads in English: POLITICS, NOT WAR.

'Is Bin Laden popular here?' I ask Barou.

He nods his head. Barou explains that whenever fights break out these days, the most common cause is a disagreement over what happened to New York City on 11 September 2001. Many Malians, Barou says, worship Bin Laden like a god and are quick to celebrate the attacks on the United States and to praise the deaths that resulted.

'People are stupid,' Barou says, shaking his head. Other Malians to whom I've broached the subject have been much less fervent in their denunciations of Bin Laden. When I've asked the question, 'What do you think about the September 11 attacks?' the most common response has been, 'Look what the Israelis are doing to the Palestinians.' Unlike most Malians, Barou considers himself pro-American. This isn't because he's a Dogon animist rather than a Muslim, either. As he and his brother have their lucrative business selling African trade beads and Malian tribal art to dealers in the States, the two brothers can attribute much of their wealth to American connections,

whereas many Malians have never even met an American in person. It's easy for us to become a concoction of myth or hearsay here, too. Cheap Hollywood flicks show Americans spending all their time machine-gunning bad guys with Arnold Schwarzenegger or cavorting on California beaches in skimpy bathing suits. One of America's greatest contributions to Mali thus far: gangsta rap.

Barou stops his car. We get out and walk past adobe homes to the village's small central square. Before one of the houses, under a shade tree, sits a group of chatting men, all of them facing an old man with a long white beard, dressed in pure white robes: Big Father. He is much lighter-complexioned than most of the men around him, suggesting Arab ancestry. His soft, moist eyes gaze out at me as we approach, and I feel caught in the arresting placidity of his presence. Barou tells me that Big Father is eighty-two years old – remarkable, as the male life expectancy in Mali is only fifty-one. I sense that there is something truly special about this man.

Marabouts like Big Father are all men who possess a strong knowledge of Arabic and the Koran. They are, in effect, Muslim sorcerers: they write magical text for charms, foretell the future, appease wrathful genies and bring about good fortune through spells. Their work is closely tied to and sanctioned by the Koran, which gives them leave to work with the supernatural realm on behalf of others. For all divinatory requests, the marabout makes use of his Islamic training and customs as a basis for the answers.

In addition to being a marabout, Big Father is also an imam, or prayer leader, at the village mosque; the two *métiers* often go hand in hand. Barou tells me that some unscrupulous imams become marabouts in order to cash in on the lucrative job of telling people's futures, but the most sincere marabouts are the wealthiest ones because the process of divination works on a donation basis: the most earnest and successful individuals receive the largest numbers of devotees, and thus the most money. Big Father is just such a marabout, renowned throughout Mopti for both the integrity and the accuracy of his services.

Big Father ushers us inside his hut, and I sit on a mat opposite him. We look at each other for a moment. I've been wondering if he'd balk at the idea of helping a non-Muslim, but there's nothing but sincerity and generosity in his eyes. He strikes me as a very venerable man. I offer him a generous donation, which he takes humbly, with a nod of the head.

Barou tells me the way it works, that I won't be able to receive answers today. Big Father will take my questions and wait until night, when he will enter into a deep prayer and trance. He will stay up all night, if necessary, until he receives information about my problems. Often it's in the earliest hours of the morning that he feels his greatest power and a communion with his divinity, at which time he'll be told what I need to do in order to bring about my desires. Barou says that all marabouts work after dark, and that most are descended from previous marabouts. It is a sacred and ancient vocation.

Barou asks Big Father a few of his own questions first. When he finishes, he instructs me to ask my own, translating for me.

I ask: 'Will I get to Timbuktu?' I have Barou explain that I'm travelling alone by kayak on the Niger and that it's been difficult so far.

Big Father listens patiently to the translation, casting his eyes on me from time to time. When Barou finishes, he nods. He has understood my question, and tonight he will ask it.

He says something and Barou translates: 'You have more questions.'

'I do?' I say.

Big Father speaks, and Barou translates: 'He wants you to tell him what is troubling you.'

I hadn't been planning on asking anything else. I guess it's too surreal to me, addressing personal questions to this respectable eighty-two-year-old man sitting before me. I sigh. 'I don't know. Just out of curiosity, does he see a man in my near future? You know.'

It's a question for some psychic hotline, not a Malian marabout. I feel silly. But I get curious like anyone else.

Big Father nods and waits.

'And then my job,' I say, feeling as if I'm on a roll now. 'How can I make more money? What can I do? I work hard, so I don't understand what the problem is.'

He stares at me with his bright eyes, full of a gentle kindness, as the translation is given.

'That's it,' I say.

Big Father nods. He asks for my name, and as I say it he writes it down in Arabic on a piece of paper and checks with me to make sure he's pronouncing it right. He says he will be repeating my name tonight while praying on my behalf. When I return tomorrow, he'll have answers for me.

It's the next morning, and I go back to see Big Father. This time I take Assou along, so he can more precisely translate what's said into English. Assou's never seen Big Father and is still partial to Salla, the man who insisted I will have four children some day.

Big Father is in the same place where we found him before, under the shade of a tree, ringed by a small crowd of his devotees. He looks up as we arrive and smiles kindly, getting to his feet. He enters his hut and we follow, taking our shoes off at the door.

Big Father sits on a mat across from us, waiting patiently for the chattering Assou to end a story he's in the middle of telling me. When he finally finishes, Big Father starts speaking, telling Assou the answers he received to my questions. He speaks for a long time, Assou stopping him every once in a while to translate.

'So he says that you'll reach Timbuktu,' Assou says. 'He's made a *saphie* for you, to protect you, and he's blessed it.'

'This charm will really protect me?' It seems too superstitious a notion to me.

Assou laughs. 'Of course,' he says.

He listens for a while longer. 'Big Father says you have a

strange job, and you travel from place to place. He says you won't make money this way. He says you need to stay in one place and do something there for many months – this is how you'll make money. He's certain of it.'

'How does he know about my job?' I ask. Because I never told Barou that I'm a writer, only that I'm travelling in a kayak on the Niger.

Assou asks him, and Big Father nods as he answers.

'He hears these things,' Assou says.

I feel a tingling on my neck. For the first time, I'm starting to think that maybe this man has access to some realm most of us don't – *maybe*.

'He heard about them late last night. He asked your questions and prayed for a long time, and a voice told him the answers.'

Big Father talks again. Assou starts laughing as he listens.

'This is very interesting, Kira,' Assou says. 'He's told me about you and men.'

'Oh, no. Tell him I don't need to hear about that.'

'He said he's seen your life with men. He's seen all the men you've ever been with. He says some of these men were not kind to you, so sometimes you can be . . . how do you say it? . . . *paranoid* about men, and you run away. He says you'll get married, but how soon depends on you.'

Assou is enjoying this consultation immensely now. As most Malian women get married when they're teenagers, the reason why I'm single has been a source of curiosity and amusement to him ever since we met.

'Big Father says you must be patient with the men you meet, not scared of them. Then you'll meet the right man because you'll let him enter your life, and he will be kind to you. He says you need to stop pushing men away. It all depends on you.'

'Great,' I say.

It's strange to be told something like this on the plains of West Africa, by an old, white-bearded sorcerer who could have come right out of a Tolkien novel.

Big Father tells me the sacrifice I must make: I need to buy one live sheep and seventeen metres of white cloth. Both must be brought to him for a blessing, and then given away to a poor woman. Doing so will help enlist certain divine forces to act on my behalf in all the things I asked him about. He hands me a small, folded piece of paper upon which is written a verse from the Koran: my *saphie*, meant to protect me during my journey to Timbuktu and beyond. He instructs me to have it sewn inside a leather pouch, which I can wear for good fortune.

I thank him and give him some more money as a gift. How tantalizing it all sounds! White cloth that, when blessed, will correct irregularities in my life. A live sheep that will bring love and prosperity and safety. A *saphie* to ward off evil with magic words. Fifty dates given away here, a hundred rice cakes there, to send away malign spirits. If only life were so efficiently regulated. If only so easily understood. I hold the *saphie* in my palm and stare at the folded paper. How badly I want to believe it holds some power, some efficacy beyond what I can comprehend.

I thank Big Father and get up, promising to send him some white cloth and a sheep for his blessing – as long as he assures me that the sheep won't be killed. He reassures me that all will be well for me – though, as he's said, much will depend on me. He will be praying for me. He hopes I will like Timbuktu.

CHAPTER EIGHT

ASSOU TELLS ME THAT HE'S JUST BEEN TOLD THE location of one of the most powerful witches in all of Mali, in case I'm interested. Her name is Yatanu, and she lives in the midst of Dogon country, in a tiny village called Niry in the Bandiagara Escarpment, a few hours south-east of Mopti. I feel a bit witched-out at the moment, but he assures me that I've never seen the likes of this woman. When she was ten, her parents, witches themselves, cut open her left arm and put a scarab beetle into the biceps, sewing the skin back up. Presumably the beetle died, but a spirit named Deguru remained, with whom she converses to obtain knowledge about people's pasts and futures. She can also summon up the power of her beetle spirit in order to bring about particular events, so that most Dogon people live in terror of her.

I admit it sounds impressive. I tell Assou that I'll hire a Land Rover to take us out there. I'm fascinated by the idea

of someone having a monopoly of power over other people's lives.

The Dogon living around the escarpment are mostly animists, having protected their beliefs from invading Islamic armies by retreating into the rugged, rocky country of eastern Mali. Here they constructed adobe huts high in the cliff walls, not unlike modern-day Anasazi, allowing them to continue their traditions virtually unmolested. To this day, they remain proud and suspicious of outsiders, rumours abounding that they still conduct human sacrifices – a fairly commonplace practice for them not so very long ago. Park himself wrote about a people living in this part of Mali who were known for their cannibalism, and it's quite possible he was talking about the Dogon: 'To the best information I was able to collect,' he wrote, '[the inhabitants] are cruel and ferocious; carrying their resentment toward their enemies, so far as never to give quarter; and even to indulge themselves with unnatural and disgusting banquets of human flesh.'

Rain has come to the Dogon country of Mali more often than around Mopti, and the usually dry, inhospitable terrain has turned to a verdant landscape. Groves of squat, bulbous baobab trees open enormous red flowers to the sun. The distant mountains of the Bandiagara Escarpment shimmer with fresh green shoots. Here is the view often associated with the sub-Saharan plains of Africa: acacias, savannah, monkeys scampering into brush. The Sahara hasn't taken over this greenery yet, though I know that the desert country lies disturbingly close to the north.

As we travel the dirt track to the escarpment, I have the driver of the Land Rover stop at every poor village or congregation of kids I see along the road so I can pass out some of my hundred rice cakes and fifty dates. As per Binta the witch's instructions, I make sure I only give them to beggars, or kids under twelve. It took Assou and me a couple of hours this morning simply to procure enough of the cakes from street vendors, so that I was seriously thinking of just forgetting this whole 'sacrifice' business, but Assou insisted I not offend the spirits by ignoring their orders. Meanwhile, I had Barou drop off the seventeen metres of white cloth and the sheep with Big Father. It's been a long and expensive day of appeasing spirits and obtaining blessings. I much prefer my Buddhism.

I've discovered, though, that I'm really enjoying fulfilling my sacrifice duties. I give out goodies to little girls balancing huge bundles of washing on their heads, and to young boys gathering firewood in the dusty savannah. This is poor country, and the dates and rice cakes are city luxuries that they probably never have out here. We pass a field where some skinny, malnourished-looking kids are herding goats. I order the car stopped so I can fill their arms with rice cakes. Our driver, an enormous, bullish man who would make a great full-back, steps out of the car to call to the kids. They run off in terror, hiding behind rocks. I send Assou instead, and pretty soon the kids are surrounding the car, smiling and thanking me with outspread hands. It takes a while before I'm able to give everything away, and I see that behind the obvious superstition of this practice,

behind my scepticism and left-brain resistance, is the act
itself: basic generosity between people. Nothing silly or
irrational about it.

We decide to spend the night in a large Dogon village
called Banini, which rests on the edge of the escarpment.
Assou and I make arrangements to visit the witch first
thing tomorrow. This village is well frequented by packs of
tourists during the cool months of the winter season, as it
sits beside an impressively high waterfall that plummets
hundreds of feet to grassy slopes below. Though Banini sees
few people at this time of year, its collection of tourist shops
remains open for business, full of the kind of low-quality
kitsch that foreigners presumably buy in large enough
quantities to persuade the local people to keep making the
stuff: crude masks of fertility figures, Bambarra antelope
carvings, wooden key chains. I can't escape the incessant
solicitations from the store owners and so enter each place
for a brief look. The most widely sold items are imitations
of Dogon granary doors. Obtaining a genuine antique door
has long been a coup for collectors of African art, so that the
best way to find one is not to go to the Dogon villages any
more but to art galleries or private homes in the West. The
doors are renowned for their representation of ancestral
figures, but the imitation ones improve upon the features
and are more elaborately carved. The theory seems to be:
give the tourist more bang for his buck. I see a pile of newly
carved doors lying in the grass behind a Dogon hut.
They're left out in the sun and rain for a few months
until the wood warps and gets stained by mildew,

giving off the appearance of something ancient and sacred.

I walk with Assou through the village, staring at ancient Tellem ruins in the crevices of cliffs higher up. The Tellem were the former occupiers of this land until the Dogon came along, driving them into extinction. It's not known what happened exactly, the Tellem vanishing but for their decaying cliff dwellings littering the countryside. The Dogon now use these homes as places to deposit their dead. Tourists frequently sign up for Tellem tours, the highlight of which is visiting some of the more accessible mud dwellings to see the human bones within.

What's left of the Tellem people's culture – some old bronze sculptures, fetish figures, burial necklaces made of crude iron links attached to centuries-old trade beads of glass and stone – are sold to tourists in a hush-hush sort of way by local entrepreneurs. Most of these things were obtained by grave-robbing, which involves rappelling down cliff faces with crude baobab-bark ropes and raiding the crumbling adobe structures, but the Dogon express little repentance in the face of the great financial incentives. This way of making spare change has become common-place enough to require more daring manoeuvres into higher, harder-to-reach crevices, as well as scouting the surrounding countryside for new caches of artefacts. If one village runs out, another further down the escarpment has probably found something.

Banini is a typical Dogon village, in that it's built among the rocks of the escarpment, each squat adobe hut having its own little courtyard and a cylindrical granary building

topped with a cone of thatch. 'Cute' is the word that comes to mind. The village looks cute and benign, like a kind of hobbit land, with its granaries of different sizes – tall ones for men's food, short ones for women's – built among huge boulders. It sits at the base of that high waterfall that plummets down the rock face and pools beside a few baobab trees in full bloom. I'm hesitant to use the word 'Eden' to describe this place, but it does look very pristine and untouched, very innocent. Goats wander the hard-packed earth, chased by naked children. The kids' umbilical cords were cut a couple of inches from their bellies so that their navels sprout an additional appendage. An old chief sits in an open-air meeting house, called a *toguna*, that's covered with a low, millet-stalk roof. The roof is designed in such a way as to prevent anyone from getting enflamed during a village squabble and standing up to make angry threats. Every year the *toguna* gets a new roof of millet stalks on top of the previous layer, so that it resembles a Chinese pagoda.

I follow Assou around the village, and he talks and talks endlessly. He does it with the intention of being helpful, as he knows a lot about Dogon country, but by keeping my attention on what he's saying, I constantly miss the scenery. I haven't had the chance to just be present. I sit down on a log and stop listening to him finally, taking in the beauty of this place – its waterfall, the enormous red flowers that fall from the branches of the baobabs like autumnal leaves.

The Dogon believe that everyone is born twice. The first birth is our entry into mortal life, replete with its struggles

and hardship. But during this experience, we can have a moment of 'sight', becoming aware of a state known as the *sigi*, or second birth. When you experience this *sigi* birth, you will never be the same. You have seen another world, one beyond time. You know the feeling of transcendental knowledge, the truth of all things, and there is no going back. The Dogon believe that the *sigi* birth must happen to all of us, if we are to become whole. There is no time to spare. No time for dallying. The path awaits.

Understandably, the Dogon believe that the 'road of the *sigi*' is a long, arduous undertaking, and so every sixty years the Dogon villages in these parts commence a special five-year-long ceremonial period designed to help people 'see the *sigi*' through dance and ritual. Such is the importance of knowing a wisdom greater than oneself. There seem to be obvious equivalents of the *sigi* in Western and Eastern religions. In Christianity, particularly its mystical tradition, it might be seen as gaining entry into the 'interior castle', where one may progress through the 'beautiful mansions' to ultimate union with God, as described by St Teresa of Avila. In Judaism, it is like the pursuit of the kabbalist, following the twelve stages of the *tzaddik* (righteous person) to the 'throne of God' and ultimate realization. In Buddhism and Hinduism, it is the transformational understanding of non-duality, selflessness, and the impermanence of all things. But regardless of how a religion might explain its own experience of spiritual 'rebirth', the goal seems to be the same: transcendence of self and a joining with universal truth.

*

I return with Assou to the guesthouse where we're staying, telling him I'm going to take a walk for a while – alone. Silence is like music to me, and I need some time to myself. Like me, Mungo Park was usually quite reticent, though every person of any importance in London wanted to have the famous explorer at his or her dinner table after Park's narrative became a bestseller. Still, it was reported that the great discoverer of the Niger River detested small talk and had no interest in attending dinner parties or being publicly acknowledged for his achievements, leading a spurned London hostess to say that he had 'the manner and dignities of his Niger kings'. Good for Park.

I walk up a rocky hill and sit to watch the sun set behind the escarpment. I breathe in the stillness, feeling a peace settling upon me that's otherwise hard to find in Mali. Even when I paddle on the river, there's always somebody around – a Somono fisherman in a distant canoe, village people onshore, a shepherd staring at me from the edge of the riverbank. It's a luxury just to be alone for a while, having nothing to listen to except the sounds that come at me from the evening's quiet. I think of the Dogon idea of second birth; I imagine never being able to see the world around me in the same way again.

I return to the guesthouse. Assou finds me, asking if I'm angry with him.

I insist that I'm not. 'People aren't all the same,' I explain. 'I just need to be alone sometimes.' But I get tired of trying to explain to some people that I value privacy and

solitude as much as they value socializing. If I don't have time to myself each day, I get stir-crazy. I'll just run off, needing to escape from a place. But in countries like Mali, with strong tribal traditions, that must sound virtually incomprehensible, as family, religion and social order provide a crucial structure that sustains people and prevents discontent. Back home, being alone might be considered a kind of independence, but here it is pathology.

We reach Niry village, where the witch Yatanu lives. It sits high on a rocky plateau, a collection of low adobe dwellings mingling with tall, thatch-topped granaries. Dogon women crouch in the tiny, beehive-like menstruation huts to protect the village from the devilry of their periods. I imagine being one of them, stuck in the hot huts once a month, banished and accursed for being female. Assou instructs me to carefully follow the path that he takes, as walking arbitrarily might cause me to step on some taboo spot of ground and call forth the wrath of the spirits. Little boys gape at us: this isn't a village that ever sees tourists.

We climb up the rocky slope to the huts perched above, searching for Yatanu's. Assou has never met this woman, but he says he's heard about her: she's at least seventy years old, one of the Dogon's most powerful and feared witches. It's hard to get a consultation with her because she doesn't like most of her visitors and sends them away, but I've brought along a village officer who happens to be related to her, hoping he'll help the cause.

We stop at a mud hut, and the Dogon man walks inside.

After a short moment, Yatanu appears before us: a toothless and wizened woman, breasts lying flat against her chest, scrappy indigo sarong tied about her bony waist. She stands in the shadows of her hut, staring at me. Assou tells her that I'm here to ask for a consultation, and will she grant me one?

She steps forward into the sunlight, sits down on her haunches and studies me. I smile at her nervously, looking into her cataracted eyes. She says something in Dogon to the man I've brought along, who then translates to Assou, who translates to me: 'She likes you.'

Sighs all around. I give her a wad of money in gratitude, which makes her face erupt into a grin.

'She likes you even more,' Assou whispers.

I ask my question: 'Will I be able to get to Timbuktu?'

She puckers her lips and nods as the question is translated. She places her left arm tightly against her chest and speaks to the muscle where the beetle spirit supposedly lives. All at once, something on the biceps leaps up and hops around. I've never seen such a thing, nor has Assou – our mouths are hanging open. I lean forward to look for scars on her arm, but see nothing.

'That's too weird,' I say to Assou, an object now seeming to strain and lurch beneath the skin, as if trying to escape. It's about the size and shape of a large gobstopper, and the movements are so severe that I find myself taking a step back.

Yatanu reports her findings to me: 'You'll get to Timbuktu.'

172

Assou asks some questions of his own now, and whenever the answer is yes, the muscle leaps up and dances.

'I'll ask her if you'll ever get married,' Assou says to me, grinning.

'Don't ask her that,' I say.

'It's too late! She says you will. This man will be from your country. She says she is asking Ama for special help with this.'

I ask who Ama is, and it turns out that he is the head Dogon deity, who speaks through the beetle spirit intermediary in her arm. As most Dogon are animists, it's not surprising that they have an entire pantheon at their disposal, but Ama is the head honcho, a deity of fickle temperament who demands constant propitiation. Below him are other gods, like Lewe, god of the earth, who reveals himself as a snake, as well as Nomo, god of the water. Then there are a whole slew of lesser spirits: *yeneu* enter people and exchange body parts; evil *atywunu* live in the brush around a village and have been known to attack people. *Yeba* spirits live just outside a village as well, but are less dangerous, while the *jinu* roam throughout the countryside, ambushing unsuspecting travellers. All these spirits, in addition to the gods themselves, require such care and respect that it couldn't be an easy thing keeping yourself secure and everybody happy in the spirit world. Just to be on the safe side, many Dogon men carry around a magical horsehair switch, which they use to fend off spirits.

Yatanu says that she wants me to know a few things. The first is that she's Ama's élite messenger among mortals. She

has a close relationship with him and has personally asked him for things on my behalf: success reaching Timbuktu, help with bringing the right man to me for marriage, and general prosperity. She says that with the assistance of Ama and his helpers there is no doubt of these things happening. When one thing comes true, I must send thanks to her, which she will then send on to the gods on my behalf. It is customary that I show my gratitude for the gods' intercession by also sending her a gift – be it money or women's clothes or whatever. But the point is this: when the gods help you, you must show them your appreciation; if you don't, you will offend them and they might spoil whatever has manifested in your life.

She also wants me to know that she's doing me a favour by allowing me to see her. Such consultations cost a Dogon witch days, weeks, even months of her life. Each time she performs a divination, she loses some of her lifespan by way of payment to the spirits. Also, she's not only shown the future of her clients each time, but also her *own* future, including her death. Thus, it can be frightening to perform any divinations at all, but Yatanu knows that this is her duty in life, and so she follows the path she's been given. She declares that she's not scared of her calling.

Yatanu answers some of Assou's own questions, and he starts looking very pleased. 'She says I will make a lot of money,' he tells me with a flash of a grin, turning back to her.

I'm wondering how reliable beetle spirits are. But, not wanting to further deplete Yatanu's lifespan by more questions, I ask Assou if we can leave.

He agrees. He's looking a bit troubled now. 'I think,' he says, 'it's not good for us to speak to any more witches. We've spoken to enough.'

'You'd be right about that,' I say.

We watch the beetle spirit hopping around in Yatanu's arm.

'A lot of witches have helped us with their power,' Assou says. 'Many spirits have been called upon, you know? This is dangerous power. I think we shouldn't see any more people. And you must remember to give each witch a gift in the future, to show your appreciation when things start to happen. This is very important.'

'OK,' I say.

Yatanu goes inside her hut for a moment. She comes out with a small wooden carving and hands it to me. It looks not unlike one of the faces carved on Easter Island.

She speaks, and Assou gets the translation from the Dogon man. 'This is a good-luck charm for you,' Assou says. 'It will protect you whenever you carry it with you. It will help you on all your travels.' And now Assou laughs. 'Yatanu likes you very much. What did you do to her?'

CHAPTER NINE

IT'S TIME FOR THE JOURNEY TO CONTINUE: TIMBUKTU OR
bust. I estimate I'm about two weeks away, give or take a
day. That's roughly 350 miles left to paddle. *Jesus*, I think.
Three hundred and fifty miles. My respite in Mopti has
spoiled me, and I find myself resisting all the uncertainties
that lie ahead, clinging to the comfort and security found in
town. By now I feel qualified to make some predictions
about what will come: much hotter temperatures, hippos
galore and the difficult crossing of Lake Debo. And then,
of course, there will always be the mercurial moods of
the Niger. Something Mungo Park wrote echoes my
thoughts: 'All these circumstances crowded at once on
my recollection; and I confess that my spirits began to fail
me.' Or try to fail me, if I let them.

Rémi meets me in the hotel lobby early in the morning,
eager to take advantage of the good lighting for his
photographs. He looks well fed and in a chipper mood. For

him, today is the continuation of what has amounted to a river safari on the Niger. He insists on putting my inflated kayak in his boat, so he can shuttle me back to the town dock where there are more picturesque crowds and marketplace hustle-bustle for the background of his shots. All I want to do is *really* leave, get this trip under way again. I'm like a runner sitting in before-game limbo, nerves getting frayed. But I humour him, getting in his boat and backtracking a mile to the docks, where I put my kayak in the water. I paddle back and forth past the crowds gathering on shore. I try to look like Serious Kayaker, like Hardened Adventurer Leaving Mopti. Whatever such a person would look like. I career past the pirogues tied to the piers, waving at the kids, waving at the fruit vendors and fishermen and salt sellers, feeling like some goddamn good-will ambassador. I feel really stupid.

Rémi's pirogue circles behind me as he takes pictures with several different cameras. He calls out directions – paddle that way, paddle towards him, paddle by the crowd over there. I do it all, over and over, and at last he gets enough Mopti shots for the magazine's needs and bids me a prompt goodbye, best wishes on the Niger, and I'm not sure when or where I'll run into him again.

My five-day break in Mopti reveals itself in slower paddle strokes, my stamina not up to peak strength as when I first arrived in town, but I know this will soon change. The weather has been holding up so far, and I don't have to battle any fierce winds. But in its place are the fishermen's nets, which I hadn't counted on. Back by Old

Ségou, the river was so wide that this hadn't been a problem, but by Mopti the Niger is about a third the width, so men string their nets across nearly the whole river. They only move them for the rare river barge, meaning that I have to pass over each one I come across. Often, I can't see any net below the water and don't realize I've hit one until my kayak's rudder gets caught, yanking me back. The nets like to get caught in the rudder's screws, meaning I have to jump into the river and tread water, trying to untangle the mess. This is tedious, but my real worry is that the fishermen who own the net are going to see and get pissed off. Or – God forbid – some hippos will find me instead. I still haven't shaken my fear of them, perhaps because the fear is actually a reasonable one out here. I get things untangled as quickly as possible and jump into my boat, as if this craft of rubber and air can protect me from two-ton beasts.

I spend the morning paddling and untangling myself from nets, my progress pathetically slow. I can still see Mopti's radio tower behind me, faintly visible. When I take off the rudder, my boat flies all over the place and I can barely steer. As even the slightest breeze sends me swirling, I put it back on again. Without that rudder, I realize, I would have never been able to do this trip; Timbuktu would have remained just another mysterious name on a map.

I go more slowly, staying on the lookout for nets, pushing them down with my paddle and crossing over them, or paddling around the larger ones, even if this means crossing the entire river. This amuses the fishermen, who are

usually sitting in a canoe somewhere close to shore, watching; but as soon as a big barge starts speeding up the river, they race to pull in their nets. In this way, I pass village after village, some largely populated with adobe homes, some with a mere hut or two. The people come out to stare at me. Sometimes they're friendly and open, waving as I pass; other times they merely stand there and watch me go by, demanding I come over and give them money, or *cadeaux*. This latter reaction is relatively new. During the first part of my trip, all people really wanted was to ask me questions or yell out greetings. But north of Mopti, barges frequently tote tourists to Timbuktu, two to three days distant by motorized boat. And so I become yet another of the wealthy tourists going by.

It's nearly three o'clock, and the western sky is starting to turn dark red. Blood red. Black clouds block out the sun, giving a taste of dusk to the early afternoon. A violent wind begins churning the waters of the Niger, sending large waves and spray against me. Panicked birds shoot across the river, screeching. Herds of goats buck and stampede on shore, and all fishing canoes leave the water. It's as if Armageddon is coming. I can tell already that this storm is going to be much worse than anything I've seen yet on the Niger. Which is saying a lot. I have to get off this river – fast.

Mungo Park called these storms 'tornadoes', which was hardly an exaggeration. His second trip took place in the midst of the rainy season, and he blamed the weather for

the death of so many of his soldiers. His letters from that journey are littered with accounts of being stuck in violent deluges. At one point he wrote:

> We were overtaken by a very heavy tornado, which wet us completely. The ground all round was covered with water about three inches deep. The tornado had an instant effect on the health of the soldiers, and proved to us to be the *beginning of sorrow*. I had proudly flattered myself that we should reach the Niger with a very moderate loss. But now the rain had set in, and I trembled to think that we were only half way through our journey. The rain had not commenced three minutes before many of the soldiers were affected with vomiting, while others fell asleep as if half intoxicated.

I keep thinking about that line of Park's – 'proved to us to be the *beginning of sorrow*'. He even underscored the words. I can feel his dread, can see it now in the clouds taking over the sky. I struggle to get to shore, careful not to be caught off-guard and flipped over by one of the large waves.

The dark clouds spread across the sky, extinguishing the last patches of light. I pull in to the nearest village. There's no time to be circumspect about where I stop; I can only hope these people will be welcoming. The village is sizeable and has its own mud mosque. As there are no Fulani cattle around, the people are most likely Bozos. I think of the last Bozo village I was at, Koa, and the Osama bin Laden poster

hanging up in the middle of town, and the crowds that had to be beaten back with sticks. I've come to fear Bozo villages.

As I paddle my kayak on to shore, kids surround me, adults running to see who I am. Before long, I'm aware of something being off about this village, something not feeling right.

I ask them where I am, and the people yell, 'Wameena!'

'Where's your chief?'

They point to a nearby tree.

'Where are you going in this boat?' one man asks loudly in French.

'Timbuktu,' I tell him.

He yells this to the crowd in Bambarra, and a great uproar ensues.

'Timbuktu?' the man asks. 'Are you crazy?'

'Probably,' I say.

And now I think I understand what's strange about this place. Everyone shouts here. It's a shouting village. No-one speaks at a normal volume. I ask what people they are, and they tell me Bozo. I sigh. Pulling my kayak onshore, I hoist my backpack on to a shoulder and squeeze my way through the crowd, asking for audience with the chief.

The sky becomes a deeper, darker maroon as the wind picks up. I follow the French-speaking man to the village. Several kids pick up my kayak and carry it behind me, as if it were an additional piece of my baggage. Along the way, the crowd is so close that I'm being constantly bumped and jostled: I've become the town freak show. The kids keep up

a chant in the only French they seem to have learned: 'Donnez-moi l'argent! Donnez-moi l'argent!' Give me money! Give me money! Which tells me that this place has seen its share of tourists, probably from Mopti. One enterprising kid, a boy whose parents sent him to an Islamic boarding school in Nigeria, asks me for money in English. He also informs me that he's making himself my translator. Whether I need one or not.

I meet the chief in a small courtyard behind the village's mud mosque. He appears to be a friendly man, a trait augmented by the money I hand him as a gift. He breaks into a smile and immediately deposits my backpack and kayak in one of the rooms of his large adobe house. He urges the crowd to leave me alone – which they do, for the most part, people backing away. No-one leaves the courtyard, though, which by now doesn't surprise me.

One of the chief's wives comes over and asks me, shouting, if I'd like dinner tonight and if rice would suffice. I still can't get over how everyone shouts here. I've been to my share of villages around the world – ones deep in the jungles of Borneo and New Guinea, ones hidden in the rice paddies of Bangladesh – and this is the first time I've experienced such a phenomenon. I thank her, giving her some money. Outside the courtyard, the coming storm has started ripping and tearing across the countryside, threshing the manes of donkeys and sending clouds of dust into our faces. The red clouds slowly engulf the village, and people lose their curiosity about me, staring up fearfully at the sky.

The rain comes all at once, hard, like a punishment. The drops flail our skin, and everyone runs into the nearest hut – everyone but me. I want to see this storm. I leave the courtyard for an open field beside the village. For once, no crowd is around me and no-one approaches. The storm has granted me a reprieve from the stares, at the price of a wind that nearly knocks me over. I guard my eyes from the moving vortexes of dust, which swirl and twist through the passageways of the village like genies come to life.

The Niger flows backwards, large whitecaps assailing the shore, causing the tied-up canoes to strike each other with loud, hollow thumps. I've never seen a storm as bad as this one – not even back home, growing up in the Midwest. The rain stings my skin, soaking my already river-dampened clothes. Thunder doesn't offer the occasional boom, but consumes the entire sky with noise, so that the earth quakes and vibrates with apocalyptic vengeance.

'Hoo-eee!' I yell into the might of it all. There's something about the power of this storm, the magnificence of it, that fills me. Nothing bothers me any more. Nothing scares me. It's just me and the world, meeting head-on. 'Hey, Mun-go!' I yell. 'Mun-go Park!'

The village people stare out of their huts at me. I let the violent winds hold me up and twirl me around. They try to tear my skirt and shirt from me, try to knock me down. The people point across the river to a particularly bad wind that's tearing up soil and spraying it into the Niger. The violent wind hits trees nearby, trying to pull off branches. It whips my hair about my face

183

and knocks me to my knees. I wait. I don't feel any fear, only curiosity. I wonder what's going to happen next.

After several minutes, the storm loses strength and releases me from the grip of its winds. I feel as if I've been returned to earth. I walk back to one of the huts, passing a man squatting silently in a corner of the courtyard, his clothes soaked from the rain. The boy who has commissioned himself as my translator comes forward to explain that this man is 'stupid and crazy' – the village out-cast. I look at him again: he sits as if in his own world, his expression peaceful though the world around him just threatened to blow him away. As the storm renews its strength, the chief runs out to pull the crazy man into shelter, putting him beside me. I glance at him, envious of his unperturbed face. We all wait and watch. For calamity? For death? No-one is speaking. Even for the people of Wameena, who have lived here all their lives, this is a bad storm.

At last, the storm discharges its fury to the east of us, taking the bloody skies with it. The adobe homes have lost a great part of their walls, clay trickling away in the streams of water that escape from the courtyards. The women immediately get to work, bringing out large pails of dry river clay and patching the parts of their homes that have fallen in. The chief smiles benignly at me and shrugs. Just another storm. The children start begging for money from me again, the surest sign that normality has returned.

While the chief's wives cook dinner for his large, extended family, I sit in a chair in the courtyard and look

around. I feel changes taking place in me, yet it's hard for me to pinpoint how or what. My thoughts are a jumble in my head, and I still feel electrified by the strength of the storm. I think of how I struggled for hours today to untangle my boat from the fishnets. I keep wanting everything to go *my* way on this trip, without delays or mishaps or defeats. But when I stood in the storm just now, an extraordinary thing occurred: all fear left me and, with it, all demands for the way things should be. I stood there as the earth fired out everything, the worst it had. And to my great surprise, the show ended. It passed.

There are times when I'm travelling when I forget that things pass, and then the so-called benefits of an experience elude me and I can think only of the difficulties. I find it hard to appreciate anything with the sweat running off my face and burning my eyes, the sun's heat scorching my skin, my body aching from holding the paddle. What room for 'experience' when there is only a wish to get to the next place faster, so that the end might be nearer?

I stare at the Mali I see around me – the chickens pecking at wet clay, naked children walking through mud puddles. The goats on the riverbanks look at me accusingly, as if I had somehow caused the storm. A crowd gathers near by to stare at me, the kids asking me for money in incessant whispers. There are just too many of them to give money to. And beyond that, what would I be teaching them? Only the same lessons the other tourists have: that white people represent money and nothing more. Maybe it's foolish, wishful thinking that I want to be more to the

people I meet. It seems crucial that I become more, that we understand each other, know the commonality of our existence, know how we can help one another. But here in Wameena we have only a single night together, and the women are busy patching houses and cooking, and the men are discussing plans, language difficulties separating us more easily than continents ever can, and with much more finality. So here, too, is something I should probably learn to accept.

I offer to help the women repair their houses, but they laugh and wave me away, so I sit down to write. Sometimes when I travel I'll remember what I left behind in the States, those things I used to think about all the time, as if they deserved the full weight attributed to them by my mind. (The children are surrounding me, watching the cryptic scribbles coming from my pen. The boy with the English is demanding I go to the local market and buy him a camera. A *camera*, he insists.) I think of all sorts of things. The journey does this. The moment I take a rest, it steps in to remind me of where I've been, not just where I'm going. Inevitably, I think of the past relationships of my life, wondering what happens to the feelings that people have for each other. And why does lost love feel like a kind of death? But what place for such thoughts *here, now*, in Wameena village, among the chattering kids demanding money, and the yelling adults? Those times feel as evanescent as the storm that came and passed on the Niger this afternoon. In a moment my mind forgets them for other things. Like the sight of the village women repairing

their adobe houses. Like the crazy man, who once more crouches outside, looking for the storm that left him behind. I see the clay caked to my sandals, the damp shirt I wear, the rooster that has mistaken dusk for dawn and crows into the coming night.

I eat dinner with the chief's wives, alternating between slapping mosquitoes and bringing handfuls of rice to my mouth. People in Mali traditionally eat with their fingers, so they always rinse their hands in a bowl of water before they start. The right hand is used for putting food in the mouth; the left, meant for sanitary cleaning only, is kept at one's side. There is no use of toilet paper whatsoever, so the indispensable left hand and a jug of water must fulfil all hygienic purposes. Being a lefty, I frequently forget which hand is for what when I eat, shocking hosts and causing a ruckus at nearly every village I've been to.

I listen to the women chatting – or I should say shouting – to each other in Bambarra. While we eat, a TV man arrives from upriver. He brings with him a large colour TV, an antenna and a portable gas generator, setting these things up on a table in the middle of the chief's courtyard. It is technology and modernity come to Wameena for a rare evening's entertainment, and the entire town packs in to watch the show. I sit in the midst of the throng, my expectations as high as everyone else's, the excitement among us palpable.

It is a long wait, as the equipment must be set up and made to run, and it's an old, unruly TV. At last the set is

turned on. We lean forward to try to discern shapes from the fuzzy images, while the TV man makes a final, impressive adjustment that brings colour and sound all at once, leaping out of the set into the starlit village.

No movies come on. No Bruce Lee or Rambo taking on the world. Here in Wameena, we watch nothing but Malian commercials and public health service announcements. There are advertisements for luxury hotels in Bamako, showing large swimming pools with turquoise waters, smiling attendants, contented white customers in suits and ties. Cameras pan over banquets, where Malian businessmen toast each other and gleeful families skip across posh halls.

The little naked children around me watch this, mouths ajar, eyes transfixed on images that must be utterly foreign and fantastical to them. They see shots of white women with blond hair, not unlike mine, wearing pretty dresses, high heels, gold jewellery. They see impressive luxury cars pulling up before the chandeliered hallways, emitting Malian families on holiday.

At last the commercials give way – not to a movie, though, but to a Malian woman demonstrating how to wash one's hands. She speaks in French, urging viewers to prevent the spread of infectious disease, holding up a bar of soap before vigorously washing her hands under a village pump. The people around me watch this with the same rapt attention they gave to the commercials. Movies, if there are any, don't come, but I see that just having the TV is the point. Having the images to watch, the scenes to

marvel over. Unlike me, everyone appears absolutely content with whatever comes.

I see Rémi's boat parked along a barren shore, near the ruin of an adobe house. He stands and waves to me, and I paddle over to him. He and Heather rest on cushioned benches under the shade of the boat's canopy, their cook preparing dinner for everyone. He tells me they've had fish for the past two meals, and so they stopped at every village along the river, trying to buy some chickens. But to no avail – no-one has chickens to sell.

I try to commiserate. I offer him a shake of the head.

'This is a French boat,' Rémi says. 'You see? The cuisine is very important.'

I laugh. 'I've noticed.'

I feel culture shock every time I come across Rémi's boat. Just his talk about the day's menu. And then everyone inside looks so *clean*. They wear dry clothes, drink from bottles of mineral water. I glance at my own sweaty clothes, my mud-smeared bottles of filtered water tasting of iodine tablets.

As if reading my mind, Rémi offers me a bottle of water and invites me inside to rest. I try to find a way to climb in without getting their things wet or sullying their boat cushions. My sandals are hopelessly covered with river clay, my clothes are soaked with the river water that I splash on myself to try to cool off, and with all my sweating I don't smell like daisies these days. It's strange to suddenly care about cleanliness and propriety, as being muddy and sweaty

and wet have become such a part of this trip that anything otherwise would feel abnormal.

I take my sandals off and lie down on a bench in his boat, closing my eyes. It's the first time all day that I've had the sun off me, and for a moment I forget what world I'm in. With the mineral water, sizzling fish and French fries (with ketchup, no less, or mayonnaise if I prefer) awaiting everyone for dinner, I can't be entirely sure *where* I am. All I do know is that if I can manage to stick around long enough for dinner, there's a good chance they'll feed me.

Rémi asks me if I'd like a Coke or a Fanta. He has Orange Fanta or Apple Fanta. But there is also beer.

'You have Fanta?' I can't believe it.

He points to a large clay pot, which is filled with cold water to keep the bottles inside cool. 'Orange or apple?'

'Uh, orange,' I say. The order is sent back to the cook, and sure enough, a cold bottle of honest-to-God Orange Fanta appears from the giant clay pot and is handed to me.

It turns out that this boat is fully stocked with Coke, Fanta, beer and bottled water, so that finding Rémi feels like coming upon a kind of mini-bar in the middle of the South Sahara.

Rémi explains his plan to me. He'd like to take some 'bivouac' shots of me – Kira by Her Tent, Kira Writing in Her Journal by the River, et cetera. And, hopefully, if the weather turns bad, he can also get Kira Plaintively Surveying the River. He's chosen this spot because he likes the adobe ruin nearby. He was thinking, if I wouldn't mind, of having me set up my tent next to it.

I study the ruin. It's very poetic, in a grim sort of way. 'Bleak,' I say. And it occurs to me that such an adjective wouldn't be far off when it comes to describing parts of my trip. Bleak. Yes. Kira Enjoying a Bleak Trip.

Rémi smiles. I shrug. What the hell. I know that there are certain types of shots he must get of me, a kind of checklist. Gear shots. Tent shots. Paddling shots. Native-interaction shots. And now, bleak shots.

We wait until the sun is starting to set and the good lighting arrives, and I go on shore to set up my 'bivouac'. I put up my tent smack next to the ruin and hang my wet clothes on its sides to dry. At Rémi's request, I carry my kayak from where it's docked in the river and put it along-side my tent, laying it out in such a way that it looks photogenic to him. He asks me to take out my map of Mali, so now I become Kira Intently Studying Her Map. A local girl finds us, and Rémi gives her some candy and sweet-talks her into holding my kayak paddle. He's got a way with the kids out here, could rival Mr Rogers, and pretty soon he's got the terror-stricken girl holding my paddle and smiling feebly at the strange *tubab* with all the cameras. I sit near her in various poses, as per Rémi's instructions, and try to look Adventurous.

At last, he announces that he 'has the shots' and declares an end to the photo shoot. He pretends to find a hidden piece of candy in his shirt pocket and produces it for the girl as a parting present. I quickly make my escape, to write. Writing in my journal is the one thing I always enjoy on my trips, the one thing I count on for rest and comfort. I

wander along the shore, the mud bank rising some ten feet from the water so that I have a special vantage point from which to watch the sun set over the river. I find a little nook in the bank, out of sight of the others in the boat and the fields behind me, and insert myself inside. I sigh and shut my eyes. Even at six o'clock, the sun is hot and scalding. I pull my hat low on my head and lean back. My journal rests in my lap, but I don't write yet. I just want to breathe in the peace for a while.

I think about today. What of it? Just a lot of paddling. Virtually non-stop. Nine hours' worth of paddling. And the heat, as usual. And the aching of my arms and hands. And the feeling of foolishness that I ever decided to do such a trip, and also the gratitude for all I've seen and learned. But mostly the exhaustion. Rémi told me he's photographed other people who have taken similarly 'physically challenging' trips, and he's wondered if such people lose sight of the beauty around them. It had struck me as a retaliation of sorts, as if I had just pointed out to him the relaxing way he's decided to do his own trip on the Niger. I admitted that, yes, at times I forget to see the beauty for all my sweating and paddling and exhaustion. What I did not say was that beauty doesn't forget me, that it intrudes even in the midst of my slow, often tedious way of travel. It surprises me in clouds of birds shooting across an early-morning sky outside Mopti. Or shows up in the white butterflies struggling across the Niger, beating fragile wings. Or in all these evenings spent in thatch-hut villages, the nights dazing me with stars. It is beauty

enough for me. Too much beauty, at times, so that I must shut my eyes to it all.

I hear a familiar clicking sound: Rémi's camera. He's found me with his enormous telephoto lens, and he crouches discreetly at some distance away, capturing the closest thing he's had yet to a Real Me. Perhaps he realizes that I'm not trying to be anything for anyone now, which has otherwise been my biggest chore in life, bigger than paddling a river six hundred miles, certainly, or doing anything else. When I give up the burden of trying to please others — a number one priority for my life these days — I become someone who secretes herself away from the world, revelling in anonymity.

CHAPTER TEN

I CAMPED WITH RÉMI LAST NIGHT, AND NOW HE CONTINUES up the river, leaving me with instructions to meet him at a village called Barga. The village lies at the place where the Niger enters giant Lake Debo, a convenient spot for him to get pictures of me crossing the lake. I've been dreading this crossing, just as Park must have dreaded it centuries before. In many ways it is the most treacherous part of the journey, as it takes an entire day to cross, and is so large that it's like travelling over an inland sea. Getting lost in the middle of it is a major concern. And then if a storm should catch me, overturning and separating me from my boat, the nearest land would be many miles in any direction, and there's a chance I could drown.

In the hopes of alleviating this possibility, the captain of Rémi's boat has urged me to follow their route across the lake. Without such guidance, I could literally get dis-orientated in the vast waters, having no sense of where the

Niger begins again. It's a warning I take seriously, and so I agreed to meet them at Barga, spend the night there and then proceed across the lake in their wake.

Given this plan, today's travel sounds delightfully straightforward and easy: I keep going until I reach Barga, a mere four to six hours of paddling away (according to Rémi's captain), and then I spend the remainder of the day resting at the village and preparing myself for the all-day crossing of Debo the following morning.

I love when things are straightforward and easy. Still, I know the Niger hates plans, and so I'm apprehensive of what sounds too good to be true. But I paddle along with my spirits raised: Lake Debo, no more than six hours away. Rain comes – inevitably – soaking me and my things, but it's a timid storm with no wind. I like these kinds of storms the most, as clouds block out the intense heat of the sun and the rain cools me off. The air has a gentle smell of verdant fields, heavy raindrops hitting the placid spread of water and sending out circular ripples.

Gradually the storm passes and the sun starts to re-appear, its reflection on the water blinding me. The heat returns, my thermometer reading 96 degrees and climbing. I paddle with barely a pause. Noon comes. Goes. And now one o'clock. Two. Three. No sight of an end to this river. No Lake Debo. No Barga.

I've been paddling for over six hours now, and the river narrows to only fifty feet across – the narrowest it's been to date – but it doesn't seem to be going towards anything resembling an enormous lake. I put my hopes on each new

bend in the river, assuring myself that I'll see Lake Debo finally. But the lake remains elusive, and I can see why Mungo Park was told that the Niger flows 'to the end of the world'.

I feel a clutch of panic when my watch reads four o'clock. I keep looking for Rémi's boat in the distance. Surely he knows that something is wrong by now. But my anxiety is no good, it gets in the way, so I decide upon a new paddling strategy: I will simply accept my predicament. This works for a total of about fifteen glorious minutes, during which time I stop paddling to rest and eat a Snickers (my first meal since this morning), letting the speedy current carry me along. Mud banks rise high on either side, preventing any view of the surrounding countryside and creating a claustrophobic feel to my journey that I've not experienced before. But with my new strategy of being with what is, I just float along and rest my feet on the sides of my kayak, basking in the sun.

Up ahead, a man squats on the top of the bank, watching me. With the river so narrow, I can't avoid people even if I want to. I'm within earshot and eyeshot of everyone. As I float past, he stands and starts yelling at me, ordering me to come to him. I do the opposite: I paddle away. I feel like some child caught in the midst of a forbidden act, yet I have no idea what it is I've done. He runs after me along the top of the bank, shouting violently. No-one owns the Niger; there aren't tariffs to pay for passing on it. (At least *that* much has changed since Mungo Park's time.) I can't think of a single reason why this man would be so fiercely angry

at me, and I'm starting to get so curious about it that I slow down for a minute, let the panting man catch up.

He stops and yells out in broken French: 'Give me five thousand francs!' Which is the equivalent of about a week's wages for your average Malian. And while I believe in charity, I don't believe in paying off yelling lunatics. He's literally jumping up and down now, repeating his demand and waving his hands. I find myself in a precarious position: I'm a woman travelling alone on a stretch of river where there's absolutely no-one around except some pissed-off guy trying to extort money from me. And what if I don't pay him? Will he come after me? Will he send runners to wait for me up ahead and ambush me on the river? Such things are possible – probably more possible than I think.

I decide to ignore the man and paddle as hard as I can. He runs after me for a while but finally gives up. So much for my fifteen minutes of in-the-moment bliss. The fear is back, sitting like a bad meal in my gut. Every time the river curves, I look ahead for sight of men lying in wait for me in canoes, the river getting more and more narrow. I realize, but without surprise, that I've lived with constant fear on this trip. Fear of being chased, assaulted, robbed. Fear of bad weather and waves that might capsize my boat. Lots of fear. Fear of the wind, of harsh storms. Fear of hippos, crocodiles. Fear of being harassed by young men in passing boats, or of having my things stolen if I stop at villages. Endless fear. Fear of getting lost. Fear of not being able to find anyone if I do. All kinds of fear. My God. There's a

large part of me that can't accept that a trip of mine isn't what you'd call 'relaxing'. There ought to be *some*thing, my mind reasons, that rises above all this unpleasantness.

The Niger forks abruptly. One branch heads north-east, the other west. A village of thatch and adobe huts sits at this juncture, and as my map of Mali is inaccurate and all but worthless, I consider going there to try to ask which route will get me to Lake Debo. The village people have noticed me, and they line up on the top of the riverbank to scream at me. No-one responds to my greetings in Bambarra; they just holler and wave their arms, insisting that I paddle over to them and give them money. I wonder what it is about this stretch of the Niger. Why are folks so friendly and warm down by Ségou and so aggressive up here? What accounts for the change?

Park's guide, Amadi Fatouma, the sole survivor of his final journey, mentioned that their expedition encountered serious problems in the region of Lake Debo, then called 'Sibby'. Fatouma wrote: 'In passing Sibby, three canoes came after us, armed with pikes, lances, bows and arrows, etc., but no firearms. Being sure of their hostile intentions, we ordered them to go back, but to no effect; and were obliged to repulse them by force.' I have nothing with which to repulse anyone, except for some police-quality mace that I smuggled on to the plane from home. It's said to be effective on everything from human beings to grizzly bears, but I'm hoping I won't have to discover its real efficacy first-hand.

As my map is no help, I decide to simply pick a direction.

I have a fifty-fifty chance of screwing up, which isn't the worst odds I've ever faced. I choose west. The people in the village scream at me as I go by, and they don't stop screaming until I make it around a bend. Incredibly, the Niger, once a mile wide by Ségou, is now barely thirty feet across. I see no sign of civilization, which stumps me. If there's a big lake ahead, and a village called Barga, there must be other villages too. And certainly there must be canoes or boats heading to those villages — which is the strangest, most unsettling aspect of this entire experience. *Where are the boats?*

None of it makes sense, and as the sun is now setting, I'm starting to panic. The villages — what few there are in these parts — all seem to be hostile. I contemplate camping alone on the top of one of these mud banks, in full view of anyone who wants money or anything else from me. And if I can manage to make it safely through the night, I'll still have no way of knowing if I'm heading towards Lake Debo in the morning.

I try to think about my predicament as reasonably as I can. It seems that the best thing to do would be to stop and ask someone where Lake Debo and Barga are. But I have to be careful who I ask. I paddle along, hoping to run into someone who might be willing to assist me. And now I hear the distant sound of women's voices floating down from the riverbank.

I try to find a place to pull over. I see a fissure in the high clay bank and manage to lodge my kayak in it. Pulling and clawing my way up the muddy slope to the ground above,

I see before me a vast green expanse, a floodplain, which surely proves the presence of a nearby lake. Yet I can't see the lake. In the distance are two small thatch huts, a couple of women standing before them and chattering to each other.

I wipe the mud from my arms, straighten my hat on my head and walk towards them. They keep chattering away, not seeing me. One woman, unclothed from the waist up, perfectly round breasts exposed, pounds millet in a stone mortar. Her friend sits near by, nursing a baby in her lap. A young girl, entirely naked but for a gold band in each ear, spots me before the adults do and lets out a cry that could signal the end of the world.

'*Tu-bab! Tuuuu-bāaaab!*'

The women look up, astounded by the sight of me. They stop what they're doing, tattooed mouths hanging open. I might be some kind of apparition, come back from the dead. They look petrified with fear and wonder.

The little girl is still screaming and crying in terror: '*Tuubaab! Tuuu-baaab!*'

I smile and greet the women in my best Bambarra. 'Hello,' I say. 'How is your family?'

They don't move.

'*Barga be mi?*' I ask. Where's Barga?

The woman nursing the baby bursts out laughing and repeats what I said, her eyes linked to mine.

I ask it again – 'Where's Barga?'

She repeats my words again, saying them exactly as I had, imitating the poor pronunciation. The woman

200

holding the pestle looks at me wild-eyed now, and violently slams it into the mortar. Again and again, she slams it down. Her large biceps quiver.

I consult my meagre list of Bambarra words and phrases, written on the back of my notebook.

'What is the name of this village?' I ask, as clearly as possible.

'*Tuu-bab! Tuuuuu-bab!*' the little girl wails.

The nursing woman repeats what I say, laughing. I seem to be getting nowhere with them, though I can't figure out why. Surely they still speak Bambarra in these parts.

'Where's Lake Debo?' I try.

'Ai-eee!' the woman with the pestle yells, slamming it down with a head-crushing *whomp*.

'Is Lake Debo over there?' I ask.

'Ai-eee!' she screams.

'Uh,' I say. 'Well, it was nice meeting you all.'

I turn around and quickly head back to the river, the woman still slamming her pestle down with ferocious zeal. 'Ai-eee!' she calls after me. 'Ai-eee!'

I wonder if this day can get any worse. I slide down the mud slope and free my kayak's rudder from where it's stuck in the clay. Getting inside, I start to paddle off. Just as the strong current takes hold of me, the two women call after me. They're standing on the top of the bank now. I crane my neck to hear what they're saying. Directions to Barga? Information about Lake Debo?

Then I hear them: '*Tubab – argent!*' White person – money!

*

I've been paddling for nearly nine hours now, virtually non-stop, for a destination that should have arrived hours earlier. I still have no idea if I'm going in the right direction to meet up with Rémi. Only the fast current is encouraging, helping me travel quickly for the first time during my trip.

The river curves and bends, and I see it broadening up ahead. A village! Many villages, all in a row, up and down the shore on both sides. Could the elusive Barga be one of them? But I don't see Rémi's boat parked anywhere. And there's no lake.

As I paddle past the shore, scores of people come running from thatch huts to watch me go by.

'Where's Barga?' I ask them in Bambarra and French.

No-one seems to know what I'm talking about. They just stare and assail me with the ubiquitous calls for money. I look for men on shore, repeating my question to them as they're likely to be the educated ones and might know some French beyond the words for 'money' and 'give me'. I ask every man I meet where Barga and Lake Debo are, but they shake their heads.

I slow down by one village, where a young man entreats me to repeat my question. There's something reassuring about his eyes, his demeanour, and he has excellent French. I ignore my fear of stopping at these villages and pull over.

He tells me his name is Aboka, though he prefers being called 'Le Boss'. From the cows grazing all around him, I assume he's Fulani. He scolds a crowd of kids nearby, telling them to be quiet and leave me alone so he can

hear me. When he learns that I'm American, he smiles broadly.

'I study English in Bamako,' he says. 'Peace Corps teach me.'

I'm thinking, *Thank God for the Peace Corps*.

'I need to find Barga,' I say slowly, enunciating the words.

'Barga? Yes. Over there.' He points down the river, to where it branches again. He points to the branch going to the left. 'Barga is at the end.'

I ask him where the lake is, and he assures me that I'm very close, that Barga is on a small island where the river ends and the lake begins.

The sun sits on the horizon now, dropping behind evening mists. Time always seems to pass most speedily at the very end of the day, the sun scampering for cover. I thank Le Boss and leave him, paddling quickly down the left river channel, which is only an incredible twenty feet across, the current refreshingly fast and doing most of the work. At last, after coming round a small bend, I face the giant Lake Debo. It's like coming upon a vast ocean. All I see is water on all sides – water that reaches to the very end of the wide horizon before me – smack in the middle of the South Sahara. I can hardly believe it.

And Barga now, directly ahead. The teeming village of round, squat thatch huts rests on a narrow island at the mouth of the Niger.

I start making my way over, and people catch sight of me. In a matter of moments, the village is in an uproar. An

enormous crowd collects onshore, watching, gesturing to me, demanding money. I don't see Rémi's boat anywhere, although it is so large it's usually hard to miss. I search the lake for sight of him, but I see no-one. He should have arrived here many hours ago. I pull up to the island and dig my paddle into the mud to hold my kayak steady. Before I can do anything, the crowd descends upon me, trying to pull my backpack and dry bags from the kayak. The crowd is so thick that I can't move. Hands pull and clutch at my clothes, my body. Everything I own, including myself, is up for grabs.

'Whoa!' I yell. 'Back off!'

The people are momentarily startled. I raise my paddle and grab back my bags. I can feel the adrenalin coursing through me.

Someone suddenly steps forward with a large stick and threatens the crowd with it. This man speaks some French, and I ask him if he's seen a Frenchman in a large *pinasse*.

'No,' he says. 'I don't see them. But you must ask the chief.'

I don't want to ask the chief, not if it means getting out of the boat and leaving my stuff here, unguarded. When I tell him that, he calls over his friend, a man with ripped T-shirt and muddy pants, and orders him to fend off the onlookers while I'm gone. This man nods and steps into the water, hovering over my kayak. He swings a large stick menacingly at anyone who comes near.

'Lovely,' I say, watching this.

I can relate to poor Mungo Park on his final journey: he

absolutely refused to stop anywhere or get out of the boat. And here I am onshore, breaking Park's cardinal rule. The crowd is close against me again, barely allowing me to move. A zillion hands pinch, squeeze, poke me from all sides as I follow the guy with the French. I'm so exhausted from paddling all day with very little in my stomach, am so on edge from the crowd all around me and the futile search for Rémi, that I feel on the verge of losing whatever is left of my patience and sanity. I feel hot-wired, about to blow.

The current of the crowd carries me to the middle of the village. Thatch huts overrun all available space on the tiny island, the muddy, trampled ground showing no patches of green. The air holds an omnipresent smell of human urine and animal dung. The crowd stops me before a large thatch hut, and a man comes out to greet me. He's older, his hair showing traces of grey. He smiles at me in a strange, almost lascivious sort of way. When he shakes my hand, he won't let go of it, so that I'm forced to pull my fingers from his.

I greet him in Bambarra and get straight to the point, wanting to return to my kayak as soon as possible. I ask him if he's seen two *tubab* in a large boat. A man and a woman. The man is French, his name is Rémi. The woman, Heather, is an American.

'Where are you from?' the man asks, as if he never heard my question.

'The US,' I say. 'Have you seen this Frenchman?'

'You are from America? What is your name?'

I tell him. I tell him my first and last names. At his insistence, I pull out my notebook and write it out for him.

'Ki-ra,' he says, reading the letters.

'Yeah.' I ask him again if he's seen Rémi.

'Are you married?' he replies.

I can feel my patience fizzling. 'Please.' I entreat him with my eyes. 'Will you tell me if you've seen these two people?' Which shouldn't be hard to answer – they're probably the only white people to have set foot in Barga in the last *year*.

'What are their names?'

Though I have already given him their names, I give them to him again. He asks me to write them down for him, so I do. I write down 'Rémi' and 'Heather' in big letters. He needs help pronouncing Heather's name, and it takes him several tries to say it correctly. I feel like a TEFL instructor.

'Do you have a boyfriend?' he asks.

I sigh. I scan the shore of the island, looking for Rémi's big boat, seeing nothing.

The chief repeats Heather's name a couple of times again, then looks up at me. 'I haven't seen them,' he announces.

'All righty,' I say. 'Thank you.' I turn around and head back to my kayak, pushing through the current of bodies as if wading upstream.

'*Madame! Madame!*' The chief chases after me and grabs my arm. He looks excited.

'Yes?'

'Money, *madame*.' He smiles and shrugs.

I fish into my pocket and pull out a bill, dropping it into his palm.

Other men in the crowd rush forward. '*L'argent, madame! Madame! Madame! L'argent!*' They press against me, holding on to my arms.

I was afraid of this, that the minute I went passing out money the crowd would go nuts. But I, too, am going nuts. I know that nothing can hold back my temper now. I know that in a matter of moments I'm going to be completely out of control. I try to escape to my boat, but the hands still hold me back. All at once, I lose it. My elbows fly out and my arms are swinging against the hands that hold me. People step away, alarmed, and I break through the crowd, pushing aside bodies, my steps not faltering for anyone.

'*Pardon!! Pardon!!*' I yell out, flying through the crowd. Startled people back up, allowing me passage to my boat.

The man with the torn T-shirt and large stick is still there, fending off the crowd. I give him some money for his assistance, and he smiles, touches the bills to his forehead and waves his club with renewed vigour. Everything about this scene is absolutely surreal. I glance to see if my things are where I left them in the kayak, then I press them down, securing them. Picking up my paddle, I pull my boat into the water and get in. The crowd makes one final grab for the kayak, and my protector jumps forward, grimacing at the people and yelling until they let go. I paddle off quickly into the dusk, travelling against the current and back up the Niger, the crowd shouting after me.

I head to Le Boss's Fulani village, figuring it's my best bet for security tonight. The current is so strong that I crawl up the river, inch by inch. I wouldn't be able to do

such strenuous paddling were it not for all the wild energy that still rushes out of me. I paddle furiously, wondering where Rémi is. Does he know how hard it is to locate him when I'm paddling alone in a kayak in the middle of West Africa, people freaking out on me? The hell with the pictures he wants of me crossing Lake Debo. The hell with all that bullshit. I'll just hire some local person to show me the route across the lake tomorrow.

I finally reach Le Boss's village, called Guro. I pull my kayak on to the bank, my clothes drenched with sweat, my body shaking. Le Boss comes to the bank and greets me. He says he's glad I came back, and he encourages me to eat dinner with his parents and spend the night here. I thank him, amazed by the difference between villages barely a mile apart: Barga's madness compared to Guro's blessed sanity. I've no sooner tied up my kayak than Le Boss hands me a calabash full of warm, foaming, freshly drawn cow's milk.

'Please, just sit for a moment,' he says to me, concern in his eyes. 'Drink and rest, OK?'

I do as he tells me. I sit down on the riverbank and drink the cow's milk. No crowds surround me in this village. No-one asks for money. Le Boss brings some of his younger brothers over to help unload my backpack and dry bags from the kayak, then the boys return to carry the kayak itself into the village. I sit with my knees up, head resting on them, observing my quivering hands. I feel the familiar up and down movements of river waves, as if I were still paddling on the Niger. I shudder at the thought of passing Barga again tomorrow.

I finish the milk, and Le Boss leads me to the village. Cows graze between the thatch huts, staring at me like sentinels as I pass. I go to meet his parents. His ageing father, Hamaduna Ba, sits regally on a mat in a blue *grand bubu* shirt, inviting me to take a seat beside him. He's married to three wives, who busily prepare a meal for all of us. I give Hamaduna some money as a gift and thank him for his hospitality. He shakes his head deferentially.

'It is my pleasure,' he says in perfect French. 'Perhaps you'd like to change into dry clothes?'

'Yes,' I say.

He has a son carry my backpack into his thatch hut, and Hamaduna himself pulls a mat over the door to give me privacy. It smells warm and soft inside, like dry hay, the family's few possessions – clothes, a storage chest, a stool – lined up neatly against the far side of the dwelling. I shed my wet clothes, enjoying the luxury of putting dry cloth over my skin.

Hamaduna waits for me outside with special Malian tea prepared, and I join him on the mat again. It's a thick mint tea, syrupy and sweet. As per the Malian custom, I completely finish my glass and pass it along to Le Boss to drink from. Together we watch the sun go down, night settling around us. Hamaduna tells me that he recently went to Paris for his fiftieth birthday. He and his first wife stayed in a fancy hotel and drank Bordeaux and rode the Métro. I try to imagine this man beside me, sitting before a hut made from woven thatch, cows gathered all around him like minions, riding the Paris subway. But Hamaduna is a

wealthy man by Malian standards; he tells me his cows are worth about $380 apiece. And he has a herd of nearly a hundred, with an additional twenty-five calves.

'Do you eat chicken?' he asks me.

I tell him I do, so Hamaduna sends the kids running after some birds.

Hamaduna asks what brings me here. When I explain that I was supposed to meet some friends at Barga who never showed up, he asks for further details – how many people, what kind of boat – and then passes on the information to a couple of his sons. The boys leave in canoes, going to the different villages in the area to ask if anyone has seen Rémi. I'm dazed by Hamaduna's generosity and assistance. It is as Park discovered two hundred years before: no two villages in Mali are alike and nothing is predictable.

While I am talking to Hamaduna and Le Boss, one of Hamaduna's sons runs over to tell me he's seen Rémi's boat on the river nearby. The captain of the boat is shining a spotlight in the darkness, trying to find me. I go to the shore, and sure enough, there's Rémi's boat. He's calling out to me.

I wonder what happened. Did he take another branch of the Niger? Did he encounter trouble somewhere? Was he searching for me on Lake Debo?

I call to him, and he stands on the side of the boat to greet me. The barge brushes up against the shore, stopping, and he jumps on to the ground.

'Hello!' he says.

'I was at Barga, asking around, but I didn't see you,' I say in a rush. 'The people said you never came. I didn't know what to do.'

'I was on that hill. You see? Over there.' He points to the east, to a distant, high hill, its top outlined in the moonlight. 'Kira, it was so beautiful. I climbed the hill and I was taking pictures from the top. Ah, it was incredible! The sun was setting. It was perfect.' He sputters his lips and shakes his head. '*Parfait.*'

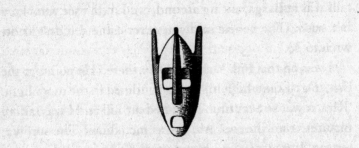

CHAPTER ELEVEN

LAKE DEBO TODAY. THE WEATHER WILL MEAN EVERYTHING. I wake up early and lie in my tent, nervous about the crossing. The sun hasn't risen yet and it's grey out, so I can't tell if a storm is coming. Even if there isn't one now, one could come later in the day. Hamaduna told me that if a storm hits while I'm in the middle of Lake Debo, the waves can be dangerously large. I remember seeing the lake last night: just a sheet of water as far as the eye can see. No land, nothing until I get to the other side. Half the challenge of crossing Debo lies in the fact that I must complete the journey in a single day; there can be no stopping if I get tired, no dallying.

The cows of Guro gather around my tent, chewing on grass and staring at me. I sit up, my whole body aching as if I'd spent all of yesterday climbing up a mountain. *Up a river*, I think. I get out of the tent and take it down. Guro would be quiet were it not for the roosters' head-splitting

calls. I'll need to wait for Rémi to get up. I walk over to a calf tied to a post and scratch its neck. It stretches out its forelegs like a dog and wags its tail, letting out satisfied *humphs*. To the west, across a green flood plain, I can see Lake Debo covered with morning mists.

I wonder what troubles Park had when he crossed it. According to Fatouma, the group was attacked on the lake, but nothing more is known. Still, Park made it across somehow, and the thought of his success renews my feeling of determination.

Le Boss emerges from a nearby hut and waves to me.

'Kira,' he yells, looking at me petting the calf, 'you can buy that cow and take it back to America with you!'

'It'd be hard to get on the plane.'

'I'll sell it to you for cheap.'

'I don't think the National Geographic Society would pay for it.'

Rémi and Heather are getting out of their tent near by. They head on to the boat for some Earl Grey and rich tea biscuits, their Malian cook coming over to take down their tent. The roosters are finally shutting up, strutting between the huts and jerking their heads. I carry my backpack to the shore and secure it inside my kayak, being careful about weight distribution. If the weight is even slightly greater on one side, my kayak's nose will veer off in that direction — not unlike a car with poor wheel alignment. What this means in terms of a full day of paddling is that one arm will have to work harder than the other to keep the kayak straight.

I sit on the shore, eating a Snickers for breakfast. Seeing this, Rémi comes over to invite me to breakfast in his boat, and I walk the gangplank to join them. Forgetting my manners, I heap sugar and cream into my cup of tea, wanting to get as many calories into me as possible. Rémi and Heather encourage me to help myself to the biscuits, which I do. I plough through the packet. Meanwhile, we chat and joke about stuff, and I'm glad for their company and this diversion, as it helps calm my nerves about the paddling. Part of me wants to delay what I know will be a hot, gruelling crossing. The sun already burns over the water from the east, melting the newly applied sunscreen from my face. Another hot one. No doubt about it.

I finish up and leave the boat to say goodbye to Le Boss and his father. I get in my kayak, the whole family standing on the shore to wish me a safe journey. The current sweeps me towards Barga, with Rémi's boat puttering past.

At this time of day, Barga looks sleepy. The narrow Niger expels me into huge Lake Debo, and I pass the island village without drawing much of a crowd. Rémi's boat motors ahead of me, trailing back and forth as he takes photos of my paddling. I feel as if I'm in a *Sports Illustrated* photo shoot now, so I do my best to look Athletic, though my tired arms and upper body don't feel like co-operating today. What I need is a few days of downtime, which I don't anticipate having until – or unless – I get to Timbuktu.

It's not long before the horizon shows only a meeting of sky and water on all sides of me, the waves sizeable and

unruly. I've read that this part of the lake is 160 feet deep, which makes my crossing feel all the more hazardous. If I were to overturn, lose my things, there would be little hope of recovering them. But perhaps there is something to be said for a Dogon witch's assistance, because there's still not a single cloud in the sky and no hint of a rising storm. Such a day is a total fluke at this time of year, wind and rain the norm.

Rémi's boat leaves me behind, becoming a small brown dot on the horizon up ahead. I keep following that dot. A river steamer passes me, so loaded with people and baggage that the water nearly overtakes the gunwales. The ship overshadows me like a giant, her crew cheering and howling, the passengers craning to get a look at me, this woman in her tiny red boat, paddling feverishly beside their swift passage.

I'm starting to find this crossing rather intimidating. Without landmarks to reach, it can seem, in the midst of such a great spread of water, that I don't go anywhere. I have to keep reminding myself that I still make progress: as long as I keep paddling, I can be confident I'll get somewhere. Before long, I see white buoys in the distance, meant to guide boats to where the Niger picks up again. I reach one buoy and then the next, all sight of land gone and Rémi's boat a speck to the north-west now. The heat starts to become intense, my thermometer reading 106 degrees. The hottest day yet. But there can be no stopping.

I catch up with Rémi finally, where his boat is tied to a buoy. I grab hold of the side, taking the opportunity to rest

for a few minutes and drink some water. I see a sandbar rising in the distance, proof of how shallow Debo can be in spots, the rainy season coming later and later in recent years, drying the lake up and encouraging the Sahara to encroach further south.

My crossing becomes straightforward now: I just follow the buoys. Which is a relief. Still, Rémi waits for me at intervals so that I have a chance to rest by his boat every half-hour or so. Heather cheers me at each leg of the journey, which really helps to make the crossing more pleasant.

More islands start to rise from the lake, and soon I'm entering a wide channel, heading towards land and the mouth of the Niger. Hippos peer at me from the shallows – the first hippos I've seen – their heads rising and lowering, air spraying from their nostrils. Lake Debo, the part I'd worried about most, barely stirs behind me.

I decide to stop off in the first village after Debo, a town called Aka, to see if they have any mangoes or other supplies to sell, as my food stocks are getting low. The kids of the village see me coming and crowd on to the shore, shouting and pointing. It's the largest concentration of kids I've seen to date, and I hope things will go more smoothly than at previous villages.

As I near the shore, the kids swim into the river *en masse* to check out my kayak. This has never happened before – usually when I'm on the water, I'm safe. Before I can paddle to deeper water, the crowd surrounds me and threatens to push me out of my boat. Kids are everywhere,

trying to climb into my kayak or pull it to shore. I decide to humour everyone this time. I pick up a little girl to lift her into the kayak, but the minute my hands touch her she screams and stiffens all her limbs, refusing to get inside. Another girl volunteers, but when I touch her, she screeches as if in pain. There is obviously something terrifying about being touched by a *tubab*, though I can't figure out what.

Now a boy steps forward – a remarkably brave boy, given the risks of a white person's touch – and he actually tries to pull himself inside my kayak. I lift him up and put him inside, and his friends look on with fear and wonder as he makes himself comfortable in front of me and waves at them. *This boy*, I'm thinking, *is destined for greatness*.

We go for a ride together, and now his face of confidence and equanimity breaks into a look of terror as the kayak wobbles back and forth. He hollers and braces himself with his hands, as if riding on a rollercoaster for the first time, but quickly calms himself and regains his composure. The kids all yell and cheer him on, and when he's at last sure he won't fall out, he raises a fist of victory like Muhammad Ali.

I deposit him beside his friends again, and they all slap him on the back and crowd around him. They shoot out questions, as if he'd just returned from the dead. It turns out that Aka doesn't have any food to sell, so I turn my kayak around and paddle on towards Timbuktu.

It's been one of those strange days on the river. I spent the entire time paddling but seemed to make no progress.

The river curved and dipped but got me nowhere, and half the time I was fighting against the wind. I'm beat and nearly out of food, and with the sun going down, I approach a prosperous-looking village to try to buy a meal and lodging for the night. Stopping at villages is always pot luck. What tribe will I get? Will they have food to sell me? Will they like me?

I'm greeted by the usual crowd of fifty-plus people, naked kids swarming around me and yelling excitedly. They tell me that this large collection of adobe huts is called Berakousi, and that it lies at the spot where the Koula River enters the Niger. I see goats nearby; women pound millet. I ask what people this is and am told they're Bozo.

As I go in search of the chief, it quickly becomes evident that they don't want me here. Young toughs, one sporting a black T-shirt with Osama bin Laden's face printed on it like a rock star's, start harassing me in pathetic French. Where's my husband? Would I like to have sex with them? What man back home allowed me to travel here by myself? Their faces are covered with indigo head-wraps, in the manner of North African Tuaregs, just their eyes peering out at me. Obviously it's cool to look Tuareg here. I ignore them, nearly being knocked off my feet by the crowd of pushy onlookers as I try to move forward. I've noticed a fine but palpable division between curiosity and aggression towards outsiders along the Niger, and Berakousi village clearly crosses the line. I don't want to stay here. But food is important, so I need to find the chief.

He's out in the fields, so I sit on a wicker chair to wait for

him. I refuse numerous requests from women who keep trying to pass me their babies, wanting me to breastfeed them. The sun is fast departing and I'm worried now, because the river's too choppy and mercurial along this stretch to make night paddling safe, and I didn't see an alternative village nearby.

Finally the chief appears, an old man named Gardja Jemai, who walks over and surveys me, frowning. I give him a large sum of money as *cadeau*, explain as best I can that I'd like to buy a meal if possible. And if he can't spare any food, I'll just be on my way. He stands there, frowning, saying nothing. I pass money to the best French speaker in the crowd and ask him to translate my request. There is a brief exchange and I'm told to wait.

I wait, and wait. The sun, I notice, is nearly gone. Too late to go elsewhere. The village people continue to crowd around me. I sigh and try to resign myself to the situation, asking the chief if I can sleep on a patch of ground nearby. He holds out his hand for more money, and when I give him a wad of bills, he nods. The young men sit around me, demanding money too. One guy tells me that he wants the watch and flashlight that I've just taken out of my back-pack. He picks up these things and fingers them. Meanwhile, I am the subject of a large, communal conversation, my title *tubabu* – 'whitey' – being exchanged excitedly by members of the crowd.

A woman, one of the chief's four wives, comes over and announces that she has food for me. I thank her and give her some money, and she drops a bowl in front of me.

219

Inside sits a rotting fish head, blooms of fungus growing on its skin.

'*Mangez*,' the woman says. She puts her fingers to her lips.

And I'm so hungry and fatigued that I do. I just don't care any more. I crack open the mottled fish skin and pull out bits of white meat. Everyone laughs heartily, and I see that this is a joke, feeding me a dog's dinner. When I finish, I notice that Osama and Co. have requisitioned one of my pens. I decide to just let it go, hoping that the situation won't escalate. I recall a grim passage from Park's narrative, about his Moorish captors: 'They had recourse to the final and decisive argument, that I was a Christian, and of course that my property was lawful plunder ... They accordingly opened my bundles, and robbed me of everything they fancied.' The young men nudge me, speak threateningly to me through their Tuareg face-wrappings, the chief – traditionally my benefactor – standing by and doing nothing. When one man puts his hand around my wrist, I wrench my arm away, holding up a fist.

'Don't touch me,' I say.

The village people laugh. I get up, scolding myself for my loss of temper, scolding the fear within me that caused it. I put on my backpack, heading to the shore. Can I still get out of here tonight? But it's darkness all around, the Niger churning madly before the confluence of the Koula River. I'm stuck. Nothing to be done.

I wish I didn't feel such fear and anger now. But I do. Those emotions stay. My time in this village tonight, with

the young men taunting me, feels like a miniature pro-
duction of larger world events. Fear begetting fear. People
feeling threatened, alienated, enraged. Not wanting to
provoke anyone, or to be further provoked, I sit for hours
on the dark shore, slapping mosquitoes, hoping that the
people in the village will get bored waiting for me and go
back to their huts. It feels like a true Mungo Park moment:
'I felt myself as if left lonely and friendless amidst the wilds
of Africa,' he wrote in one of his last journal entries. Yes.

When I finally return, the village has cleared out, and
one of the chief's wives smiles in pity, bringing out a foam
mattress for me to sleep on. I lie down and wrap myself in
my tent's rainfly, my clothes becoming soaked with sweat.
Fleas and other assorted insects crawl up my legs, up my
clothes, get caught in my hair. They bite me incessantly. My
chest burns, and I shine a flashlight down my shirt, seeing
my breasts covered with bites. I slather on 100 per cent
DEET bug repellent, the stuff that melts plastic. I don't
even care. I shut my eyes to wait for first light, when I'll
leave this place. It is one of those nights that I know I must
get through, that promises no sleep.

I escape from Berakousi in the first light of dawn, just as
the roosters crow out their ear-popping paeans to the
morning. It was Mungo Park's same strategy – to leave
before any of his tormentors had a chance to wake up.
('Early in the morning,' he wrote, 'before the Moors were
assembled, I departed.') I've learned a lot from Mungo
about how to do this trip. More than simply teaching me

how to greet village elders, handle crowds and escape from unpleasant villages, he emphasized the importance of patience and acceptance of whatever comes, no matter how difficult the events.

Being as silent as possible, I stuff my flysheet into my backpack and slip it on, grabbing my paddle. The village slumbers, except for a couple of women who fetch water from the Niger. It's too dark to see if any of my things have been pinched during the night, though I doubt it: I was awake nearly the whole time. I have that heavy, sunken feeling that no sleep gives me, as if my body were functioning on slow-speed. This state has allowed a mix of dark emotions to rise to the surface of my mind, leaving me feeling absolutely defenceless before them. There is depression that I chose to do a trip that has proved so exhausting and difficult. Disappointment over getting so angry in the village last night. Despair at how much further I have to go, through the storms and heat and increasingly hostile country.

I try to push all the emotions away. It's my only option, given where I am, given the circumstances. I must suppress everything into blissful apathy. And after a few moments, I succeed. With a feeling akin to indifference, I watch the waves of the Niger slapping the shore and reaching out to me. I put my backpack into the kayak. Getting in, I paddle hard, leaving Berakousi far behind me.

If I'm learning anything on this journey, it still feels shady and inconclusive. But I do know that a lesson repeats itself every time a fisherman passes in his canoe, not

bothering to return my greeting, just asking for money or gifts. People don't seem interested in me much beyond what I might be able to give them. They see my white skin and reduce me to an identity I can't shake: Rich White Woman, Bearer of Gifts, nothing more. This is an important lesson – the way people so easily label and dismiss each other. I'm dismayed by how simple it is for me to get caught in the same game, to start seeing every passing man in a canoe as a threat or as someone who only wants something from me. In this cordoning off of the people I meet, in this mistrust, I deny them their humanity. Do we ever greet people without wanting something from them? Without hoping they'll give us certain things in return – love, money, approval? Without wanting them to change, or to do what we want, or to see us the way we want to be seen? What's stopping us from simply finding joy in another's presence? I'm miffed by it all.

My stomach grumbles from no breakfast, but I keep paddling north, into the great bend of the Niger that does a 180-degree turn through the South Sahara on its approach to the town of Niafounké. Whenever the river curves, winds tend to blow directly at me. This stretch is no exception, a fierce wind striking my face, sending large waves against me, the current trying to pull my kayak towards shore. Attempting to paddle into such strong winds and giant swells feels futile, but the alternative is to wait around all day, hoping for a respite from the weather, which means making no progress whatsoever. And because this is the rainy season, the longer in the day I wait, the

more susceptible I am to late afternoon storms. So I paddle hard to stay on course, my arms crying out in pain, though I've taught myself to ignore it. None of this is fun or challenging or exciting – it just is. I take whatever comes, my body too busy with paddling to give my mind a chance to protest.

No-one is out in this kind of weather. That's one thing I've learned about river travel on the Niger: if the locals are out in their canoes, it's safe to paddle. These people have been fishermen for millennia, and they know a bad day when they see one. Still, I don't wait for good days as they do; I want to know that, with every minute that passes, I'm getting closer to Timbuktu. I travel from landmark to landmark, hoping as I edge around each bend that the wind will shift behind me and offer me its assistance. But as the hours go by, I'm still fighting this river. My concentration stays fixed on the large whitecaps that strike my kayak from the side and try to flip me over.

At midday, opposite a sizeable village, I pull over to take a rest. My arms are smarting, and I haven't eaten anything since the rotting fish head the night before. I burn so many calories from the constant, hard paddling all day that I'm perpetually hungry. I search deep in my backpack for some forgotten food and am rewarded for my efforts: a smashed Snickers. It feels like a gift from the gods. I sit down to eat it, only now noticing how the current carries over raw sewage from the village across the river and deposits it up and down the shore – human shit everywhere, congealing in the sun. But with the apathy still left over from earlier

this morning, I don't care. The villages along the Niger have their own wells for drinking water; everyone knows not to drink from the polluted Niger, the river acting as washing place and communal toilet for thousands – if not millions – of people by the time it reaches its termination in Nigeria.

As I eat, a canoe passes close to the shore with a couple of families inside. I wave to everyone and say hello in Songhai, the new lingua franca of these parts. Men standing on either end of the canoe, poling it along, yell out, '*Cadeau, madame! Cadeau!*' They hold out their hands for money. The kids start taking up the chorus: '*Cadeau, madame! Cadeau! Cadeau!*'

I look down at my feet until they pass.

CHAPTER TWELVE

FOR THE FIRST TIME, IT FEELS AS IF TIMBUKTU IS GETTING close. Perhaps it's the sight of large dunes bordering the river, or maybe it's the heat that grows each day, well over 100 degrees. But the desert country has arrived, almost unnoticed, slowly altering the landscape with each mile travelled, making it drier, thirstier for the waters of the Niger. I don't see anything green any more, as I had at the start of my trip. No jungle-like views along the river. No trees except for the rare ones planted in a village. Another day ends in this scorching country, the sun low to the west and the light getting soft. I remind myself that I've been paddling for weeks already. No-one to really converse with to help me pass the time. No major diversions until the very end of each day, when I pull over at the nearest village, never knowing what's going to happen.

Before my trip, it had seemed daunting, the idea of being alone on this river for so long, with nothing to do but

paddle. But I've grown used to it by now. The West, with all its rush and stress, has trained me to believe that I must fill every moment of every day with something 'important'. What counts as 'important', though, is never entirely clear. I know that spending weeks paddling a kayak on the Niger would *not* have been important by my former criteria. In fact, the idea would have been an all-out affront to that old frame of mind. Paddling doesn't seem worthy enough, somehow, or practical, or sensible enough. It seems like an abhorrent waste of time. But what would I be doing instead? I smile at the answer: finishing my Ph.D. in English. Writing dreary seminar papers. Reading countless books – volume after volume of stale critical theory written by people who are convinced they have the right answers. Listening to the endless lectures about so-and-so and such-and-such, with titles like 'A Revolutionary Aim: Serialization and the Role of the Temperance in Delaney's *Blake*'. Mulling over a dissertation 'statement of intent', being told that all worthwhile endeavours have clear and definable objectives from the start. That all worthwhile endeavours must yield something tangible, something valuable, which furthers one's career or brings in money or achieves a certain standing. *These* are the things I would be doing instead, if I weren't on this river.

I laugh. I laugh loud enough to send some nearby birds squawking away. I see my life now as if it were all finished and laid out before me. I see the things I did in order to get somewhere, to do something else. I see the things that once mattered to me, and now don't. So much of it seems so

strange and so silly and so tragic, all at once. All of it a way to bide time, a way to wait and plan and plot for the kind of life I wanted. But paddling on the Niger — now that is a real doing. For the first time, I feel as if I have no influence on the outcome. I just keep paddling, and this life of mine shows me what it thinks I should know. It tells me what it thinks is actually important.

Travelling as I am, slowly, deliberately, I memorize every nuance of this river. Every bend, every curve. The way the land seems to jut sharply from a distance, only to smooth out upon my approach. The persistence of the winds that are always carving and shaping the high white dunes, sending sand whirling into the Niger. As I've become entirely dependent on the weather and other natural conditions, I've learned to be acutely aware of my environment. I recognize the cause of various eddies, smell changes in wind and weather, feel the ever-so-subtle pull on my kayak's rudder that tells me how best to alter my course. I can tell the time from the position of the sun, am accurate nearly to the minute, though such accuracy has become unimportant. I no longer wear a watch, don't want one. When the sun goes down, I know it's time to pull over. That simple. And I take whatever I get. A friendly village, a hostile village. I take whatever comes.

I feel a new patience that requires no effort on my part. It results naturally from each day, from an understanding that no matter how hard I paddle, it makes little difference. Timbuktu stays far away, and these hours don't pass any faster. I have no obligations out here; my mind can't scold

and cajole me into a new project. I'm not bothered by calls or e-mail or people at my door. Here, I have no choice but to be completely present in each moment of my life. Mali slowly, meticulously, imprints itself on my mind.

New, more basic concerns replace the old, tedious, programmed ones. For example, taking meals. I've learned to eat only when the sun reaches a certain spot in the sky and not before, regardless of my stomach's protests. To eat too much too often is to be wasteful and not ration what little food I have – which is almost nothing now, just some dried fruit and granola from home. Rationing takes self-discipline, though, and has been one of the hardest things I've had to teach myself. Not only do I refuse to eat food from my stocks more than twice a day, but the portion must be conservative – a handful of granola, say – as I can't rely on villages to have food to sell or dinner to offer, and I need enough to get me to Timbuktu.

There are also paddling concerns. I must try to get the majority of my paddling done before or after the midday hours, when the sun is hottest and the wind is strongest, both thwarting my progress. As I'm now well into the Sahel, the South Sahara, I'm also experiencing a different kind of weather during the rainy season from what prevailed down by Ségou. Here, violent storms arrive late in the afternoon or during the night, so that I need to paddle hard to find a secure place to sleep by the day's end.

Which brings up concerns about where to sleep. Do I camp or do I stay in a village? Before, I chose villages for

greater safety, but lately this has seemed just as dangerous an option as camping alone along the Niger. Though I always pay the people I stay with, I don't want to go to a village where I'll be a burden to anyone, or where the people might feel hostility towards outsiders. But it's hard to know the status of a village when I'm simply paddling by and must go on appearances, so camping has become an attractive choice again – as long as I can find a remote place where no-one will visit me, and I can get a good night's sleep.

Still, I prefer staying in villages and getting to know the people. Usually, I look for places with cows, which will probably be Fulani villages. For some reason, the Fulani have invariably been among the most welcoming of the peoples I've encountered. And their cows, of course, mean the possibility of milk to purchase. But lately I haven't seen many Fulani villages, so I look for other signs to help me choose. Generally, if people don't yell out requests for money or gifts as soon as I go by, that's a good sign. Even better if only a few kids run to shore. The less people react to my being an oddity, the more privacy I can usually expect to find. I try to avoid larger villages too, as huge crowds tend to overwhelm me in these places. My main concern is avoiding a repeat of my experience with the fish head and the young toughs in Berakousi.

I see that I have about an hour of light left, so I look for a place to pull over. I pass a fisherman heading back to his village and start up a conversation, enquiring how close I am to the large town of Niafounké.

'It's over there,' he says in French, pointing to a distant bend in the Niger that would take nearly two hours to reach. Then he says, in a quiet, polite sort of way, 'Money, miss?'

I slip him a bill. He asks where I'll be spending the night and when I shrug he suggests his village. It seems to fit all my criteria: it's small, has no crowds, and there are some cows nearby. When I ask him if I can camp beside the village, he smiles and nods his head, encouraging me to come to shore. I follow him, tying up my kayak next to his long canoe. This village, he tells me, is named Dagougi; the people are Songhai. As women come to the shore to greet me, I see that they're unadorned but for gold earrings. Unlike the Fulani, they don't have any facial tattoos. They watch me set up my tent outside the village, donkeys wandering about and noisily cropping grass.

Dagougi sits on a hill overlooking the Niger. It's composed of neat, rectangular adobe homes, their backs facing out so that they form a large defensive square with a single entranceway. I began to notice this 'fortification' layout shortly after I crossed Lake Debo, and it's a widespread characteristic of Upper Niger village architecture. Not so very long ago, people in these parts needed to keep themselves safe from desert marauders, such as Arabs coming from the north or tribes invading from further south. Hence, their villages took on the form of mini-garrisons. The degree of fortification depends on the village, though I've passed places so completely surrounded by high adobe walls that I could see nothing inside but the tops of the minarets. Along the Upper Niger, the architecture speaks

of a rich and often brutal history, empires vying with each other, entire villages living in fear of enslavement or slaughter.

The great Songhai Empire reigned in these parts, off and on, from AD 1100 to 1600, meeting with periods of defeat from the invading Tuareg or Malian Empires. The German explorer Heinrich Barth, who made it across the Sahara to Timbuktu in 1853, would comment on the 'excellent historical works' of the Songhai people, noting their strong place in the scholarship of the region and of Africa as a whole. The Songhai didn't enjoy true power here until their greatest leader, Ali the Great, expelled the Tuareg from Timbuktu in 1468. He then reigned for twenty-eight years, conquering most of the country that I've paddled through and wresting the great commercial city of Djenné from the Malian empire of Bambarra. Ali was succeeded by his general, Askia the Great, who strengthened his empire's association with Islam and made a famous journey across the Sahara to Mecca. The experience greatly inspired him: he started a series of holy wars against neighbouring tribes shortly after he returned, conquering as far east as present-day Niger and reaching as far west as the Atlantic Ocean. Before long, the Songhai ruled over a kingdom that extended a thousand miles east to west, enabling cities like Timbuktu to prosper as never before. It was this prosperity that Leo Africanus wrote about in his book *History and Description of Africa and the Notable Things Contained Therein*, and that encouraged Europeans to reach Timbuktu.

*

I pass the town of Niafounké early this morning, the Niger starting to look more and more interminable. I figure it's the heat getting to me. My sunscreen doesn't really work any more; I sweat so badly that I'm constantly wiping my face, and whatever remains rolls off with the perspiration. I put on my long-sleeved shirt, which makes things much hotter but protects my skin. Before me the Niger goes on and on, beginning a long straight stretch. I've become a good judge of my paddling speed, and usually I can accurately estimate how long it will take me to get to a distant landmark. In this case, though, I don't even see a curve up ahead to act as a point of reference. Still, I must be getting closer to Timbuktu, and that's encouraging. I'm starting to believe I may actually make it, that this crazy trip of mine might actually be successful.

After a few hours of paddling, I reach the end of the straight stretch. The Niger curves to the east, splitting around an island. Rather than taking the longer, outside curve, I opt for a short-cut down the shallower channel. This is preferable, too, because I want to avoid passing the villages that border the other branch. The screaming, incessant calls for *cadeaux* have been getting much worse with each day that passes.

I paddle through what appears to be a kind of marsh-land, passing dark brown objects floating in the water. Used to seeing such fishermen's floats attached to under-water nets, I think nothing of them until one rises and spurts out air, two eyes peering at me: hippo! Hippos

233

everywhere – I've never seen so many in one place. A whole hippo colony, and I'm stuck in the middle of it.

This is the worst of my nightmares. I've often debated what I would do if caught in such a situation, and I never had any good answers. During the first half of my trip, I didn't see hippos at all – most of them had been shot by locals, the teeth sold on the black market. But in this part of the Niger, for whatever reason, the hippos are flourishing.

All I know about hippos is what I've gleaned from PBS shows, that they're cute but bad-tempered critters whose skin produces a natural sunscreen. At night, they come on shore to forage, which is when you want to be sure you don't run into one. I've heard that hippos are more dangerous than lions, more vicious than crocodiles, and that they readily protect their young to the death. And I see baby hippos here. Park noted the local people's fear of them: 'We saw three hippopotami close to another of these islands. The canoe men were afraid they might follow us and upset the canoes. The report of a musket will in all cases frighten them away.' It's all the advice I've received: try a loud noise.

'Nice hippos,' I say to them. 'Good hippos.'

The hippos just watch me. My rubber boat would be no match for their teeth, yet they seem lazy enough, a mother and baby lounging near by. I slowly turn my kayak around, and all at once I paddle in a fury against the current, back towards the other branch of the Niger. I paddle as if I were going through a minefield, trying to retrace my original route. Hippo heads rise as I pass,

making sounds like whales as they shoot air from their nostrils. The dark eyes watch me from just above the surface of the water, assessing, granting me passage.

As if hippos weren't bad enough, the Tonka rapids are coming. This is a natural aberration in the landscape, a strange rocky cleft that cuts through the sand of the South Sahara and enters the Niger, disturbing its course. The river flows in a tight S shape at this one spot, after millennia of trying to meander its way past the blockage. Boulders of black rock form a wall across the river, compressing it and speeding up its current; during Mali's colonial days, the French cleared a small passageway in the middle to allow the passage of river barges. But the boulders remain everywhere under the surface, threatening boats and tossing the waters; during bad weather the rapids can become nearly impassable.

I approach the middle of the wall of rock, paddling towards a buoy that marks the place for safe passage. Though the weather is relatively calm today, wind churns the water, creating swirling, tugging eddies that try to take over the manoeuvring of my boat. The current reigns here, seizing my kayak and hurling me towards a rocky bend. I paddle hard to reach a sandy bank on the opposite shore, finally making it. I decide I'll wait for an approaching river barge to show me the best route across the final part of the rapids. Loaded with people and supplies, the boat travels slowly over the fierce eddies, skirting large black rocks that rise from the water. I paddle immediately in its wake,

successfully passing the dangerous parts, until the river
spurts me into a long strait. So much for the dreaded rapids
of Tonka. Dunes rise on either side of the river, baking in
the Saharan sun.

To my right, I see the familiar brown 'floats' again,
which I now know to be hippo heads. This time, though, I
stay at a safe distance from them as I paddle in the middle
of the river. A couple of boys in a canoe start spreading out
a fishing net behind me, heading straight for them.

'*Hang-ya! Hang-ya!*' I say in Songhai to them. 'Hippos!'
I point at the creatures.

The boys glance to where I'm pointing, then look back
at me and laugh. They put out the last of their netting
within fifteen feet of the animals and calmly return the way
they've come.

The land along the shore seems to get drier, more forbidding. Trees have all but vanished, and only the
occasional scraggly bush dots the horizon. Still, given the
starkness of this country, the people live in increasingly
refined adobe dwellings that show a level of artistic
achievement I haven't yet seen along the Niger: doorways
and window frames ornately carved, the mosques with
decorated walls and sharply angled minarets.

As night comes, I pull over to a small village of round
adobe huts named Nakri. My reception here is unusual
compared to what it's been at most other Bozo villages, as
the people don't crowd around me and no-one asks for
money. I think that's half the reason why such enormous

crowds have met me at other villages: the people wanted to be near by should I decide to pass out goodies or spare change. But here in Nakri, a couple of women greet me with the sole intention of finding out what I'm doing on the river. When I ask them if I can spend the night in their village, they enthusiastically say yes.

They lead me to their chief, who's building a canoe near by. He and the men helping him invite me to look at their work. The canoe is being constructed from a combination of wide slabs of rain-forest wood and some remnants from older canoes. The used pieces look in pretty bad shape, have jagged edges and holes, but the men work at joining them to the new pieces of wood as if putting together a puzzle. They fasten the pieces together by heating and applying a sticky tar, securing them further with wooden pegs. Other men take long planks meant for the hull and curve them in wooden vices laid along the ground. The canoe itself will be a large one when it's finished – maybe thirty feet long and eight feet across. The process looks laborious as there's no electricity, no professional tools to help with the building. The men must do everything by hand.

Their construction method is probably similar to Mungo Park's back in 1805, when he sat in Sansanding trying to create a boat for his Niger journey. In Park's case, though, he only put together a couple of rotten canoes sent to him from Mansong, King of Bambarra. Just doing that took him an entire month.

The chief stops his work and leads me up to the village, laying out a mat for me to sit on. His wives – he has three,

as far as I can tell – offer me some rice for dinner. No-one has asked for money or *cadeaux* yet, which is virtually unprecedented. I can only conclude that the people have never had any tourists visiting their village before, and so they've never had any reason to associate white people with money. And they probably don't have a TV man coming here either, bringing images of posh Bamako hotels and pampered white guests enjoying cocktails.

The issue of money creates a quandary for me. I want to be generous, paying the women and the chief's family for allowing me to stay and eat with them. People in Mali make on average about $10 a week, if that much (for many, it's barely half that), so I always try to pay the families I stay with the equivalent of a couple of weeks' wages. In particular, I slip something to the wives and other women, who have less of a chance to make their own money. At the same time, though, I don't want to change Nakri village's image of white visitors for ever by passing out bills in front of everyone. So I decide to be secretive about it. I go to where the chief has started working on his boat, and I slip him some money as a gift.

Giving money to the wives, though, proves to be my downfall. I follow them to their cooking area and surreptitiously pass them something, but an old woman catches sight of the bills changing hands and all hell breaks loose. Within half an hour the female populations of both Nakri and the nearby, much larger, village of Tindirma have started congregating around me, asking for money. Tindirma, it turns out, borders a dirt road that leads to

Timbuktu, and so the people there are especially familiar with white tourists and government workers going by in slick new Land-Rovers. Some of them know a little French, and they offer me reasons why they need the money. Sick children, injury, illness. Some of them actually produce children with ailments, but it's not possible for me to help everyone, and I don't want to further damage matters by indiscriminately handing out cash. As for the sicknesses, I probably have the antibiotics that would cure some of the ailments but, lacking proper medical knowledge, I don't want to play doctor with people's lives.

I do have some bottles of ibuprofen that I brought to Mali to pass out as gifts, and when a couple of old women with painful arthritis come forward I ask a young woman who speaks really good French to translate my instructions for taking the pills. When I hand the bottles over, the old women are so happy to receive them that they hold their hands towards me and start crying. I look down, feeling completely ashamed. Ashamed for all I have, and for all they don't. Ashamed that while American babies live, theirs must die. Mali has one of the highest infant mortality rates in the world: twelve of every hundred babies die. And what to do about any of it? I know that the economy of my own country often flourishes by exploiting other countries' poverty and suffering. Sitting here in Nakri, in front of all these people, I feel a certain culpability from simply being American.

The crowd finally disperses, everyone going home, and peaceful Nakri returns to normal. I walk down to the

Niger just as the setting sun is streaking it with orange light. A storm is coming from the south-east, but I know it will take an hour or so to get here. For now, I study the waters, sighing, thinking about the crowd of women who had surrounded me. I hear a voice and turn to see a woman holding a sick little boy. I recognize her from before; from the descriptions she gave, her child probably has dysentery or giardia: life-threatening ailments without antibiotics.

'Please, *madame*,' she whispers in French, holding out her hand. '*Argent*.'

I place some bills in her hand. It is all I can do.

I wake up in Nakri to the rooster calls, day only a grey suggestion to the east. My stomach lurches, my guts feeling as if they're being stripped from me. I barely make it out of my tent and through the village to the Niger, where I keep vomiting up bile. Everything in my body feels as though it's turned to liquid. I'm so faint that it's hard to stand, so I kneel and hold my head. Only two days to my goal, and now this.

Some kind of dysentery, probably, though I can't say which one — amoebic, bacillary? I'm hoping it's the latter, which is easier to cure. Still, when I return to my tent to take antibiotics, I immediately throw them up. A group of village folk have risen, and they watch me and *tsk*. Poor, sick white woman. The children stare, silent and un-comprehending. All I can think about is getting to my goal, reaching my goal, where I can finally stop and lie down, and not have to do anything any more.

I wash off my face, smooth down my T-shirt. I'm getting to Timbuktu if I have to crawl. The women are still *tsk*ing as I take down my tent and load up my kayak. They insist that I stay, but the journey calls. I've come too far to fail now. Hunched over, I get in my kayak and wave goodbye, paddling off towards the morning sun nudging its way through the clouds.

I travel slowly through the intense, rising heat. When I feel too faint, I stop for a while, letting the current take me. But it's a sluggish current, and virtually no help. I try taking some more antibiotics, knowing they would help cure me if I could keep the pills down, but I quickly throw them up. That's the way it goes: vomit, paddle, vomit, paddle. There's been no food in my stomach since the previous evening, but I don't try to eat anything. My appetite is gone, replaced by the painful spasms in my gut and a headache that registers in red spots of faintness before my eyes. Timbuktu feels further than it ever did. Two days might be two centuries away.

And this is the hottest, most forbidding stretch of the Niger to date, great white dunes swelling on either side of the river, pulsing with heat waves. The sun burns in a cloudless sky that offers up not even a hint of breeze. Strangely, the shores here are more populated than ever, desolate adobe huts regularly breaking the monotony of the desert. The lucky village has a single scraggly tree to provide shade, its branches hanging despondently. I use these tiny settlements as my guideposts, reaching and passing one and then the next, amazed by the Niger's tenacity

as it cuts through the Sahara, a gloriously stubborn and incongruous river.

I wonder what Park felt on this stretch. We can never know for sure, having no written record and only unreliable hearsay from Amadi Fatouma, the sole survivor of the expedition, who claimed that Park and his men had to shoot their way through these waters. Everyone, apparently, wanted Park dead out here.

Which might explain why I'm assailed with angry shouts at every turn, entire villages gathering on shore to yell at me, so that I stick to the very middle of the Niger and carry my can of mace in my lap, paddling as hard as I'm able. Gone are the waves of greeting and friendship from local tribes that I'd experienced at the beginning of my trip. Inexplicably, the entire tone of this country has changed. When I wave hello to people out here, they invariably gesture for me to come and give them money. Add to this the dysentery, which makes me so ill that I frequently have to go ashore, and I spend a great deal of time worrying about where I can stop, and whether, while in the middle of being sick and unable to defend myself, someone might try to rob or hurt me.

Meanwhile, my map becomes even more worthless. None of the turns is where it says it's supposed to be. Short-looking stretches go on interminably. My muscles ache from the dysentery, and my thermometer reads 110 degrees. This is a kind of heat that I've never experienced before, not even when I lived in Tucson for grad school. This heat dissolves into my skin, burns through even the

strongest sunscreen, enervates and debilitates. I throw my paddle down, splashing myself with water in an attempt to cool off, though I know by now that it won't work. There is nothing to be done.

There is a certain moment when all resolve goes, when even the most determined person faces the knowledge that they've done the most they can do and the only choice left is to give up. I don't want to admit that I may be at that point, but it sure feels that way. Faint and dizzy, I hold my head down before the midday sun, trying to resist the urge to throw up.

Angry men are shouting at me from a nearby shore, demanding I give them money or *cadeaux*. When I glance at them, they wave wildly and stamp their feet. I speak to them in English, though I know they can't understand. I ask them if they've seen any good movies lately. I say hello and enquire after their families. I whistle and make strange, enigmatic signs in the air.

The men stop yelling and study me as I float by. It occurs to me that I'm acting like a crazy woman. Which isn't so bad. I actually kind of like it. Not caring any more.

'Hey, Mungo Park – can you hear me?' I ask the river. 'Hey, Mungo – help me out here.' I wipe a film of sweat from my face.

Silence. The river's current is so slow that algae grows on the surface of the water.

'Hey, Mun-go!'

I pick up the paddle and start moving again. I pretend

it's Mungo Park assisting me, his spirit arriving *deus ex machina*-style to get me to Timbuktu.

Below a large orange dune, I see the long, rectangular shape of one of the enormous river barges that ply the Niger. Usually they hold about sixty people plus baggage, are so overloaded that the gunwales barely rise above the water. In this case, though, the boat is nearly empty: must be Rémi's boat. I never know when I'll run into him, was certain he'd be at Timbuktu by now, taking in some air-conditioning and waiting for me to eventually get there. This unexpected meeting is a blessing: not only are they great for mooching, but their boat's canopy is the only shade to be found anywhere on the Niger. I feel as if I could pass out from the sun. Red dots of dizziness have been filling my eyes, regardless of all the water I drink. I could use a secure place to rest for a while.

Rémi waves at me in greeting, and I pull alongside their boat. Heather is reading a copy of the *New Yorker* – for the third time, she tells me – her legs propped up on the table. Rémi attends to his cameras. Behind them, their cook prepares lunch. Will it be boiled chicken with tomato and herb sauce and noodles today? Or just fried river fish with French fries? I'm wondering what gave me the dysentery. The rice gruel I had the previous night? Or the rotting fish head at Berakousi?

'How are you doing?' Heather asks me.

'Other than throwing up at a village this morning, I'm fine.'

'You catch something?'

'A little dysentery.'

'Well,' she says, 'if it's any consolation, you don't *look* sick.'

Which I suppose I don't. I try to keep these matters to myself usually. And I'll reach a certain point – which I reached long back – where discomfort becomes the norm. All the heat, the sweating, the aching of my body, the dysentery – all of it normal. So that any luxury, like the bottled mineral water Heather is giving me from their personal stash on the boat, becomes an incredible novelty. I reach deep in my backpack and give her a damp, wadded bundle of pages in return: an issue of *Harper's*.

'Maybe you can dry it out and unstick the pages,' I say.

With the shade of their boat's canopy over me, and a bench to rest on, I swallow some antibiotics again and lie down with my hat over my face, knees pulled in against me to try to counter the stomach cramps. Doesn't work. I feel hopelessly nauseous. I hear Heather's comment, *You don't look sick*, as I get up, almost mechanically this time, and lower myself into the river to go onshore to throw up. Before I know it, I'm collapsing into the water.

I wake up half in the water, half on shore, retching into the sand. My only hope is that Rémi isn't taking pictures of this. I glance back at the boat to check. Heather is politely feigning an interest in her *New Yorker*. Rémi still seems to be fiddling with his cameras. The three Malian crewmen look out at me, shocked, unsure what to do.

I just lie by myself onshore, retching for a while, unable

to get up. The sun is like a glaring heat lamp, weighing me down. It occurs to me that I might call to the others for assistance, but this seems strangely impossible to me. I feel a universe away from them, as if we inhabited different planets; my voice could never possibly travel the light-years' distance. One part of me is fascinated by the fact that I seem absolutely incapable of asking for help. But this is in keeping with my personality. Not to mention that I *chose* this hell, I actually asked for it, and so now I must bask in it – alone.

I slowly get up and trudge off behind a nearby dune. It's strange to no longer see the waters of the Niger before me. This country is all sand and scrub brush. A wasteland. I sit down and stare off at the Sahara. I know it goes on and on for many hundreds of miles. Just the endless sand. To leave the Niger would be to die.

Why did I come here again?

My stomach calms itself and my faintness subsides to a gentle clarity: the post-vomiting high. I look without look-ing. Like seeing through a window, but no-one doing the seeing. Sand dunes flowing towards the horizon. A few bushes. Birds wheeling in the sky.

I know I have two choices: keep going or quit. It's really that simple. But I've come too far now. My goal is too close. All I want to do is paddle again, and keep paddling until this elusive place called Timbuktu is reached, or until I'm unable to go on.

I walk back to the Niger, wading through its waters and getting into my kayak. Rémi hesitates, then says, 'I'm not a

doctor, but maybe it is good to think about this paddling. Your health is important. You don't have to continue if you're sick.'

'I've got to paddle or I'll never reach Timbuktu,' I say. I dip my hat in the water and put it on my head.

'I don't want to tell you what to do, I'm not a doctor, but here is my boat. You know what I'm saying?'

I nod. He is offering me the chance to quit, to be taken to Timbuktu in his boat. No-one would probably ever know.

'I'm going to paddle,' I say.

He holds up his hands. 'OK.'

Heather comes over to the side of the boat. 'Kira,' she says, 'just remember that we're here for you.'

'Thank you,' I say, humbled, and I paddle off into the midday heat.

CHAPTER THIRTEEN

ONE MORE DAY — I HOPE. IF I CAN PADDLE ABOUT THIRTY-five miles today, I can get to Timbuktu by night, but that's quite a distance in a river so sluggish, with my body so weak. I camped in the dunes, awake most of the night from the discomfort in my guts, but I managed to keep down some antibiotics, so that I feel stronger now. Or at least as strong as I'll ever get, given the circumstances.

I start early, at first light. I don't have any food left, so I don't eat. Even at eight in the morning, my thermometer reads over 100 degrees, great dunes meeting the river on either side, little adobe villages half buried beneath them. It is the land of the Tuareg and Moor now, fierce nomadic peoples who crouch down close to shore and stare out at me from their indigo wrappings, none of them returning my friendly waves. Park admitted fearing these people most, nightmares of his time as their prisoner plaguing him long after he managed to run away from his captors and return

to England. It does not escape my attention that the Tuaregs boast a long history of killing nearly every European traveller who ever tried to reach Timbuktu, including the first woman to make the attempt, in 1869. Only by learning to speak Arabic and disguising himself as a Moor did the Western traveller have a chance of making it to the fabled city alive. In later years, when France claimed Mali as part of its overseas empire, the colonial government waged nearly non-stop battles against the Tuaregs, but with only limited and short-lived success. They remain an indomitable people, never subjugated, never conquered.

I can imagine Park's trepidation on this part of the journey in particular, as an island splits the Niger, creating a narrow channel on either side. The narrower the river, the more vulnerable you are. Village people are closer to you, can reach you more easily. There is less opportunity for escape. And this is the most populated stretch of the river to date, sizeable villages dotting the shore wherever I look, so that I can't evade detection. All I can do is paddle as hard as I can, the people on shore screaming and scolding me as I pass. Crazy people now, people so determined to catch me that they swim into the river after me. I have no way of knowing exactly what their intentions are, though I can tell they're not good, so I follow my new guideline, learned from Park: Don't get out of the boat – *for anything*.

When I float along for a moment to drink some water, men on the shore see it as an opportunity and leap into their

canoes, chasing after me and demanding money. I keep my can of mace in my lap and paddle like a madwoman, managing to outrun them. One man comes close enough to hit my kayak with the front of his canoe, nearly grabbing my lead rope with his hand. I'm able to see his face and his wild eyes as I strain to get away. I know one of us will have to give up – him or me. I pace my strokes as if it were a long-distance race, and he stays on my tail for several minutes before falling behind. Swearing at me, he returns to his village.

But it is more of the same at the next village, and at the next after that, so that the mere sight of the pointy canoes on the shores frightens me. No time to drink now, or to splash myself with water to try to cool off. To stop is to give them an incentive to come after me. I round the great bend of the Niger, the sun getting hotter and hotter, my head aching.

The river widens, and I don't see any villages on this stretch. I stop paddling and float in the very middle of the river, nauseous again, and faint, my thermometer reading 112 degrees. I squint at the Niger trailing off into distant heat waves, looking as if it's being swallowed by the Sahara. When Park once asked a local man where the Niger went, he'd replied: 'It runs to the world's end.' Yes.

'This river will never end,' I say out loud, over and over again, like a mantra. My map shows an obvious change to the north-east, but that turn hasn't come for hours, may never come at all. To be so close to Timbuktu, and yet so immeasurably far away. All I know is that I must keep

paddling. I *have* to be close. Determined still to get to Timbuktu's port of Korioumé by nightfall, I shed the protection of my long-sleeved shirt, pull the kayak's thigh straps in tight, and prepare for the hardest bout of paddling yet.

I paddle like a person possessed. I paddle the hours away, the sun falling aside to the west but still keeping its heat on me. I keep up a cadence in my head, keep my breaths regular and deep, in sync with my arm movements. The shore passes by slowly, but it passes. As the sun gets ominously low, burning a flaming orange, the river turns almost due north and I can see a distant, square-shaped building made of cement: the harbinger of what can only be Korioumé. Hardly a tower of gold, hardly an El Dorado, but I'll take it. I paddle straight towards it, ignoring the pains in my body, my raging headache. *Timbuktu, Timbuktu!*

Bozo fishermen ply the river out here, and they stare at me as I pass. They don't ask for money or *cadeaux* – can they see the determination in my face, sense my fatigue? All they say is, '*Ça va, madame?*' with obvious concern. One man actually stands and raises his hands in a cheer, urging me on. I take his kindness with me into the final stretch, rounding the river's sharp curve to the port of Korioumé.

I see Rémi's boat up ahead; he waits for me by the port, telephoto lens in hand. It's the first time during this trip that I'm not fazed by being photographed. I barely notice him. I barely notice anything except the port ahead of me. All I can think about is stopping. Here is the ending I've

promised myself for weeks. Here I am, six hundred miles of river covered, with the port of Timbuktu straight ahead.

Something tugs at my kayak. I'm yanked back: fishnets, caught in my rudder. To be this close, within sight of my goal, and thwarted by yet one more thing. The universe surely has a sense of humour. I jump into the water, fumbling at the nylon netting tangled around the screws holding the rudder to the inflatable rubber. It's shallow here, and my bare feet sink into river mud full of sharp pieces of rock that cut instantly into my soles. I try to ignore the pain, working fast, pulling the netting off until I free my kayak. When I get inside, the blood from my feet mixes with grey river water like a final offering to the Niger. I manoeuvre around the nets, adjust my course for the dock of Korioumé and paddle hard.

Just as the last rays of the sun colour the Niger, I pull up beside a great white river steamer, named, appropriately, the *Tombouctou*. Rémi's boat is directly behind me, the flash from his camera lighting up the throng of people gathering on shore. There is no more paddling to be done. I've made it. I can stop now. I stare up at the familiar crowd waiting in the darkness. West African pop music blares from a party on the *Tombouctou*.

Slowly, I undo my thigh straps and get out of my kayak, hauling it from the river and dropping it onshore for the last time. A huge crowd has gathered around me, children squeezing in to stroke my kayak. People ask where I have come from and I tell them, 'Old Ségou.' They can't seem to believe it.

'Ségou?' one man asks. He points down the Niger. His hand waves and curves as he follows the course of the river in his mind.

'*Oui*,' I say.

'Ehh!' he exclaims.

'Ségou, Ségou, Ségou?' a woman asks.

I nod. She runs off to tell other people, and I can see passers-by rushing over to take a look at me. What does a person look like who has come all the way from Ségou? They stare down at me in my sweat-stained tank top, my clay-smeared skirt, my sandals both held together with plastic ties.

I unload my things to the clamour of their questions, but even speaking seems to pain me now. Such a long time getting here. And was the journey worth it? Or is it blasphemy to ask that now? I can barely walk, have a high fever. I haven't eaten anything for more than a day. How do you know if the journey is worth it? I would give a great deal right now for silence. For stillness.

My exhaustion and sickness begin to alter this arrival, numbing the sense of finish and self-congratulation and replacing it with only the most important of questions. I've found that illness does this to me, quiets the busy thoughts of the mind, gives me a rare clarity that I don't usually have. I see the weeks on the river, the changing tribal groups, the lush shores down by Old Ségou metamorphosing slowly into the treeless, sandy spread near Timbuktu. I'm wishing I could explain it to people – the subtle yet certain way the world has altered over these past few

weeks. The inevitability of it. The grace of it. Grace, because in my life back home every day had appeared the same as the one before. Nothing seemed to change; nothing provided variety. It had felt like a stagnant life.

I know now, with the utter conviction of my heart, that I want to avoid that stagnant life. I want the world to always be offering me the new, the grace of the unfamiliar. Which means – and I pause with the thought – a path that will only lead through my fears. Where there are certainty and guarantees, I will never be able to meet that unknown world.

Night settles on the shore, and Rémi pulls his boat up alongside the cement dock. I deflate my kayak for the last time and pack it up, carrying it and my things on to the boat. Heather and Rémi both give me a hug of congratulation, but I'm still too numb to really comprehend that I've done it yet. To celebrate, Rémi offers me my choice of their on-board selection of soft drinks. I take an Orange Fanta. Outside, barely discernible in the darkness, the crowd of onlookers continues to discuss what I've done. I can hear them exchanging the word 'Ségou', and I wonder if they believe that I've paddled this far. But it doesn't matter. I lie down on one of the benches. My head feels hot, and it aches to the metronome-like beating of my heart.

Rémi has gone onshore and tries valiantly to get us a taxi into Timbuktu, but the driver of the only car available at this late hour demands an exorbitant sum of more than $150 to drive thirty kilometres. It is the first time I've seen Rémi get so blustering and assertive, and he argues

passionately for a lower sum. We are all hoping for what we've promised ourselves tonight – a hotel room in Timbuktu with blessed air-conditioning – but the driver won't budge his price, thinking he has us. As we're all nearly out of our magazine expense money, I suggest we camp, and go to Timbuktu the next morning when there are sure to be plenty of taxis to take us there at a reasonable price. For the first time, I see this disappointment as just another uncontrollable part of life, like the storms that arose on the Niger. Nothing personal.

I point to the opposite shore as a place to camp away from the crowds. Rémi and Heather agree, and so the great boat is started up and we speed over the Niger beneath a sky dazed with stars. We ground the boat on the opposite shore, and I go about setting up my tent. I'm too sick to fully acknowledge the end of my trip. Rémi offers me a beer to celebrate, but I know I wouldn't be able to keep it down. I do manage to swallow some antibiotics and anti-nausea pills, which quiet my stomach enough to allow me to eat a mango and some of the noodles Rémi's cook has made for us. As I sit to eat, I'm swaying back and forth in my mind, as if I were still careering over the waves of the Niger. I've heard that this happens to sailors, that they get so used to being tossed by the waves that they have trouble readjusting to solid ground. For me, it is as if the Niger still keeps a part of me, as if to tell me that I finally belong to it.

Before bed, I sit outside my tent and stare up at the stars.

'Mungo . . .' I whisper, the Niger licking the muddy shore in the moonlight.

By the dim light from my torch, I read the last two letters Park ever wrote, right before he left Sansanding in 1805 to head down the Niger, never to return. The first was to his sponsor, Lord Camden, in which he declared, 'I shall set sail to the east with the fixed resolution to discover the termination of the Niger or perish in the attempt ... and though I were myself half dead, I would still persevere; and if I could not succeed in the object of my journey, I would at least die on the Niger.'

The last letter, different in tone, was to his wife, Ailie:

I am afraid that, impressed with a woman's fears and the anxieties of a wife, you may be led to consider my situation a great deal worse than it really is. It is true my dear friends Mr Anderson [Ailie's brother] and George Scott have both bid adieu to the things of this world; and the greater part of the soldiers have died on the march ... but I still have sufficient force to protect me from any insult in sailing down the river to the sea. We have already embarked all our things, and shall sail the moment I have finished this letter. I do not intend to stop or land anywhere until I reach the coast. We shall then embark in the first vessel for England. I think it not unlikely but I shall be in England before you receive this.

I don't think Park believed he would really reach some kind of 'coast' and return to England again. His letter to Lord Camden, though resolute and brave, seemed to

suggest a kind of futile determination. The Niger's termination was still a mystery to him; he couldn't have known where the river would take him or where he would end up. But what he could be certain of was the heat, the hostility, the myriad dangers at every turn. I think he realized, on some gut level, that those two letters would be the last he would ever write.

And so Park left on his final journey. When he didn't return to England in what was considered a reasonable length of time, the colonial Governor of Senegal sent Park's trusty servant Isaaco into the interior in search of him. Years would pass. Then, in 1810, Isaaco reappeared in Senegal with news that Park was dead. What we know of Park's last days comes from the written testimony that Isaaco had collected from Amadi Fatouma, Park's guide during the ill-fated river journey. According to Fatouma, Park had reached Timbuktu's port, where locals started a bloody skirmish: 'On passing Timbuctoo we were again attacked by three canoes, which we beat off. We were reduced to eight hands; having each of us fifteen muskets, always in order and ready for action.'

According to another account told to the German explorer Heinrich Barth, who visited Timbuktu years later, Park had actually landed near the city and made contact with the locals, only to be chased away by Tuaregs. And in a final account brought back by the British explorer Hugh Clapperton, Park had made it to his Golden City and was received warmly by the prince. Regardless, he ended up dying on the Niger as he had prophesied, getting as far as

Bussa, in modern-day Nigeria, before he disappeared in the river. Drowned? Killed by natives? We'll never know. The Lander brothers, British explorers who visited Bussa in 1830 in an attempt to learn of Park's fate, recovered only his hymn book and a nautical almanac. Inside the almanac they found some of Park's old papers – a tailor's bill and an invitation dated 9 November 1804 that read 'Mr. and Mrs. Watson would like to have the pleasure of Mr. Park's company at dinner on Tuesday next, at half-past five o'clock. An answer is requested.' The great Mungo Park, survived by a dinner invitation.

I catch myself smiling. In the end, I suppose it doesn't really matter what happened to Park. For him, as for me, the journey must be enough.

CHAPTER FOURTEEN

TIMBUKTU.

It is the world's greatest anti-climax. Hard to believe that this spread of uninspiring adobe houses, this slipshod latticework of garbage-strewn streets and crumbling dwellings, was once the height of worldly sophistication and knowledge. The 'gateway to the Sahara', the 'pearl of the desert', the 'African El Dorado' is nothing now but a haggard outpost in a plain of scrub brush and sand. After having had such a long and difficult journey to get here, I feel as if I'm the butt of a great joke.

I must content myself with simple rewards. The cold bottle of Coca-Cola I buy from a street vendor. The mango – a mango! – I purchase for the equivalent of twenty cents. Shade trees under which I can stand out of the sun. Shade, a blessing to me now. Such simple things. I stand under the awning of a shop and etch a trail through the dusty clay with the toe of my sandal, the sun like an officious

presence, burnishing my skin with heat. I came to terms with it a couple of weeks ago, paddling into the Sahara, our relations cordial now.

The people of Timbuktu stare at me in my T-shirt and skirt, many of them covered as if for a snowstorm, encircled from head to foot in a long black chador or indigo wrappings. I wander along a labyrinth of streets, nodding and smiling at them from behind my sunglasses. I'm looking for some vestige of what the explorers of old had promised me I'd find in Timbuktu. Here is the 'great object' of Mungo Park's search; in his narrative, he'd described what he'd heard about it: 'The present King of Tombuctoo is named *Abu Abrahima*; he is reported to possess immense riches. His wives and concubines are said to be clothed in silk, and the chief officers of state live in considerable splendour.' I walk past the baking adobe buildings, taking care to skirt piles of refuse, dung and rotting kitchen scraps tossed beside the streets. How did everyone get it so wrong?

When Park wrote of this place, the city's true heyday was long expired. Generations of Europeans never knew that a blue-eyed eunuch from the Moroccan court, a Spanish Moor named Judar, had led a mercenary army to Timbuktu in 1591 and sacked it. From that point on, Timbuktu would never be the same. Its riches were seized. Its great institutes of scholarship all but vanished. What remained of its former greatness was little more than its name, coined after a woman slave. But 'Timbuktu' hasn't lost its power and charm, still inspiring countless people to visit.

During the fourteenth century, this city had been the domain of one of Timbuktu's most famous patriarchs: Mansa Musa, the Emperor of Mali, who amassed huge wealth from the sale of gold, salt and slaves. He actively sought the conversion of all his subjects to Islam, succeeding in 1336. (The conversion still holds solid, Timbuktu remaining a devoutly Muslim city; its one Protestant mission, around for nearly two decades, reportedly hasn't claimed any converts.) Musa himself made his renowned six-thousand-mile pilgrimage across the Sahara to Mecca in 1324, accompanied by sixty thousand escorts and a hundred camels carrying three hundred pounds of gold each. As he passed through Egypt, he gave away so much gold that he caused the metal to depreciate in value for the next ten years. When Musa returned to Timbuktu, he built its most impressive edifice yet, the Great Mosque.

Musa's death led to a period of decline for Timbuktu, marauders and Tuaregs taking turns sacking the city. Ali the Great, ruler of the Songhai Empire, finally seized control in 1468; he promptly executed thousands of local leaders, but also ushered in a great cultural renaissance that would later inspire the European imagination with tales of an 'African El Dorado' deep in the Sahara.

It could be argued that the person most responsible for establishing the myth of Timbuktu in the West was Leo Africanus, the Moor who wrote about his experiences in the city in the early 1500s. Exiled from Spain and then captured by Christian pirates, Africanus was freed by the Medici pope Leo X, and taught Italian. *The History and*

Description of Africa and the Notable Things Contained Therein was published in Italy in 1526. It was translated into English in 1600 and became a popular authority on the mysteries of the desert kingdom. Leo wrote dazzling accounts of Timbuktu:

There is a most stately temple to be seen ... and a princely palace ... Here are many shops of artificers, and merchants, and especially of such as weave linen and cotton cloth. And hither do the Barbary merchants bring cloth of Europe. The inhabitants, and especially strangers there residing, are exceedingly rich, insomuch that the king that now is, married both his daughters unto two rich merchants.

The rich king of Tombuto, hath many plates and sceptres of gold, some whereof weigh 1300 pounds. And he keeps a magnificent and well-furnished court. Here are a great store of doctors, judges, priests, and other learned men, that are bountifully maintained at the king's expense.

And hither are brought diverse manuscripts or written books out of Barbarie, which are sold for more money than any other merchandise. The coin of Tombuto is of gold without any stamp or superscription; but in matters of small value they use certain shells brought hither out of the kingdom of Persia. The inhabitants are people of a gentle and cheerful disposition, and spend a great part of the night in singing and dancing through the

streets of the city; they keep a great store of men and women slaves.

Understandably, European governments with colonial aspirations were eager to see if this account was true. Little matter that Africanus also described 'cottages built of chalk and covered with thatch', or that he incorrectly described the Niger as flowing westward. The legend was born. Westerners scrambled to be the first to reach the fabled city. The Englishman Gordon Laing chose to get there by crossing the Sahara. He travelled undisguised and with only a local guide, leading many modern historians to believe that he was out-and-out suicidal. Miraculously, he reached Timbuktu in 1826 – the first European to have actually entered the city – but he paid a heavy price for the honour: just before he reached his goal, Tuaregs attacked him. They riddled his body with gunshot wounds and sword slashes, cutting off his ear, breaking his jaw and nearly severing his right hand. Laing spent weeks in a mud hut in Timbuktu, recovering, only to be strangled to death by Tuaregs when he attempted to return to Europe across the Sahara. Well into the twentieth century, his bones in their lonely, sandy grave outside Timbuktu made for a popular tourist destination.

Timbuktu's golden myth wasn't officially debunked until the Frenchman René Caillié disguised himself as a Moor, learned Arabic, and crossed the Sahara to reach the city in 1828. History credits him as being the first European not only to get there, but actually to *return* to tell about it –

a distinction that was no small feat at the time. He reported what few had suspected: that Timbuktu's wealthy heyday was long over.

The German explorer Heinrich Barth was the next to make it to Timbuktu, in 1853. When he finally returned to Europe, he published a book in 1857 that refuted Leo Africanus's lavish descriptions, announcing that the Golden City was 'sand and rubbish heaped all round'. Others would try to follow him to see for themselves. In 1869, an intrepid thirty-three-year-old Dutchwoman wanted to be the first European woman to get there, but Tuaregs killed her before she made it. Finally the French military moved in, taking steamers up the Niger, battling local tribes and raising the tricolour over Timbuktu in 1893 – less than a hundred years after Park had been the first European to gaze on the city from the Niger. The French fought the Tuareg for years, defeating them in 1902 after a series of bloody desert battles; the Golden City remained in their hands until Mali's independence in 1960.

I walk Timbuktu's dusty streets. It is 115 degrees already and barely noon, so that I bow under the weight of the sun and every action feels unusually ponderous. I pass wasted-looking donkeys scavenging in rubbish heaps, am careful to avoid the streams of fetid wastewater trailing down alleyways. I visit the homes of past explorers, the Gordon Laings and René Cailliés of history who risked their lives to get here. They were just as disappointed at what they found. Caillié would write that the city and its

landscape 'present the most monotonous and barren scene I have ever beheld'. Later, in 1897, the French explorer Félix Dubois expressed his own unbridled disgust: 'These ruins, this rubbish, this wreck of a town, is this the secret of Timbuctou the mysterious?' But I like best what Tennyson said, who had tried to imagine the golden city in his poem 'Timbuctoo' before any Westerners had got there:

> your brilliant towers
> Shall . . . shrink and shiver into huts,
> Black specks amid a waste of dreary sand,
> Low-built, mud-wall'd, barbarian settlements.

The tourists, mostly flown in on package tours, wilt in the sun as they trudge past me through the streets, searching for whatever it is that Timbuktu had promised them. I fear they too have been disappointed, though this end of the world knows enough to sell them air-conditioned rooms at inflated prices and *faux* Tuareg wear. I'm learning to move just as slowly, so as not to exert myself in the heat, my every step feeling hazardously close to truth. I see that Timbuktu is better off left to name and fancy. It is a place that's not meant to be found.

I wander around Timbuktu after dusk. I'm told that this is dangerous, that unsavoury elements may be lurking about, but there is nothing else to do other than sit in my hot room back at the hotel, sweating through my clothes, the overhead fan panting out air. I'm still too sick to eat a full meal

or drink a beer at the hotel restaurant, though at least my antibiotics have taken control of the illness.

I had promised myself an air-conditioned room at my journey's end, but the day before I arrived a contingent of foreign aid workers invaded Timbuktu in their brand new Land-Rovers, seizing all such rooms in town. Rémi is back among them, drinking beers. He spent part of this afternoon trying to secure an air-conditioned room for Heather and himself, bribing and cajoling hotel managers. He failed, and so he has vowed – as I have – to leave this city as soon as possible. He said he has never, on any of his prior travels, experienced a heat as bad as Timbuktu's. I would have to agree. Strangely, the night offers no respite from the hot temperature, and only the occasional whiff of a breeze gives faint relief. At any rate, it is better to remain outside at all costs.

The stifling heat lasts well into the night. I make my way past the empty market, walking between adobe houses. I casually look around for *antars* – genies. Most of the people in Timbuktu believe in these spirits. There are black and white ones, the whites considered more powerful. They show themselves in a number of different ways. Most often, they appear as a black spot on the ground ahead of you, which expands into enormous size if you stare at it. They also come in the form of stray dogs or cats, which vanish as soon as you go near them. Some genies take the appearance of short, squat, black-skinned men with long beards and feet that point backwards, which cause mischief in people's houses.

Walking outside at night, as I am, is supposed to be the best way to come in contact with them. During a full moon, genies will throw stones at you. They can also smell a man who has just had sex with a woman, and they will beat him as he walks home. Cat genies speak your name as you pass by, and if you turn to answer them, they'll show you something so terrible that you'll go crazy. People regularly go crazy from genies (I'm told). They also fight with genies, die from genies. Genies have been known to kidnap people and cause them to disappear in the desert. Especially evil genies enjoy filling the streets of Timbuktu with vagrants and insane people. Witches are the only ones who willingly cavort with the genies of Timbuktu, performing secret *holo-hori* dances, during which they summon the genies to a spot in the desert and become possessed by them. Then they will dance so crazily that they'll actually die if people don't severely beat them with sticks to make the genies leave their bodies.

I look for dark spots on the ground ahead of me, but see nothing. Timbuktu keeps its secrets. Only a stray cat walks by, forgetting to call out my name.

I don't want to leave Mali without trying to free a couple of slaves, an objective I've had since the beginning of my trip. I carry a couple of large gold coins from home, thinking that if I'm able to free anyone, they can start a business for themselves with the money.

It's not an easy thing to free slaves in a country where slavery is technically illegal, and where the government

will readily insist that no such thing exists. But it does. There is an entire underclass in Mali known as the Bella people, a race of West Africans who have been the traditional slaves of the Moors and the Tuaregs for centuries. It is a classic and tragic lesson in human irrationality. Mali's Tuareg, with their olive complexions and light-coloured hair and eyes, believe themselves to be a Caucasian people, and therefore distinct from the Bella, who are darker-skinned and have physical features associated with sub-Saharan Africans. The Tuareg can thus claim a superiority over the Bella, which helps justify the oppression of them.

This prejudice extends to Malian culture at large, where a Bella is thought to be stupid, ugly, poor, worthless. One does not eat with a Bella, not even in the worldly towns of Mopti and Bamako. To call someone a 'Bella' is a grave insult, a way to pick a fight. The rare Bella who does manage to make something of himself will usually tell everyone that he's a Songhai, being completely shamed into denying his heritage. Or, if he has the courage not to hide who he is, he faces the jealousy and wrath of other Malians, who believe that the Bella, as eternal slaves, don't deserve any success.

I have been increasingly dismayed by what I've learned about the situation of the Bella in Mali, which is why I'd like to help someone if I can. In Timbuktu, I go in search of them, and find them living in haggard huts near the garbage dumps. Most of these people work for the Tuareg in one capacity or another. The women do all a

Tuareg family's domestic duties, from the cooking, washing and cleaning to hairdressing; Tuareg males will also force them into sexual acts. The male Bella acts as a Tuareg man's personal servant, or he is a shepherd or farmer. Occasionally, the Tuareg master will offer the services of his Bella to others, getting any monies received. Most Bella who are still slaves are not allowed to keep their own wages and must rely on their masters for all things in life.

I've contacted Assou, sending him a round-trip bus fare to come up from Mopti. I'm thinking he can help me look into the possibility of freeing a slave or two, as he grew up in Timbuktu and knows the right people. Assou has refused to accept any money for his assistance, wanting to free the women as badly as I do. He is fond of saying to me that 'What you do for others, you do for yourself.' His eyes get moist when he speaks of the Bella. Back in Mopti, he told me a secret: that he considers himself one of them. Though he's Songhai by birth, he was breastfed by his mother's Bella friend, which by Malian standards makes him part-Bella. 'The Bella are in my blood,' he told me. It was a daring admission for him to make, and I had to swear not to reveal his story to any Malians as he thought it could hurt his career. But he said that his parents had always stood up for people like the Bella. They always treated everybody the same. And he had learned from them.

I meet Assou at my hotel, and I ask him if we can go together to visit a Tuareg family. I want to see how they interact with their Bella servants. The family we visit lives in an adobe hut on the outskirts of Timbuktu. I greet three

corpulent women who are spread out on mats under a thatch awning. They have light complexions and straight black hair, looking not unlike women from India. They wear large gold earrings, and the henna on their hands and feet makes it seem as if they wear maroon-coloured gloves and socks.

The head woman works with leather, so I ask her if she could put my prayer paper from Big Father into a special leather *saphie* pouch. She agrees, greeting us cordially and offering us chairs and cups of tea. It is a young Bella woman, however, who brings us these things. The girl is lanky, scrawny, barefooted, her hair in crude cornrows. She wears a ratty *pagne* and moves with slow deliberation, her eyes making contact only with her feet. She doesn't speak and isn't spoken to except by way of an order.

'Is that girl a Bella slave?' I ask Assou in English, a language the *saphie* woman can't understand. We watch the girl serving the Tuareg women some tea.

'Yes, of course,' he says.

'How do you know?'

'I know this family. They don't pay her money. She belongs to them.'

'Couldn't she just leave if she wanted to?'

Assou laughs. 'They'd find her and bring her back. She *belongs* to them.'

'They'd punish her?'

'Yes. Look,' he says, 'how they don't feed her anything, but they are all fat. Look.'

I glance from the skinny Bella girl to the well-fed

Tuareg women. The one who is busy fashioning a piece of leather around my prayer paper suddenly snaps out an order. The Bella girl rushes forward to take away our teacups, and the Tuareg woman glances at us as if to say, *It's hard to find good help these days*. It is my first glimpse of the relationship between these two peoples.

I leave with Assou, my *saphie* hanging on a string around my neck. I think I can understand why the Bella have remained in a perpetual state of servitude. Their condition goes beyond the fear of a Tuareg master's coming to reclaim them or punish them if they run away, beyond the economic poverty that keeps them reliant on their masters. I see that it stems from an entire frame of mind that batters their self-esteem into submission from the very day of birth. They are not born to their mothers, but rather to the Tuareg family that owns them. I wonder if they believe they could ever have the means to achieve anything better for themselves? It is the consciousness of the downtrodden.

CHAPTER FIFTEEN

HISTORY STILL PERVADES TIMBUKTU, SLAVERY BEING ONE of the most secretive and ongoing of all the old institutions. If you mention the idea of slavery in Mali to some experts, though, they'll be quick to cite the 1971 law that supposedly abolished it, insisting that the Bella are now paid workers, having freedom of movement and civil rights. In short, they're not 'slaves' any more. But people living in Timbuktu tell a completely different story: that the Bella are slaves by deed if not by word, are still a form of 'property' that the Tuareg refuse to give up, are often raped or beaten by their masters, forced to live on the fringes of society and to turn over any money they earn. So is it 'slavery', then, or is it not? But beyond the semantic debate rests a more fundamental question: where does all this wordplay leave the Bella at the end of the day?

When researching the slavery situation before my trip, I was perplexed by recent US State Department reports that

conclude that *de facto* slavery still exists in Mali. Why had an entire group of people remained the equivalent of slaves in a country that claims that slavery isn't happening any more? Was there no recourse for them? Which is when I mulled over the feasibility of actually freeing someone – which isn't without its own degree of controversy. Some people familiar with the region asserted that it wasn't possible, that I'd only be duped by those involved in the negotiations. Others argued that, at least on a psychological and economic level, the Bella remain hopelessly tied to their Tuareg masters, so that even if I could free someone, they'd be left without the means to provide for themselves.

Yet, suppose I really *could* free someone? Just suppose. And then, what if I gave someone enough money to start up a business and become self-sufficient? Wouldn't this be preferable to the alternative: dehumanizing, often brutal servitude for the rest of one's life? After studying and debating all the facts, I finally concluded that it was worth a try.

My understanding about the situation in Timbuktu is that it mirrors what's happening a bit further to the north, in Mauritania, where the slavery issue is well publicized and is starting to be addressed by aid organizations and the government alike. Mali, however, seems to be in a state of denial. I've learned that some of the Tuareg living in the Timbuktu area would release their Bella from servitude if someone would simply compensate them for officially letting them go. Before the 1971 law was passed, the Tuareg could sell their Bella, contract them out, or put them to

work for the master's family, keeping all monies the individuals made, so that the idea of simply 'giving these people away' because of a decree made in distant Bamako seemed akin to tossing away valuable merchandise for no good reason. After all, what do those rich men in the government know? Many Tuareg refused flat out, and though they'll claim their Bella are free to come and go as they please, it is just subterfuge – they have to say that. (Just as people have spun me the official line: 'There is no female genital mutilation in Mali; it's against the law' – when organizations like Amnesty International and the World Health Organization have estimated that at least 90 per cent of Malian women still undergo the procedure.) And with no-one in the Malian government willing to investigate the matter, and no authorities willing to charge people with the crime, the tacit slavery flourishes as if no law had been enacted at all.

This isn't to say that some Bella didn't take charge and leave their former masters after the emancipation law was passed – many did. I found some of them living on the outskirts of Mopti or Bamako, in squalid thatch huts, on worthless plots of land or on the edge of city garbage dumps. Suddenly becoming free without sufficient funds to start life anew meant that even those Bella who managed to obtain a guarantee of emancipation were forced to live in the same villages where they had been kept in servitude, psychologically and economically dependent on their former masters as if they were still enslaved. All of this emphasizes that freedom is worthwhile only if Bella have

274

the means of starting businesses *independent* of their former masters, which is what I want to arrange if I can actually free someone.

To that end, Assou has been helping me out. His Tuareg friend has been acting as middleman, speaking to the head of his own and other Tuareg families to see if they could spare a female Bella or two. In addition, Assou has enlisted the help of his 'second mother', the Bella woman who had once breastfed him. She is speaking to the elders in various Bella families, trying to identify a couple of young women who might benefit the most from being freed. I've requested that they be women, who face a very real possibility of seeing themselves or their daughters raped.

And now a breakthrough: Assou has found a Tuareg chief willing to sell a Bella or two. Assou and I work to ensure the legitimacy of this arrangement, though everything must be done in secret because 'slavery doesn't exist in Mali'. Assou will be the one to pass on the money to the women's Tuareg master, 'Zengi' (he didn't want to reveal his real name). He must pretend to be the one in charge of the negotiations, or none of this can happen. He has told Zengi that he's freeing the women as part of his college 'research' and that I'm coming along to help him take notes. Also, he needs a couple of photos for his research, and so there will be someone along to take photographs. This is what has been approved by Zengi. Under no circumstances must Assou let on that I'm a writer, or that any of this is my idea.

Negotiations settled, Assou and I arrive at the Bella

village with Rémi. We sit in the midst of the small thatch huts. The Bella have been told that Assou is arriving today and that their Tuareg master has requested their presence in the village. So they are all sitting here now, staring at us – old and young, children half clothed, women cradling infants. Assou admits he doesn't know which two women have been chosen to be sold to me, so that I stare back at each of them, trying to know what it is like to be them. To wake up each day knowing you are owned by another, unable to marry without the master's permission, unable to travel without his leave, unable to earn your own money or buy your own shoes. Zengi is sole arbiter of their lives, and I want to see this man, look into his eyes, know some inkling of what lies in his heart, what drives him.

There is a brief wait, as he lives separately from them, among his own people; the Bella here report to him and his family each day for their work duties. A car arrives and Zengi steps out. He is cloaked in indigo wrappings, the Tuareg man's traditional desert wear. I can see only his eyes as he daintily holds the bluish material over his nose and mouth, as if afraid of catching a cold. He sits down on a mat before 'his Bella', as he calls them. He coddles one older man, stroking the man's arm and patting him as one might a favourite pet.

I have Assou ask him if these people are his slaves.

'Slavery is illegal in Mali,' he says calmly.

'But they are *your* Bella?' I ask.

He nods his head.

Rémi comes forward with his camera to take a picture of

him, and Assou angrily waves him back. 'Not yet,' he says quickly, and glances at Zengi to see if he's on to us: that this event isn't about Assou's 'research'.

Fortunately, he looks unfazed.

'Are they paid monthly wages?' I ask.

He tells me, through Assou, that he gives them a place to live, stock to raise, the clothes on their back. When one of them gets married, he provides animals for the bride price. This, I'm to understand, is their 'pay'.

I turn to a middle-aged woman who is sitting near by. 'If she wanted to leave here, go to Mopti and not come back, could she?' I ask him.

Zengi's face-wrapping falls for a moment, revealing a trace of a smirk. 'Either I kill her, or she kills me,' he says, which is to say, 'Over my dead body.' He readjusts his face-wrapping again, just his hazel eyes visible.

There are words in the Bella language for the distinctions between master and slave. *Terché* refers to those Tuaregs who have slaves; *aklini* is the actual word for 'slave', which is still in everyday use. The fact that they have these words, still *use* these words, speaks of the tacit master–slave arrangement that continues to exist among these peoples.

I ask which women are to be freed and whether the money I passed on to Assou is sufficient for the purchase of one or two people. They talk for a while, and Zengi holds up two fingers. Assou says that he will free two women, household helpers that he has decided he can spare as he has three others already, and sufficient Bella babies to fill

future vacancies. Their price is to be considered a bargain and a sign of his beneficence: the equivalent of $260, more than Mali's GDP per household for one year.

He motions to a couple of young women standing at the edge of the crowd. They approach us with apprehension.

'These are the women,' Zengi says. He orders them to take a seat on the mat before me. One of them, I notice, holds a sickly-looking baby girl.

'She has a baby,' I tell Assou. 'Ask him if he can include the baby with her mother.'

Assou does, and a brief discussion ensues. 'He won't,' Assou says.

'Then ask him how much the baby is.' I can't believe such a sentence has come out of my mouth, but Assou is asking him now and Zengi is sitting up regally, shaking his head.

'He won't sell the baby,' Assou says. He leans closer to me. 'He's already giving us a favour by selling two people. It's best, when a person gives you a favour, not to ask for more.'

Which I take to be a warning. No more will be sold, Assou tells me, because they're too valuable. A little boy nearby, for example, is to be Zengi's son's personal servant. The value of 'his Bella' depends not only on age and occupation, but on how closely the Tuareg family relies on their services. In the case of the two women sitting before me, they're fairly dispensable and replaceable, and thus cheap.

I'm staring at the little girl, wondering what will become

of her, but there is nothing to be done. While I know that her mother can still live in this village and won't be physically separated from her child, the girl remains bound to a life of servitude to Zengi's family as soon as she's big enough to work. I already feel that tell-tale numbness coming over me, that suppression of emotion that I invoke whenever I can't deal with something. Better not to feel anything. So I stand up and tell Assou I'd like to get this over with. Pay Zengi his money. Buy these people already.

Zengi follows us behind a nearby hut – he doesn't want 'his Bella' to see him receiving money for their family members (apparently even he is capable of the rare twitch of conscience) – and Assou hands him the money. My personal money, which I never seem to have enough of and which I certainly don't want Zengi to get. But there is no way around it. And the Tuareg man pockets the bundle of bills and leads us back to the crowd of waiting Bella. With a regal wave of his hand, he directs the two women to us.

'Go with them,' he tells them. 'You belong to them now. I'm finished with you.'

And the shocked looks on their faces are hardly what I expected. Hell, I don't know what I expected, but definitely not this. The two women obediently follow us as we walk away from the throng. I have no idea what to say to them, and I ask Assou to tell them that I did this – bought them – so that they'd be free. So that they won't belong to anyone, and can go and get a job if they'd like, earn some wages, live without having to bow down to another.

The women just stand in front of me. One of them,

Fadimata, is smiling, but the other, Akina, looks as if someone's just smacked her in the face. I hand them each a gold coin I brought from home for this purpose, worth about $120 apiece, as well as some Malian money. I have Assou tell them that this was all my idea, and that this money is meant to help them start a business, get a footing somehow.

The women nod. Fadimata is thanking me, but Akina holds her head down silently. I don't understand what's wrong, so I ask if we can go somewhere to be alone, away from Zengi, who is standing near by, mummy-like in his indigo wrappings, explaining the situation to the other Bella. We head into a thatch hut and sit on the sandy floor. The women sneak glances at me, Fadimata holding her – or perhaps I should say Zengi's – baby in her arms. They have hidden the gold coins and money in their palms, and now they really look at them for the first time.

I've never been good at small talk, particularly not with people I've just purchased.

'So will you start a business now?' I have Assou ask them.

Fadimata replies: 'I'll try to get some millet or rice to sell in the Timbuktu market.' Though she'll probably stick around this village because of her baby, she'll be self-sufficient. Any produce that she sells in the market, any money she makes, is hers now. She won't have to report to Zengi.

'Have you liked working for him?' I ask her.

'No,' she says immediately. 'I want to live my own life and have my own business.'

'What do you think about your baby belonging to him?'

'I have no choice,' she says, glancing down at the child and caressing her head.

Akina holds her head down and says nothing. I ask her if she liked working for Zengi's family.

'No,' she mumbles, looking at her hands.

'Are they nice to you?' I ask.

She shakes her head, refusing to look at me.

'Do they hurt you?' I ask.

Softly, she says that they beat her. Fadimata nods in affirmation. She says that they beat her too.

I don't know how to ask the next question, but I feel I must. I ask them if any of the Tuareg men have ever taken them . . . raped them.

The women are silent.

I have Assou tell them that they're safe talking to me, that I'm not going to tell any of the Tuareg what they say, that I'm their friend.

'It didn't happen to me,' Fadimata says. 'But it happened to my friend. She told me.'

Akina nods in agreement but says nothing. She looks downright scared, and she fingers her dress, frowning.

I have Assou ask her if she's OK. She looks up at me, looks into my eyes for the first time. 'I feel shame,' she says, 'about what happened.'

'Shame?' I ask Assou.

And it comes out that she feels ashamed that she was

sold like some animal. She feels ashamed to be sitting in front of me.

'No,' I say. 'Tell her not to.' I reach over and take hold of her hand. She stares at me; we've got tears in our eyes. I keep squeezing her hand. 'Tell her not to feel ashamed.'

Assou tells her, and it is as if a transformation comes over her. Her whole countenance changes, relaxes, and she is able to look into my eyes. When I ask her if she'll tell me how the Tuareg have hurt her, she becomes animated. She stands, and she imitates someone beating another person on the back. Her hands come up and down with an imaginary stick, as if trying to drive it through the body of another. When she stops, the expression on her face is one of pure rage, pure hatred. Both women tell me that they're beaten daily, for no reason whatsoever.

They explain to me that they must do everything for their Tuareg masters, and it is a description I've heard from other Malians – that the Tuareg consider themselves an aristocratic race, above performing everyday tasks. The domestic servants buy food for the family, prepare it, farm the land, cook, pound millet. Basically, they do all the work, so that the family has leisure.

'So if a Tuareg's sitting here and wants a bottle that's out of reach,' I say to the women, 'do you have to bring it to him?'

They both smile and nod adamantly. 'We have to bring everything to them,' Fadimata says. She imitates a Tuareg woman holding her hand out. 'Like this: take and bring.' We all laugh – Akina the loudest. It's nice to see her smiling.

I enquire how old the women are, and their answer surprises me – maybe eighteen or nineteen. They don't know for sure because no birth certificates were drawn up. But they look much older than that; they *feel* much older, as if their unpleasant experiences with Zengi's family have aged them irrevocably.

I ask the women if they can move away now, go to Mopti if they want. I'm wondering what guarantee there is – if any – that they won't be reclaimed the minute I leave.

'No, he can't,' Fadimata says. Akina nods in agreement. 'We're free now. We have his promise. When he told us to go with you, that meant everything. "Go" is a guarantee that means, "You're free".'

I can only hope they're right. Still, in a society that refuses to acknowledge the ongoing reality of slavery, there can be no official papers drawn up, no receipts. If Zengi is honourable, upholds his part of the bargain – as the women assure me he will – then they have nothing to worry about. And the fact that they are already planning their futures, telling me about the millet they will buy, is enough to reassure me. For now. At any rate, perhaps they won't be beaten or humiliated any more.

When I get up to leave, shaking each of their hands, they tell me that God will bless me, will take care of me for what I've done for them. They keep repeating *albaka* – thank you – over and over. I'm grateful to see their happy expressions, though I don't know what to say. Maybe Fadimata can buy her baby if she makes enough money. I don't have words.

*

I can't seem to forget the two women back in the Bella village. All I want to do is leave Timbuktu, go home. But before I do, I ask Assou if he will take me to the Djingarey Berre mosque to see the door that – if opened – will end the world, according to local legend. This mosque is Mali's oldest, built by the great Songhai king Mansa Musa in the fourteenth century after his return from Mecca. It has survived the centuries virtually intact and now sits on the edge of town, spiked adobe minarets reaching skyward, garbage swirling about its walls.

We have the mosque to ourselves, the caretaker busy with tourists on the roof. Inside, it is dim and cool. Faint light trails down from skylights, exposing the clouds of dust kicked up by our feet. It is hugely empty here, the adobe walls revealing the pressing of ancient hands.

The special door is in a nondescript wall along the far side of the mosque, hidden behind a simple thatch mat. Assou tells me that no-one is shown the real door any more. He doesn't know why. Perhaps it's too dangerous. He once glimpsed it when he was a boy, but he doesn't remember it.

'I want to see what it looks like,' I say.

Assou laughs. 'I never met anyone as curious as you.'

'I'm serious.'

'Then go look.' But I notice that he himself is scared.

The empty mosque rings with our voices. Dust swirls in the shafts of light. Kittens lie in the shadows of the columns, their ears flickering to the sounds of our voices. There are more kittens here than I've ever seen in one

place, their bellies gently rising and falling, their eyes half closed and Buddha-like.

I creep forward and gently pull back the mat. And here it is: the door that can end the world. It is made exclusively of wood, the middle part rotted away. It looks un-remarkable, like a piece of faded driftwood. Suddenly, impulsively, I stick a hand out and touch it.

The world doesn't quake. The waters don't part. The earth continues on its axis, churning out immutable time.

'The world hasn't ended,' I declare, my voice echoing along the far walls.

'You must *open* it,' Assou says, laughing.

And I could open it, standing here as I am with the care-taker blithely unaware on the roof of the mosque. For an insolent moment I pretend I hold the world in my hands. I think of Zengi and the slave women. I think of the Fulani women teaching me how to cook. I see that Bozo fisherman in his canoe, cheering me on to Timbuktu. It is such a kind yet cruel world. Such a vulnerable world. I'm astounded by it all.

EPILOGUE

HOMEBOUND, FINALLY. I LEAN BACK IN MY SEAT, MY flight to Bamako making a complete mockery of my kayak trip. From this height, all those weeks spent on the river have been reduced to mere seconds as we speed by. I look out of the window. Park's majestic Niger appears as a feeble trail of grey, cutting through desert plains, winding around pale hills and emerging in an unassuming puddle that is Lake Debo. It took me a day to cross that lake, and another two days to battle around the northern buckle of the Niger that empties from it, those days surrendered now to a shuddering passage at fifteen thousand feet.

Clouds block out the scene. I turn the air-conditioning knob to full power and shut my eyes, feeling utterly exhausted. Is this what it's like to enter a second birth? But there are no Dogon around to ask. I know only that there's no returning to the way I was before this trip. I finger the seatbelt, slack and useless around me. This is the airline –

286

Air Mali – that the US State Department advised me against using. Well, I've broken my last rule then, but I wouldn't paddle up the Niger if all the geniuses in Washington paid me. There is one thing that Mungo Park never understood and that I finally have: the journey will always tell you when it's over.

FOUR CORNERS
A Journey into the Heart of Papua New Guinea
by Kira Salak

The Beach meets *Heart of Darkness* in an extraordinary travel memoir charting 24-year-old Kira Salak's three-month solo journey across Papua New Guinea.

Following the route taken by British explorer Ivan Champion in 1927, and amid breathtaking landscapes and wildlife, Salak travelled across this remote Pacific island – often called the last frontier of adventure travel – by dugout canoe and on foot. Along the way, she stayed in a village where cannibalism was still practiced behind the backs of the missionaries, met the leader of the OPM – the separatist guerrilla movement opposing the Indonesian occupation of Western New Guinea – and undertook a near-fatal trek through the jungle.

Selected by the *New York Times Book Review* as a Notable Travel Book of the year, *Four Corners* is both a gripping true story and a parallel journey into the author's past, where she revisits the demons that drove her to experience situations most of us can barely imagine.

'KIRA SALAK IS A REAL-LIFE LARA CROFT'
New York Times

'A LUMINOUSLY WRITTEN, THOUGHTFUL
ACCOUNT . . . EXEMPLARY TRAVEL WRITING'
Kirkus Reviews

'A REMARKABLE WORK . . . HER ENCOUNTERS WITH
FIERCE-LOOKING MEN AND WOMEN ARE SURPRISINGLY
ACCURATE AND FULL OF CHARM'
Tobias Schneebaum, author of *Where the Spirits Dwell:
An Odyssey in the New Guinea Jungle*

0 553 81550 4

BANTAM BOOKS

'Two men go on a journey: flat, direct and more dangerous than either will admit. The narrative is deliberately unbranded, unspecific. The enthusiastic, inexperienced partner goes by Nine. This pushes the narrative into an allegorical space, even as we are up close and personal with the two on their trip from south to north. Eggers has been writing fiction that tells a story of America in our present moment, and often that moment is characterized by decline. To environmental devastation, violence, the power of social media, the loss of the middle class, we can now add Americans abroad, over their heads. Darkly funny' *Los Angeles Times*

'The ever-incisive, worldly-wise, compassionate and imaginative Eggers maintains the tension of a cocked crossbow in this magnetizing, stealthily wry and increasingly chilling tale' *Booklist*

'Eggers may be the only living American writer for whom the term "Hemingway-esque" meaningfully applies. Eggers ably weaves in a host of ethical questions over one man's responsibility to the other, what makes help transactional versus simply kind. An unassuming but deceptively complex morality play, as Eggers distils his ongoing concerns into ever tighter prose' *Kirkus*

'A testament to Eggers's expert skill at point of view. *The Parade* is a deeply felt book that defies easy labels. This is a book you can finish in a single sitting. And you will'
Tony Romano, *New York Journal of Books*

'An eye-opening political fiction. Eggers's tense and intricate storytelling reveals complex moral and ethical issues'
Christian Science Monitor

'Eggers is able to see the world as it is, while also holding on to his vision of how the world should be'
Chimamanda Ngozi Adichie

PENGUIN BOOKS

The Parade

'It partakes of a complex of anxieties about America's role as an affluent superpower of dubious virtue' *Financial Times*

'Fable-like, stylish and slick' *i*

'Eggers's commitment to social and political issues continues' *Mail on Sunday*

'A heartbreaker and a mindbender. It is a novel of ideas that packs an emotional punch that left me reeling. With clear, unadorned prose, Eggers lays bare the costs of war, and of peace' Tayari Jones, author of *An American Marriage*

'This is a tale for our time, an allegory about intervening in foreign lands without knowledge, and so a nightmare vision of our endless wars' Thomas E. Ricks, author of *Fiasco* and *Churchill and Orwell*

'A parable of progress, as told by J. M. Coetzee to Philip K. Dick' Richard Flanagan, author of *Gould's Book of Fish* and *The Narrow Road to the Deep North*

'In *The Parade*, the anxiety grows with every page and every mile to reach an ending that turns everything upside down and sends us into the heart of darkness. A minimalistic, merciless novel. A powerful allegory and a painfully concrete contemporary story – Eggers is a true virtuoso of that synthesis' Georgi Gospodinov, author of *The Physics of Sorrow*

'In an unnamed country, two unnamed employees of a foreign road-building corporation arrive for a twelve-day assignment. Eggers differentiates between Four and Nine solely through their reactions to the post-civil-war devastation around them. How this setup reduces the two men to their willingness – or refusal – to see others is

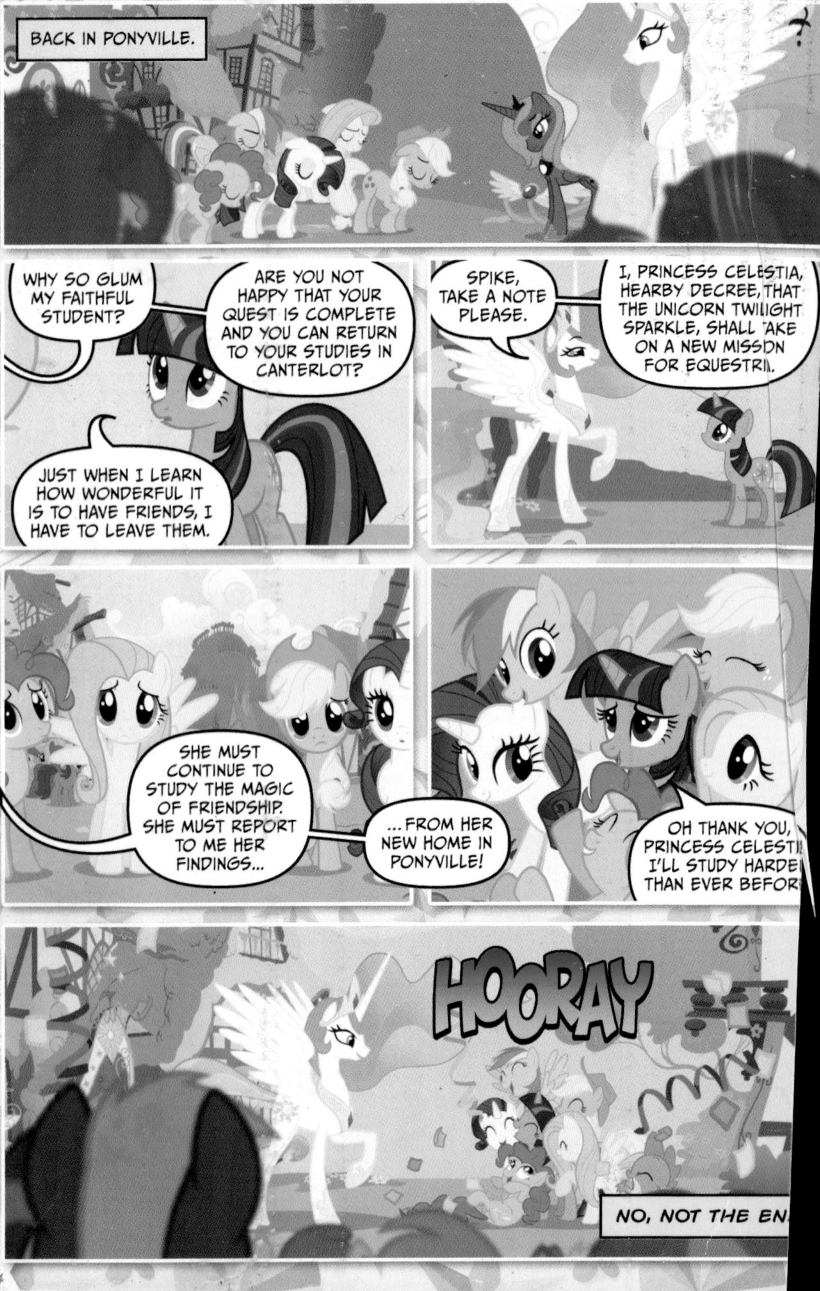
BACK IN PONYVILLE.
WHY SO GLUM MY FAITHFUL STUDENT?
ARE YOU NOT HAPPY THAT YOUR QUEST IS COMPLETE AND YOU CAN RETURN TO YOUR STUDIES IN CANTERLOT?
JUST WHEN I LEARN HOW WONDERFUL IT IS TO HAVE FRIENDS, I HAVE TO LEAVE THEM.
SPIKE, TAKE A NOTE PLEASE.
I, PRINCESS CELESTIA, HEARBY DECREE, THAT THE UNICORN TWILIGHT SPARKLE, SHALL TAKE ON A NEW MISSON FOR EQUESTRI
SHE MUST CONTINUE TO STUDY THE MAGIC OF FRIENDSHIP. SHE MUST REPORT TO ME HER FINDINGS...
...FROM HER NEW HOME IN PONYVILLE!
OH THANK YOU, PRINCESS CELESTI I'LL STUDY HARDE THAN EVER BEFOR
HOORAY
NO, NOT THE EN